NOVEMBER MEMORIES

INSIDE THE CHRISTOPHER PORCO CASE

ISBN 978-1-4357-0387-2

Cover Design By Alvin Tostig

Published by Lulu.com

Electronic and print version can be purchased at:
Lulu.com
Keyword: Porco
OrLulu.com/content/1332510

NOVEMBER MEMORIES
INSIDE THE CHRISTOPHER PORCO CASE

By

STEVE FERENCE

Author's Note

This book uses a variety of sources to bring together facts, impressions, and even misinterpretations by witnesses that are each part of any true story. Those sources include direct testimony from pre-trial hearings, direct trial testimony and evidence, private interviews, public statements, press conferences, and, in some instances, personal, but obvious, observations. Original court documents are interspersed in an attempt to give readers the best insight into what was being discussed at the time. Original source documents have been transcribed verbatim, keeping as close to the original format as possible. Typographical errors in the original documents are mostly recorded unchanged, without the typical (sic) notation. The documents are all cited in the bibliography by chapter for further reference. Sources who gave information confidentially are not listed in the bibliography. One of the goals of this book was to be as transparent as possible, to bring readers through the case and help them understand the players and information. Therefore, such sources are used rarely and only when necessary.

All dialogue is the result of direct testimony or interviews and intensive note taking in and out of court. Dialogue came from statements that were written down as close to verbatim as possible.

The goal of any journalist is to get as close to the truth as possible. It is a goal made difficult by competing interests and the fog of emotions surrounding an awful event. Where some witnesses contradict others in their memory of a certain event, every effort was made to show both sides and let the reader understand the claims.

Using this framework, the story strives to be as accurate as possible while allowing you, the reader, to be the final judge on what you think really happened early that November morning.

PART I
MURDER

I

Delmar, New York
November 15, 2004

Later, everyone in Judge Cardona's office would realize it was too quiet. For now, morning chatter and the movement of papers kept the gears of justice moving in each room.

The New York State Appellate Division office in downtown Albany, New York, handles cases ranging from burglaries to murders. It also includes civil cases from unemployment to family issues that are often serious disputes. Ask anyone in the courthouse, they'd probably tell you it's the cases involving the emotional family issues that can be the most difficult and draining.

Peter Porco would know. For years the middle-aged law clerk had worked on such cases. At least once Peter had received a threat against his family as a result of his work – a threat serious enough to warrant a police check-up as his two young boys, Johnathan and Christopher, were whisked away from school.

If that event was traumatic for the boys, it was likely even more so for their mother, Joan. The elegant woman had an air of intelligence – of confidence about her. She took pride in her family, of protecting her boys, and tried to keep surprises at bay through organization and planning. She attended daily mass. A police report would later state she "was very straight, to the point of being stiff," though when she spoke with you, her soft eyes would usually hint only at kindness.

Nothing ever came of the threat that forced their children to be taken out of school. After all, it had happened years ago when both Johnathan and Christopher were still boys. But they had grown up. After High School, Johnathan had graduated ROTC and left for nuclear submarine training. Christopher had taken the typical college route, enjoying the full spoils of life at Rochester University. According to college officials, he rarely attended classes.

The threat wasn't the last the family would face. Living in Delmar, a small suburb of Albany, the Porco family could have lived a quiet life in their large but unassuming colonial. They kept their yard well groomed, just like the others on the street. In fact, both Peter and Joan had just raked the leaves that had fallen around their Brockley Drive home. The house certainly didn't stick out among the others, but police had visited it before to look into several burglaries. They had never made an arrest.

"Have you seen Peter?" one of Cardona's law clerks asked. Peter occasionally worked at home, but that didn't preclude the question from being asked. Many Albany attorneys, judges, and law clerks knew him not only as a competent worker, but also as a gentle, caring man with whom you could share a laugh. One co-worker would later say Peter was the kind of guy you felt comfortable being around. If you asked how his family was doing, you already knew he wanted to know even more about yours.

In fact, no one in the office had seen Peter. But that wasn't surprising. Yesterday, he had made two phone calls to his boss, Judge Cardona, as he worked from home. But today, there were no phone calls yet, and *that* was unusual.

In the law business there is always the small chance someone might let discontent with their case coalesce into the more sinister act of violence. That chance, hanging ever-present over any legal worker, was enough to be cautious, though it certainly was no reason to panic. By 10:30 in the morning – there had still been no phone call. It was time to put any concerns to rest.

Ring. Ring. Ring. The Porco's phone rang without anyone picking up. Now those concerns seemed a little more justified – enough concern for one of the secretaries to offer to drive over and find out what was going on. Worries grew. Cardona and the security team dismissed the idea of her leaving and came down on the side of caution. They decided to send court officer Michael Hart. He was armed and knew the protocol in case something had happened. There was a logical explanation for almost everything – even if no one had heard from Peter.

The uniformed court officer from the New York State Office of Court Administration nodded his head when the judge asked if he would go. He immediately left the courthouse, jumped in his car, and traveled through the downtown Albany traffic, finding fewer cars on the winding country roads 20 minutes away in Delmar.

As the court officer slowed to a stop outside the Porco's home, nothing seemed out of place. He tried the Porco's home phone one more time from his cell phone before getting out. It just kept ringing. He closed the car door - by far the loudest sound in the quiet neighborhood. The sun heated the cool November air as Hart walked up the paved driveway. Suddenly, he stopped. A key with two or three rubber bands tied around the end sat in the front door lock. His suspicions grew. His heart began to beat faster.

"Peter?" he asked through the closed door as he knocked loudly. No one answered. His hand gripped the knob with the key still in it, and he noticed a red streak on the doorknob. Two or three drops of blood spotted the cement steps where he stood.

Officer Hart thought a second and walked to the garage door to see if it had been left open as well. It was locked. He used his Nextel to instantly connect to his boss, Chief Costello. "Do you want me to go into the home?" he asked.

The phone chirped back. Costello said he could, but warned him to be careful.

Hart heard the Porco's old golden retriever barking from inside as he called Costello on the cell to keep each other on the line. He clicked on the speaker function so they could talk easily. Hart decided to go in.

He took a breath and turned the front doorknob slowly. He pushed the door open – then stopped in his tracks.

He tried to comprehend what he saw. In front of him a large bi-fold closet door, coated with blood, had been ripped from where it had hung and came to rest on the floor. Blood was everywhere. Blood droplets on the floor had dried hours ago. To the right of the front entrance at the base of the stairs, lay the body of Peter Porco. His eyes were wide open, his shirt stuck halfway up his chest. His arm reached above his head as if he had struggled to pull himself up the stairs. Peter's forehead had taken the brunt of the attack. It looked as if someone had slashed him deeply using a very large knife.

Hart held onto his gun in his right hand, cell phone in his left. "This is a crime scene. Call an ambulance – Peter's not breathing," he shouted into the phone. Costello quickly complied.

Hart heard a beeping sound coming from another room. Carefully scanning for any movement that might tell him the killer was still inside, he found a cordless phone charger by the slider. It was disconnected from the house phone Hart had tried to call earlier. Through the cell, Costello told him to leave the house immediately.

The call went out as a man down with injuries, and police arrived quickly. The Bethlehem Police Department was located only about a dozen blocks away, so within minutes the first of many police cars showed up, cracking the November silence outside.

The first officer briskly walked over to Hart, and the men decided to clear the house before the others arrived. They walked past Peter's body and through the kitchen. Nothing. Then they made their way down the stairs to the basement where the door was shut. The Porco's dog, Barrister - Barr for short - stood behind it, wagging his tail. Besides the dog there was nothing else except bookcases of law-related pamphlets and papers, a computer desk, and a corner crammed with typical family junk. The two went back up to the kitchen. It seemed messier than the other rooms.

From there, the two men walked around the body of Peter and went upstairs. Blood streaks coated the banister every foot or so. The Bethlehem Police officer went to the right. Hart went to the left. Time to clear the bedrooms. Opening the doors one by one, ready for anything, the cops found only clean, organized, and untouched rooms - the obvious attentive touch of Joan Porco. The only thing that seemed like it had been touched was the bed of Johnathan Porco where the sheets were turned down, though no one noticed.

Hart walked down to the bedroom at the end of the hallway. He would later testify about that moment, telling the courtroom…"and then I walked into that bedroom." The sight was one he would never forget.

A person was lying on the bed -- not lengthwise, but widthwise. Blood was spattered all over the wall in back of the bed – even on the reading lamp above. The sheets were saturated where two people usually slept. A 3-foot-long ax handle stuck out from the center of the bed, its head slicing through the wet sheets.

Joan Porco, who was hardly recognizable from the large, bloody wounds to the upper part of her body, moved her head slightly. Hart later recalled, "her face was black."

Hart left the house as the other officer called down to let the arriving investigators and EMT's know they had found someone alive. Detective Christopher Bowdish had also arrived by now. Others would later be involved too, including detectives Anthony Arduini and Sergeant John Cox, both veterans of the force with over 60 years of combined experience. As Bowdish stepped out of his unmarked car, he saw an officer rush inside the home. Hart stood near the front as the detective walked up to the porch. He noticed the key still in the opened front door and went in.

Immediately, he was nearly overwhelmed by the scene. Blood was everywhere. "*A sure sign of a struggle*," he thought. In one of the bathrooms, little bits of tissue covered the floor, all stained red. Bowdish winced at what he saw before him. Blood all over Peter's body, all over the closet door. He took in the awful scene and remembered those past burglary investigations he had worked on at this very home.

The white-haired detective, with the corresponding mustache and the hardened look of a man who had already seen too much in his career, went upstairs. Walking through the blood-smeared walls of the hallway, Bowdish took it all in. Two EMT's followed. He motioned them to come with him to the master bedroom, where Bowdish saw Mrs. Porco lying on the bed. Somehow, she held up her hand, as if motioning them to come in.

The bed jutted out diagonally from a corner of the room. Joan wore what looked like a nightshirt which she had pulled down to more properly cover herself as she lay saturated in her own blood.

The two EMT's, Kevin Robert and Dennis Wood, began their work to get Joan to the hospital as safely as possible. Her face was full of hack marks, similar to Peter's. One of her eyes was split open, and one side of her jaw had been nearly severed from her face. Joan's blood pressure was dangerously low – almost nonexistent. She grew more agitated as the EMT's worked on her. Then, they realized her eyes seemed to be following their movements. She was trying to hang on.

Bowdish radioed to Lt. Heffernan. He again recalled those unsolved burglary investigations and remembered the Porcos had two sons. Bowdish took pictures of Joan and the room as he waited for a response. After a moment, Lt. Heffernan reminded him of the boys' names. "Christopher and Johnathan."

Bowdish tried to clear his head as thoughts, theories, and questions raced through his mind. He asked the paramedics if he could ask Joan some simple, fast questions.

"Quickly," Robert responded, giving Bowdish a tiny window to ask Joan the most burning of questions before the only witness would likely die.

Bowdish leaned over Joan's face. "Can you hear me, Mrs. Porco?" he asked.

She seemed to nod her head yes.

"Did a family member do this to you?" he asked even louder.

Again, she moved her head up and down. *Yes.*

"Did Johnathan do this to you?" Bowdish continued as the medics looked on.

This time her head moved from left to right. *No.*

"Did Christopher do this to you?" he asked, the words of this question picking up speed.

Joan shook her head up and down.

He wanted to be sure. He asked her again if Johnathan "did this to you." Again, she shook her head no.

"Christopher- did Christopher do this to you?" he asked.

Again, Mrs. Porco nodded her head. *Yes.*

"I'm sorry," said Detective Bowdish, apologizing to her out of what he later attributed to pure human compassion at the sight of her awful injuries.

The medical team continued to try and save her. They held Joan down as the needle of an IV stung her arm to sedate her. They didn't want her to further injure herself. Joan tried to yell, but nothing came out. Slowly, and ever so carefully, they put her small frame on a stretcher. They carried her to the ambulance through the tight hallway, down the stairs, and over her husband's body, which would not be moved for hours as the crime scene was sealed off. Sirens blared, and the ambulance brought Joan fifteen minutes away to Albany Medical Center.

Detective Bowdish realized the sheer magnitude of the scene and called the State Police Forensic Unit. He continued to click away with his camera, preserving what he saw on digital memory. As he took pictures of the outside, he noticed a small group of people had gathered near the property. News vans covered with their station's logos soon began to pull up. Reporters clutching pens and small pads of paper stepped out, ready with questions for officials.

Bowdish ignored the small crowd and walked over to the side of the house. His search for clues had only just begun, and already other officers notified him a phone wire had been left hanging off the telephone pole in the Porco's backyard. Bowdish walked over. Five feet above the ground the wire that should have continued toward the Porco home dangled in the air.

Bowdish dusted for fingerprints – and got one. He lifted the print and repeated the process, giving himself two copies to send in for analysis. He took a few more pictures.

Within an hour, the state police arrived and took control of the scene, taking most of the evidence out of the house and finding even more tantalizing clues.

It's called amino black processing. A chemical is added to any surface that might have blood on it – blood that might be too small to notice with the human eye alone. It was a process that would slowly turn doorways, molding, and floors in the Porco home a dark, purplish-black color wherever blood reacted with the chemical.

By now, police tape surrounded the property as state and local police continued to comb through the house. Peter Porco's body had been brought to the morgue at Albany Med.

Now, the grueling police work began. Six state police investigators would look over every inch of the house for the next six days.

Investigator Drew McDonald was one of them. He had responded to thousands of crime scenes, but this one was particularly gruesome. He and the others wore special white suits, latex gloves, and booties, to keep from contaminating the crime scene any more than it might already have been from the frantic rush to figure out what had happened.

Numerous local police and EMT's had come through the house as they attempted to save Joan Porco's life.

McDonald took note of the bloodstains as he walked through the first floor of the cream-colored house. He looked at the front door. It seemed odd to him that the key in the doorknob seemed to have come from a hollowed-out portion of the planter sitting on the front porch – a so-called "hide-a-key." Few people would have known about that.

Rochester, New York
November 15, 2004

It had been a quiet morning for John and Barbara Balzano, who live just outside the city of Rochester. John, the balding, retired school administrator, had yet to find out his sister had been brutally attacked, her husband murdered. But around lunchtime he got the worst call he had ever received.

The call came from the elderly Father David Noone, Joan's first cousin, a well-known priest from Loudonville. "Come quickly," he told John. "Joan's in serious condition." Noone said he would meet John at the hospital - three hours away from the Balzano's Rochester home.

Trying to put it all together as he hung up the phone, Balzano's mind jumped to his nephew, Christopher, a nearby student at the University of Rochester. Balzano had made the trip to the University several times before. Each semester they'd usually see each other a few times, especially for holidays when Christopher might not be able to get back to Albany. Sometimes they even met up to play golf. Few weeks went by when Christopher and his uncle didn't talk by phone.

Balzano knew it would take about a half-hour to get to the University of Rochester and pick up his nephew for the trip to Albany. Then it would be at least a three-hour trip from there. His mind raced. His wife called Christopher to tell him something had happened to his parents. His uncle would pick him up. She continued to quickly pack some basic supplies for a couple of days stay in Albany. She took her own car.

John Balzano's drive to campus took about as long as he had expected, but he just couldn't get there fast enough. The private university, with just over 6,000 students, sits only a few miles outside the actual city of Rochester. John had been there enough to know where to park near Christopher's dormitory, the Munro building. It had the scent of a place inhabited by college students. The hint of cigarettes and old beer wafted through the air. A few students milled about in the hallway as John felt the pressure to find Christopher quickly. The 2nd floor was typical – a bunch of closed doors leading into rooms with small fridges and other college paraphernalia. Though he looked at the faces of students as he walked by, he couldn't find the one familiar to him. He quickened his pace, searching.

And then he saw him - surprising himself at the same time. He hadn't noticed Christopher right away. "Christopher!" he almost yelled. In fact, John had walked right by his nephew, partly because Christopher wore a dark sweatshirt with the hood pulled over his head. Later, John would wonder whether it was the day or the lighting or a million thoughts clouding his mind that made it difficult to recognize him. "Chris…" he said, as the two hugged.

The pair quickly left the building once Christopher grabbed a few things for the trip. With the young man now sitting in Balzano's car, they sped off campus.

Breaking the speed limit, it would take just over three hours until the two could meet up with family and friends at Albany Med. Over three hours until doctors would let them know how well Joan was clinging to life. Three hours.

As the rural scenery of upstate New York passed by, plenty of questions floated around in John's mind. He would later testify that few words were spoken, and that the long trip to Albany was mostly quiet. Christopher looked out the passenger window.

Then, a call came to Balzano's cell phone. It was Father Noone – with shocking news. He told Balzano not to say anything, but that he should keep Christopher close because the driver's nephew might be a suspect in the murder of at least one of his parents. In fact, police had just put a "be on the lookout," or BOLO for him:

HOMICIDE
DATE 11/15/04
TIME/12:50PM
LOCATION/36 BROCKLEY DR DELMAR NY 12054

DESCRIPTION OF CRIME/HOMICIDE TWO VICTIMS

WEAPON USED/UNK

DESCRIPTION OF SUSPECT(S) /CHRISTOPHER PORKO 7/9/83 W/M
POSS DRVING 04 JEEP WRANGLER. NY CWG2494 UNK
DESTINATION USE CAUTION SUB POSS ARMED
IF SUBJECT LOCATED HOLD VEHICLE FOR EVIDENCE

CASE #/18415
INVESTIGATING OFFICER/DET CHRISTOPHE BOWDISH

*

Balzano kept on driving, his nephew a car seat away.

Meanwhile, more and more friends and family members arrived at Albany Med as the hours passed and the day gave way to night. No one really knew what to think, or how to comprehend what was happening. They exchanged details about the incident, trying to put together an awful puzzle to which they only had a few of the pieces. All they really could do was offer support to each other as they waited for any good news about Joan's condition.

John Polster and his wife, Lynn, had also come to the hospital as soon as they had heard the news. John's career path had led him to become best friends with Peter – an accident of the alphabet that had Peter Porco sitting next to John Polster when the two studied law back in the 70's. Joan and Lynn had quickly become friends as well, raising their children together. Over the last few weeks, the two families had been planning a three-day vacation to New York City that would never happen.

Polster knew Christopher was a suspect. The lead story on the radio and television was the attack at 36 Brockley Drive. Police were saying publicly that the two Porco boys were not suspects – but that they did want to talk with them.

In fact, several Bethlehem Police officers walked the hospital hallways, giving a different impression. Father Noone spoke with one who had heard the priest call Balzano on his cell phone. The officer demanded to know if Noone had warned Christopher that police wanted to question him. Noone explained he only spoke with Balzano to give him a heads-up and prevent police from questioning him without an attorney.

"John will never honor that request," the officer said. "He will tell Christopher. Do you realize you have jeopardized this investigation?" The officer didn't want to risk losing any crucial information. "Disgusting," the cop said as he walked away.

Polster needed a break from the tense waiting game going on at the hospital and a break from the police who seemed to be everywhere. Walking to the cafeteria to get something in his stomach, he sat with his wife and Mary Louise Ruby, Joan's cousin.

The conversation immediately turned to why police seemed to be focusing on Christopher. They agreed that it seemed time to calm the rumors and possibilities. It was important to talk about what was really going on before someone might mistakenly say something and cause the police to further scrutinize family and friends who hadn't even begun to grieve. "How do you think Chris could have done it – gone to Albany and back?" Ruby asked the others at the table.

Polster shook his head. "I think it's impossible Christopher could have traveled there and back." The discussion continued for several minutes. Everyone said it was important that Christopher had an attorney. Given Peter's background in the law, as well as Polster's, it wasn't surprising that everyone believed it was what Peter would have wanted. The small group left the cafeteria and went back to wait for any hopeful signs that Joan would survive.

Kenneth Gregory had been the Roman Catholic chaplain at Albany Medical Center for nearly a decade. Years ago, he had even worked at St. Thomas the Apostle Parish in Bethlehem, so he was familiar with Joan and Peter Porco.

Gregory learned from a doctor that Joan had been admitted to the Emergency Room in critical condition. The doctors explained the surgeries they would begin once she underwent a CAT scan to reveal the extent of the damage to her face, head, and arms, which had also been slashed.

It was difficult for the human mind to comprehend how serious Joan's injuries were, though they were detailed in page after page of medical records. At the time the paramedics had found her Joan's blood pressure was 70/0. They would later testify in court that number usually meant death.

When she first arrived at the hospital, doctors had to deal with a four to six-inch laceration running from the top of the right side of her forehead to just above her left eye. Another four-inch gash went from just above where her left eye should have been to her nose. Doctors could see her brain through the top of her head – gray matter mixed with blood and bone fragments. A deep half-a-foot long laceration cut the left side of her mouth where her jaw was no longer connected. Teeth were missing. On the bottom of one of her arms, there was another four-inch cut, though the bleeding was controlled there. Her right pupil was dilated and non-responsive. At first Joan didn't respond to any questions, but doctors noted that amazingly, she was later able to shake her head to communicate "yes" or "no."

Joan was intubated, a process by which medical personnel place a tube in the patient's throat to clear the airway. They gave her anesthesia as they suctioned away blood. Doctors were unable to assess how much pain Joan might still be in.

They made sure everything touching her was sterile. They knew that even if Mrs. Porco made it through the first surgery, or even the second, infection would likely set in. They could only do so much to stop it.

With the initial treatment completed and the patient stabilized as much as possible, Father Gregory walked over to Joan Porco. He saw her head and face covered with bandages. Joan was about to have a CAT scan, but there was little hope. Gregory leaned over and gave her the Last Rights of the Roman Catholic Church.

John Polster approached Detective Charles Rudolph, one of the members of the Bethlehem police force who had been walking the hallways of the hospital for several hours now. Polster explained he was an attorney and gave his card to the detective. If Christopher wanted an attorney, Polster said he would fulfill that role. Rudolph gave his business card to Polster along with his pager number. It was just before 8:00 at night.

Christopher Porco arrived at the hospital with his uncle. Polster would later describe the 21-year-old as "dazed and visibly shaken," as he was hugged and given condolences. The red-haired attorney pulled Christopher into a small room nearby, asking the people who had been waiting there to leave. He needed a few moments to discuss the situation. As a former assistant district attorney in neighboring Schenectady County, Polster had seen too many situations where police - rightly or wrongly – had interrogated someone and a carelessly misspoken word led to unnecessary accusations.

Polster got right down to business. He told Christopher that police considered him a suspect in the attack on his parents. "How could anybody think I could do something like this?" Porco asked. Polster told Porco that police wanted to question him and that he could act as the young man's attorney if desired.

The conversation continued as Dr. Elaine LaForte and Dr. John Kearney walked into the room to see how their young friend was holding up. Christopher worked with them at the Bethlehem Veterinary Clinic while he was home from school. They had been impressed with his love of animals and his work ethic. Kearney and LaForte shared concern that their tall, quiet, and soft-spoken friend could be accused of such a crime. As soon as they found out police wanted to speak with Christopher, the two also told him he should have an attorney - just as two police officers walked in.

Bethlehem Police Detective Vincent Rinaldi grabbed Christopher by his left arm. "We'll take him," Polster thought he heard the man say as they walked away. More officers joined them as they walked out of the hospital. Two officers had already sat in the front seats of an unmarked police car - waiting. Detective Rinaldi placed Christopher in the back seat, and then followed him in. Detective Rudolph opened the other rear door, sandwiching Christopher in the middle. There was no way to get out. Christopher noticed they were all armed. By now, the group of officers who had accompanied Christopher to the car filtered into separate police cruisers. A marked Bethlehem Police SUV led the way to the Bethlehem Police Department. It would be a long night.

As the unmarked police car made its way to the police department, Detective Rudolph's pager beeped. It was Polster. Rudolph immediately called the number, and Polster asked to speak with Christopher who was handed the cell phone.

"Hello?"

The two quickly discussed if Christopher wanted Polster as his attorney, then the phone was handed back to

Rudolph. The detective listened for a moment to Polster and then said, "OK."

Polster would later explain he told the detective that he "was going to represent" Christopher. "Don't do any questioning until I get there." But what really happened when Christopher was questioned would be the subject of continued debate.

Christopher remained cool. He had shown little emotion so far and seemed determined not to let the police make him say anything he didn't want to. He was ushered into a room cluttered with boxes and papers and sat down at the table in the middle. In the corner up by the ceiling, a camera quietly recorded the scene in black and white, catching every word.

John Polster arrived at the police station only a few minutes later after a quick discussion amongst the adults at the hospital. All of them had decided Christopher should have an attorney present.

In the silent police station Polster walked up to the dispatcher's window. Determined to assert his client's rights, he asked to speak with Christopher or one of the officers who had taken him in back. The dispatcher made a call, then told Polster to wait. He would be waiting awhile.

Only a few feet away, Detective Bowdish began the interrogation. He told Christopher the attack was a big deal in Bethlehem. The media was all over the story. "I'll probably end up talking to a lot of different people," said Bowdish. Porco sat and listened. "Hopefully I can talk to your mother, too, I guess."

"I haven't seen her yet, so..." Christopher Porco's voice trailed off.

"Right. Right. But whenever we talk to anybody, we always have to...we're supposed to read everybody their rights. All right? Nobody is under arrest. Nobody - that's not the deal here."

Porco sat silently. There was no emotion on the face Bowdish was trying to read.

"I'm trying to gather information, but if I don't do it all right..."

"I understand," said Christopher.

"It's a sheet, all right? Look at it like this." Bowdish slid a piece of paper on the table towards Christopher. "You know, it says, you've got the right to remain silent, refuse to answer any questions. Anything you say can be used against you in a court of law. I'm trying to gather information here, all right? That's all I'm trying to do," Bowdish said, trying to convince the young man.

"I understand," said Porco. He signed the paper.

Time to eliminate variables, thought Bowdish. "Do you know if your brother has been around lately at all?"

Christopher answered in an even tone, "Not to my knowledge. I haven't talked to him in probably a month.

"Okay," said Bowdish.

Porco continued: "Not to my knowledge, no. In fact, no. He's on active duty. You can't just leave."

The interrogation continued with one question after another. Porco didn't flinch from any of the scrutiny. The dispatcher told the investigators in the back room that a man was waiting to see Christopher. He had said something about being an attorney.

Detective Rudolph jumped in on the questioning. "OK, is he representing you?" he asked.

"He couldn't probably because of his relationship with my family," he said.

Rudolph pressed the issue: "OK, but you're OK talking to us?"

"Uh huh."

"You know, I mean, this is something that we," Bowdish paused. "I told you we're collecting information, right?"

Outside the dispatcher's window Polster paced in the hallway. The dispatcher informed him that police had been told he was there. "He waived his right to counsel," said the dispatcher.

"That can't be," said Polster. He knew that technically it was impossible to make the decision without your attorney present. It simply didn't mean anything, at least not legally.

Polster pulled out his cell phone and the business card he had been given at the hospital. He called Detective Rudolph, but the phone's answering machine picked up. Polster usually came off as a calm guy, but he was livid. He identified himself to Rudolph's cell phone as Christopher

Porco's attorney and demanded that all questioning stop until he was allowed to see his client.

Just to the right of the police window, the town court's doors were open. Polster walked over to one of the desks and put down a few papers he had been carrying. He took out a pen. With his legal experience he knew some careful notes could be helpful if the police persisted and eventually brought charges against Christopher. According to his notes, at 8:39 PM he had asked to see Christopher. At 8:52 he asked again. He called again at 8:55. Every twenty minutes he demanded to see Christopher at the dispatcher's window. When someone was there, Polster would say through the glass, "I'm here. I'm Christopher's attorney. Can I see him yet?"

Several hours had gone by, and the interrogation continued. Everyone was beginning to feel drained from the day, but Porco remained cool.

Bowdish had told Christopher over 30 minutes ago that his mother "says you were involved here." But now, the conversation returned to the attorney question once the detective mentioned the word "polygraph."

"I want to have a lawyer present for that," said Christopher.

"Why is that?" asked Bowdish.

"Because I'm not sure that I'm being treated fairly."

Bowdish assured Christopher that he was being treated fairly. "Are you accepting to take it?"

"I will take one," replied Porco. "After I've spoken to a lawyer."

The minutes ticked by, and Bowdish got nowhere with the polygraph question. He tried a different route. Bowdish insinuated he knew Porco had killed his father.

"I was not home," explained Christopher. "I don't know how to say it any plainer to you."

"Mmm? Excuse me?" asked Bowdish.

Porco's voice was still calm. Unemotional. "I don't know how to say it any plainer. I was not home. I was nowhere near my house, and the bottom line is I would never do this, ever."

"That's why I want you to take it," Bowdish said, still pushing the idea. "Because otherwise, you'll just, you know, you'll just be charged."

"There's a trial before, right?" asked Christopher.

"Yeah. I don't want it, you know?"

"I don't want a trial either," said Porco. "Obviously. But, you know, I feel I've been very cooperative."

Polster had been ignored hour after hour. It was approaching one in the morning. He fought the sleep that tugged at his eyes. All the awful news, all the raw emotion, the pressure from police, and it all led him back to the loss of his best friend. Joan would probably die too. Polster sat in the silent courtroom, exhausted.

Detective Rudolph had taken over the questioning. Porco had been offered food, but declined several times. All the stress from the day made food the last thing on his mind.

Christopher drew a crude map on a piece of paper of where he said he had jogged on the University of Rochester campus about 17 hours ago and before he had found out what happened. "Did you have a conversation with anybody while you were running?" Rudolph asked. "Did anybody that you know of see you? Any of your friends see you running?"

"I don't think so," said Porco. When I got back, some people were around."

Rudolph wasn't convinced. "I'll be honest with you. I'm not on the fence. I'm on the other side of the fence, and I'm convinced that you did it."

The camera silently recorded every word.

Porco's voice, again, didn't change from its calm tone. "I understand how you feel, and I'm sorry. Not correct," he told the detective.

"All right," said Rudolph. He had had enough. "All right. So between you and me, right? There is nobody else in here to witness it. Why don't you tell me what happened because nobody else is going – just me anyway with no witnesses – because I know you fucking did it."

"I didn't do it," Porco responded.

"You did it!"

"I most certainly did not," said Porco. "I'm sorry if my reaction is not what you want."

Rudolph didn't like Porco. He didn't like the young man's responses. His parents had just been killed – well, so far the mother wasn't dead yet – and he didn't seem to respond like someone who had just lost at least one parent. Also, he hadn't really pushed to leave to see his mother, another reason why Rudolph was convinced the kid did it. The police had simply told Christopher he couldn't go to the hospital because they believed him to be a threat to his mother. "I've been around doing this long enough to know," Rudolph told Christopher.

"Dealt with a lot of murderers, huh?" Christopher asked sarcastically. The Bethlehem Police Department was relatively small, dealing mostly with smaller infractions in the cozy, suburban town.

"Enough," Rudolph shot back. "Let me guess, there's an insurance policy?"

Again, Porco didn't show any emotion. "I wouldn't kill my parents for money."

The interrogation lasted over six hours before the police let Christopher leave. They couldn't charge him – yet. But he had given them plenty of leads on which to follow up. Just a few rooms down, Polster had been nodding off inside the courtroom and finally decided to leave. He wasn't getting through to anyone, anyway.

He drove his car away from the police station and saw a tall person walking along the side of the street. He slowed down to see who would be walking at this hour of the night. Polster realized it was Christopher and stopped the car. He told him to get in. As they drove back to the hospital, Polster said he had been trying to stop the interrogation and had wanted to talk with him all night. Christopher said he didn't even know Polster had been there at all. He was confident he had told the police he did not and could not have done it. But Polster was concerned – and relieved – once he finally saw Christopher.

Detective Bowdish sent two detectives to the University of Rochester to interview students and continue to gather evidence.

II

From: "Porco" pporco@nycap.rr.com
To: chrisporco@sprintpcs.com
Cc: "Chris Porco" Jeffsalosa@hotmail.com
Sent: Saturday, January 10, 2004 4:47PM
Subject: Urgent you call home.

Chris,

Regret to inform you that you have been academically separated from the U of R. Go to your campus mail box to obtain a copy of the Dean's letter and enclosures explaining withdrawal and tuition refund.

Your grades for the Fall Semester are:
Principals of Economics: D
Intermediate Microeconomics D
Calculus IA E (Rpt)
Leadership & Management II B
General Physics I D

Current GPA: 1.14
Cummulative GPA: 1.51

Immediately upon arrival on campus, please go to the Center for Academic Support (Lattimore Hall Room 312), submit and sign a withdrawal letter and ask for a copy of the instructions for withdrawal Procedure and Refund Policy if you didn't get them at your post office mail box. You must have completed withdrawal from the University before classes begin for us to obtain a full refund for the Spring 2004 semester! Then, inform John Heidkamp and pack up your things. Return all Navy property to the ROTC and sign whatever is needed to separate you from the unit. Mom will be arriving with the van on Tuesday, January 13, 2004 between 3:30-4:00 p.m. to pack you up and bring you home. Please call as soon as possible. Dad

From: "Porco" pporco@nycap.rr.com
To: "Chris Porco" Jeffsalosa@hotmail.com
Sent: Wednesday, January 14, 2004 7:32PM
Subject: Call us between 9:30-10:30 tonight PLEASE!!!!

1/14/04

Hi Christopher-

I imagine that you've had a busy day. Your family is wondering where you stand at U of R. we need copies of letters and your new transcript immediately. Our fax at home is --. I'm sure the dean would allow you to fax the info to us. I would also think that we would receive a letter from him to verify this change since we now have quite a few letters saying that you have been academically separated from the university.

Hope that you are well. I am thinking of coming up Friday night to see you.

Please give some thought to your schedule this semester and how to improve your use of time so that you can get a superior cum…

With mixed feelings I sign off, Your mother
XOXOXOXOXOXOXOXOXOXOXOXOXOXOXOXOXOXOXO

From: Chris Porco cp002m@mail.rochester.edu
To: Peter Porco PPORCO@courts.state.ny.us
Sent: Friday, Jan 16, 2004 11:27 AM
Subject: Re: Moving Out

hey dad,

i got your email, I will be ready.. just bring the blue bins from the basement, I think that should be all I need, I really don't have that much, and I am going to leave the fridge and microwave for JP for awhile at least… Thanks,
Chris

*

Delmar, New York
November 16, 2004

"I'm not saying there's a maniac on the loose," explained Albany County District Attorney Paul Clyne to the line of reporters clutching microphones and pads of paper. "But it is possible the homicide is the result of a random burglary." It was the DA's attempt at calming the fears of the tight-knit neighborhood. The latest television news reports still said Joan was in critical or serious condition, depending on which channel you flipped to. And there had been no arrests.

Few knew police had interviewed Christopher for hours. Journalists simply said Christopher and Johnathan both were with their mother as she did her best to recover from her first surgery. The officials who were allowed to talk to the crowd of cameras said both sons were "not suspects at this time." The local reporters wanted answers for a nervous community. Police wanted answers that would lead them to the killer – answers they hoped would stand up in court.

They continued to come across tantalizing clues at the Porco house. The first was obvious as the investigation took a more methodical, scientific approach. On the side of the home, about six feet above the ground, they found the garage window was left open only a few inches.

Investigators would later learn Peter had bolted the top window to the bottom window for added security. He had made it one solid sliding piece that could only open a few inches at the top or the bottom of its frame.

The outside screen had also been sliced from top to bottom in the shape of a "C." The flap rested against the lower part of the screen, leaving a space that a small puppy might be able to fit through – if it could get that high and if the window hadn't been turned into one piece. A police forensic expert took several pictures of the window and the cut screen.

Investigator Drew McDonald continued his study of every detail outside and inside the house. The extra key that still sat inside the front door's lock had blood smears on it, but after dusting for fingerprints, none were found on the metal surface.

McDonald walked inside. Nothing unusual in the living room. No blood. The dining room – clean. Silverware, china, and crystal all remained. An open pocketbook sat on one of the tables. It held credit cards belonging to Joan Porco, a few family photographs, along with the typical female accoutrements. McDonald noted that nothing seemed to have been taken. Then he realized the brown leather chair in the living room did have blood on it. The cushion held a portable phone in its grasp. On the nearby wall, more blood.

Looking at the details in each room, McDonald made his way to the messier kitchen. Cabinet doors had been left open. Blood spots dotted the floor. Red-stained paper towels and tissues covered the countertop. The nearby sliding glass door was slightly open. He looked down and saw a piece of wood in the track. A small amount of blood had dried on the door's handle.

He walked over to the sink and noticed the dishwasher. Dishes filled both racks, which had been pulled out as if someone were about to put the cups and forks away. Dark red drops stained the floor below the opened dishwasher door. Even the inside of the door had blood on it as if the killer had stood over the open dishwasher. But tests would later reveal the blood was Peter Porco's.

Then McDonald noticed something else. On the top rack of dishes, resting on the mugs and plates, he saw a cashier's check from SEFCU, a credit union, with a smear of red in one of the corners. It had been made out to the Saratoga Springs City Court in the amount of $100, and was signed by Peter. More camera clicks captured the scene.

After looking in the garage, more questions needed to be answered. Both overhead doors remained closed and locked. One of the Porco's vehicles had been parked close to the wall that separated the garage from the inside of the house. McDonald noticed some more blood on the car's blue hood, and there was also a broken bottle nearby. Soon, all of the red blood would look purplish from the amino black processing. It would take five more days to finish that process and catalogue the evidence.

McDonald went back inside. Near the front door on the wall at about eye level, someone had smashed a Time Warner security alarm panel. Every few moments it beeped. The alarm system had either been damaged enough so that it didn't work, or it had been turned off. Nearby, in the downstairs bathroom bits of red toilet paper covered the floor.

Soon, Kurt Meyer, an alarm system technician, arrived at the house. He met with McDonald and took a look at the alarm panel. The LCD screen had been destroyed, but Meyer had a hunch the system would still give them plenty of information.

McDonald brought Meyer downstairs. Veterinarian friends of the Porco's had come a little earlier to get Barr, who had been staying in the basement as police worked upstairs. There had been some discussion, but investigators eventually agreed to let the vets take the dog. It helped eliminate variables from the crime scene by getting a shedding, tail-wagging dog out of there.

The downstairs looked like most finished basements. The cement floor had been covered with a light-colored carpet. Peter Porco had made a mini-office for himself with a computer desk surrounded by filled bookcases. McDonald took more pictures of the scene. The computer seemed untouched, though it would soon be sent away to be mined for any information it might hold. The investigator walked over to the washer and dryer. The dryer had various clothes inside it, most likely Joan's and Peter's. Here, there was no sign of blood.

In the corner of the room behind some junk kept in the basement, McDonald took a picture of another computer tower as Meyer went in to take a look. This one was part of the Porco's Time Warner security system. Meyer and McDonald both knew that even if the smashed keypad didn't work, technicians at the state laboratory might be able to find out when the break-in had occurred. They might even find out when that wire in the backyard had been cut. Tests of the system might help pin down a timeframe for the attack, giving the police one more brick with which to build their case.

It turned out the alarm system wasn't the only "brick" found downstairs. Investigators noticed one fingerprint on the outside of the downstairs door after dusting. Just like the one they had found near the cut phone wire, they hoped that the latest one they had found would lead them right to the killer. But the basement print would be the only one that matched someone other than the two victims.

Albany, New York
November 16, 2004

By now, Christopher Porco's signature bright yellow Jeep Wrangler was in the Armory Garage in Albany surrounded by police tape. Signs in the windshield warned anyone who might be working there not to get anywhere near this large piece of potential evidence.

Porco had purchased the Jeep recently. If you knew Christopher, you knew of his vehicle. After all, who could miss it? He had tricked it out with the coolest and most expensive features. The $17,000 yellow Jeep had extra wide tires that stuck out of the sides by several inches. A winch and fog lights sat on the front grill. Even the seats had been upgraded. The headrests were really speakers that gave both the driver and passenger the feel of luxury, even while driving off-road. Police had brought it by flatbed from Rochester to Albany. It was basically the same trip they believed he would have made only a few dozen hours ago if their suspicions proved true.

Rochester Police officer Michael Cotsworth found the vehicle. Another officer had asked him if he had recently seen a yellow Jeep. Since he had driven by one earlier, he knew exactly where it was parked.

Cotsworth headed towards Genesee Street on the South Side of the city, where there were plenty of college students who spilled into the neighborhood from the University of Rochester campus. He parked his police car and walked over. It turned out he was right. The Jeep was registered to a Christopher Porco.

Cotsworth called the State Police and blocked off the street to eliminate traffic. He pulled out a roll of yellow police tape and formed a perimeter around the vehicle. He looked inside. Some Wendy's hamburger wrappers were crumpled on the floor. A Dunkin' Donuts cup stuck out of the center cup holder, filled a quarter of the way with a brown liquid. Because it was dark, he didn't see much else.

Soon the Jeep rested on top of a flatbed truck for its journey to Albany, where investigators would scour the vehicle for anything that might link him to the crime.

Delmar, New York
November 18, 2004

As news crews outside continued to speculate about what had happened inside the house on Brockley Drive, forensic investigators walked near the yellow police tape that by its very sight reminded everyone something absolutely awful had happened. The police ignored the journalists and small groups of curious onlookers who wanted to make some sense of the murder scene.

Reporters had begun to dig deeper into the story. They found a history of police visits to the Porco's home.

The last had been almost a year ago. November 29th, the Friday after Thanksgiving, police had been called around dinnertime for a burglary. A Bethlehem Police Officer had met Joan and Peter at the front door of their home. Joan seemed shaken. Peter was concerned. They walked over to the front of the house where Peter showed the officer the damage. The officer looked over the cut window screen in the cold air.

The family then showed the officer where their computers had been. The burglar had taken two laptops – a Mac and a Dell, one of which was Joan's computer from her work as a school speech language pathologist.

The officer walked away from the house after being told a camera had been dropped in the yard. A dusting of snow covered the electronic device that the burglar had apparently dropped while making his getaway.

The burglar would never be brought to justice for the crime. For years, it would remain an open case. But it had spooked Peter and Joan enough for them to put an alarm system in the house and was likely the reason that garage window had been bolted together.

Delmar, New York
November 19, 2004

Police continued their work. Inside the home they noticed a man's smashed Timex watch in the bed where Joan had been found. At first it didn't seem out of place. But Peter's watch had already been accounted for.

While investigators pondered what that could mean, officials from the University of Rochester dropped off a variety of items a little before five in the evening. They had confiscated clothes and other personal belongings from Christopher Porco's dorm room back in Rochester, hoping if their suspect was in fact guilty, they'd find a telltale clue.

Meanwhile, some of the remaining members of the Porco family hired well-known Albany-area attorney, Terence Kindlon. He ran the successful Kindlon & Shanks law firm, with offices only a block or so away from the center of New York's capital city. Kindlon would represent Christopher in court if necessary, but until then he told police to leave the young man alone. If they had evidence, they could charge him with a crime. Absent any charges though, Kindlon didn't want police falsely pointing to Porco. His client had proclaimed innocence from the start.

Calling hours for Peter Porco were held November 20th, from 9:30 until 11:30 in the morning at Saint Frances

DeSales Church in Loudonville. Still in the hospital, his wife was unable to attend. Peter, the father of two and friend to everyone at the office, had been killed at the age of 52.

III

From:	"Porco" pporco@nycap.rr.com
To:	chrisporco@sprintpcs.com
Sent:	Friday, March 19, 2004 8:32PM
Subject:	Failing Grades-You did it again!!!!!!!!!!!!!!!!!!!!

You just left and I can't believe my eyes as I look at your midterm grade report. (F, F, F, IP) How could you LIE to us like you did. You know what they say, " Three strikes and you're out." Explain yourself. Mom and dad

From:	"Chris Porco" cp002m@mail.rochester.edu
To:	"Porco" pporco@nycap.rr.com
Sent:	Saturday, March 20, 2004 9:15AM
Subject:	Failing Grades-You did it again!!!!!!!!!!!!!!!!!!!!

Hi im in london, ive been touring around with sarah a bit. I don't know why my grades would say that. I assure you, I didn't 'do it again'. One reason may say that is of when I registered, my teachers initially had no record of me in their classes. I would assume that is all that needs to be fixed, although it shouldn't have been a problem, I have been getting grades. Maybe it just hasn't been reflected in the computer for some reason. But obviously they are incorrect... my lowest grade that I have gotten anything is a B on a physics test. My grade in that class shuold be a low A though because I got an A on the first test. Im emailing the registrar now and ill see what they say. Don't jump to conclusions, im fine. London is wonderful, ive seen most of the major sites today, the cathedral, big ben, parliament, the bridges, westminster abby, some other stuff. Ill try to call you tonight. Love you
chris

*

Albany, New York
December, 2004

For the next several weeks Joan would hold onto life as best she could. Only a day after the attack she was brought into the operating room. Doctors wrote in their reports that she tolerated the operation to remove excess blood well. Plates and screws were used to repair the most extensive damage to her head. The surgeons and doctors worked hard to keep everything as sterile as possible to avoid septic shock.

The day after the initial surgeries - the day after all those bandages covered her face and her left arm - Joan Porco had been able to roll over in bed in what doctors call a "log roll." But for several weeks, Joan would remain in a medically induced coma. There were signs she would make it, but no one knew for sure. The dressings on her facial wounds were changed regularly.

While lying in her hospital bed, Thanksgiving came and went. The Balzanos still spent much of their time at the hospital by Joan's side during her recovery. They even rented a small apartment from Albany Med so they could stay near the hospital. The Polsters visited often. Christopher visited most days as well.

They weren't the only ones. District Attorney Paul Clyne had also made several visits to the hospital. He wanted to see if Joan could remember anything that might solve the crime that had left her with a broken family. But he had to wait. The one person who might be able to explain what had happened – a speech language pathologist, nonetheless - couldn't communicate.

Sure, Detective Bowdish had told Clyne of the head nod. That would certainly be helpful for prosecuting Christopher if it came to that. But Clyne wanted to be sure. Perhaps she knew something else, another piece of the puzzle that could transform the brutal attack into a closed case. Either way, some would forever doubt what she communicated.

But then, finally, as the unusually warm days of November gave way to the cold of December, there was good news. Joan awoke from her coma. Clyne asked her doctors if he could interrogate her. They gave him the OK. But while Clyne tried to interview Joan from her hospital bed, she was unable to give him much information. It seemed to Clyne that Joan couldn't remember anything about the night she and Peter had been attacked. Doctors explained to the DA that it might be temporary memory loss resulting from the drug-induced coma.

Clyne hoped that's all it was. Temporary. It would be nice to tie up the case with a big ribbon and hand it to a jury for an easy decision. After all, he only had a month left as the DA. After a messy re-election bid, Clyne had just been beaten by David Soares, who had worked under Clyne until he was fired.

Joan Porco never did regain her memory of the attack. It would create legal dilemmas and allow some to speculate that perhaps "having no memory" was her way of protecting the remaining members of her family. Such speculation would turn out to be wrong.

Though Joan was alive, the loss of her memory from that dreadful night essentially meant the loss of the most important witness. While there was no one to blame but the attacker, her loss of memory would cause the investigation to last far longer than it otherwise might have.

Albany, New York
December 2, 2004

Terence Kindlon enjoyed a view of the federal courthouse through the windows of his corner office. That courthouse used to be a large U.S. Post Office for the city of Albany after it had been constructed in the early 1900's. But Kindlon wasn't paying much attention to the view. As Christopher's attorney, he had been poring over the mounds of documents that had filled up half of the room next to his office. That wasn't all. He had also been fielding calls from the media, offering to comment at some point about the whole mess. He felt it was necessary because the public already had his client pegged as the killer. Kindlon was appalled by it all. He had spoken with Christopher, of course, and he knew Christopher to be the victim. The young man had lost his father and had nearly lost his mother.

Kindlon had practiced law in the Capital Region for years. Though he spoke with the passion and energy of a much younger man, the lines on Kindlon's face and the thinning brownish-gray hair gave his true age away. He had married his current wife, Laurie Shanks, a law professor specializing in closing arguments and cross-examinations, years ago. Their children had grown up. One of his sons would soon head out to Fallujah with the Marines. It was a place that would become the scene of some of the worst fighting in the Iraq War. The elder Kindlon, a Marine who had survived being shot in the head in Vietnam, had returned from that war and graduated from Ithaca College. The politically liberal Kindlon had learned to be skeptical of the government and of people in power, perhaps from his experience in Vietnam. His views may have also stemmed from his work in cases that had caught the public's attention over the years. At one point he had battled in court to prove that some police had been trained to plant evidence. He had won that battle, shaking up the system in the process.

But with the government's financial help in the form of the G.I. Bill and lots of studying, he had passed the bar exam. And as the years went by, the cases became more serious. While he had been involved in several high-profile trials like the evidence planting case, this murder case – which was far from going to trial – was already getting plenty of media attention.

Kindlon's powerful but raspy voice, his tall frame, and his Marine-straight posture, gave the impression that he was in control - and he wasn't averse to what some might call dramatics in the courtroom. He hadn't given too many of his famous sound bites to the cameras yet, even as the pressure on his client had become overwhelming. As people from Delmar and the Town of Bethlehem remained concerned a killer was on the loose, Kindlon believed the police – or the District Attorney's office - had already unfairly painted the picture that his client was guilty through a few key leaks in the local newspaper. While Laurie worked behind the scenes, Kindlon was ready to set the record straight for his client who was just old enough to legally buy himself a drink.

In fact, Kindlon had begun kicking his side of the public relations war into high gear. Especially after inquiring reporters found out that subpoenas had been handed out to dozens of people, including University of Rochester students who were mostly friends and fraternity brothers of Christopher's. A grand jury was scheduled to meet tomorrow, Friday, December 3rd. They would look at the evidence, hear testimony from witnesses like those students, and then decide if they should indict anyone for the murder in Delmar. If they did, it could lead to a trial.

"Instead of conducting a proper investigation," said Kindlon to the cameras that surrounded him, "they've spent the last few weeks on a scavenger hunt." Kindlon would continue to say that police had been investigating Christopher and not the crime. Investigate someone long enough, he argued, you might start to convince yourself you had found the person responsible.

The night before the grand jury convened, Kindlon's face filled television screens across the Capital Region, explaining Christopher may not have been officially or publicly named as the suspect, but police were treating him that way. Already, he said, the Bethlehem Police Department had turned down resources offered to them from the Sheriff's Department and New York State Police. Kindlon knew that meant they thought they had their man. Still, no one had been charged with any crimes.

"I hear him being accused of murder everyday," Kindlon told the cameras. "And there's nothing he can do to defend himself."

Albany, New York
December 3, 2004

All the big names walked through the front door of the Albany County Justice Building. Michael McDermott went off to the side of the metal detectors, clutching a large briefcase full of papers for the day. The thin, tall, graying, and soft-spoken Chief Assistant District Attorney was still hoping to stay on the case even though the new DA would take over operations in only a few weeks.

Clutching his own heavy briefcase, Kindlon walked in as well, ready for the long day ahead. While all the players made their way to the proper room, no comments were made to the media because of the secret, private nature of the grand jury hearings.

As everyone already knew, a grand jury typically decides if there's enough evidence to indict someone in a crime, which then usually leads to a trial. But earlier that day, McDermott hinted about the other use for the grand jury. With witnesses under oath, the process could act as yet another tool to get information out and keep the investigation moving along.

Television news reports would be filled with the best speculation of Albany's reporters as the grand jury met. The witnesses who testified had to be figured out through back-channels. Occasionally - and off the record - those "in-the-know" would tell reporters. But with no one from the public allowed in – what was said behind closed doors remained a mystery. At least for now.

However, the witnesses were easy to identify, at least on the first day as University of Rochester students walked into the courthouse. Reporters on the evening news surmised that prosecutors were picking apart Porco's alibi – his assertion that if he was on campus at the time of the attack, then it was impossible he had been in Albany. Kindlon later told reporters the students "confirm Christopher was on campus late Sunday night and again early Monday morning. I don't know where the DA is going."

Rochester, New York
November 14, 2004

All the students at the University of Rochester called it "Munro." It was a place that had become more known for its parties and student get-togethers than for being a good place to sleep at night. It wasn't too different from most other college dorms, where students become nocturnal and mornings are quiet.

Most members of the University's chapter of the fraternity, Sigma Phi Epsilon, lived in the building after the fraternity moved from Wilder Tower to Munro that year. At its weekly chapter meeting Christopher joined over a dozen of his fellow frat brothers.

The conversation was nothing out of the ordinary. Plans for upcoming fraternity events. A check of the group's finances. A brief discussion about the visit by the fraternity's regional director, Jason Wortham, who would arrive later in the evening. The brothers discussed where Wortham would sleep. It was usual practice for someone to give up his bed for the guest. The truth was, another brother had already offered his bed, but then he had taken back his offer, telling his friends he just couldn't do it. The young men frowned. To go back on your word in Sigma Phi, well, it just wasn't done. Discussion of their options followed, and then Christopher Porco told them he would volunteer his bed. It was no big deal, he assured them. He would sleep on the couch in the lounge instead. Problem solved.

Some of the brothers were still upset Porco had offered his bed – allowing his brother to get away with reneging on his offer. But he reassured them. Besides, the brothers knew Christopher had plenty of other places to stay if he wanted. The quiet young man with his short, dark, spiked hair and piercing eyes had a way with women. Whether it was with a friend or just camping out in the lounge, he surely had a place to stay.

The meeting continued with the "gavel pass" where each brother says something about his week. Lewis Ortiz, Vice President of Sigma Phi Epsilon, who was taking classes at the medical school, updated his friends. The others followed. Christopher said he had gone home to Delmar to see his girlfriend who attended a different school. He said he had left last Friday the 12th and had returned the following day. It was nice to see his blonde haired, blue-eyed girlfriend, Sarah. He said he hadn't had time to see his parents. He then told them he didn't feel good – some sort of cold or something - which had tired him out.

After the meeting, Christopher and some of his friends walked to the charity event known as "Anchor Splash" which involved selling T-shirts, holding "a beautiful eyes contest," and a swim relay. Porco had been an accomplished swimmer in high school. However, he hadn't followed up on any of that talent in college, except at the charity, even though he was built for the sport. The event raised a couple thousand dollars for Delta Gamma's foundation, Aid to the Blind and Sight Conservation, to get Braille books and other important resources to the blind.

By the time the event ended it had been dark out for several hours. Porco met up with friend and dorm-mate, Marshall Crumiller, along with another acquaintance, Travis Johnson. They grabbed dinner at "the pit," a favorite spot on campus, around 9:30 at night. Christopher joked around about parking his Jeep on campus in back of Munro – that he would stick it right on the grass by the building.

Crumiller shared the laugh and then offered to drive Porco to get his vehicle that had been parked off campus as usual to avoid parking enforcement. Christopher hadn't paid to park on campus. He took Crumiller up on the offer, especially since it was cold and he didn't care to walk to his Jeep; they were in Rochester, with a significantly higher crime rate than Delmar's.

Porco parked the Jeep by his dorm and went inside. Everyone was getting ready for a relaxed night before another week of classes began. A small group of students hung out in the lounge where Chris had told his frat brothers he would sleep. There, they watched the movie, "Shrek," until two or three in the morning. Students came and went. Some chatted and most drank - one reason why no one remembered exactly what time everyone left the lounge.

Porco's parents were attacked only hours later.

Rochester, New York
November 15, 2004

Rachel Boylan, who would later graduate from the University of Rochester to become a Lieutenant in the United States Marine Corps, lived in Gale, another dorm on campus. She awoke and threw on some sweatpants and a sweatshirt. At 8:45 in the morning, there was just enough time to grab some food on the way to class – aerobics class, really. Boylan walked over the Phase Bridge, a pedestrian walkway. She noticed someone in shorts - a tall person, jogging below her - making his way towards a parking lot perhaps. She recognized Christopher Porco and kept walking. She had attended ROTC the same as he had, so she knew of him, though he had quit after only a brief stint. Thinking nothing of it, she continued on her way.

Albany, New York
December 8, 2004

Joan Porco continued her recovery. Doctors noted that she was responding to her medications well. They were able to reduce the overwhelming amount she had to take. Still, the scars that ran across her face were apparent to everyone who was there offering support.

Her recovery had just begun, and Albany Med had only so much to offer her. They had done their job. Joan Porco was brought to the reputable Sunnyview Rehabilitation Clinic about a half-hour away in Schenectady. There, she would get the treatment she needed. It wouldn't be days or even weeks, but almost a year before Joan would be seen in public.

Before he left office, District Attorney Paul Clyne set up a camera and interviewed Joan from her hospital bed, saving her answers on tape for the grand jury.

Albany, New York
December, 2004

The grand jury continued convening each Friday, listening to witness after witness tell their stories. A female friend of Christopher Porco's apparently testified – his girlfriend – though no one was sure that's who she was – and she was already distancing herself from the Bethlehem Police Department's "person of interest." The Times Union, the newspaper delivered to thousands of homes in the Capital Region, had broken news (as it would continue to do in the case) that a neighbor thought he might have seen Porco's yellow Jeep in the driveway the night of the attack. The grand jury learned about Peter and Joan's financial status. Reports on the matter got the public suspecting that investigators thought an inheritance could be the motive. Overall, little information was leaked about what was happening behind closed doors, but what did get published seemed only to increase the Capital Region's suspicions that the well-off preppy college kid had committed murder.

As the public grasped for any detail that had to do with the case, and the investigation progressed quietly and methodically, rumors spread like wildfire. Some were true, many were not, and some were simply unverifiable. The newspaper reported that investigators were looking into whether Christopher had a gambling habit. Bethlehem Police wouldn't comment.

The fourth time the grand jury convened, on December 21, was the last time before the holidays and the last before the new District Attorney took over. As usual, no one would comment about any witnesses or the testimony. But every reporter waiting outside the courtroom knew what was going on as soon as it happened. It wasn't an uncommon sight, but audio/visual equipment was wheeled in on a large cart. The doors closed. Then everyone heard a slightly muffled voice coming from inside that could only belong to Joan Porco. The taped interview played because it was still impossible for her to be there in person.

Time ticked away, the holidays passed, and December became January. In Delmar and around the Capital Region, the case continued to make for intriguing conversation. Everyone had a theory. From the impossible: his brother had to have done it - where was the military man? To the more believable: someone angry with Peter Porco's legal work had done it.

It seemed most people thought there was enough evidence to put Christopher away for life. The rumors came from everywhere. Even closer to the actual case, it was hard not to hear word that an indictment was imminent. But nothing happened.

Just after Valentine's Day in 2005, the news picked up on the fact that Christopher had found not one – but two - GPS tracking devices on his yellow Jeep, the same Jeep that continued to draw stares wherever he drove it. At first, according to his angry attorney, his client didn't even know what the devices were. "They're just grasping at straws," a very frustrated Kindlon told the local 24-hour news channel. "The next time we find one on a car, I'm going to take it to the Thruway and stick it to the side of a truck and let it take a ride to Buffalo."

Officials wouldn't comment on the specifics, but it turned out the devices were placed on the vehicle by the State Police. Being able to track Christopher's every move through his car's travels wasn't only perfectly legal, it was a great way to see if he would lead investigators anywhere interesting. He hadn't, and instead he continued to check his car for similar devices.

Meanwhile, the minimal flow of information continued as investigators remained relatively tight-lipped. "We can't comment on ongoing investigations" seemed to become a popular phrase for officials. Then word came that Christopher himself might testify in front of the grand jury where progress seemed to stall as February turned to March. Then Spring became Summer. All the while, talk of how Christopher had to have done it filled the collective conversation of the Capital Region.

Joan Porco – who had not been seen in public – apparently had enough of it all. On August, 24, 2005 the Times Union printed a letter from her that made the paper's front-page headline, and served to add even more fuel to the speculative fire:

JOAN M. PORCO

August 23, 2005

Albany Times Union
Box 15000
Albany, NY 12202

Dear Editor:

On November 15, 2004, my world tragically changed. The happy life that my beloved husband, Peter, and our sons, Johnathan and Christopher, had was lost forever. Johnathan was just starting his career. Christopher was early in his college life. Peter and I were contemplating our retirement and planning on being able to enjoy the rest of our lives with our many relatives and friends. On that horrible day, Peter and I were victims of a brutal attack. Peter died from his wounds. Thanks to wonderful doctors, numerous medical treatments and surgeries, I have survived. I continue to improve, and even though I have suffered grievous injury, both physical and emotional, I thank God for my life.

Unfortunately, the horror and unbearable sadness I continue to feel as a result of the loss of Peter has been dramatically intensified by the trauma that our cherished son, Christopher, has been forced to endure. I have been told that within hours of us being found in our home, the Bethlehem police declared Christopher to be a suspect in the murder of his father and the attack on me. Incredibly, the police have told the media that Christopher and his father had a difficult relationship and that he therefore had a motive to kill him. Although dozens of family members, friends, and neighbors have told the police that these statements are lies, the Bethlehem police continue to spread vicious rumors about Christopher and our family.

I want to say unequivocally that, although I have no memory whatsoever of the attack, either because I was asleep or because of my injuries, I am absolutely positive that my son was in no way involved in this heinous crime. He is an intelligent, compassionate, peaceful, and loving person, and no one could ask for a better son. He, Peter, our older son Johnathan, and I have always had a wonderful relationship, and Christopher would never hurt any one of us.

I implore the Bethlehem police and the District Attorney's Office to leave my son alone, and to search for Peter's real killer or killers, so that he can rest in peace, and my sons and I can live in safety.

Sincerely,
Joan M. Porco
Joan M. Porco

*

Because she stood by her son, reporters challenged officials: was Christopher a suspect or not? If not, then why the intense focus? It seemed only to torment his recovering mother and divide the family in two.

But officials responded. District Attorney David Soares made his own headlines when he called Christopher the "s-word" - a suspect - for the first time. "I believe we have enough information and evidence to say Mrs. Porco is wrong," he said.

Soares' statements were buttressed just a couple months later. Just before Halloween and after yet another grand jury meeting, officials leaked more information to the Times Union. It didn't look good for Christopher. One of the two computers that had been stolen from the Porco residence back on November 29th, 2003, had been traced back to him. It would later come out that police had found several electronics in a small safe Christopher kept at the Brockley Drive house.

Albany, New York
November 4, 2005

The grand jury reconvened, and everyone knew what was about to happen. After almost a year and plenty of criticism from the public on how slow the process seemed to be going, the grand jury indicted Christopher Porco in the murder of his father and the attempted murder of his mother, even though she still supported him. With his trademark nonchalance, Porco was led out of the courtroom in handcuffs as he and Kindlon failed to dodge the bright lights of the television cameras.

Kindlon continued to deny his client's involvement, telling the thick throng of reporters "there really is nothing here. There's never been anything here as far as Christopher's concerned…when we can look at the evidence - that will be established beyond dispute." Porco was escorted out of the building to a police vehicle, and was transported to the Albany County Correctional Facility. The judge set his bail hearing for two weeks later.

DA David Soares addressed the reporters. They wanted to know how his office would sort out the conflict between prosecuting Joan's son for her attempted murder while she had publicly stated he couldn't have done it. "Ultimately the issue here is in order to get justice for Joan Porco, we have to find her son guilty," he said in his understated, calm tone of voice.

Prosecutors spoke over the next couple weeks about the relative strength of their case and how they had left "no stone unturned." Kindlon continued to argue that police ignored information that might take them to other suspects. Both sides bickered through the media about how much Joan's take on the crime was being considered. Kindlon repeatedly used Joan as an example to show how officials were only looking at evidence that met their assumptions. "Joan complains it's been over nine months since anybody from the police department or the District Attorney's office has talked to her," Kindlon told several news channels. Prosecutors said that was completely inaccurate.

Either way, November 14th made it one year since the attack. *One year*. And yet, even if some sort of closure might be possible for family and friends – such a feeling seemed so far away.

Albany, New York
November 16, 2005

Bail hearings are typically straightforward affairs. Both sides show some of the cards they're holding – but rarely reveal any aces. The process allows both sides to explain why a suspect may or may not flee the area to try and avoid a trial. Prosecutors reveal some of the evidence that might give the judge reason to think a suspect will "disappear" beforehand. The defense attorneys try to argue that a suspect will indeed show up. The defense asks that if bail is set, it should be lower (or in some cases nothing or next to nothing) than what the prosecutors argue to ease the burden on the defendant and his or her family and friends. Either way, this bail hearing would only increase the public's appetite for more information about the case as Christopher Porco's comfort over the next several months depended on the judge's decision.

Most times, bail can be set rather quickly. But not this time. Christopher, still in handcuffs, came into the Albany County Courtroom through the maze of hallways inaccessible to the public. His mother and brother had already written the judge asking for his release on bond:

JOAN M. PORCO

November 13, 2005
Hon. Jeffrey Berry
Albany County Courthouse
Albany, New York 12207

RE: Christopher Porco

Dear Judge Berry:

I understand that you will be presiding over the trial of my son, Christopher, and that you will be the person making the decision as to whether or not he will be released on bail pending trial.

I am sure that you know that the present charges against Christopher result from a brutal attack on November 15, 2004, upon my husband, Peter, and me. Peter died as a result of his wounds. Thankfully, I survived.

Even though I am still in the process of recovering from the attack, I have had many occasions to be with Christopher. During all of those times, he has been the same loving person that Peter and I raised, and continues to treat me with the same respect that he showed before the attack. I have no fear being in his presence.

Based upon everything that I know, and that I have heard about the investigation, I firmly believe that Christopher is innocent. In saying this, there are some things that I would like to bring to your attention. I have heard through the media that the police and district attorney's office are claiming that Peter and Christopher did not have a good relationship. This is a false allegation. Their relationship was excellent. While there were some disputes that caused problems, those disputes never reached a level that would have destroyed their relationship, let alone caused one to attack the other. Further, after the DA's office questioned me while I was at Sunnyview Hospital, in Schenectady, they asked if I might be available for further questioning. Even though I have been living outside of the Capital District area since December, 2004, I have always been available to travel back to Albany. Never in the 12 months since the attack has the DA's office contacted me to come to the Grand Jury so that I could answer questions about my family. And I want the court to know that I am appalled about the lies that have been told about my family. I was also disappointed that I did not know about the Grand Jury vote to bring charges against Christopher. Had I known that he was going to be in Court, I would have been there to support him.

I am imploring you to set bail, and that you set it in a very modest amount. I plan on using all resources available to me to post bail for my son, Christopher.

On behalf of Christopher, and in hopes that my family will not be further torn apart, I thank you for your consideration.

Very truly yours,
Joan M. Porco
Joan M. Porco

JOHNATHAN D. PORCO
Saratoga Springs, New York

November 13, 2005

Hon. Jeffrey Berry
Albany County Courthouse
Albany, New York 12207

RE: Christopher Porco

Dear Judge Berry:

I am sending this letter on behalf of my brother, Christopher. I am told that you will be presiding over his trial, and deciding whether or not he will be released on bail pending trial.

Chris is charged with the murder of my father and attempted murder of my mother. I am firmly convinced that he is innocent. I have not heard or seen anything from him or any other source that would indicate to me that he is guilty.

I am currently in the military. Because of that, my time and location are determined by my orders. Currently I am in the Saratoga area and, to the extent that my position will allow, I will do whatever I can to assure the Court that my brother will be in Court whenever he is supposed to be. I would also like the Court to know that, had I known Chris was going to be in Court as a result of the Grand Jury action, I would have been there. I didn't know until it was happening, and could not make it.

I support my brother and am requesting that you set bail in a very modest amount.

Thank you.

Very truly yours,

Johnathan D. Porco

*

Joan's letter was signed, Johnathan's had not been.

Meanwhile, dozens of television and print reporters and their photographers followed Joan as she moved as quickly as she could through the hallway to the courtroom. She tried her best to ignore the crazy scene. Cameras clicked away. Flashes lit up the room. To shield her body from the cold air and hide her extensive injuries, Joan kept the hood of her white winter jacket over her head. A pair of wide, black sunglasses wrapped around her deeply scarred face. A few reporters would later say she looked like a completely different person. They talked about the difference as an old photograph of her with Peter continued to be shown on the evening news.

Just minutes after her son entered the courtroom, Joan took her seat. The arguments would last for hours, taking several days until a decision was reached. Chief Assistant District Attorney Michael McDermott asked that no bail be set so that Christopher would have to wait for his trial in jail. But Kindlon argued that was ridiculous. After all, hadn't Christopher remained around his hometown even through all the intense investigative – and public – scrutiny? "The DA wants you to believe he's some terrible person," Kindlon said and would continue to say to reporters in the coming months.

McDermott said Christopher wasn't a terrible person – at least not all the time. He told the judge he believed Christopher was a manipulator who would behave one way to his friends and family, but then act another when no one was looking. "One of the things Mr. Kindlon's been stressing," McDermott told reporters outside the courtroom, "is that he had no criminal record, that he had never been in trouble before. We put forward facts that he'd been engaging in criminal activity." Officials would later say the extent of that supposed criminal activity was even greater than what the judge would allow to come into court.

As the first day came to an end, the judge didn't make a decision as to whether Christopher would get bail or not. He needed more time. Just as he had arrived at the courthouse, Christopher was brought back to the Albany County jail in handcuffs.

The hearing would continue a week later, but before then, Times Union reporter, Brendan Lyons, struck again. The newspaper shared e-mails that gave the public an inside look at communications between Christopher and his parents right before the attack:

Peter Porco - $31,000 loan and Car loan

From: Peter Porco
To: Christopher at U of R
Subject: $31,000 loan and Car loan

Chris,

The Bursar says you owe the school $16,003.26 for the current semester. They have no record of any tuition waiver or exemption for the current semester. They tell me you will not be allowed to register for the Spring semester until this sum is paid. They also inform me that you have not signed any type of payment agreement. Obviously you have not been truthful with us about the status of this semester's costs. You must be planning to use the current $15,500 installment to pay for the current semester and are counting on the receipt of the second installment in January to pay for the Spring Semester. I've contacted the student financial aid office and instructed them to return the $15,500 electronic installment they are to receive because it was not authorized. They have agreed to do so. In addition, Citibank has been directed to stop any future installments on the loan and they have agreed to do that. You need to contact Citibank right away at -- and either rescind the loan or drop me as a co-signer and I expect written confirmation from them faxed to me at the office and at home that they have done so. You should tell them that the U of R has been contacted and agreed to return the electronic installment. If I'm to incur any further debt in connection with your college expenses for the <u>current</u> semester, it will be on my terms with the lender I choose. I'm certainly not gong to agree to a loan at an interest rate of prime +.5 with a cap of 25%! I can do better with a Plus loan at 4.75% with a cap of 9%.

As if this isn't bad enough, I just learned from mom that Citibank auto finance has been calling over the last two days saying that you must pay both the past due October payment and your November payment right away or you will be in default on the loan and that will affect my credit rating since I am an owner of the car. Mom's been trying to e-mail you but you have not answered. You have a lot of explaining to do. It's time to stop the bullshit and call me at the office right away. Dad

---

From: "Porco" XXX@nycap.rr.com
To: Chris Porco" XXX@springpcs.com
Sent: Monday, November 08, 2004 4:05PM
Subject: 11/8-Monday- Call tonight or I'll be there tomorrow

Chris-
Dad and I are very upset about your not communicating with us. We don't know if you are well or mentally stable. Uncle John and Aunt Barbara and Uncle David will be here tonight and we may need to discuss your behavior with them as well. Dad is about to have a nervous breakdown. Do you understand that you are not behaving responsibly? If you don't call I will be there to see you tomorrow. For God sakes, call, MOM

*

The e-mails were only part of the prosecution's arsenal. They hoped the writings would show a different side of Christopher and the darker relationship they believed he had with his parents, something Kindlon would continue to argue against in court. "Chris Porco had no history of violence at all," he said. "Because his credit cards weren't paid and his marks at school were bad," he would later ask the courtroom, "we're supposed to believe he wanted to kill his parents?" Kindlon, who had several kids of his own, told reporters on more than one occasion that most families with college students would likely be guilty of having similar conversations.

The e-mails angered John Polster. He told several reporters that no one was talking about the last e-mail that Peter sent to Christopher. That note would later come out, but for now, Polster said it showed a father and son who had worked out their problems - problems, that once again, were not too uncommon for families putting children through college. Christopher's supporters argued debts were certainly not good enough of a motive for the young man to actually try killing both of his parents.

Albany, New York
November 22, 2005

The scene looked nearly identical to the one from just a week ago. Reporters filled the courtroom. Christopher looked calm. His short, dark hair was a bit rumpled and without its normal gel or mousse.

Judge Jeffrey Berry, who presided over cases in Orange County, had been given this case to prevent a conflict of interest since Peter Porco knew the Albany legal community well - including judges - and they of course knew him. The case was assigned to a downstate venue where it was decided Berry would be the proper man for the job.

He had started out as a judge in Newburgh in the mid-1980's and had risen within the ranks through the years to his current position. He was known for his ability to handle tough cases, though he was also known by some for his slightly different style in the courtroom. Berry often stood up and paced behind the bench, something that seemed to surprise attorneys. As cases progressed and the pacing continued, they grew accustomed to it and would make their arguments just the same.

Judge Berry decided to set bail at $250,000 in cash or $1 million bond. Prosecutors may have been surprised, but they didn't show it. Everyone would claim victory. Soares told reporters after the courtroom emptied that such bail "is unprecedented in Albany County." Sure, prosecutors had wanted Porco to wait for trial in jail, but they simply downplayed the decision by saying it only meant a trial was coming.

The defense team, however, was visibly excited. Because bail was unlikely for someone accused of such a vicious crime, they considered it one of the first "wins" in what they hoped would become a pattern. Christopher Porco spoke briefly with Kindlon, then returned to jail as his family and friends began putting together what they could to bail him out. They would literally mortgage houses to do it, Polster told Capital News 9.

And sure enough, only six days later, $250,000 in cash had been raised, not only allowing for his release, but making another court appearance unnecessary. As Christopher walked out of the Albany County Correctional Facility a free man, he stopped in front of a group of reporters. One asked Christopher how he felt. Kindlon reassured his client it was all right to talk. “Well, pretty good…actually,” he said slightly awkwardly, like a young student trying to do his best delivering a speech in school. “I’d like to say that I’m absolutely innocent, and I’m looking forward to trial.”

“OK,” mumbled Kindlon as he put his arm around Porco and the two escaped the reporters. Porco spent the weekend at a hotel near Albany International Airport with his mother. Kindlon told reporters Mrs. Porco was excited to see her son. The case would only get more bizarre in the coming months.

In early December, the Albany County Bar Association honored Peter at their annual memorial service.

PART II
PRE-TRIAL

IV

Albany, New York
January, 2005

Sometimes Judges put conditions on those fortunate enough to make bail, but there were no exact rules for what Porco could or couldn't do. All he had to do was stay in the area and not break the law.

He wouldn't violate either of those two promises to the judge. But that didn't stop the public from ratcheting up the gossip about the otherwise seemingly collected young man. And some of the gossip was true.

Downtown Albany, with its proximity to several colleges, always seems to get busy once the sun sets and the dinner crowds leave for suburbia. With about a dozen bars around Pearl Street - from sports bars to clubs, from the upscale to the cheap - most people can easily find their right crowd. Many of these establishments have specials to bring in the undecided customers, but several bars also hold what's called "trivia night." Come in. Drink. Answer random questions, and win prizes.

Christopher Porco was often seen downtown enjoying himself, taking part in the trivia games at which he was quite good. Every once in awhile, someone would recognize him as the guy on TV and would ask to have a picture taken with him. That especially included cute college-aged girls who thought Porco was good-looking. Many didn't really know the story – or at least they said they didn't. Several local internet blogs posted pictures of Christopher out enjoying himself.

"Doctors, lawyers, Indian Chiefs, truck drivers, and everybody has an opinion about this case," Terry Kindlon would later say. Reporters and a few knowledgeable attorneys wondered why Porco hadn't been advised to keep a low profile so whatever he did wouldn't taint the potential jury pool. Others thought perhaps Porco just wasn't listening. Many theorized he was trying to show he was innocent, but some wondered how he could do such a thing even this soon after the attack.

Bethlehem, New York
March 30, 2006

It was to be the first of too many tragedies for the Bethlehem Police Department. Cancer took the life of Detective Sergeant John R. Cox, Sr. He had worked with the department for over three decades. He was involved with all the major investigations, including the Porco case, and had been at the crime scene that first day.

Chief Lou Corsi released a statement to the media: "John should be remembered as one who never minced words and always told you the way it was. Never short on comments, he was a decent, proud and humble man who loved his family and friends."

Hundreds attended his service.

Throughout the next couple of months, as Christopher Porco visited the bars, prosecutors were busy gathering evidence. They thought about what fit – and what didn't. Assistant District Attorney David Rossi, a young, up and coming prosecutor with dark eyes, an inquisitive look, and short, black hair combed forward, was confident in the case they were building. The team from the Office of the District Attorney studied detail after detail. They made a visit to the University of Rochester soon after the attack, talking with whomever they could to find out if and when Christopher had gone missing. They spoke with campus officials about what those security cameras high above the sidewalks might have seen. They took statements from Porco's fraternity brothers. They brought in a specialist to measure the gas in the yellow jeep after it had been impounded. They spoke with people who cooperated and those who didn't. And they spoke with neurologists and doctors to find out all they could about Joan's condition.

As the months progressed, the evidence filled box after box. All the containers were brought to the basement of a government building on State Street, just about a block from the Capitol. Because prosecutors had thousands of pages of papers related to the case, so did Kindlon. Although he had so many documents, he made it clear he was not happy with what he thought they were doing. "It's called a document dump," he said. "Prosecutors are supposed to give the defense all the evidence, all the paperwork. They do, but they bury it in as much as they can so we have to sift through it. It's filling up the room right next to us right now."

Prosecutors denied using the tactic. On more than one occasion, McDermott or Rossi would say there was simply a lot of evidence and paperwork, and it was their job to make sure the defense has access to everything. Then, they'd slightly smile.

In the meantime, the typical back-and-forth motions began to be filed by both sides. Kindlon filed a motion to dismiss the charges, arguing there wasn't enough evidence. It was time to let his innocent client go free from further baseless accusations.

Prosecutors fired back. They filed a response using statements from Detective Bowdish, among others, to argue Joan had not only known her attacker, but had told Bowdish by nodding her head that her son had done it. In fact, a doctor at Albany Med had already sworn that Mrs. Porco had been responsive when he first looked at her.

STATE OF NEW YORK
COUNTY COURT
COUNTY OF ALBANY

THE PEOPLE OF THE STATE OF NEW YORK

- against -

AFFIDAVIT

CHRISTOPHER PORCO

Hon. Jeffrey G. Berry

Defendant **Index No. DA 845-05**

STATE OF NEW YORK)
)SS:
COUNTY OF ALBANY)

John Dalfino, M.D., being duly sworn, deposes and says:

1. I am a third-year resident in the neurosurgery department at the Albany Medical Center Hospital.
2. That on November 15, 2004 I was the neurosurgery resident who participated in the care and treatment of Joan Porco, both in the Emergency Department and later during her surgery.
3. Mrs. Porco arrived at the Emergency Department via ambulance sometime shortly after noon on November 15th, 2004. When I saw her she was intubated.
4. I evaluated Mrs. Porco in the Emergency Department. Her most obvious injuries were traumatic wounds to her head and face which included an open skull fracture and injuries which caused both her eyes to be swollen shut.
5. I performed two neurological examinations on Mrs. Porco while she was in the Emergency Department. These exams were performed within 15 minutes of each other. Mrs. Porco had been started on sedation and pain medication upon her arrival at the hospital. Due to her head injuries, medications with a short half-life were administered. These medications are short-acting and their effects wear off shortly after they are discontinued. I ordered these medications discontinued prior to my neurological evaluations.
6. My examinations of Mrs. Porco found her to be responsive to my commands. She was able to move all four extremities upon command and was able to appropriately answer "yes/no" type questions by nodding or shaking her head.
7. As part of my exam, I evaluated Mrs. Porco using the Glasgow Coma Scale. This test is used to quantify a patient's level of consciousness following a traumatic brain injury. The test score represents the sum of the numeric scores assigned to three categories: eye response, verbal response, and motor response. The highest score on

the test would be a 15; the lowest score would be a 3.

8. Because Mrs. Porco was intubated and could not speak at the time of the evaluation, she received a score of 1 in the verbal response category (the lowest possible score). Likewise, because her eyes were swollen shut as a result of her injuries, she received a score of 1 in the eye response category (again the lowest possible score). However, she received a 6 in the motor response category (the highest possible score). This was due to the fact that she was able to follow my commands and appropriately respond to "yes/no" type questions. Accordingly, I determined Mrs. Porco to have a technical score of 8T (the "T" refers to the fact that she was intubated) on the Glasgow Coma Scale.

Sworn to before me this
27 day of April, 2006.
John Dalfino, M.D.

Notary Public, State of New York
My Commission Expires: ______

THOMAS E DOLIN, JR.
NOTARY PUBLIC-STATE OF NEW YORK
No. 02D06039338
Qualified in Albany County
My Commission Expires March 27, 2010

*

Kindlon wasn't able to get the charges dismissed as he had hoped. In addition to the affidavit, prosecutors filed a "Memorandum of Law Regarding the Admissibility of Communications Had Between Joan Porco and Members of the Bethlehem Police Department and Albany County Paramedics at 36 Brockley Drive on November 15, 2004." In the 37-page document prosecutors argued the head nod should be allowed at the trial. "Mrs. Porco indicated to a police detective and the paramedics by nodding her head and gesturing with her hand, that her son Chris had attacked her. The People submit that while one cannot predict with total accuracy how the evidence and strategies of the parties will unfold at trial, at this stage of the proceedings, Mrs. Porco's on-the-scene identification of the defendant to police and paramedics is admissible at trial on four separate and independent grounds. Specifically, Mrs. Porco's statement is admissible for the truth of the fact stated under the excited utterance exception to the hearsay rule."

It sounded complicated to someone not trained in legal arguments. Basically, the memorandum stated Joan was close to death when she supposedly nodded "yes." Therefore, if she implicated her son in the attack, she had no reason to lie about it. Prosecutors also argued the head nod would be a necessary part of the trial to refute expected defense claims that police had no reason to go after Christopher.

Kindlon was angry that these documents inevitably led to news stories because the news stories kept people talking. He was afraid that fewer and fewer potential jurors would be able to serve. In fact, Kindlon had already begun printing out all the articles on the case, ready to fix the problem. The pile would only get thicker.

Albany, New York
April 17, 2006

Soon, it sounded like things were finally beginning to take shape. The trial of Christopher Porco was set for late June, with jury selection taking place around the 15th of the same month.

In the meantime, more news kept the case on everyone's mind. Media outlets got a hold of documents the District Attorney's office had released.

The 19-page memorandum, a Molineaux/Ventimiglia application in lawyer-speak, read in parts like a rap sheet in essay form and further led the public to believe Christopher Porco was guilty. If that was true, the question for many people who casually discussed the case became: Would Chris get away with it because he had Kindlon as his attorney?

ALBANY <u>COUNTY</u> COURT

The People of the State of New York,

- against –

Christopher Porco

Memorandum of Law

P. David Soares
Albany County District Attorney
Attorney for Respondent
Albany County Judicial Center
6 Lodge Street
Albany, New York 12207
Tel. (518) 487- ----

David M. Rossi
Of Counsel

Katie Harris
Law Clerk

STATEMENT OF FACTS

UNIVERSITY OF ROCHESTER

The defendant attended the University of Rochester as a freshman in the Fall of 2002. At the end of his first semester, he was placed on academic probation. At the end of his Fall, 2003 sophomore semester, the defendant was involuntarily separated from the University of Rochester for poor academic performance. In the Spring of 2004, the defendant registered for classes at Hudson Valley Community College. He didn't complete any of those classes. In August of 2004, the defendant reapplied to the University of Rochester sending them a forged Hudson Valley Community College transcript which indicated that he had received three A's and a B for the Spring semester. The defendant was accepted back at the

University of Rochester for the Fall of 2004. He informed his parents that the University had mistakenly separated him from the college because a professor had lost an exam he took. He told his parents that the test had been found and because of the mistake, the University had agreed to pay his tuition for the Fall of 2004.

On October 7, 2004, the defendant informed his father that he wanted to take out a loan for $2,000 to help with some school expenses. Peter Porco sent the defendant work and tax documents as proof of employment agreeing to cosign a $2,000 loan. On September 23, 2004, the defendant used those documents to secure a $31,000 loan from Citibank. On November 3, 2004, Peter received a letter indicating that his $31,000 loan had been approved. Peter immediately cancelled the loan and attempted to contact the defendant to discuss it. After being informed by the Financial Aid Director, Sean Hanna, that the defendant was already obligated to pay for the Fall, 2004 semester, Peter secured a loan to pay the tuition for that semester only.

In early November, Peter ran his credit report and found that the defendant had also forged Peter's signature on a Capital One Auto Finance check in the amount of $16,450 to buy a Jeep. The defendant had previously informed his parents that this Jeep was given to him by a customer in Florida as part of a computer swap deal.

During the Fall of 2004, there was an agreement between the defendant and Peter and Joan Porco that if the defendant's grades weren't good enough in the Fall of 2004 for him to qualify for an ROTC scholarship, that he would not be allowed to continue at the University of Rochester. The defendant was in a fraternity, was very popular, and enjoyed his time at the school very much. He consumed large amounts of alcohol and rarely attended class. On November 9, 2004, the defendant sent his parents an email which indicated that he was getting good grades. During the semester, the defendant asked a friend to take an Economics test for him. The defendant's Professors state that Chris was likely to fail every class in the Fall due to absenteeism, incomplete assignments, and failing test scores.

*

The memo went on to argue that Christopher had also taken advantage of people through computer sales on eBay – the website he apparently used often. It wasn't surprising, if only because family friend John Polster had spoken of Christopher's prowess with technology. According to Polster, Christopher had rigged up his own computer that cooled itself by cycling in water from a fish tank.

But one State Police investigator said Christopher had gotten too good at selling computers online. The investigator said Porco tried "hundreds of times" to get customers to pay money for products he wouldn't send.

The memorandum continued to outline the problems Christopher had been going through and focused on his debt that grew as his college years continued. "While a student…the defendant created a persona of a person with great wealth, often telling stories of homes in The Outer Banks and million dollar investments."

Specific eBay deals were described. "On July 26, 2004, the defendant posted for sale on eBay four Apple PowerBook laptop computers." According to the document, customers deposited $8,200 to his eBay account, then he transferred over $4,100 to his bank account. "One of the customers…did not receive his computer and made several attempts to contact the defendant," the memo read. Porco allegedly told the customer there had been a death in his family. To another customer, he sent an e-mail "using the name David Porco, indicating that his brother, Chris Porco, had been killed in a car accident."

The document explained that eBay found out about the fraud, closed his accounts just days before the attack, and demanded over $3,600 be paid back.

Prosecutors also outlined all of the debt Christopher had accumulated. He owed American Express "over $4,000 which had an interest rate of over 26%." He tried to make a payment, but that check supposedly bounced. It made for a "minimum monthly payment on his AMEX account of $362.05."

Capital One Auto called repeatedly for him to make payments. He owed them $14,000, and was in danger of defaulting when Peter had sent an angry e-mail demanding answers.

Even his cell phone bill wasn't getting paid. Another attempt at payment had been returned in the beginning of November 2004. "His October to November cell phone bill totaled $254.25 and was not paid until 21 days after the murder," Rossi wrote.

The memo also stated the University of Rochester told Christopher almost two weeks before the murder that he owed them over $16,000. He had also been taken off his parents' credit card about a week before the attack.

With the filed document prosecutors published what they believed to be the motive. The young man's financial world had come crashing down around him. By their math, Christopher was $37,881 in debt. Prosecutors said he had a *negative* checking account balance of $115.30, and a little less than $2 in savings on the day of his parents' attack.

The written argument also outlined his supposed "prior bad acts" – including a burglary at his parents' house in 2002 while he was home on Thanksgiving break. The memo stated it was made to look like someone cut the window screen and came in through that front window. It said Christopher did it again on July 21, 2003, and later put the Dell computer he had stolen on eBay.

They also alleged he took electronics from the Bethlehem Veterinary Hospital by turning off the alarm system and taking a "Sony Digital Camera...Sony camcorder...(2) HP IPA Pocket PCs, and...(a) Verizon cell phone belonging to Dr. John Kearney. After taking the property, the defendant reset the alarm" and "staged the scene to look like a burglary by breaking a first floor window and opening it." Some of the items were put on eBay, but the Verizon cell phone was found in Christopher Porco's safe inside the Delmar home after police had come looking for clues in the wake of the murder.

The memorandum argued all of this had to be allowed in during the trial because prosecutors believed it showed clear motive - not only why Christopher supposedly did it, but also how he thought he'd get away with it.

While the accusations seemed bad enough – accusations Kindlon argued sounded bad but certainly didn't mean Christopher *was* the killer – the memorandum didn't stop there. Rossi wrote Porco had become "violent at times, choking one student to the point that others had to pull him off the student, and even threatened to kill a female student who was teasing him." If he could kill his parents, get some inheritance (the amount of which is still disputed, but was likely at least several hundreds of thousands of dollars), and think he could get away with it, prosecutors thought that was all a jury would need to understand why he might murder his parents.

Yet, others who read the document thought it might have gone a little far in trying to draw similarities between the prior acts and the murder. Yes, it cited the previous screen cutting in the windows. But it also stated, "the perpetrator had a close relationship with the victims," which the defense argued was a conclusion, not a definite fact because they believed Chris to be innocent. The memo also tried to connect the dots further, explaining that the November "break-in" of 2002 was similar with the murder in 2004 because both had happened in November.

Prosecutors asked that the prior acts be allowed into court for the purpose of establishing motive. It meant the jury would hear the bad acts as a way to understand Christopher's state of mind, but not to determine what had really happened two years before.

But that was only if the information dug up by investigators was allowed in at all. Kindlon had already begun fighting to suppress evidence he thought was more prejudicial than probative of whether his client committed murder.

The defense attorney wanted the whole six hours long taped interrogation with the Bethlehem Police thrown out. He told the Times Union on April 19, 2006, "It's one of the most egregious constitutional violations I've ever personally laid eyes on…this case is really about character assassination and they want this (videotaped) statement to use in the process of assassinating Christopher's character. They don't deserve this statement. This case has to rise or fall on what proof they have of his guilt and the fact is, they don't have any proof of his guilt."

STATE OF NEW YORK
COUNTY OF ALBANY
COUNTY COURT

THE PEOPLE OF THE STATE OF NEW YORK,

- against -

MEMORANDUM OF LAW

IN SUPPORT OF DEFENDANT'S MOTION TO SUPPRESS STATEMENTS

CHRISTOPHER PORCO

Defendant

Judge Berry
Index No: DA 848-05

Defendant, Christopher Porco, respectfully submits that the statement elicited from him by law enforcement on November 15-16, 2004 must be suppressed. It was obtained while he was in custody and in violation of his indelible right to counsel. Even if the Court determines that he was not in custody, the right to counsel had attached prior to questioning and could not properly be waived outside the presence of his attorney. Further, police did not provide him with legally sufficient Miranda warnings prior to eliciting the statements.

*

The 24-page memorandum went on to explain Polster's frustrating visit to the police station and the confusion that ensued. Kindlon basically believed that because Polster was acting as Porco's attorney, Porco had no right to be questioned without him there, whether he was technically in custody or not. The document also stated that his client couldn't waive his right to an attorney without him because the attorney client privilege is created and dissolved by the two people who made the agreement in the first place.

The memorandum recalled the frustration police felt when Father Noone said he told Porco's Uncle, John Balzano, they "were interested in questioning him." It discussed the nearly dozen phone calls and messages Polster left with officers in an attempt to talk with Christopher while he was being interrogated.

Kindlon also argued his client never received a fair Miranda warning. "At the outset of the interrogation, Christopher signed an Acknowledgment of Rights form after he was given only a matter of seconds to review and sign it while the officer placed his hands over a portion of the form and spoke to Christopher," Kindlon said. "Police did not read the Miranda rights aloud from the form. Rather, Detective Bowdish provided Christopher with an abridged version of the warnings, which completely omitted any mention of the right to an attorney."

On the tape Christopher repeated over and over again how he didn't do it and that it wasn't him. Either way, Kindlon knew judges didn't like it when police seemed to jeopardize a person's right to counsel. If prosecutors had to rely on their own research and statements instead of what Christopher uttered during that late night stint, all the better, thought the attorney. He said his client obviously had the death of at least one of his parents on his mind at the time. As a result, he didn't want prosecutors using any of Chris' statements to form the foundation of their case, especially since an attorney had been all but knocking on the door to get in that night.

Other legal documents were also filed around the same time. The flurry of activity seemed like an attempt to "one up" the other side as the deadline for filing approached. On paper Polster told his side of the story, explaining he had been locked out and unable to reach Christopher the night he was interrogated.

Father Noone also told of his day, the communications he had with the Porcos, and how he wasn't happy with police. In his affidavit he stated, "at the conclusion of my phone call with John, a member of the Bethlehem Police Department approached me at the hospital. He did not identify himself by name, however, when I described him to others later in the evening, I was told it was probably Detective Arduini. Although I tried to maintain privacy, I believe that the police officer overheard my end of the phone conversation with my cousin, John."

Through Kindlon, Christopher offered his statement as well.

STATE OF NEW YORK
COUNTY OF ALBANY
COUNTY COURT

THE PEOPLE OF THE STATE OF NEW YORK,

- against - AFFIDAVIT

CHRISTOPHER PORCO,

Judge Berry

Index No: DA 848:05

Defendant.

Christopher Porco, being duly sworn, states:

1. I am the defendant in the above entitled action.
2. I learned on November 15, 2004 that my father had been killed and that my mother had suffered very serious injuries and was being treated at Albany Medical Center Hospital.
3. At the time, I was a student at the University of Rochester. My uncle, John Balzano, who lives in Rochester, picked me up at my dorm to bring me to the hospital to see my mother.
4. I was extremely upset at the death of my father and the attack on both my parents.
5. When I got to the hospital, I was not able to see my mother because she was in surgery. Some of my relatives, my friends, and friends of my family were present in the hospital and tried to comfort me and give me information about my mother's injuries.
6. One of my father's closest friends, John Polster, who is an attorney, brought me into a small room and told me that the police considered me a suspect in the attack on my parents. I was completely shocked and asked how anyone could think that I would hurt them.
7. John Polster told me that the police wanted to question me. He said that he would act as my lawyer if I wanted him to. I told him that I did. John Polster is not only an attorney but someone I have known and trusted my entire life. He is like an uncle to me and I know that he has been an attorney for as long as my father because they were in law school together. I also knew that he had been an assistant district attorney in Schenectady and knew about the police and questioning.

8. While I was speaking with John Polster, my friends and employers, Dr. Elaine LaForte and Dr. John Kearney came in the room to see me. I told them that the police wanted to speak with me. They told me that I should have an attorney and I told them that John Polster was going to be my attorney.
9. Before I was able to finish my conversation with John Polster, Dr. LaForte and Dr. Kearney, see my mother, or speak with other family members and friends, I was approached by members of the Bethlehem Police Department.
10. Detective Rinaldi took me by the arm and told me that I needed to go to the station with them and answer some questions. I was never asked if I was willing to go and felt that I had no choice whatsoever. The officer kept hold of my arm and guided me through the hospital. There were at least seven or eight police officers surrounding me as we left the hospital.
11. Detective Rinaldi placed me into the back of an unmarked police car and immediately got in beside me. Detective Rudolph then got in the back seat on the other side of me so that it was impossible for me to get out of the car. Two more police officers whose names I do not know were in the front seat. Both of the officers on either side of me had guns. I do not know if the officers in the front seat had weapons. There were other Bethlehem Police officers in other cars around the one that I was in.
12. John Polster offered to drive me to the police station but the police refused to let him.
13. When we were leaving the hospital, I saw that a marked Bethlehem Police SUV was in front of the car I was in. There was also another marked car with police officers in it behind us.
14. Within a few minutes of the time I was in the police car with four police officers, Detective Rudolph's pager went off. He called the number on the pager and it was John Polster. The detective told me that John wanted to speak with me and handed me his cell phone. John asked me again if I wanted him to be my lawyer and wanted him to be with me when I was questioned. I told him that I did. He told me to give the phone to the police officer. He listened for a few minutes and then I heard Det. Rudolph say, "O.K."
15. When I got to the police station I was brought into a big room and police began questioning me. They started out very nice but then became very angry when I kept telling them that I would never hurt my parents.

Lots of different officers came in and out of the room and took turns asking me questions. Some acted nice and others were very nasty.

16. When the police started to tape the interrogation, Detective Bowdish told me that the attacks on my parents were a big deal in the Town of Bethlehem, and he asked me if I heard about a recent murder in Bethlehem involving a love triangle. I have no idea why Detective Bowdish told me this stuff, but almost immediately after that he told me that he is supposed to read me my rights.
17. Detective Bowdish handed me a piece of paper and very quickly told me some of my rights, like it was no big deal. I assumed those were all of my rights since he had just told me that he was supposed to read me my rights. It seemed like I was given only a matter of seconds to look at the piece of paper and sign it while the officer was talking to me.
18. Since the interrogation, my attorney has explained to me that the police are required to provide me with complete Miranda warnings. I do not remember the officer telling me that I had the right to speak to an attorney before they questioned me or to have an attorney present while they questioned me. I do not remember the officer asking me if I understood my rights or if I was willing to waive my rights and talk to them without an attorney present.
19. However, shortly after I got to the police station, I asked the police whether John was there and they told me that he was not. During the entire seven or eight hours that I was at the police station, no one ever told me that he was there or that he was demanding to speak with me. If I had been told that he was there, I would have asked to speak with him immediately and I would not have answered questions without him being present.
20. At no time during the many hours I was in the police station did I feel that I could leave. Exactly the opposite – I felt that unless I answered all of the questions and gave them everything they wanted, including the clothes that I was wearing, a DNA sample and fingerprints, and raised up my shirt so they could check for bruises, that I would not be able to see my mother.
21. I was never left alone while I was in the police station and never felt that I could leave. In fact, at one point I had to use the bathroom and felt I had to ask permission from the police to do so. I was taken to the

bathroom by Detective Rinaldi, who stood outside the door and waited for me. He then took me back to the interrogation room.

22. On the way to the bathroom, I saw another room at the police department where several police were gathered. I also saw Paul Clyne, the Albany District Attorney, who I recognized as someone who knew my father.
23. The police became more and more angry as the hours went by. They kept accusing me of murdering my father and trying to kill my mother. I was afraid of them, stunned at the death of my father, and extremely worried about my mother.
24. When the police finally stopped the interrogation, they let me out of the police station between 3:00 and 4:00 in the morning without any means of transportation. They told me that I could not go to the hospital to see my mother because I was a suspect in the attacks. I started walking toward Delaware Avenue. Suddenly, I heard John Polster calling my name. He caught up with me and told me that he had been at the police station the entire time I was there. I was shocked, as I had been told he was not there. If I had ever been told that he was there, I would have immediately asked to have him come into the room. He was not only my attorney but someone who had known me my entire life. I trusted him and wanted him to be with me.
25. When John caught up with me, he said, "Why did you tell the police you didn't want to see me?" I told him that I had never said that, that I had asked if he was there and was told that he was not. He told me that the police told him that I said I didn't want him.
26. John Polster gave me a ride back to the hospital where I was able to see my mother for the first time since she was attacked.

Christopher Porco
Christopher Porco

Sworn to be me this 17th
Day of April, 2006.

Terence Kindlon
Notary Public

*

Albany, New York
April 19, 2006

As all the documents were sent off to the Albany County Courthouse, reporters noticed that Kindlon seemed to have made up his mind that the more information got out, the better chance the trial would be moved. He wanted a place where the jury pool had never heard of Christopher Porco.

Some days, the Capital News 9 reporter would leave Kindlon's office after an interview, and in the small waiting room, the local CBS crew would be waiting. Channel 10 and 13, the ABC and NBC affiliates respectively, would be there often as well, along with the Fox crew. It seemed the only day-to-day difference was which station would arrive first.

Kindlon answered all the questions that the filings inevitably led reporters to ask. He explained that investigators had gone to Chris' dorm room at the University of Rochester right after the attack to get a DNA sample from his clothing. He said there had been no DNA match with anything at the crime scene.

But for the most part, talk centered on the potential change in venue. Kindlon argued his client was getting the bad end of news coverage and that everyone in the Capital Region was tainted from the lies and false impressions. "We're not inclined at this point to request a change of venue," Kindlon said. "We're certainly ready to take that step if and when it becomes unavoidable." Kindlon explained it would be unlikely he would make the request until they went through jury selection and found too many people who had an opinion.

Additionally, because Peter Porco was a law clerk, even a potential move proved complicated. Normally, the Albany Appellate Division, Third Department, would make the decision. But that's where Peter had worked. Instead, an appellate court in Brooklyn would take a look at the circumstances, and then they would likely move it to Goshen, in Orange County, according to Kindlon. After all, that's where Judge Berry worked. "It has its advantages," Kindlon told a number of news stations. "Orange County seems to be 16 yards outside of this television and newspaper market...The more of this garbage they publish and propagate, the more likely it is we're not going to get a fair trial and the less likely that the trial will be conducted here." Though Goshen fell right between the media markets for Albany and New York City, most Orange County residents got their news from the City, so almost no one had heard of the case. It had been discussed only fleetingly on a few national television stations like Court TV.

Prosecutors were still hoping to have the case tried in Albany. Not only because they thought Porco could get a fair trial, but because they knew moving it would stretch the office thin, make for longer workdays, and eat up their budget to the tune of hundreds of thousands of dollars. McDermott wouldn't say much about a venue change either way: "I don't want to fuel the fire that could lead to this case being tried elsewhere," he told Capital News 9.

If the trial were to be moved, witnesses would have to be flown in, driven in, and fed. Evidence would have to be sent south. And so much of that work just wouldn't have to take place if witnesses, many from the Albany area, could simply commute. Prosecutors said any move would be a real hardship.

Bethlehem, New York
May 11, 2006

The debate continued over how tainted the potential jury pool might be. Discussions at bars and restaurants still centered around whether Christopher was wrongly accused or if he was going to get away with murder. But then tragedy and a bizarre set of circumstances stopped everybody in their tracks.

Detective Sergeant John Cox had passed away just over a month ago. Now, another man who had been working on the Porco case passed away. While the death was upsetting for anyone who knew him, the allegations made by Kindlon would also shock many in the community.

Detective Anthony Arduini was 52-years-old. He had a wife and three children. He had suffered from what doctors later discovered was a brain aneurysm. Like Cox, he had over three decades of experience with the police department. His colleagues would later say losing two men with over half a century of experience between them in such a short time devastated the small department. And not only had Arduini still been involved with the case, he was one of the first to respond to the crime scene back in November.

Chief Corsi again released a statement to the media, obviously shaken at yet another death. "Tony should be remembered as one whose sense of humor and compassion for people was always at the forefront of his personality...Never short on comments, he was a decent, proud and humble man who loved his family and friends. He was my friend." Arduini and the late Detective Sergeant Cox had been close colleagues too.

As those who knew Arduini did their best to come to grips with the awful news, the pre-trial hearings were moved a day. They had been set up for Monday, the 15th, to discuss what evidence would be allowed in the trial. The change allowed people involved with the trial to attend his services.

His wake was held on Monday evening. His funeral took place the following day at 10 in the morning with full department honors. The pre-trial hearings began later on Tuesday.

Arduini's family was private in their grief. They shunned reporters, some of whom only wanted to find out what this specifically meant for the trial.

Terry Kindlon also spoke of the tragedy. He was beginning to hint Arduini held key information that might benefit the defense. But he wouldn't say much more than that – at least for now. "We were looking to cross-examine him because a cross-examination of him as a witness would have developed some significant information," Kindlon said. He added that two deaths in such a short period of time were not only tragic, but also odd. "It's almost like this is the curse of Porco or something. Two good Police officers from a small department tragically losing their lives," he said.

But the circumstances surrounding Arduini's death were even more bizarre. "Wild coincidence," said Kindlon. "My associate, Kent Sprotberry was taking his daughter, Emma, to piano lessons the other night. He came around a corner and saw a man lying on the street." Sprotberry lived nearby and was the one who dialed 911.

Town Supervisor Terri Egan told Capital News 9 that Arduini was "just a phenomenal family man, dedicated to his wife and children. Anyone who knew him has to miss him because he was one of those types of people you just knew was there."

V

From: "Porco" pporco@nycap.rr.com
To: jeffsalosa@hotmail.com
Sent: Wednesday, September 01, 2004 9:58PM
Subject: speedpass- I need an explanation

9/1/04

Hi Christopher-

Please call us tonight. I just got a call from Mobil Speedpass- you had charged over $60. In snacks/food for three days straight. Do you have any money on your card or food at school? What has happened at HSBC?

Please take note. I have just temporarily stopped the use of your speedpass device. I can reactivate it when I am assured that you will only use it for gas when you are unable to pay for it yourself- that is- once in a while.

Please call and let us know what is happening with classes as well. Love you and I am concerned with these behaviors- MOM XO

From: "Chris Porco" cp002m@mail.rochester.edu
To: "Porco" pporco@nycap.rr.com
Sent: Thursday, September 02, 2004 12:22PM
Subject: hey guys

Hey guys,
Quick update.. I cannot locate my speedpass, Its not on the keychain where I normally keep it. I will be on the lookout for it. In the meantime, just cancel it. Also, my junk mail filters were set too high on my email, so I wasn't getting stuff from you. I have to run to class, but I will stay in touch. Say hey to john for me, tell him good luck with the storms. Hope all is well, talk to you soon.
love
chris

*

Albany, New York
May 16, 2006

It was a beautiful, sunny Tuesday for the beginning of the pre-trial hearings - and for the services that would be held later in the morning for Anthony Arduini.

Just as few clouds filled the sky, few parking spaces could be found around the Albany County Judicial Center. The defense wouldn't need any of the spaces, however. Kindlon's office was situated a mere two blocks away, so they walked. A few minutes before the hearings were set to begin at nine in the morning, Kindlon walked in back as Mrs. Porco linked her arms with Christopher's. Photographers from the various news stations moved backwards with their cameras on their shoulders, recording each step. Mrs. Porco's face had healed well since she had last been seen in public. Though her wounds remained obvious, she still walked side by side with her son to the courthouse in a show of unwavering support.

Once inside, Christopher placed the contents of his pocket in a tray to be x-rayed. He then stepped through the metal detector with his mother right behind him. They both picked up their belongings and walked to the elevators on the right as the cameramen continued to record their every move.

Everybody filed into the courtroom through the double doors and took a seat. Christopher sat on the right side of the room next to Kindlon, his back to the public. Both were dressed in sharp looking suits. A producer for "48 Hours" feverishly talked on her phone to one of her colleagues. She was trying to figure out a last minute way to make sure they were on board with an attorney hired by some of the local news channels to argue the proceedings should be open to the public and to news coverage.

Prosecutors McDermott and Rossi also took their seats as Judge Berry entered. For the next hour the media attorney argued it was everyone's first amendment right to be in a courtroom for the proceedings. He cited case law off the top of his head to prove his point. He said the media had a right to take a look at the interrogation tape. He believed it was on the defense to show the requests would be detrimental to the defendant's rights.

"The tape may be admissible," said Judge Berry. "We'll figure it out. Whether the tape is admissible in and of itself (in the trial) may be a question of agreeing on words, the transcript of it," he added, possibly looking for a compromise on the subject. He told the courtroom he had watched the entire interrogation to make sure the transcript and the tape matched.

Then, it was Kindlon's turn. He asked that the pre-trial proceedings be closed to the public. He said he had enough of the bias he thought everyone had from reading and watching the news. The other day "someone passing my office yelled an obscenity," he said. Discussion of the videotape or the supposed head nod, said Kindlon, "would only serve to inflame the public and affect the ability to hold a fair trial, at least in Albany County." After all, the public would soon become the jury pool for the case. What should be done, he asked, if some of those pieces are thrown out, but the bias remains? In the end, he wanted the press excluded. Simple.

Judge Berry was not quick with rulings. Attorneys who had worked with him before said he would often take weeks if he could to carefully craft each decision. Here, there wouldn't be an official, written ruling for several days. But Berry gave everyone a good idea what he would do. As for the closure issue, Berry said it came down to the probability of prejudice. "It's clear everything's been brought to the public…I have no problem" offering to open the court to the press, he said. "Almost everything has been disclosed already that was discussed today." Cameras, however, would not be allowed in. The cameras that had been rolling up until now were taken off their tripods and brought out to the hallway. The video that had been shot inside would be replayed, reused, and recycled as needed for the next couple of weeks on the news.

Then, Berry announced a lengthy recess so prosecutors and others could attend Arduini's funeral from 10AM until 1PM.

Scores of people went to show their respects. But things wouldn't get easier for those who knew him anytime soon. Accusations were going to be made that would surprise and anger many in the Capital Region.

For the next few days the proceedings would be focused on just three main questions that would make a big impact on the eventual trial. Would the taped interrogation be tossed out? Would the supposed head nod be allowed in? And finally, would the alleged "prior bad acts" of Christopher Porco be heard by jurors?

John Balzano, the man who had driven his nephew from Rochester to Albany, had an understandable look of constant concern on his face. He was the first to take the stand after the court reconvened a little after 2PM. He looked over to his wife who sat in the public seating area, then briefly looked at Joan and the Polsters, who were all sitting together. Mrs. Porco sat still, occasionally whispering to a few of them.

Balzano, like the other witnesses, started off by answering basic questions: what his name is, how it's spelled, and what's his address. All of this was for the record, and the simple questions often seemed like a waste of time, but were the basis for the more important questions and answers.

Balzano spoke about how often he saw Christopher. He said it was convenient his nephew attended the University of Rochester. He talked about November 14th, when he received a call from Father Noone. He said that's when he had first heard about the assault. "The first thought that came to me was that Chris was at Rochester. I thought I'd pick him up." Balzano added that he thought Chris would need all the support he could get, even though at that time he said he didn't know much about what had happened.

"We had a good relationship," said Balzano. "We'd go golfing." He said it took 25 minutes to get to his nephew's dorm room and when he got there, he had to look for what seemed like a few minutes. He didn't recognize Christopher at first. Balzano said Chris had on a sweatshirt and had "a hood on his head...We drove back together. It was quiet. He was dark. I'm not sure if it was the lighting or the day," he said. Balzano told the courtroom that was the best he could explain it.

Balzano spoke about arriving at the hospital and seeing all the concerned family members and friends. Since it seemed police were eager to speak with Christopher, he said there was also worry from some that his nephew didn't have an attorney. Balzano said Christopher didn't feel he needed one. He told the courtroom Porco had told him, "I have nothing to hide." He said his nephew thought of Polster as a friend – not an attorney at that time.

Balzano soon stepped off the stand. Father Noone was next. "I was concerned he didn't talk with a lawyer," he said. When he took Chris to get some food, Chris reiterated that he had nothing to hide. Noone said, "There was very little, if any, reaction" when he spoke with Christopher. The priest said the young man told him John Polster was his father's friend, "but not my attorney."

Father Noone stepped down after spending about 20 minutes on the stand. Then, Mary Louise Ruby opened the swinging door that separated the attorneys from the public area and calmly walked to her seat. David Rossi stood up and thought about his questions for the witness. Joan's cousin recalled eating with the Polsters at the hospital after they had been there for a few hours. She said it was difficult to believe "Chris could have done it and gone to Albany and back." She added that "he said he'd be willing to talk to police and didn't do anything wrong."

She said she saw police escort Christopher away from the group of people. That was when family members agreed. John Polster should go to the police station.

Laurie Shanks stood up. The Albany Law professor would handle the questions for Lt. Robert Berben. The two discussed when he was paged and how often. She pointed out he had even been given Polster's business card. Shanks hinted that most police officers would probably know they were on thin ice once an attorney had handed them his card, let alone when an attorney had called a few times.

Then it was Rossi's turn. He jumped up quickly as he liked to do. He had only a few points to make – and managed to get the witness to add some doubt to the question of whether Polster was, in fact, Christopher's attorney. He brought up the man's business card. "Attorney is not written near John Polster's name, is it?" he asked.

"No," said Lt. Berben.

Already, it was approaching dinnertime, and while the judge seemed to hint that he was hoping the hearing would wrap up in a day, that would be impossible. He asked everyone to return at nine the following morning and dismissed the court.

Christopher stood up as the day came to an end. Joan walked over to talk with her son. They spoke softly with each other as the chatter from the courtroom drowned out what they were saying. Joan shook her head from side to side. Either she was concerned about certain aspects of the testimony, or she was just listening intensely to her son. He seemed to be agreeing, perhaps reassuring her.

Reporters emptied their seats, walked through the thick double doors, and grabbed their pens, pads of paper, and microphones. Terry Kindlon and his wife walked out, followed by Joan and Christopher. The cameras followed the Porcos, who were led by Shanks as her husband stayed behind to answer questions. Reporters bumped into each other, doing their best to get the sound bites they'd need for the evening news.

Kindlon addressed the fact the judge denied his motion to close the pre-trial portion to the public. "This is not surprising," he said. "The burden that has to be sustained by the defendant who seeks to close the hearing was extraordinarily high…In the interest of wearing a belt and suspenders at all times and leaving no stone unturned, we felt it was only prudent to bring the application." Kindlon pointed they had at least gotten cameras barred from the courtroom, even though New York law rarely allowed cameras inside during court proceedings anyway. Judge Berry just happened to believe in freedom of the press more than New York legislators did.

"The question of whether or not the interrogation tape will be made available to the media is still open," Kindlon explained. If the tape, or parts of it came in as evidence, the media would have access to it anyway, unless Berry thought otherwise.

"How is Joan Porco doing?" one of the reporters asked.

"Joan Porco has been all throughout these proceedings extremely supportive of her son. And she's here because she's his mom, and this is a very important event in his life. She's here so that she can support him and demonstrate her support to everyone who may be interested in this case," Kindlon said.

He also told reporters Judge Berry had asked him to file for a change of venue in order to "streamline" the process. "I think there's been no mystery about that, obviously we've been contemplating a change of venue for quite some time now. It is virtually impossible to avoid people who have already formed an opinion on this case."

Albany, New York
May 17, 2006

The second day saw a very similar scene. Christopher walked up the street with his mother and into the Albany County Judicial Center. They walked purposely, trying to look calm but obviously aware that half-a-dozen video cameras followed them closely.

Judge Berry entered, and everyone in the courtroom stood. He took his seat and then motioned for everyone to follow his lead. He asked Kindlon to explain a motion that he had filed. Kindlon stood up and rolled his shoulders back as if he suddenly recalled a Marine drill instructor barking commands at him to improve his posture.

"Your honor," he said loudly. "We have a motion to disqualify the DA's office." People sitting in the public area perked up. Kindlon mentioned first that he was unsure what three attorneys seated on the prosecution's side in back of McDermott and Rossi were doing there. But his main point was that Paul Clyne, the former District Attorney, and McDermott, were too close to the case because they had given advice to the Bethlehem Police Department during Christopher Porco's interrogation. He wanted to put members of the DA's office, past and present, on the witness stand. He argued the indictment should be dismissed because "prosecutors cannot simultaneously be a witness."

The judge acknowledged Kindlon's motion and asked for the prosecution's response.

McDermott stood to answer the allegations. First, he explained the three attorneys were from the New York Prosecutor's Training Institute. Basically, they were sitting by to help in any way they could. As for the main point, "our function was simply to provide advice," said McDermott. He said no one from the DA's office actually conducted the interview as Lt. Berben had already testified, and they "were not present for the reading of rights or for questioning." McDermott said it is quite common for members of the DA's office to offer legal advice to police on sensitive matters and that if what they did was wrong, then "every DA's office would then be witnesses."

Kindlon stood up as soon as McDermott finished. "This is not a typical case," the defense attorney said to the Judge. "This is not a typical case since all these legal folks knew and loved Peter." He said there was likely "anger over his death." Kindlon said his client's rights were at stake. McDermott and Clyne - "we need to talk to them to make sure."

Judge Berry thought for a moment as Kindlon took his seat. In his stern but thoughtful voice he said, "It's common in southern New York for District Attorney's to work with police. In this case the degree of involvement was advice. They may have fed questions to the interviewer. But the advice claim will be enough for now...But you do have the right to call the DA's to the witness stand. I'm not going to stop the hearing to do it...You are entitled to go into their role and to get to the true relationship of Christopher Porco and John Polster."

Kindlon was back on his feet. He wanted to make sure the Judge understood his point. "It's not just that prosecutors participated – but it's the degree of involvement. The magnitude of the action," he said, "and the impact on the case."

The judge said the hearing had to move forward. If Kindlon wanted to pursue the issue, he could once he began calling witnesses.

Once Judge Berry pacified Kindlon for the moment, David Rossi began asking questions of Detective Charles Rudolph, who had put in 14 years with the Bethlehem Police Department. Rudolph said he had spoken with Polster briefly at the hospital, but there wasn't any talk about lawyers at the time. Nonetheless, he said he gave his business card to Polster. Then, he helped escort Porco to the police station along with several other officers.

Rudolph said he was paged by the man he had just met and promptly called him back. He said Polster wanted directions. "He didn't tell me he was a lawyer," he explained to the courtroom. And "Porco didn't ask where Polster was."

Rossi proceeded with a discussion of the interrogation. The video, which was about to be played in parts, lasted about six hours. Prosecutors said VHS and DVD copies had been made for the defense. Kindlon raised a concern about being given a 406-page transcript, but a few days later, he had received another 410-page transcript with the changes left unmarked.

The issue was noted, and Rossi continued as the lights dimmed and a courtroom television was turned on. It was hard to see from almost any spot in the courtroom. The black and white video looked grainy, and the interrogation camera was placed just far enough to make it difficult to determine which figure was Christopher Porco and which was Detective Rudolph. Det. Bowdish also made an appearance and asked questions after Rudolph. The video played for several minutes. The transcript could be read like closed captioning.

DETECTIVE RUDOLPH: Did you hire – you didn't hire an attorney today, did you?
MR. PORCO: No, the guy John I talked to, he is an attorney, but just a friend.
DETECTIVE RUDOLPH: Okay. Is he representing you?
MR. PORCO: He couldn't probably because of his relationship with my family.
DETECTIVE RUDOLPH: Okay, but you're okay talking to us?
MR. PORCO: Uh-huh.

*

Several video clips were played for the court to see. Christopher discussed jogging on campus the morning of the 15th. He even drew a diagram of the route he said he took and added the date and time for police.

The prosecution seemed satisfied and called Detective Bowdish to the stand. He calmly walked up, sat, and took a sip of water.

Bowdish corroborated what he could from Rudolph's testimony. He said Christopher had signed and dated a piece of paper that listed his Miranda rights. He spoke about the back-and-forth with Porco, specifically, when he tried to get him to take a polygraph test. Prosecutors played part of that conversation. In it, the young man spoke calmly and without emotion. Porco told the detective, "after I've spoken to a lawyer, I'd be happy to take one."

The video continued with Porco saying he knew he was entitled to speak with an attorney. He also told Bowdish, "I don't know how I could kill someone when I was that far away." Later, the detective told Christopher he couldn't leave to go to the hospital because "you tried to kill your mother and will try to do it again."

In the front seat of the public seating area, Joan Porco shook her head from side to side, very clearly showing those who noticed that she disagreed.

Rossi asked Bowdish if he had seen McDermott or Clyne at the police station that night. Bowdish said he was "not aware members of the DA's office were there at the office until later." He had not asked for any legal advice, according to his testimony.

Then it was Laurie Shanks' turn to cross-examine the detective. She flipped through a few notes and then pointed out that Bowdish had only read two out of the seven Miranda rights listed on the piece of paper. More importantly, he didn't read the right to an attorney part, she said. He agreed. "So you didn't read the sheet," she said. "You could have stopped this interview at any time, but you continued the interrogation for six hours." It was her way of asking a question.

Bowdish said Christopher "could have stopped it at any time if he wanted."

"But you didn't tell Chris he had the right to refuse a saliva DNA sample," she asked, sounding concerned.

"He knew," Bowdish said, though he added that he didn't say it was specifically for a DNA sample.

Shanks hammered away on the point, saying Bowdish had made Porco lower his pants and take his shirt off "and didn't say to Chris he could refuse it."

Bowdish said he only wanted to check for blood or DNA on Porco's clothes. He also wanted to see if Porco had any bruises on his body – a sign of physical struggle. There were none.

Bowdish finished answering Shanks' questions by saying he "knew" right *after* the interrogation that Polster was there.

Then McDermott asked one final question of Bowdish, to which the officer answered that he "never told Christopher he was under arrest." It was important because McDermott would later explain for the cameras waiting outside the courtroom, "if your freedom of movement is restricted and you're not allowed to leave, the police have to read you your rights."

Bowdish had survived the grueling cross-examination - at least that's what his fellow officers told him later as they left the courtroom. But first, it was once again John Polster's turn to take the stand. He was the first defense witness, and he hoped to prove Christopher's rights were violated so the interrogation would have to be thrown out. The defense knew if the interrogation - and therefore the video of it - were not allowed in court, prosecutors would not be able to use information they had obtained as a result. Referred to as the "fruit of the poisonous tree," it meant prosecutors would need a separate basis from which to introduce evidence. It wasn't a big deal if prosecutors had already made the proper adjustments to their case. But Kindlon figured they hadn't and wanted to deal them a good setback from the start.

Polster said he had practiced law throughout the area. He discussed the attorney/client relationship and said an oral agreement could retain a lawyer; money has nothing to do with it. He said he and his wife had been planning a three-day vacation to New York City with Mr. and Mrs. Porco.

He said he spoke with Mary Louise Ruby at the hospital about whether Christopher could have done it or not. He felt it was impossible that "Christopher could have traveled there and back." Christopher, he said, seemed "visibly shaken" when he first saw him.

Polster told the court he had given his card to Det. Rudolph around that time. "I explained I was a family friend and an attorney," he said. "I would be representing Christopher if he wanted me to." He and Christopher talked for three to five minutes in a private room at the hospital before the police grabbed the young man for questioning.

While in the room, Polster said Christopher had wondered aloud, "How could anybody think that I could do something like this?" Polster said he knew police were saying Joan's head nod indicated Christopher had attacked her. He thought it was important to talk to Porco about obtaining a lawyer.

Joan, who had been listening intently to the testimony shook her head once again when she heard her friend mention the head nod.

His testimony continued. As police were about to grab Porco, Christopher apparently pointed to Polster, saying that he could use his father's friend as his attorney, the witness said.

He spoke about his frustration at the police station when he was not allowed to see Christopher. He said he told a policeman, most likely Detective Rudolph, that the "questioning must stop until I see him." Polster said he demanded to see Christopher at 8:33, 8:39, and 8:52. He said he called at 8:55, and went to the dispatcher's window every 20 minutes after that.

Already it was approaching the end of the day in court, so Polster left the stand. The judge advised everyone to return for 9:15 the following morning.

Outside the courtroom it was a familiar scene as Kindlon, and then McDermott, stopped to speak to journalists.

"This is a collection of bar exam questions wrapped up in a made-for-TV movie," said Kindlon – a quote he would reuse throughout the proceedings. "John Polster was maybe 30 feet away from his client Christopher Porco and separated by a door and a wall. Everyone knew he was there," he said. "The question was, 'did you have a lawyer?' But given the normal understanding it's 'oh yeah I gave a lawyer some money and he now represents me.' Attorney- client relationships are formed when there's an agreement between a client and a lawyer. Once it has formed, it is unbreakable, and unless and until the lawyer is in the presence of his client."

Reporters also asked about making members of the District Attorney's office testify. It was something expected to happen in a day or so. "Paul Clyne, Mike McDermott, Dave Rossi – the DA and two of his top assistant DA's - were in the very next room, and police officers were passing between that room where the DA's were and the room where the defendant was." Kindlon said it was likely all they had to do was walk a few feet to get fed the next question to ask.

Whether there had been wrongdoing or not, Kindlon said he had to call the prosecutors to the stand. "We would be less than zealous advocates if we failed to do that." A reporter asked what would happen as the prosecutors testified. "Well, obviously they'll have to call in some backup assistant DA's in the courtroom while they…are being witnesses." Bottom line, said the defense attorney, "it's a question of degree. If you are simply offering legal advice and that's all you're doing, that's one thing. But if you're duking it out with the cops and with everybody else, you're not offering legal advice, you are materially participating in the investigation."

Kindlon thanked the throng of reporters, saying he had a lot of work to do that evening.

McDermott didn't speak for long. He said he had plenty to do too. But he did say there would be no conflict of interest for those in the DA's office. He was ready to prove just that by testifying.

Albany, New York
May 18, 2006

The pretrial hearings had already lasted longer than Judge Berry expected, and he hinted he was ready to wrap things up. There was talk that if the issues were not resolved, he was willing to stay until midnight. Everyone was already exhausted from the intense work it took to make such complicated legal arguments, but thankfully, no one would have to stay late. Yet, as the day began, many braced themselves, especially since they hadn't even addressed Joan Porco's supposed head nod yet.

Polster returned to testify once again. His wife sat next to Joan in the first row of benches. The red-bearded attorney described the three pages of notes he had kept from November 15. He wrote about a conversation he said he had with Christopher, who asked if it would be proper for Polster to represent him. The notes stated he talked with Det. Rudolph and told him Christopher was "going through a lot." Polster wanted police to "wait till I get there" before any questioning began. Then Lt. Berben came out and identified himself. At that point Polster's notes stated he told the officer, "I represent Chris. All questioning should stop."

He said after hours of this, the police station seemed even quieter to him. He decided to leave, having accomplished little, and saw Christopher walking along the side of the road as he drove away. "It was obvious they never told Chris I was there," he told the court. "Chris said, 'they told me you weren't there.'"

Polster explained he became even angrier several hours later when he watched the news. He said they were making the arrest of Christopher Porco seem likely. "The press was out of hand," he said. "There was no warrant. An arrest was not imminent."

Polster also had to consider some legal realities. Hoping to avoid a conflict of interest, or at least the perception of a conflict, he said he spoke with Kindlon. After all, the attorney who eventually agreed to take the case enjoyed helping people whose rights might have been violated.

In fact, it's what pushed Kindlon to become an attorney in the first place. He had seen a man with little or no ability to speak English get put on trial with what he thought was inadequate representation. It had happened while he was in the Marines during the Vietnam era. Kindlon took Christopher as his client days after being contacted by Polster, who remained Joan's counsel.

McDermott stood and began asking questions after the defense finished their direct examination of Polster. Judge Berry clarified for the court that "a person who believes he's in custody has to be read their rights." The defense team smiled briefly, wondering if that was a sign of a decision to come.

McDermott brought Polster back to his memory of everyone at the hospital. "You're an experienced attorney. Did you tell police your client wasn't going anywhere?"

"No," said Polster.

"Did you say you hadn't finished interviewing your client?"

"No." Polster added that he briefly told Christopher about his Miranda rights, but was cut short.

Polster then shared his notes that he said were written while his conversation with Christopher was still fresh in his mind.

> JRP – would you feel better if I was there with you while they (talked w/ questioned) you?
> CP – would that be proper (or something like that)?
> JRP – oh yeah.
> CP – yes.
> JRP – ok – wait until I get there to talk. Give the phone back to
> (the police/ the detective/ the officers).
> CR – yes/hello?

*

Polster made the point that he clearly said he would be Christopher's attorney. But McDermott didn't buy it. "Would you feel better if I was there," was not what an attorney would say, he argued. "So you let your client –

suspected of murder - leave with police?" he asked incredulously.

"Yes," answered Polster.

McDermott's cross-examination ended, and Laurie Shanks shot up from her seat to hammer home the defense's contention that their client's rights had been violated. She said Polster had given his card to police, which did, in fact, have "Attorney at Law" printed on it. She reiterated that Polster wanted whomever had committed the crime to get caught. He surely didn't want to impede the investigation. After hours of testimony, Polster stepped down. Whether he was ever Christopher's attorney or not would be determined by the judge. If he thought Polster had acted as Porco's lawyer, then the taped interrogation would likely never be seen by jurors at trial.

Of course, there was still one major question to be resolved concerning the interrogation. The prosecutors shuffled their roles accordingly. Rossi left the courtroom, and McDermott took the spot where Polster had been all morning.

Kindlon asked McDermott if he knew police were going to the hospital for the purpose of getting Christopher. McDermott said he had known that. He then went to the police station and "set up shop" in a nearby detective's office. "We went over to provide legal advice to the police," he said. When he first arrived, an officer told him Detective Bowdish was interrogating Christopher at the time.

"Are you aware Mr. Polster was in the station?" Kindlon asked McDermott.

"Lt. Berben said a man named Polster was at the window who is an attorney, who says he's Christopher's attorney." Kindlon was trying to see if perhaps members of the DA's office would end up proving his point that everyone knew Christopher's attorney was being denied access to his client. But McDermott said one of the officers told him they had asked Christopher about Polster, and Christopher had said he "was just a family friend."

Kindlon asked if McDermott knew the exact question used to determine Polster's relationship with Christopher. That way, McDermott could have been sure the interrogation was legal.

"I was not sure of the exact question to Christopher posed by police," the Chief ADA answered.

"Well you should have," scolded Kindlon. Judge Berry gave a look to Kindlon, urging him to continue without the comments.

McDermott explained he later found out he could watch the interrogation through the closed-circuit television system at the station. He caught the last two hours or so of questioning. He also said Det. Cox had come to him and said Porco had been "Mirandized" and had waived his right to counsel.

The questioning of McDermott only lasted a few minutes, and then he left the courtroom. Assistant District Attorney David Rossi took the same seat. He told a similar story: Lt. Berben told him about a man who said he was an attorney. "My understanding of the law is that if he's his lawyer then you have to let him in," Rossi said. "But you don't have to let him in unilaterally."

Kindlon pressed the issue, asking what impression Rossi had of the situation. The ADA didn't mince words: "the impression I had, was that this was some nutcase off the street."

Kindlon did get Rossi to admit that no one from the DA's office went to verify who Polster was.

Christopher Baynes, an ADA who said he was not there that November night, made the final point as he questioned Rossi. He concluded that no one from the DA's office had verified who Polster was. And that was the point. Because they didn't get involved, McDermott and Rossi didn't have a conflict of interest in the case, he argued. Baynes said his colleagues were not in the same room with Christopher and didn't talk with either Porco or Polster, so they were fit to continue.

Rossi's time on the stand had come to an end. Kindlon presented his conclusion: "The defense has established they are competent witnesses as to whether rights were violated." He added that they therefore should not be allowed to continue as prosecutors on the case.

Baynes disagreed. "The central issue is the interaction of Rossi and McDermott with the principals in this case. They didn't give any advice they couldn't have given over the phone," he said.

Kindlon fought back. "You don't have to be there in person," he said, sounding slightly frustrated, as if Baynes wasn't getting it. "It is the gathering of material evidence that moves you to being one thing to a witness." Kindlon argued the prosecutors "can't be deliberately blind to what happened. And there's the question of whether failure to act by the DA's has the effect of making them witness advocates." Kindlon said he wanted the indictment dismissed because the prosecutors in question had presented the indictment in the first place.

Judge Berry thanked both sides for their arguments and issued what was to be a rare, immediate ruling. "I don't believe the DA's office has a conflict or should be disqualified. There are times they are called upon to give advice to law enforcement agencies," he said. "I will not order them off the case at this time."

*

After lunch, the hearings continued with some of the most difficult testimony. Judge Berry would have to decide whether Joan's supposed head nod actually occurred and whether it was meaningful or not.

Judge Berry began by summing up the facts. EMT's treated Joan Porco. The People allege she shook and nodded her head to answer several key questions, but Joan has no memory of it. The question is "whether it's a hearsay part of the evidence, or legitimate evidence," said Berry.

Kevin Robert, one of the EMT's who treated Joan in her bedroom, began telling the courtroom the gruesome details from that day. He said when he found her, he knew he had limited time to ask any questions. He explained that "she didn't answer immediately, she just tried to move." He said he broke down the rapid-fire questions into smaller parts. "Did Johnathan do it?" he said he asked. She shook her head from side to side. "I asked if Chris was involved, and she shook her head up and down – vertical," Robert said. He also witnessed her one eye following him – a sign she may not have been as disoriented as they otherwise would have expected.

McDermott had been asking the questions of Robert, but now Shanks took her turn, starting off with a stern voice, as if she was trying to put pressure on Robert. "Are you a doctor?" she asked.

"No," he answered. After a flurry of other questions, he said that Joan was quickly sedated once the brief questioning ended. She had low blood pressure, "consistent with someone who lost a lot of blood." One of Joan's eyes seemed completely damaged. On the Glasgow Coma Scale, her initial score was 11 out of 15. "After she was sedated, I gave a three-score," he said, "which is almost the same as being not alive." An unconscious person could get a three.

Though Robert said the top priority was to take care of Joan's airway, Shanks wanted to make her point. The questions may have been asked of Mrs. Porco, she said, and she may have made movements. But it is also common practice for health professionals to determine if a patient is oriented to who they are, where they are, and what the date is. "No one asked her if she knew who she was, did they?" Shanks asked.

"No," said Robert.

"No one asked her any base questions. Did anyone ask questions she already knew the answer to, to see if she understood the questions?" She sounded astonished at the thought.

"Not that I can recall," the EMT answered.

Shanks said she was also confused about who asked the questions to Joan in the first place. Robert replied that Detective Bowdish had asked the questions at first – "did Johnathan or Chris do this to you?" There was no verbal response, said Robert. He said he saw Joan's jaw trying to move, but no words came out. Then Robert said he asked two questions: "Was Christopher involved?" and "Was Johnathan involved?" Mrs. Porco gave no verbal response, he said, but gave the head movement. Then, with the help of another EMT, he sedated her with an IV so she wouldn't move from the pain of being transported to the hospital.

"No one asked if she heard anything or if she had been lying there for hours?" asked Shanks.

"I thought she might not survive because of her injuries," answered Robert, staring at the attorney. "She had major damage to her face and head."

The Judge thanked Robert, and the next witness, Bethlehem Police Sergeant Robert Helligrass, walked up.

His testimony was nothing new to most people in the courtroom, but it left no doubt about how awful the crime was. The sergeant described the blood on the floor throughout the house. He talked about how Peter Porco had been at the bottom of the stairs. He said someone had found a person alive upstairs and remembered running up to offer help. That's when he saw a woman on the bed. He noticed lots of blood in the room. Blood soaked the bed. Blood covered the walls. He said he saw a large ax sticking out of the bed. Joan appeared coherent as she pulled down her bloody nightgown to properly cover herself.

He added that he had watched Detective Bowdish ask Joan, "Do you know who did this to you?" He said he "observed a response." Bowdish asked the next question – if Johnathan did this – and said Joan shook her head from side to side. Then Bowdish asked if Chris had done it. Sgt. Helligrass said Joan nodded her head yes.

Joan, who was listening to every word as she sat next to her friends in the front row, leaned over, but didn't say anything. She appeared to be uncomfortable hearing the graphic details of the crime and how she had been so close to death. Laurie Shanks was about to begin with a few questions for the sergeant, but instead, the Judge noticed Joan and stopped Shanks for a moment as Christopher brought over a cup of water to his mother. She sipped it, and Shanks continued.

Sergeant Helligrass said Joan didn't appear to be "writhing in pain. I saw EMT's put a mask on her face to give her oxygen," he said - - and was cut off.

Joan's friends created a small commotion as they made sure she was OK. She seemed emotional and shaken, and very weak. Some of the reporters left the courtroom to tell their cameramen who were waiting outside to get ready. Others waited to see if she would be all right. Judge Berry said the testimony would continue after a 15-minute recess.

Joan, supported by the Polsters, walked to the elevator in the hallway and out of the building. She had help getting into a car that quickly drove off. She was utterly exhausted.

After a few minutes passed, the witness finished his testimony, saying that he saw Detective Bowdish ask all of the questions.

Dennis Wood, another EMT who was at the scene, testified next. He told the court he saw Robert treating Joan. "There were just massive amounts of blood everywhere," he said. The ax was on the bed. He tried not to move it while he treated Mrs. Porco. Not only did he see her shake her head as the others had explained, he said she also raised her index finger and waved it back and forth as she shook her head "no," or up and down as she nodded "yes."

Bowdish then returned to the seat he had already occupied as Wood left the courtroom. The detective said he knew the Porco boys' names because he had called the dispatcher to get the names of the people who lived at the home. Then, he went upstairs. "I asked if she could hear me," he said. "I asked if a family member had done it. She nodded her head up and down. If John had done this to her. She shook her head in a 'no' indication from side to side. I asked if Chris had done it. There was a 'yes' indication. I asked again – did Chris do this to you?" He said she gave another 'yes' indication. "I thought she could die," he said, so he ended the questions there, "and then I apologized to her."

The Judge let Bowdish leave and told the courtroom that the hearings were complete. Judge Berry would determine if Christopher's prior bad acts would be allowed at the trial without courtroom arguments. He asked both sides to submit their briefs by next Thursday. Ten days after that he would likely have his rulings on the taped interrogation and the head nod.

Both prosecutors and the defense attorneys answered reporters' questions, but all were eager to leave after the long day so the interviews were brief. Kindlon said Mrs. Porco was all right. The testimony had just gotten to her. "Peter Porco died again in this courtroom," he said. "She lost him again in this courtroom and it had to tear her heart out."

Kindlon also said it was an important day for the defense, as different witnesses told different stories about which questions were asked, how many were asked, and by whom.

McDermott was also concerned about Mrs. Porco. And now, he wanted to talk with John Polster to see if Joan remembered anything after hearing the gruesome testimony. McDermott also told reporters he expected Joan to take the stand at some point during the trial.

Soon, the courthouse cleared out. Television reporters wrote their stories in the large news vans out front where cameras from each station were placed in a row for live shots.

VI

From: "Chris Porco" cp002m@mail.rochester.edu
To: "Porco" pporco@nycap.rr.com
Sent: Wednesday, September 15, 2004 9:49PM
Subject: Re: cal us tonight!!! 9/15

Hey guys,
Your phone is busy, has been for about an hour…I will try more. I am doing well. I am sorry I havent talked to you recently, ive been busy. My fever went away today, all im left with is an annoying cold. For Thanksgiving, if you are planning on seeing john id love to go too. Ill keep trying you guys, in the meantime im doing physics hw.
love
chris

From: "Peter Porco" PPORCO@courts.state.ny.us
To: "chrisporco@sprintpcs.com
Sent: Monday, September 20, 2004 4:47 PM
Subject: Your car loan payment is overdue

Chris,

We received mail on the weekend indicating that your car loan payment was overdue and that you had 5 days to pay it before they begin collection activities. You need to take immediate action on this.
Dad

From: "Chris Porco" cp002m@mail.rochester.edu
To: "Peter Porco" PPORCO@courts.state.ny.us
Sent: Monday, September 20, 2004 5:05PM
Subject: Re: Your car loan payment is overdue

Yo pops,
I paid it last week… im sure there is some delay, and that's why you got a notice. I was waiting for my new credit card to come through. The payment is nowset up on automatic deduction, so there shouldn't be any problems. If I could, could I have you and moms social security numbers and your ny state drivers liscense numbers, I need them for paperwork related to financial info for next semester. Hope your having a good day,
love
chris

*

Albany, New York
June 2, 2006

Two weeks went by and the pre-trial rulings had yet to be made by Judge Berry. An article in the Times Union said prosecutors had a strong piece of evidence that no one had heard about until now. It was a tollbooth ticket, allegedly with "mitochondrial DNA" on it that could link Christopher to the crime by putting him on the highway the night of the attack. Kindlon said he heard about the supposed evidence while he had the rare opportunity to escape from his office. He was changing his plane's oil when Times Union reporter, Brendan Lyons, called to ask him what he thought about it.

Soon after the revelation, another letter by Joan Porco appeared in the Times Union.

Joan M. Porco

June 2, 2006

Mr. Rex Smith
Times Union
Albany, New York

Dear Mr. Smith:

As you know, in November of 2004, my beloved husband, Peter, was murdered and I was attacked and left for dead. As the victim of such a horrible crime, I knew that my life would never be the same. I did expect, however, that the police and the DA's office would investigate and find the people who committed this crime. I expected that they would be in regular contact with me, giving me information and asking me questions.

Instead, I have learned that the police decided within minutes of finding me lying in bed, covered in blood, and severely injured, that my son, Christopher, was responsible for killing his father and injuring me. They say that I nodded my head when they asked me about him. I have no memory of the day at all, but can only assume that I heard my child's name and wanted him with me.

For months, my family has been disparaged in the press. The relationship between my husband and I and our son has been characterized as filled with anger and threats. Nothing could be further from the truth. Christopher is one of our adored children. We would never reject him because of bad grades or credit card bills and he would never hurt us for any reason.

In the 18 months since this crime was committed, neither the police or the D.A. have come to see me to ask if their "theories" about my family are true. Finally, a week or so ago, I was informed that Mike McDermott wanted to speak with me. In spite of the numerous times that I have been deceived by the authorities, and in hopes of having the truth finally come out, I agreed to speak with him. I arrived in the area last night to attend a meeting scheduled for this afternoon.

This morning I was confronted with an article on the front page of the Times Union. After making some inquiries I have learned several facts. I was told that, at least as of sometime late yesterday, there was no written report of any DNA test in the possession of the District Attorney's office. Further, no report was provided for review to the Law Office of Kindlon & Shanks, the firm representing my son, Christopher. Even more distressing, the purported existence of the report was leaked to your paper by either the police or the DA's office.

The only conclusion that I can draw is that the authorities want to obtain a conviction at all costs, in any manner possible, without any regard for their oath to seek justice. And more importantly, they seem to want to try this case in the press, where there is no defense, rather than to follow proper procedure in the courts where evidence is received only within legal grounds. Why would a rumor of such a DNA test be given to the press? The only purpose of the leak to your paper could be is to influence public opinion and taint potential jurors.

Because circumstances are the way they are, I now no longer see any benefit, for either Christopher or justice, to my meeting with the DA's office. They do not speak for me or for Peter and are clearly not interested in learning the truth.

I ask that you publish this letter, with my name. Because I am telling the truth, I do not have to hide behind an "anonymous tip."

Very truly yours,
Joan M. Porco
Joan M. Porco

cc. Michael McDermott
Bethlehem Police

*

Albany, New York
June 6, 2006

"As of last week, there had been 230 major stories," Kindlon told the Capital News 9 camera, flipping through page after page in his stack of printed articles. "We feel as a consequence there has been a tremendous level of conventional wisdom about this case. To be prudent, we are filing a motion with the appellate division for a change of venue." Now it was official. The defense had filed to move the trial out of Albany.

Kindlon said the jury would likely get picked before any decision was made. The change of venue paperwork would already be in the system so that if jurors seemed to be tainted, the motion would theoretically allow for a quicker move. No one knew at the time it wouldn't work like that at all.

Kindlon said he had to try to get the change in venue as a result of all the information leaked to the media. "It has been persistent. It has been prejudicial. A lot of it has been flat out untrue. This has been mentioned in our motion," Kindlon said.

Rachel McEneny, spokeswoman for the District Attorney's office, responded to the motion by saying, "Terry Kindlon's filing of a change of venue is premature. We're looking forward to next Thursday's trial date."

But it wasn't the motion that shocked anyone. After all, many had said for weeks that this trial was headed somewhere else. What happened next led to a blistering Police Benevolent Association response, a frustrated Arduini family, and a concerned defense team. Kindlon went on the offensive.

He said he was fed up with finding leaked information in the newspaper or television news reports several days a week – and pointed his finger. "I don't know if it's the Bethlehem Police, or if it's the DA's office."

He also took the opportunity to criticize the apparent DNA find. "Everyone's been conditioned to think that DNA is conclusive evidence," he said. "Everyone who watches TV says, 'oh my God...DNA!' But this is the low-grade trashy stuff." Indeed, the DNA in question was not nuclear DNA, which can be matched with someone specific. Instead, it was mitochondrial DNA, which experts said could only rule out groups of people from having contributed the sample.

Kindlon wasn't only looking at the type of DNA, but also at how it was obtained. "We think it's tremendously significant that the New York State Police scientific laboratory, arguably the finest, most publicly funded laboratory in the United States today, had this toll ticket for 18 months, and they didn't find a drop – a molecule - of DNA on this. But when the District Attorney's office sent some of the taxpayer's money to some outfit in Pennsylvania, which operates out of an office which has a suite number - so we're talking small time here - that this outfit was able to find DNA evidence in about three days flat," said Kindlon.

Kindlon not only questioned the validity of the DNA results, but he also said the chain of custody had a broken link. In the course of any trial, prosecutors have to show who handled each piece of evidence throughout the investigation. It was a way to prove there was no chance for the evidence to be tampered with. But Kindlon said there was a big problem. One of the papers filling the 29 large boxes in the room near his office held a curious concern for the defense. Kindlon said the document stated that a witness told police that in the course of their investigation, "Anthony Arduini showed me a toll ticket." It seemed innocent enough, and certainly had a purpose behind it. But Kindlon said, "The chain of custody passes directly through the hands of Anthony Arduini. He is no longer available to anyone as a witness. That could be a very dramatically difficult problem here as far as the chain of custody."

Kindlon argued that if the tollbooth ticket had been handled, it was therefore tainted and useless. Not only that, but police - and Arduini in particular - had good reason to plant the evidence, he alleged. He said Christopher had dated one of Arduini's daughters. Then, he said, Christopher had possibly dated his other daughter. It was all the more reason a man might plant evidence, according to Kindlon. He said his client had broken up with both girls.

The defense attorney didn't stop there. "Sometimes they plant it out of frustration because they're so intensely interested in getting a conviction." Kindlon said he almost considered Christopher to be framed - "frame is a good word, I like that."

He also said the few e-mails seen by the public were only part of the story. "What was left out of the final e-mail was that it said everything's under control, everything's cool. Come on home this weekend, your mom and I look forward to seeing you," he paraphrased. "They didn't bother putting that out in front of the press."

Nor, did they show Chris for who he was, he said. "He works in a vet shop and loves animals. He was the captain of the swim team at Bethlehem Central High School." And besides, "Joan Porco doesn't remember anything about that night, but she does remember the twenty-odd years before that and her relationship with Christopher. And she knows because she has a mother's knowledge of her son, that it could not have been him."

Albany, New York
June 13, 2006

Just days later, the Supreme Court of the State of New York Appellate Division, Second Judicial Department, made a decision on Kindlon's motion for a change of venue. The ruling explained that it is unusual to grant such a motion before "voir dire," where potential jurors are screened through a series of questions. It cited "the identity of the victims, the nature of the crime, and the intense, localized, and prejudicial pretrial publicity" as the reasons why the trial would be moved several hours south of Albany. Judge Berry would preside over the case from his usual courtroom in Orange County, New York.

*

Albany, New York
June 14, 2006

Even with the change of venue ruling, it was unclear if the Albany County jury pool had truly been tainted. Prosecutors felt there were enough potential jurors who had not heard about the case, or at least enough who just didn't really have time to care. One Albany resident on lunch break outside the Capitol told Capital News 9 she had heard "that he's guilty. But I think somebody is, you know, innocent until proven guilty. But I don't know. It's a tough case. We definitely talk about it. It's kind of like O.J. Simpson, you know?"

A college student on his way to class told the reporter, "It's hard to be objective about it, having heard so much." He said that the case was constantly talked about in college circles.

One Delmar resident said he heard plenty, and really didn't have an opinion. The coverage hadn't made him think one way or the other. Several attorneys thought it was a risky move; they thought the defense might not get jurors in Goshen who were more sympathetic than the Albany jurors might have been.

Albany, New York
June 15, 2006

All the attorneys returned to court one last time before the trial headed to Goshen. Basically, it was one last chance to air any last minute issues. That way, any controversies wouldn't slow down the schedule.

Judge Berry told the attorneys he didn't expect the trial to last longer than a month. Even though it would be moved, he hoped jury selection would still begin on the 26th. He said he had his decisions on the pre-trial hearing issues, but he wanted to withhold them a bit longer. They weren't "finely tuned," the judge told the courtroom. After meeting with Berry later, both sides said they had an idea what his decisions were, but said they were unable to discuss them. The public would have to wait to find out what would be allowed at the trial.

After the procedural information was discussed, Kindlon made it known he was frustrated with prosecutors. He said the mitochondrial DNA "evidence" merited more discussion. He reiterated it was "the trashy kind" of DNA and questioned whether the conclusions could be respected by scientists and accepted in court.

More importantly, he said, the chain of evidence had to be addressed as well. "The ticket was in Anthony Arduini's possession for some time." Kindlon said he had concluded the DA's office is "not in a position to concede that the location (of the ticket) can be established." Bottom line, Kindlon said Arduini was unable to testify, so no one could be sure how trustworthy any DNA evidence might be.

The attorney didn't stop there. "Detective Arduini, in his life, expressed a most extreme disapproval of Mr. Porco, who dated one of his daughters." He didn't think Christopher was a good person, he said. "After he dated Detective Arduini's older daughter, he established a relationship with his younger daughter." Kindlon paused. "On the morning Mr. Porco's remains were found – and immediately, without stopping at Brockley Drive - he went to see his daughter and make sure he didn't run away with his daughter," he said. "I don't mean to sound like a wild-eyed conspiracy theorist, but sometimes evidence gets planted...There is no way to establish a reliable chain. Given the fact that no one claimed there was DNA, and it was in the possession of the New York State Police lab for 18 months, we have been given concern Detective Arduini may well have contaminated the ticket."

Kindlon claimed Arduini had access to Porco's shirt and his Jeep. That meant he had access to Porco's DNA. He also wondered if Arduini and the others had used gloves or if they had handled the ticket without taking the proper precautions.

The Judge thanked Kindlon and agreed with him that prosecutors failed to provide him with information in a timely manner. Then, McDermott stood to counter Kindlon's accusations.

In a calm but loud tone of voice, McDermott said the State Police had photographed the tollbooth ticket, and Arduini couldn't have contaminated it, because he only had a *photograph* of it. The police had to chop up the actual ticket to run their tests – and so it couldn't even be read by the time Arduini had shown it, said the prosecutor. He added that the chain of custody had nothing to do with Arduini. He was confident the evidence would pass muster.

Kindlon resumed his argument. "The document I received says 'the ticket,'" he said. "Nothing about a photograph."

McDermott said it "was definitely a photograph."

The two went back and forth. Next, Kindlon accused McDermott of a document dump once again. The defense attorney said he had received over 150,000 pieces of paper so far, over 1,500 just a day ago. McDermott countered that he had given the attorney months to go through the evidence. Kindlon wanted to know if there would be anymore discovery material to expect in the next few days. "This is a trial by ambush," he said.

McDermott moved on. He told the court that prosecutors were putting together an animation to help jurors understand the murder scene. It would show the attack and animate the blood spatters so they could draw basic conclusions with the help of testimony from a crime scene expert.

But Kindlon found fault with that immediately. "Did we have eyewitnesses there?" he asked sarcastically. He guessed the animation would show one person committing the crime. "But why not two, three, or four people?" he asked. "They're speculating it was one person…I'm betting the animation will show one individual, about six foot three inches tall and a former swim team captain." If prosecutors wanted to bring it into the trial, he wanted it to be the center of more hearings. The judge agreed with Kindlon – at least as far as the animation. It would not be allowed in.

The banter continued for a bit. McDermott mentioned he wanted to bring in a video analyst who would testify that a yellow Jeep had been caught by University of Rochester security cameras apparently leaving campus the night of the attack. The vehicle, recorded on digital memory, had patterns and stains that the witness would say matched Christopher Porco's yellow Jeep exactly.

Before the day wrapped up, Judge Berry said he would allow a still photographer into the trial whose pictures would be limited by the judge's discretion. He said he would allow a pool video camera inside during opening arguments and summations. Before he dismissed everyone, Judge Berry said his official rulings on the numerous issues before him would likely come out after the 26th, once the jury had been seated.

Albany, New York
June 16, 2006

The Capital Region woke up to the latest Times Union's story. Brendan Lyons had broken yet another one. This time, his article quoted sources as saying the taped interrogation was going to be thrown out by the judge. It meant Judge Berry thought Christopher had been in custody and had not received the full reading of his Miranda Rights.

But it was also important because of the "fruit of the poisonous tree" idea. Now prosecutors would have to make sure all of their evidence came from a source other than the interrogation. And it complicated matters because some key parts of the prosecution's case were difficult to explain without it. One of the problems, for instance, was that Kindlon claimed Arduini had planted the DNA evidence on the toll ticket. *If* it had happened, it would have come *after* Christopher had provided DNA samples during the interrogation. And now, as far as any jury would be concerned, there was no interrogation.

Capital Region attorney Paul Der Ohannesian, who often provided insight into the legal nuances of the case for a couple of the news stations, told Capital News 9, "the defense has to be careful that it doesn't open the door to the admission of evidence that's otherwise excluded."

Meanwhile, McDermott continued to call Kindlon's accusations of police misconduct completely ridiculous.

All of this came as Judge Berry had yet to rule on whether the head nod would be allowed in or not – or, perhaps, his decision just hadn't been leaked yet.

Albany, New York
June 19, 2006

It was moving day. The DA's office spokeswoman, Rachel McEneny, spent the morning coordinating the transportation of box after box after box of evidence from downtown Albany to downtown Goshen. "Our staff is on the ground speaking with realtors, exploring office space," she told several reporters. She said people were already rather tired after working nearly around the clock to make it all happen.

Coordinating details of the move wouldn't be easy. Everyone expected the trial to last anywhere from three weeks to as many as six. Prosecutors planned on calling 135 witnesses from 15 states and Okinawa, Japan. McEneny said members of the DA's office were planning on meeting with the County Executive to discuss the additional cost of the move and would request sufficient funds in the hopes of a successful prosecution.

Albany County Comptroller Michael Conners said all the travel, food, hotel, office space, and miscellaneous expenses would add up quickly, making it quite costly for taxpayers. "We were ball-parking the additional cost of the move to be between $250,000 and $350,000," Conners told the News 9 reporter.

McEneny thought the cost might actually be lower because Goshen was further south than Albany. "It's actually cheaper to fly into Newburgh and Newark," she said, but that assumption was based on a number of variables that could change at any time.

There was some financial leeway, though, as long as there were no surprises. Half of the year had already come and gone, but only about 37% of the DA's annual $5.6 million budget had been used, according to Albany County officials.

Bethlehem, New York
June 20, 2006

It had taken several days for those who knew Anthony Arduini to respond publicly to the controversial accusations that he had planted evidence. "It's upsetting to us as members of the community and as policemen that Terry would stoop that low," Bethlehem PBA Union President Scott Anson said through his teeth.

Anson conducted interview after interview with reporter after reporter, wearing large, dark sunglasses. While his shades hid a large part of his face, he was unable to hide his anger. He looked like he was about to punch the News 9 camera simply because it was there, and Kindlon wasn't.

"I think Mr. Kindlon has sunk to an all-time low for Mr. Kindlon when he goes after deceased people that can't defend themselves. (Arduini's) integrity and honesty shined through on every case. He never tampered with evidence, he never trumped up charges." Anson's face turned redder the more he spoke.

He believed it was impossible for Arduini to have tampered with the tollbooth ticket. He was "never anywhere near it. Never in the same room with it," according to Anson. "If this police department is so bad, and this community is so unsafe because of this police department, I would wonder why Mr. Kindlon lives here amongst us and has for years and raised a family here."

Kindlon was in Rochester for the day. He had flown his plane there to save time and avoid the commercial airlines. He would return in the evening, but in the meantime, he seemed surprised by the response his statements about Arduini were getting. “If anyone’s feelings are hurt, that’s regrettable. I was given a piece of paper by the DA’s office that said the ticket was in Arduini’s possession.”

He said he was just doing his job.

PART III
TRIAL

VII

Goshen, New York
June 26, 2006

At seven in the morning, Goshen was nearly silent. About a dozen businesses line the main street near the Orange County Courthouse. Most wouldn't open for hours. One sold coffee and desserts, a pizza parlor also sold seafood, and a popular deli usually had a line to the door around lunchtime. That shop owner would make a few roast beef or meatball sandwiches, then he'd usually stop by a few tables to see if everyone approved. Steve's Deli was also the place where half of the future jurors would grab their lunches each day for the next few weeks. Nearby, stately houses clutched American flags that waved softly in the summer breezes.

Across from those homes, it was impossible to miss the odd architecture of the Courthouse. Cubes jutted out from all sides. In the back by the parking lot, two security guards who worked there saw the circus had begun. Prosecutors and their staff had been in Goshen getting ready for the trial since the previous Wednesday. They organized evidence, set up offices, and found the best places to catch a quick meal. But it wasn't the prosecutors who concerned the court officers.

Most members of the media had only arrived the night before. Some had actually started the two-plus hour trip Monday morning. Large satellite trucks pulled in next to each other – affiliates for FOX, NBC, ABC, CBS, as well as Capital News 9. One court officer arrived on his motorcycle after the oversized vehicles parked and was not too pleased to see his usual spot swallowed up. He grudgingly parked 20 feet away in the large empty parking lot that would soon be filled with scores of potential jurors.

Only one car sat in the parking lot besides those belonging to the news crews. Inside a small sedan, the Balzanos, Christopher Porco's uncle and aunt, sat quietly, staring out the windows of their car. They would arrive several hours early for the first week or so of the trial simply to sit together in the center of the empty parking lot with the windows rolled up.

Meanwhile, members of the media were told what rules they had to follow to stay on the good side of the officers. One officer told each news station to keep their cameras in back of the plastic barricades that had been set up to keep the group from obstructing the path into the courthouse. Everyone obliged. That would be where interviews of both the defense and prosecution would take place each morning and during lunch breaks.

The cameramen and live truck operators put up tents, one next to the other, on the 30-foot-wide strip of grass between the live trucks and the courthouse. As soon as the equipment was in place, some of the reporters went live, previewing the day. Joggers and dog-walkers slowed their pace to try and figure out what was going on.

It wasn't long before other cars joined the Balzanos. The large parking lot filled quickly after around eight each morning, forcing the tardier drivers to creep from aisle to aisle in their vehicles. Many usually ended up parking creatively.

Workers, potential jurors, and those with a court date all walked into the courthouse in packs of a dozen or so, happy to get out of the hot weather. Already, a yellow Jeep had quickly made its way around the parking lot. A few reporters waiting by the courthouse entrance saw it and informed the others that they were staying at the same hotel as Christopher. They said they saw him sitting with his mother eating breakfast, which happened to be a bowl of Wheaties. Mrs. Porco was apparently fussing over what Christopher was eating, the story went. He kept referring to her as "Mother," asking, "Mother would you like some cereal?" one reporter said. A newspaper reporter joked that Christopher would need his Wheaties.

Then a grayish Honda Accord arrived, and Terry and Laurie got out with bundles of papers and a few plastic containers full of documents. Several minutes later, Christopher Porco, dressed in a dark suit, carried a couple of the boxes alongside his attorneys who seemed eager to get inside and get down to business. Joan walked alongside them, staying close to her son. She wore a fashionable pair of large sunglasses that helped to hide the scars on her face. She chatted with Christopher as the cameras recorded their walk inside.

With David Rossi just behind him, Mike McDermott headed towards the barricades as well. They used a cart to bring in several boxes of documents. Already close to nine in the morning, they went right inside, not wanting to be late the first day.

Once through the heavy glass doors, it was a straight shot to the courtroom through a long hallway. Of course, you had to go through security first, which included emptying your pockets and walking through a metal detector. Some of the security guards were friendly, but a couple of them made it obvious they would much rather be somewhere else. As you made your way past the metal detectors, other courtrooms lined the long hall. If you walked by at the right time, you might hear emotions flaring inside from the family cases being discussed.

It took some time for the actual day to begin. Waiting for the Judge, Christopher Porco sat alongside Shanks who looked through a few papers. Kindlon paced the courtroom, stopping to chat with reporters. Had the reporters, including photographers, newspaper writers, and television personalities all sat together, they would have probably filled more than a few of the dozen benches in the public seating area. But the courtroom was still quite empty compared to what it would soon look like. For now, jurors waited in another room down the hall and to the left.

Judge Berry entered. Everyone stood and didn't sit back down until he said to. Christopher looked straight ahead as Berry explained how he hoped the day – and parts of the trial – would proceed.

He explained the questions he would ask potential jurors: how many have an inability to serve as jurors for four to five weeks? How many have heard or read something about the case? It was fairly typical legal stuff.

Judge Berry had a group of 80 Orange County residents enter the courtroom, which squeezed out some of the reporters. After the first round of general questions, 30 were told to come back the following day. Then the next group came in. Only knowing that this was some type of murder trial, several said they would have a hard time serving because of the nature of the crime. Six said they had heard about the case in the news. Others said they could be fair and impartial, and Judge Berry asked that group of about 30 potential jurors to return the following day to join the first 30.

Because of the sheer number of people in the courtroom, and perhaps to throw a bone to the defense, only one journalist was allowed in the courtroom at a time during the jury selection process. The rule remained, even though groups of potential jurors would exit every so often, leaving plenty of seating.

Judge Berry seated juror number 21, one of several who would return Tuesday for more questioning. He asked jurors to be honest with their answers during direct questioning, or voire dire. "Just because an answer is acceptable doesn't mean you need to give the same answer," he instructed. Berry said the case would be tried with at least three alternate jurors. He gave the potentials a chance to tell him why they couldn't serve by having them walk up to him. A few took advantage of the opportunity and explained their situations. One manager had a business merger to tend to. One man said his wife was sick with breast cancer and he needed to take care of her. They and a few others were dismissed.

But the 60 who had made it past both sides' scrutiny were told to come back for 10:45 the next morning. They were warned not to watch television, not to go on the internet, and not to find anything out about the case. Jury selection would continue for a second day.

Later, outside the courthouse, Kindlon stopped for what would become the daily ritual near the media tents: taking questions in front of multiple microphones sticking out of a makeshift stand. "The most critical thing that happens around a trial is the jury that sits in judgment of the defendant," Kindlon said. He added that he was glad the case had been moved. It eliminated much of the presumed bias that he thought would have occurred had the trial stayed in Albany County.

While the jury selection process was extremely significant, so too was the discussion about what evidence would be allowed in and what would be barred from the trial. After the first day of jury selection was complete, the Judge allowed both sides to provide their arguments on the latest defense motion. It asked that University of Rochester students not be allowed to testify, though the prosecution was planning on it.

Back in court Shanks said, "It shifts the burden of proof." She believed if the students said Christopher was nowhere to be found on campus that night, it meant Christopher had to prove he was somewhere else. But he didn't have to testify, nor did he have to prove anything. It was up to the prosecution to do that.

McDermott confidently told Judge Berry the students "are important witnesses who say he wasn't in the lounge since that's where he said he was."

Shanks immediately shot up out of her chair. "That's a hearsay account of where he was," she said. With the taped interrogation most likely thrown out, she argued there was no basis to say Christopher told people he was with his fellow students that night.

Already the day was getting late. Judge Berry asked for briefs of both sides' arguments for the following day when the potential jurors would return. He asked everyone to arrive by 8:45.

As the court cleared out, journalists returned to the microphone stand outside. Kindlon explained the motion they had only begun to debate. "It's a goofy evidence problem," he said. "It appears the prosecution wants to take statements attributed to Chris and pick it apart." He said the motion would simply prohibit the student testimony if the interrogation was suppressed.

But the whole situation was certainly hard to follow since both he and McDermott said they pretty much knew the ruling on the interrogation and the head nod. While they weren't supposed to talk about it, they both said they were waiting on the ruling to see how best to proceed. "I have an inkling of what may be in the offing, but I'm going to withhold comment until I see it," McDermott said earlier.

In the meantime, a reporter asked how Kindlon's client was doing on the first day. "How's Christopher holding up?" he repeated. "Well, he's like a runner in mile 25 of a marathon going up heartbreak hill. I mean this is tough duty. Very difficult to be a young person charged with murder on trial for your life."

Kindlon stepped back from the microphones, joined Laurie, and met up with Christopher who had begun walking to the parking lot with the others. A 48 Hours producer chased after them, working to befriend the group.

McDermott and Rossi stepped up to the cameras, filling the void left by Kindlon. The microphone stand had to be adjusted for McDermott's taller frame. He spoke about the extensive witness list that included 135 people ready to testify about some aspect of the case.

He said he still wished the trial had remained in Albany County. The move had simply complicated every aspect of his team's job. And it didn't make it easy on their families either. He was asked whether Mrs. Porco's support of Christopher might complicate their case. "It could," he answered. "That's something we're going to try and bring out during jury selection and see what the jurors have to say about it. Undoubtedly that will have some sort of effect."

He added that he would ask the judge to exclude all witnesses who might be called to testify from sitting in the courtroom throughout the proceedings. McDermott said he was concerned that since Joan Porco was both a likely witness and someone who wanted to show support for her son, the scenario could impact jurors. However, if the judge ruled she couldn't watch the trial each day, it would mean she wouldn't be able to watch as 12 random people determined her son's fate.

Goshen, New York
June 27, 2006

The day began much like the previous one. Reporters arrived, breaking the silence around the courthouse. The Balzanos quietly sat in their car until scores of other cars filled the lot. McDermott, looking a bit tired, walked into the building. Ten minutes later, Kindlon and Shanks arrived as well. Mrs. Porco joined her son as he walked in past the reporters who had been told by the defense team not to talk with their client. A few still said "hello" to them simply because the scene felt so awkward.

Seventy-one more potential jurors were screened throughout the day, but both sides realized the process was taking far longer than either had thought. "I thought I'd be able to say at this point the paint's all dry," said Kindlon after the judge had announced a lunchtime recess. "But the paint's still wet…we're not quite up to the starting line yet."

As the day progressed, Judge Berry asked question after question. "Have you ever been convicted of a crime?" In one group, eleven people raised their hands. "Did you ever have financial difficulty?" Sixteen put their hands in the air.

Both sides also discussed the potential witnesses to see if any future jurors knew them or had biases. Witnesses from GE Consumer Finance, Hudson Valley Community

College, Sprint, Citi Corp., eBay, the New York State Retirement System, investigators, daughters of investigators, friends of Peter Porco, and Dr. Henry Lee, the famed forensic pathologist from Connecticut, were all listed as possible witnesses.

The defense asked potential jurors if they "can tell what someone feels about something by looking at them," obviously trying to weed out those who might jump to conclusions about Christopher Porco's stoicism.

Sitting next to his attorneys, he took what appeared to be copious notes. He smiled as much as he could for the seven jurors – five women and two men - who had been seated by noon. The group included a middle school teacher, a retired paralegal, a bus driver, and a woman who said she enjoyed studying genealogy. Judge Berry said he wanted six alternates in addition to the 12 whose job it would be to decide whether Porco would go free, or live the rest of his life in prison.

The surprise of the day for prosecutors was that Kindlon and his wife decided to put some of Porco's prior bad acts out in the open for everyone to see in an apparent attempt to steal the prosecution's thunder. Through fancy wording of questions, they basically stated that stealing a computer from home doesn't lead to murder. Outside the courtroom at the usual spot by the media tents, McDermott later told journalists, "Yeah, I was a little surprised to hear that during jury selection, but we've got to think about that one tonight." He called it an "interesting development."

Goshen, New York
June 28, 2006

By mid-morning, another 21 Orange County residents were ready to be screened. A nurse, a purchasing agent, an unmarried teacher, a recent criminal justice graduate, and a Hungarian immigrant, were all part of the group peppered with questions until the early afternoon.

Finally, 12 jurors – and six alternates – were given specific seats to occupy for the duration of the trial. Judge Berry read them a set of instructions. At last it seemed like the trial was ready to truly get going, though it would only take a few hours before a call for a mistrial would anger the judge, surprise those sitting in court, and frustrate the prosecution.

Judge Berry told the waitress, recently retired teacher's assistant, director of information management, junior high math teacher, and the other jurors, what they could expect for the duration. Fridays would be days off because he had to have a day each week to tend to the local cases that still filled his calendar.

He said that both sides would now have a chance to explain their side of the facts during what's called opening arguments. The prosecution would go first, then the defense. Berry said when McDermott spoke, for instance, he was not stating what definitely happened, but instead "what the prosecution intends to prove at the trial…the theme and theory of the case." Basically, it was a preview of what was to come.

McDermott stood, his tall frame taking up a spot close to the bench, where he could move around, gesture, and keep the attention of the jurors. They still had little information about what the well dressed Christopher Porco was accused of doing.

The Chief Assistant DA welcomed and thanked the jurors for their service. Christopher Porco, he began, "is charged with two crimes. We will show that in the early morning hours of November 15, 2004, he entered his home while his parents were home, entered the bedroom, and attacked them viciously with an ax."

McDermott's soothing voice grew louder, even dramatic, as he spoke. "He struck his father over a dozen times." He attacked his mother, he said, "and left them for dead."

"How could this be?" He let the question hang in the air for a moment. "We'll spend the next several weeks answering that question," said McDermott. Several jurors' eyes stayed wide open. Some looked at Chris, as if trying to figure out how the kid in front of them could have done such a thing.

McDermott described Peter and his wife as Joan listened from the front row. He mentioned their professions. Christopher sat still next to his attorneys who busily took notes. Rossi sat ten feet to the side, also making an occasional note. McDermott described the four-bedroom house and explained that Christopher's brother, Johnathan, was "stationed at a Navy base in South Carolina then. And you'll hear proof Johnathan wasn't there (at the house that night)."

McDermott glanced down at his notes every once in a while, but mostly reiterated the argument from memory. He explained how Michael Hart, the court officer, came to the house after Peter failed to show up for work, how he faintly heard the dog bark. How the door was unlocked, but he didn't go in right away. How he found traces of red drops on the ground. McDermott brought jurors to the scene – speaking in the present tense. Hart "tries to lift the garage door. It's locked," he said. "Hart calls his boss, who allows him to go inside…He opens the door – six or eight inches – but it sticks. Something is behind the door."

McDermott described the crime scene further: "The bi-fold door has been ripped from the closet, covered in blood…The filing cabinet inside the closet is open. Hart sees Peter's body and its awkward position on the stairs…The court officer decides to check the rest of the house. He goes down the hallway, sees blood in the downstairs bathroom, sees blood on the floor in the kitchen, on the appliances and countertops. Hart's boss tells him to get out of there." The jurors' eyes locked on the prosecutor.

"Officers arrive," McDermott continued. They "check the house and find blood in the family room." He said they walked downstairs to the basement and opened the door. *Nothing*. "They go to the dining room on the ground level, find a purse on the hutch. But all the money, credit cards, and keys are still inside."

McDermott mentally took the jury upstairs. "There was blood on the stair railing," he said. "Christopher Porco's bedroom is right ahead at the top of the stairs." He said Johnathan's room was further down. "In none of those rooms," he said, "were there any signs out of the ordinary."

Then – they "see a sight of incredible carnage."

McDermott described the discovery of Joan Porco who was near death. He discussed the ax that had been left behind in the bed. Blood was spattered behind the bed. He said Mrs. Porco's face was unrecognizable. Then, the investigators noticed she moved, and EMT's rushed up. "They will testify tomorrow," he told jurors.

A couple reporters who sat a few rows back whispered about whether the supposed head nod was going to be allowed in. They soon got their answer, as Mrs. Porco watched everything from her seat on the defense's side of the room.

McDermott described how Detective Bowdish asked Mrs. Porco, "who did this to you?" McDermott told the jury she was simply incapable of speaking because her jaw was injured. But her arms responded. The "EMT's will say she was conscious and alert," he said.

Bowdish was allowed to quickly ask yes or no questions, he said, and she "adamantly" responded when she was asked whether it was Chris. "She was asked more than once. Then, she was intubated and went through 12-plus hours of surgery. She was in a coma for days."

He paused. He purposefully made eye contact with a few of the jurors. "She has no recollection of the attack." He paused once more. "Amnesia persists to this day."

McDermott said Mrs. Porco may not have been able to say to police who the killer was. However, prosecutors would argue her brain injuries didn't preclude her from all communication. Some of the jurors looked like they were ready to cry.

The prosecutor said investigators worked together and pursued their suspect armed with the facts. The case is not based on Joan's head nod, he said. "It's based on a year of investigation. And Christopher Porco was her assailant."

McDermott continued, knowing what he was about to say would further shock the courtroom. He began to explain how Peter Porco had gone from his blood-soaked bed – where investigators agreed the attack had happened - to the bottom of the stairs. "This is not a case where a struggle upstairs went downstairs," he said.

"At some point, Peter regains consciousness. And he goes on auto-pilot, wandering around the house." McDermott said Peter used tissues to try and stop the bleeding. "He puts on a long sleeve shirt before he goes downstairs." McDermott took a breath. "His handprints are on the wall." He told jurors blood smeared on the banister from each grip. "He goes into the fridge and then starts to empty the dishwasher. He goes into the family room and sits down. He's going through his morning routine."

McDermott paused, then told the courtroom that at one point, "he had a phone in his hand." But Peter Porco couldn't dial for help.

"He then tried opening the sliding glass door," said McDermott. "He forgot there was a broom handle in the track. So he opens the front door." The Chief ADA said a couple of drops of blood fell from Peter's open wounds and dotted the concrete steps.

McDermott would later tell reporters outside the courthouse, "It's pathetic. Every time I think about it, I mean it's one of the most pathetic things I've ever heard of. The image of Peter just wandering around downstairs is just heartbreaking. And the thing is, I really didn't want Joan in there for the openings and I brought it up to the defense counsel that I was going to unfortunately be pretty graphic and I didn't think Mrs. Porco would want to hear it. But they wanted her there so they made it uncomfortable for me. I'm sure it was difficult for her to hear."

Still in court, McDermott told the jury they would hear from State Police investigators and blood spatter experts. "There was no sign of a traditional burglary," he argued. But the crime scene also shows signs of a "staged burglary," he said. He took a moment to explain how the screen to one of the windows was cut, how someone had pushed the window up. "Telephone wires in the backyard on the pole were cut. The keypad for the burglar alarm was smashed," he said.

McDermott told the jurors it didn't add up, though. The assailant only made it *look* like someone had gone through the window. He said a year before the attack Mrs. Porco's work computer had been taken. Back then, a window had been similarly opened, its screen cut. McDermott spoke louder as he said, "The laptop was sold by Christopher on eBay. That burglary is Christopher Porco's undoing."

McDermott next talked about how the Porcos had put in a security system with a keypad after the burglary. "Smashing the keypad didn't erase the memory," he said. Every disarm and re-arm of the security system was recorded in a computer downstairs. "Peter and Joan, John and Chris, were the only ones with the code...The alarm had been turned off that night, and the master code had been used to do it."

McDermott said Christopher told all his friends and family that he slept on a couch in the lounge at school. "It's a small lounge," McDermott explained. "You will hear from his friends that Christopher was not there." – and Kindlon stood up.

"I object to this," Porco's attorney said, shaking his head in a show of disgust. "Some of this may not be admissible." Judge Berry asked Kindlon to sit back down and ordered the statement to continue.

McDermott told jurors Christopher likely took I-90 to get from the University of Rochester to Delmar. He had an EZPass, but police found it jammed down in the console. "You'll hear from toll collectors who will tell you they saw a yellow Jeep with wide tires driven by a young, white male." He also said they had toll tickets that were significant for another reason. "The toll tickets have been subjected to DNA tests."

Prosecutors planned to call other witnesses, including a neighbor who woke up early that Monday morning. "And he knows the yellow Jeep," McDermott said. "It speeds up and down the neighborhood. At 4AM there's a yellow Jeep in the driveway."

McDermott conceded they never found any direct evidence linking Christopher to the murder. The only possibility, he explained, was a "single fingerprint on the outside of the basement door." He said that was significant because the Porcos never shut their dog downstairs.

McDermott continued, hoping to show why Christopher would have wanted to commit such a horrible crime. Already, a few of the jurors, the women, kept glancing over at Christopher, trying to size him up.

"Christopher was an awful student," the prosecutor continued. "He had to take a year off." Christopher had made plenty of friends, but he said, "his parents were disappointed, paying $32,000 a year to send him to the University of Rochester… They told him he has to pack up and move. So he tells his parents the University of Rochester made a mistake. A professor lost my final exam." Not only that, but because of the mix-up, the University "would give him the next semester free," he said.

Then, McDermott outlined what he said was Chris' plan to get back to Rochester. He "would re-enroll at HVCC (Hudson Valley Community College) and prove to the University of Rochester he was serious. But he didn't go to classes…Peter saw his grades – and he was frustrated." McDermott paused for emphasis. "But he tells his dad he got the wrong grades. And he changes them to all A's and one B. He sends it to the University of Rochester…and goes back to the University of Rochester."

McDermott said Christopher also returned with a new yellow Jeep. "But he couldn't really afford it, though. He applied for a car loan. He forges his father's signature for the car loan." In the front row, Joan's head bowed down.

He described how Christopher had asked for his father's W-2 forms and other documents with personal information to secure a $32,000 loan. Peter found out what the information was really for, McDermott said, "and Chris tells his dad – don't worry. It's only $2,000."

"In the fall semester e-mails are sent like a crescendo…The pressure comes to a head around the beginning of November, and Peter decides he had had enough…He starts doing some digging. His name is forged on a $16,000 loan and on a $32,000 loan. He's worried about his son's mental health." McDermott said that was when Peter said he was cutting Christopher off. "You're insane," McDermott said, as if he were Peter. "It's time to fess up" – and Kindlon shot up from his chair.

"Objection. Objection," he said. Judge Berry motioned for Kindlon to calm down. Kindlon was angry – saying something about how Peter can't defend himself. "I'm calling for a mistrial," the attorney said. Judge Berry ordered Kindlon to sit. Kindlon made sure the court would hear his rage momentarily, as Berry told McDermott to finish up.

McDermott continued, quickly recapturing the jurors' attention. "All the deception, the deceit, the house of cards is beginning to crash around him. Porco went home to silence the voices telling him to grow up and take responsibility."

Several jurors looked away from McDermott as he spoke, their faces turning red. Some, still caught up in the moment, began to weep loudly enough that a box of tissues made it from juror to juror in the front row. "Peter and Joan had a will that explains where the estate goes after death benefits," McDermott finished. He confidently closed his binder of papers and took his seat next to Rossi.

Members of the jury were told they had a short recess. The more controversial issues would never be discussed in front of them.

Once they left through a back door, Kindlon stood up, still livid. "Judge" –

- "Don't ever say mistrial in my court," Berry said, putting the attorney in his place.

Kindlon apologized but said he was left with little choice after "imaginary dialogue between Chris and Peter – and we can't cross-examine them." Look, he said, "We've created a problem. We need to shut the trial down and pick a new jury."

But Berry said none of that would happen. He told prosecutors to be careful, and reiterated that he didn't want to hear "mistrial" again.

After several minutes, jurors reentered. Judge Berry gave a quick explanation to "inoculate" them from the legal drama that had just occurred. Then Kindlon walked over, ready to try and explain away all that McDermott had just caught their attention with.

"What's riveting about this is what's happened," he began. "Life was destroyed in the middle of the night by someone who did horrible, indescribable things." Kindlon made eye contact with several of the jurors and pointed to McDermott. "You were riveted by him." He let the words sink in for effect. "We don't dispute (Peter's) beautiful, lovely, wife, was horribly injured." If you think about what you just heard, he said, eyeing McDermott again, you heard about "one - the horrible death of Peter and the maiming of Joan. Two - Chris' life was a mess. But those two things don't go together."

"Chris Porco...received a telephone call from an intern at an Albany newspaper. 'What is your reaction to the fact your mother and father have been killed?' That's how the nightmare started for Christopher Porco. The jury forewoman began to cry, though she tried to stay quiet.

Kindlon continued, ready to bash the police department. "The Town of Bethlehem has a small police force. There are only four detectives. There's no homicide squad because there are no homicides. They do drunk driving, yell at skateboarding kids, and direct traffic at High School graduation." Kindlon described the confusion he believed the police experienced once they arrived at the scene. He threw doubt on the supposed head nod by quickly adding, "The first police officer was able to see Joan's brain through her face."

Kindlon admitted he agreed with the prosecution's conclusion that Peter had walked around the house "irrationally" after the attack. But he said, "the most important thing is that the first responders were called upstairs where it was extremely dark when (the Porcos) were sound asleep...What opportunity would Joan have had to observe her assailant? None whatsoever – and there were a number of blows."

He continued his criticism of the police. "Christopher Bowdish is a detective with 17 years experience chasing kids skateboarding in the parking lot. Bowdish tries to question her. Now consider the absurdity of that proposition. She couldn't speak, couldn't see," Kindlon said. No one was sure how long she had been there. And there was "confusion over who asked the questions to Joan- was it Bowdish or the EMT? All we know is someone said the names 'John' and 'Chris' – and she had some reaction to 'Chris.'" Kindlon said no basic knowledge test had been given to Mrs. Porco, so no one could be sure if she actually understood what she was being asked about in the first place.

He turned to the topic of his client's family. "Peter was referred to as 'gentle Peter.' He was dedicated to his wife. Christopher had made some good decisions and bad decisions. He had done some dumb things. He admits he swiped a computer from his mother and had bills through the roof. He got to college and someone said, 'let's party,' and he said, 'that's a pretty good idea.'" Kindlon then slowed his speech for emphasis and smiled. "But he's working at a vet hospital to this day and is considered by the vets as one of the greatest guys."

Then the smile disappeared. "There were hundreds of police officers on this case. The strongest piece of evidence is the nod. That's as good as it gets in this case." He then walked over to Christopher and made a motion over his client's head, as if stirring a large pot with both hands. His voice grew dramatically louder as he impersonated a prosecutor: "Then we're going to slime this guy until he's covered in green slime and you can't even see him anymore."

He continued. "Bowdish went to the Jeep to find blood." Kindlon told jurors, "blood is everywhere in the house, but not in the Jeep."

He said the vehicle was sent on a flatbed truck from Rochester to Albany for testing. "The EZPass recorded it was on the highway" during that trip, he said. But "the EZPass was still jammed down" in the console. Kindlon said prosecutor's believed it was in the same spot when, according to their theory, Christopher had traveled to commit the attack. But it hadn't registered at that point, if the trip had even happened.

"The Jeep had Wendy's wrappers – but not a molecule of blood. Nothing." Kindlon got angry. "Instead of evidence – let's have slime. There's no evidence in this case.

What there is, if you could weigh it, is six tons of wishful thinking. Questionnaires were given to kids – students – at the University of Rochester. We looked over the questionnaires. All they wanted was the bad stuff in this abomination of a case. They tried to twist the facts to fit."

Then, he dropped a bombshell. "What they ignored was this: Peter, 'gentle Peter,' had a cousin in the Mob in New York City named Frankie 'the Fireman'- a snitch. Frankie 'the Fireman' is doing 25 months on a conspiracy to murder conviction. Is that ludicrous? Do you think he made a deal? Do you think someone in the Mob was sending him a message? Did investigators pursue the lead? Did they talk with Frankie?"

Kindlon went on with another possibility. He described how Peter had worked in family court, and an individual, in the heat of the moment, had threatened Peter, the Judge he had worked for, and another attorney. He said the man threatened that "he was going to get those two 'guineas' and that 'fat kike.'" He told jurors that both Johnathan and Christopher had to leave school because of the threat.

The attorney had yet another theory he wanted the jury to consider. He said Joan reported a strange man in the driveway just a few months before the attack. "Police didn't worry (about that possibility) because they already had Christopher - even though there's not a shred of evidence that connects him to the crime." He said he would throw doubt on the neighbor's claim that the Jeep had been in the driveway the night of the attack.

"Chris has no history of violence at all...Because credit card bills were not paid, his marks at school were bad, you don't sneak over to Albany then park right in the driveway and try to kill your parents." He said Chris couldn't have done it because it just didn't make sense.

He concluded by saying the attack was undoubtedly brutal and violent. He wondered aloud if it wasn't "as violent and as efficient as two mafia hit men, perhaps?"

Christopher sat at the desk, quietly listening to his attorney. "You will hear from Christopher's employers, who opened their house to Christopher. You'll hear from Joan – as a mother. Police wouldn't talk to Joan for months because she didn't say what they wanted to hear. The reason is – there's no evidence – because he didn't do it."

Kindlon looked one last time at members of the jury and then took his seat next to his client who gave a slight smile.

Judge Berry asked everyone to be back in court at 9AM to begin hearing from witnesses.

Outside the courtroom a line of reporters went live, talking about the arguments both sides intended to make throughout the trial. They spoke of DNA, Jeep sightings, Joan as a witness, and possible Mafia involvement. They said there was no official ruling on whether the head nod would be allowed in or not. But of course, it was already part of the story jurors had heard. McDermott told reporters a "semi-ruling" allowing it in would have to suffice for now. He didn't seem phased by the call for a mistrial so soon in the proceedings. "Ah...every trial Terry does that," he said.

Kindlon also brushed off the call to shut down the trial as he spoke with reporters. "I have a habit of moving for a mistrial," he said, laughing and looking at the ground sheepishly. Laurie watched the interview from a few yards back. Christopher walked over to listen. He found a spot in back of some of the reporters as Kindlon repeated his concern that police hadn't properly hunted down all possible leads. "They spent a couple of hundred man-hours talking to college kids about Christopher Porco, but when it came time to talk about Freddie 'the Fireman,' who's a snitch for the Mob," they didn't follow up, he said. "And snitches for the Mob make some real serious enemies who do things like chop relatives up with axes."

Kindlon joined his wife, and walked with Christopher and his mother to their cars.

The trial had begun.

VIII

From:	"Porco" pporco@nycap.rr.com
To:	"Chris Porco" cp002m@mail.rochester.edu
Sent:	Friday, October 01, 2004 6:24PM
Subject:	How are you doing?

Hey Chris,

Are you feeling any better? Based on correspondence received here it looks like you're borrowing money from citibank? If that's the case and its for college, I would be willing to discuss further borrowing through a parents plus loan at about 4% than have you paying 9% or more. Why don't you call home. Also, any idea where the downstairs TV remote is? It seems to have vanished since you've been here?
Dad

From:	"Porco" pporco@nycap.rr.com
To:	chrisporco@sprintpcs.com
Sent:	Saturday, October 02, 2004 10:56 AM
Subject:	Watch the mail for a package 10/2/04

Hi Chris-

It worries me when you have not communicated with us. There is no short changing the IMPORTANT things in your life- Which as I see it are #1- academics #2 NROTC #3 your family father, mother, and brother #4 other family and friends. If you are spending the weekend with #4- you willllllllll be in trouble. Learn to say NOOOOOOOOOOOOOOOO- PRIORITIES!!!! If they are good friends they will want you to do what you need to do first.

It looked like you didn't take any slacks so I'm sending some plus your lightweight vest.

Pleasse call this weekend and answer our e-mails- with the best of your ability- asw soon as you get them - If you are procrastinating- you ARE in trouble... Paradighm shift TODAY before it's too late.

We love you and are hopeing that you will find success this semester. If not-plan on transferring to SUNY –

Love you- MOM

Now- reread this again and say a prayer....

*

Goshen, New York
June 29, 2006

Thursday, everyone arrived at the courthouse eager to finish the week. But most knew this would be a tough day. Jurors would hear some of the trial's most grisly testimony. They would see the horrendous crime scene pictures.

While few noticed at first, the jury box had a little more room. One juror had been dismissed. No specific reason was given, but attorneys all thought it had to do with not wanting to hear the gruesome testimony. Five alternates remained, giving prosecutors hope that even if a few more had to leave, they still had enough to keep the trial on track.

"The prosecution calls Court Officer, Michael Hart, to the stand," said McDermott. Judge Berry motioned for the witness to be escorted in, and within moments Hart entered the courtroom. He walked past the benches filled with reporters, as well as the defendant's family and friends.

The uniformed man gave his name, spelling it for the court reporter as all witnesses would do and then raised his right hand and swore to "tell the truth, the whole truth, and nothing but the truth." He sat down and waited for the first question as McDermott walked forward.

Hart provided background information about himself. He was the Captain in Charge. He had worked nine years for the Supreme Court Appellate Division in Albany. Then, he brought the courtroom to the moment he discovered something had gone awfully wrong.

"At 10:30AM Chief Costello informed me that Peter Porco didn't show up," he told the court. "It wasn't like him. He would have called." Hart said Porco's colleagues were very concerned for the man. Hart was asked if he could take a ride to Peter's house, so he got directions and went by himself. He said he found no cars in the driveway when he arrived.

"I called the residence phone from inside the car, but it seemed to just keep ringing," Hart said. With the help of pictures projected onto the courtroom wall in back of him, he continued to explain how he discovered what had happened. He picked up a laser pointer that had been in front of him and put the shaky red dot on the image to show everyone what he was talking about. The pictures included various images of the house.

Hart said he got out of the car and walked up to the front door. As he described the key in the doorknob with rubber bands around its end, a close-up image of the key appeared on the wall. He said he knocked. But there was only silence. No one answered. He pulled on the door and realized it wasn't locked. Then he noticed the smear of blood on the doorknob and "two or three red drops on the front porch."

The next picture came up – a shot of the blood on the doorknob. Then another showed the drops of blood on the front steps. Hart said at that point he called Costello, and they stayed connected via the two-way Nextel. Hart said he heard a dog bark from inside. He decided to go in, so he called Costello, putting him on speakerphone and creating an instant connection.

He started to open the front door and felt resistance after opening it six or eight inches. He squeezed inside and saw the bi-fold door "with a big red stain on it." The picture on the courtroom wall showed the large red streak on the white door – as if someone had taken a paint roller to it.

Then, Hart saw Peter. "He was lying at the base of the stairs, sort of on his right side, his shirt pulled up. His eyes were locked open, face covered in blood." He explained he then told Costello what he saw and said Peter wasn't breathing.

He left the house. Within minutes police arrived with their guns drawn, Hart told the courtroom. He took a sip of water, then continued. He described going back in as police cleared the house. He went into the kitchen, then the bathroom. He checked out the living room and then went downstairs where the dog wagged its tail. He walked upstairs and down the hallway. "And I went into that bedroom." Hart described how there was a person in the bed "lying not lengthwise, but widthwise." An officer in the room announced the person was alive after Joan moved her head. An EMT with a medical supply bag walked into the room, and Hart said he left the house after spending one or two minutes inside.

McDermott thanked Hart, and then took his seat as Laurie Shanks stood to cross-examine the court officer. She asked if Hart had been trained to deal with "people who might be dangerous." He agreed he had been. "People in family court can become angry," she said. He agreed. "You're charged with keeping everyone safe at court," she said, adding that Peter had been very close with Judge Cardona, who had overseen some sticky family cases in Albany.

To prove her point, Shanks talked about Cardona's secretary who said she had wanted to go to the house that day. "Cardona decided it was too dangerous…did you know that?"

Hart said that he didn't know that. Shanks asked if Chief Costello had told him to wear gloves as he entered the house. "I didn't see any red smears at first," answered Hart.

"Did you do anything to make sure you didn't contaminate the evidence?" she asked, sounding more like a mother scolding her child. He said he hadn't.

He described how it looked like there had been a struggle, and added, "Joan's face was black."

The judge thanked him for his testimony, and as Hart left the courtroom, David Rossi stood up and called the next witness, Bethlehem Police Officer Charles Radliff.

Rossi related his first questions to events inside the bedroom. Radliff, the first to find Joan, said he remembered seeing the ax on the bed next to the poor woman. He described the weapon as having a three or four foot handle. He said it seemed blood covered everything. "Had you been there before?" asked Rossi.

He said he had. He talked about how a couple years prior to the attack and around Thanksgiving, he had received a call about a possible burglary. He met with Peter and Joan. They showed him the window screen that had been ripped off in the front of the house. He saw where the computers were supposed to be. He remembered seeing a camera on the ground.

Rossi thanked the officer as Shanks rose to take her shot at him.

She asked if he had been there for anything more serious than a couple of laptops being stolen. He said he had not. She pointed out that he worked in the juvenile unit and asked if he "went after skateboarders," for example. She hinted they were the biggest problem facing an inexperienced police force.

"That's not an example. That happened," Radliff said. Prosecutors shook their heads.

"How many homicide investigations have you been involved in," asked Shanks.

"None."

"This is it?"

"This is it," he replied. The defense hoped the Orange County jurors, like the majority of folks in the area who seemed to feel they had closer ties to New York City, had some preconceived ideas about upstate New York towns.

She asked Radliff if he had noticed whether Barrister had barked or not when he was inside the house. He said he did not remember any barking. It was the defense's theory that the dog was too friendly to bark at anyone. If true, prosecutors wouldn't be able to point to a lack of barking the night of the attack as reason to suspect the attacker (or attackers), was someone familiar with the Golden Retriever.

He continued by describing the crime scene much like others had already discussed it. Blood all over. Bits of tissue dotting the bathroom floor. He said Joan had motioned with her arms once the emergency responders had found her.

"Did you make sure you didn't destroy any evidence that was there?" Shanks asked.

"No, I did not," he replied. She walked back to her desk and sat down next to Christopher and Kindlon. They had both been taking notes.

Rossi shot up in his typical style. He looked quizzically at the ceiling for a few seconds, as if for effect, and then asked about the precautions police usually take when there was still a victim in the middle of a crime scene hanging on for dear life. Radliff said they knew to take precautions, but saving Joan's life was the priority at the time. "Thank you," Rossi said. Radliff left the courtroom.

EMT Kevin Robert replaced him on the stand. Already the testimony weighed heavily on everyone in court, but it would only get darker.

Robert had a natural charisma about him, an ability to seem rather credible because he took his job seriously enough and was able to explain the events of that day in a simple manner. He looked eager to answer every question to the best of his ability. At least that's how he came off to a few of the reporters listening to the testimony.

He spoke about getting the call at 11:25AM when he was on nearby Delaware Avenue. Once he arrived, he wasn't allowed to go inside until Joan was found. He remembered he soon heard someone was alive upstairs.

Pictures of the house were displayed on the wall in back of him as he spoke. They showed the bi-fold door and then a floor plan. Next came a shot of the upstairs hallway. The white doors to the different rooms were all closed, the light-colored carpet seemed untouched. The pictures built anxiety as they moved to the master bedroom. Not only was this the path of Robert on his way to try to save Joan – it was also the likely path of the killer.

Earlier, outside the courtroom, McDermott had told a few reporters that the most grisly photos would be displayed in black and white, by order of the Judge. "Any graphic photographs depicting Joan or Peter he wants in black or white, so we've got them in black and white," he said.

Robert continued to describe the scene. He said blood was all over the sheets. He saw an ax handle sticking out of the bed. A black and white picture of Mrs. Porco lying in the bed flashed up on the wall. Several women in court put their hands to their mouths, shocked at the brutality of the crime captured in the photograph. A few people looked away. For some of Christopher's friends sitting in court, it was the first time they had seen the reality of the brutal attack.

"They're very disturbing," McDermott explained later outside the courtroom. "But the thing is they're very probative because we need to prove Joan and Peter were assaulted in bed and all the blood downstairs is Peter's and there's no other perpetrator and there's no unaccounted for blood."

Still on the stand, Robert said he couldn't make out Joan's face. He tried to deal with the three injuries to her head. He said her jaw was hanging on her chest. He saw her brain and said her eyes were not visible at first.

As Robert continued to describe the scene and discussed the process of intubation, Christopher Porco wept as quietly as he could. He wiped his eyes every few seconds, pushing his glasses slightly towards his forehead as he did so. Shanks put her arm around her client, gently rubbing his back.

Robert said he told Joan to keep still after she had begun moving her legs. He spoke about the Glasgow-Coma Scale; once he got his bearings, he gave her the highest rating for eye movement. He gave her the lowest rating for verbal skills because she simply couldn't talk.

The EMT said Bowdish had asked the victim if Johnathan was involved. She indicated no, Robert said. Bowdish then asked, "Was Christopher involved?" – but there had been no initial response, he said.

Chris continued to cry.

Robert told the courtroom he then broke down the questions for Joan, repeating Bowdish's first question, to which the men received an indication of "no." Then, he said he asked, "Was Chris involved?" Robert said Joan moved her head and her hand up and down, as if to indicate "yes."

He said she had not received any medication at that point. He repeated the two questions and received the same response. Immediately after that, he said he told her they were going to intubate her. She nodded as if she understood.

Her blood oxygen level was at 93%, but a normal reading is typically above 97%, he explained. They put her on a backboard, carried her down the stairs and over the body of her husband, placed her in an ambulance, and raced to Albany Med. From the time Robert had gotten the call to the time it took to leave the scene, only a half-hour had gone by. McDermott took his seat.

Laurie Shanks shuffled a few of her papers, and then she began to tear apart the plausibility of the EMT's testimony. "It took seven minutes to get her to Albany Med in an ambulance," she stated. "Her blood pressure is so low you can barely read it. Could that have affected her orientation?"

Robert agreed that severe pain could affect a person's orientation. He said that a sergeant had lifted the window shade to let sunlight spill into the room. He wasn't sure, but another paramedic probably restrained Mrs. Porco's legs at some point. He said after she was intubated, she scored the lowest possible score on the Glasgow scale -- that she was "dead essentially, based on the scale."

"Did you have any idea when Joan was attacked?" Shanks asked. "Was it hours? Minutes?"

"No, I don't know," he said.

She continued, talking about mental status exams. "It tells us if someone is oriented. You're trained to do it," she said. He agreed.

You have to know the answer is correct, she continued. It only works if the person who asks the questions knows the answer too. "You could have asked about the time, about the place. The location. Her identity. The name of the month or the year. Who's the president? What month is the last month?" She stopped and looked him right in the eye. "Did you or anyone ask, 'did you see what happened?'" she waited for his answer.

"No," he said, sounding a little annoyed.

Did you ask, "Did you hear anything?"

"No," he repeated.

"Or any question which you knew the answer to?"

Once again the answer was no. He looked at Shanks as she took her seat, his eyes giving away his frustration.

The day continued with Dennis Wood, the other EMT who had previously testified at a pre-trial hearing. He reiterated much of what Robert had said. But when it came to the questions asked to Joan, Wood had a slightly different memory. He told the courtroom Bowdish had been the one who asked her if any of her sons had attacked her.

After Wood recalled that November day, it was well into the afternoon. Bethlehem Police Dispatcher Briana Tice would be the final witness of the day, and she looked nervous to most people inside the courtroom. David Rossi began with basic questions of her job. Then he asked her about the two phone calls she had received from Christopher Porco on November 15, 2004.

In the first call, placed nine minutes after three in the afternoon, Chris said someone at the Times Union newspaper had called him about the attack, so he wanted to know what was going on. He sounded calm as she put him on hold. Then she asked him for his address and information. She told him to call back.

Fifty minutes later, he did. Detective Rudolph spoke with Christopher, discussing when Porco had last been in the Albany area, and when he had last seen his parents. Chris said it had been three weeks since he had seen either his mom or his dad. The last things they had talked about, he said, were his college loans.

As the testimony continued, the day grew late, and the Judge ordered everyone to return the following Wednesday for nine in the morning.

The trial had only just begun, but after such emotionally grueling testimony, it seemed both the prosecution and the defense took a bit longer to pick up their files and walk out the courthouse doors. It was as if the weight of the brutal crime had sunk in and shifted everyone into slow motion.

Outside by the makeshift microphone stand, McDermott told reporters he thought the jurors were paying attention to every word. He also dismissed the idea that Mrs.

Porco hadn't seen her attacker. "The fact that she has defensive wounds on her hands, and Peter has defensive wounds on his hands, clearly supports the argument that she was conscious for a period of time defending herself," he said. "Before this trial is over, a neurosurgeon is definitely going to testify that it is medically possible for her to perceive her attacker and relate that to the police department."

McDermott also said the defense's point that the crime scene could have been contaminated by emergency responders was ridiculous. "Again, the main emphasis is finding the victims, treating the victims, and getting them out of the house. If they were more worried about collecting evidence, then Joan Porco would have stayed in that bed until she died and there would have been two murders."

More importantly, McDermott said, was the fact that the testimony related to the head nod remained consistent when it mattered. He acknowledged there was a difference between who may have asked the questions to Joan, but he said that had always been a small discrepancy. "I think they're all consistent in the three fundamental questions," he said.

The defense also claimed victory at the conclusion of the first week of trial. "I think their theory that she was lucid is just ridiculous," said Shanks. She said the fact that the EMT's stories didn't quite match was key. "What it shows the jury is even the people there who weren't brain damaged don't have a memory of what was said." She added that the defense would have their own neurologist to testify at some point to show the difference between simply responding to a question - and understanding it.

Shanks also shared her anger over how the police had handled the phone call with her client. "To think their child called their police department and was treated as a suspect instead of a grieving child is horrific," she said. "He hasn't been given any opportunity to grieve. People are watching him. You can imagine what it's like for him to hear that his beautiful mother was mutilated."

Members of the defense and the prosecution walked to their vehicles. Most of them would get right on the road for the several hour ride back to Albany. Christopher Porco's yellow Jeep was one of the first cars to zigzag out of the parking lot. He headed back to the home of Dr. John Kearney and Elaine LaForte, the Bethlehem veterinarians who had taken a liking to the young man. They believed him to be innocent.

IX

From: "Chris Porco" cp002m@mail.rochester.edu
To: "Porco" pporco@nycap.rr.com
Sent: Wednesday, October 04, 2004 12:43AM
Subject: Re: Emergency!!!!!!!

Hey guys,
I am aware of the situation with parking, I was not present when the boot was taken off.. a couple of my friends thought they were doing me a favor.. apparently it didn't take much to get it off. It wasn't even a real boot, just a chain and a piece of metal that it was tied to. The "boot" has been returned to parking services, and it was not harmed. I intend on paying the parking bastards Tuesday, when I have time.

I have been in the library all weekend, except for my hospital visit. I am fine, just 8 stitches on my chin. I demanded a plastic surgeon, and had to wait like 5 hours for one, but I shouldn't have any scar at all.

I am sorry I didn't speak with you tonight, I just got back from doing work, and I am exhausted. I just left john a voicemail, I wil try him again tomorrow.

I will also give you a call tomorrow, I need whatever documents the loan people want, I will be borrowing probably about 2000, not an obscene amount. I will speak with you about the details tmororw evening. I really don't have a lot else to report...im just really loaded up with work now, it kind of sucks. I will talk to you tomorrow, love you
chris

*

Goshen, New York
July 5, 2006

Judge Berry usually told the courtroom he wanted to begin by 9:30, or at the latest, ten each morning. But this morning, both sides waited around for Berry to appear until it was after 11AM. Publicly, the attorneys said they understood Berry had local cases to deal with and that some delays were inevitable. Privately, some were frustrated at the waste of time.

Members of the jury had to wait in a separate room in back. They were told to arrive around 8:30 or 9:00 most days. Already many had figured out the pattern and carried in books or fashion magazines to pass the time. They had been off for nearly a week because of the July 4th holiday, but both prosecutors and the defense team believed the time delay wouldn't affect the jurors' ability to keep the facts straight. "I believe they'll be able to survive the four or five days off without losing their concentration," said Shanks.

Her husband told reporters he thought the jury was paying "very close and careful attention to this case, which is very encouraging. As far as divining what's in their mind…as the old saying goes, if I could predict the future I'd spend all my time at the track and I'd be a millionaire."

Judge Berry finally entered the courtroom, and as he would do from time to time, he welcomed the jurors back with a lengthy speech. He said he hoped they had had time to reflect on this "great nation" for the July 4th holiday. He hoped they all were able to spend quality time with their families and friends. He said there may be plenty of criticism of America, but it's "still the best country in the world."

The first witness for the new week, Sarah Fischer, looked nervous as she walked in and saw that a couple rows of seats were filled. She had shoulder-length blonde hair and piercing blue eyes. She had apparently been Christopher's girlfriend, but seemed eager to distance herself from him. At the very least, there was an obvious awkwardness between the two that several people in court said they noticed.

Fischer said she knew the defendant not because they had gone to the same high school, but because a mutual friend had introduced them in May of 2004. Their relationship soon grew from playing tennis to renting movies most nights of the week. It was convenient because they only lived five minutes apart.

Rossi asked her about how Chris would typically enter his parents' home when they would go inside for a movie night. She said they would usually get in through the front door or the garage. If they chose the latter, a keypad in the garage would have to be punched. Then they could get right into the family room. She said she knew that next to the front door there was a spare key in the flowerpot. It had been used several times by the couple to get inside. She would often wait outside while he disarmed the alarm system by punching in his code on the keypad near the door. She said she knew of Barrister the dog who rarely barked. She also said she never saw the dog in the basement while she was with him.

That fall, she returned to college in Fairfield, Connecticut, and he returned to Rochester. They managed to keep up their long-distance relationship through instant messages and phone calls. He visited her once in the beginning of October.

She said he had plans to return home November 5th, a weekend before the murder. He came to Delmar, she said, and added that she didn't see him then. She explained that he had told her he had been in an argument with his parents over money and school grades. He said his parents warned him that if he didn't pull up his average, he would have to transfer to a state school.

The following weekend, she said they both came home from school to meet in Delmar. Friday, around 5:00 at night, she went to dinner with him. Her sister, Kate, had come along as well. Later, the two rented a movie and hung out at her house, spending the night together, she said. Then, around three Saturday afternoon, he returned to school. She said they talked at night, and Christopher told her he felt bad he hadn't stopped at his home and visited his parents. Then, she said when they spoke with each other on Sunday, he told her that he did stop at his parents' home to pick up a jacket. She said he saw his dad, but his mother wasn't home. "I just let it go."

The next time they spoke, at around 2PM on Monday, the 15th, she had already gone back to Fairfield. In the conversation she said Chris told her he wasn't feeling well, that his stomach was queasy. Then – Fischer said she received a message from her sister, saying that something had happened on Brockley Drive. She passed the message on to Christopher. He told her he was nervous because he hadn't been able to contact his parents all morning. She said he asked her for more details from her sister. About 2:45PM, according to the witness, Christopher put up an away message that said his parents were dead. Rossi took his seat.

Shanks stood and got Fischer to admit it wasn't uncommon for Barrister to be downstairs. After all, his Kennel was there. She told Shanks that on Friday, they had rented a movie, Chris had fallen asleep on the couch downstairs, and she had gone upstairs. Sarah said they did not talk about any arguments between Christopher and his parents. Laurie asked if there was more to Christopher's away message or if she had any more information about the timing of when Porco may have known about the attack. Fischer told Shanks that

Christopher had said he first received a call from someone at the Times Union and then called the police.

After Rossi briefly re-examined Fischer, she left the courtroom. A U.S. Navy Lieutenant took her place. The questioning lasted no more than a couple minutes. Lt. Carter said Johnathan Porco was present in Navy school class November 15th. According to the prosecution, that made it impossible for Johnathan to have anything to do with the crime.

Next, came Kurt Meyer, a Time Warner security system worker. He spoke about the details of how the alarm system in the Porco house was supposed to work. He shared records of the security system. If the system was ever breached, he said someone would first call the house, then a call would go out to the police and the fire department. But that couldn't happen if the phone wire was cut. He said the garage window was not set up to trip the alarm, but all the other windows in the house would if they were broken or moved.

Meyer said there was one master code, 4416, and two user codes, 4235 and 4030, which could be used to shut off the alarm. While a call couldn't go out if the phone lines were cut, the system would still record the event in its computer memory. Meyer said that's what he found when he was called to the house by authorities on the 16th. The alarm beeped every so often to signal trouble. He found the keypad smashed, but saw the computer system in the basement was intact.

Jurors were shown pictures of the keypad and the computer in the basement. Meyer said the keypad still worked, even though the LCD display had been broken. "The system can't be disarmed by smashing it." He said the system kept track of the last 128 "events," including each time it was disarmed, armed, or the time was adjusted for daylight-saving time. He said the times were all 12 hours fast because someone had likely programmed the wrong AM/PM time during the last change a few weeks before the attack. Meyer's documents detailing each "event" had the times corrected by 12 hours to show the proper time of day, he said.

During questioning by Shanks, Meyer told the court that according to the system report, the alarm had been armed the evening of the 14th at 5:21PM, and was turned off at 6:17PM. At 9:54PM it was reactivated. On Monday at 2:14AM, the alarm was turned off using the master code. The phone line in the back yard was cut at 4:54 in the morning. Shanks asked if a dog moving around the house could set off the alarm. She wondered if that might be a reason someone would turn off the alarm in the middle of the night. Meyer said it was possible. He added that the programmer could put in any time he wanted, and the system wouldn't correct itself.

Investigator Drew McDonald took the stand next. Built, with short hair, he looked the part of a State Trooper. He was well-spoken, with a professional, intelligent air about him. While he would testify mostly about murder scene details, he was also testifying to prove investigators had credibility and weren't only out to get skateboarders. As part of his job with the Troop G Forensic Identification Unit, McDonald said he was in charge of crime scene processing. He said he became a "crime scene technician" in 1995. He had responded to thousands of crime scenes and had over 100 homicide investigations under his belt. He even took a moment to describe the white suits, booties, and latex gloves investigators wear to protect a given crime scene. McDonald told the court Bethlehem Police had called for the assistance of Troop G on the 15th. Six State Police investigators scoured the scene.

McDonald had taken hundreds of photographs – 260 would be shown as evidence in the trial, according to McDermott. McDonald provided commentary as picture after picture was projected on the white wall in back of him. He described the bloodstains throughout the downstairs of the house as mostly "passive bloodstain patterns," that is, "blood left at the scene that just fell."

McDonald noted that the living room had, for the most part, been undisturbed. The picture above him showed it was clean and orderly -- even though he had found blood on the wall, a picture no longer hung straight, and blood stained the leather furniture.

He said the dining room was untouched. No silverware, china, or crystal had been taken. A close-up photograph of Joan's pocketbook revealed credit cards and family photographs were still there.

Then came the photos most people in the courtroom would have trouble forgetting. McDonald continued the mental tour of the house in the kitchen, where blood spotted the counter, the floor, and was smeared on the opened dishwasher.

Christopher looked away as the pictures flashed on the wall.

McDonald said a $100 SEFCU cashier's check had been sitting on the top row of dishes in the dishwasher. It was made out to Saratoga Springs City Court for Christopher Porco. A small bloodstain dotted the lower left hand side.

The investigator paused as a photograph of Peter Porco's feet, wearing white socks, told the story. McDonald said it looked like Peter had stepped in dozens of his own blood drops as he walked around the house.

Shanks put her arm around Christopher as McDonald showed a picture of Johnathan's room. His bed covers had been turned down. Then the court saw the Porco's bedroom once again.

Picture by picture, he spoke about the different blood patterns on the floor, on the walls, and in the bed. He said the blood was so prevalent in their bed that the attack could only have occurred there. He pointed to spatters on the wall in back of the bed and on a lampshade, which he said meant the assailant had stood at the left side – Joan's side - and swung the ax. He said the blood patterns proved only one person had committed the crime.

By this time, Christopher had nearly put his head down on the table in front of him. He sobbed loudly enough that you could hear him from the public seating area. He took his glasses off as McDonald outlined which side of the bed the accused killer's mother and father had slept on that night.

The investigator continued with pictures of the master bathroom, where the sink had been covered in blood. He said they had found a fingerprint on the door of the master bedroom, but couldn't determine whose it was. He told the jurors that only about five percent of fingerprints at a crime scene are identifiable.

With the late start, the Judge said that was all jurors would hear for the day. After they stood, grabbed their belongings, and left the courtroom, Berry said he had a few announcements to make. He said the taped interrogation would not be allowed in, but the tollbooth ticket, supposedly with some type of DNA on it, would be. Of course, because of what had already gone on in court, the ruling didn't surprise anyone. The more legal-minded folks knew that if the defense somehow opened the door, the tape could still come in anyway.

Outside the courthouse, McDermott explained why McDonald's testimony was so important – especially as reporters asked where all this was headed. They wanted to know where the silver bullet was that would sway jurors one way or the other. McDermott explained there wasn't such a thing in this case. He said the investigator's testimony, however, was key. "Part of our burden," said McDermott, "is to show Christopher Porco committed this crime. That's going to mean ruling out this was a break-in gone bad, that there was more than one perpetrator, that the assault happened other than in the bedroom."

Reporters also asked the Chief Assistant DA about the cashier's check left on the dishwasher. "I don't know. That's always been an interesting question. I mean, it's obviously related to Peter's trying to clean up Christopher's mess."

McDermott also said the ruling that banned the taped interrogation was frustrating. "It's going to be much more inconvenient. More people are going to have to show up that would not have had to show up before. Some things we might not be able to establish."

Kindlon took questions from reporters right after McDermott stepped away. The defense attorney let on that he thought the defense had a good day, as tough as it was to listen to McDonald's testimony. "I couldn't look at the pictures if it was my father and you couldn't if it was your father," he told the journalists. "It's almost primal."

From there he cast doubt on the importance of the State Police investigator's testimony. "What his testimony has established, is Peter Porco was brutally murdered. Didn't have anything to do with Christopher, however. It never will." He also had a different take on the cashier's check. "I think it's very significant," he told the reporters, "because not to over do it, but with his dying breath, Peter was taking care of one of his sons and one of his son's needs."

Kindlon said he was thrilled the taped interrogation had been thrown out "because of the despicable way they dealt with Christopher." And perhaps more importantly, Kindlon said he would prove the DNA evidence wasn't good evidence at all. "By the end of the trial, you will realize from the testimony you'll hear that the DNA could have come from 60% of the population."

Kindlon's wife commented on Sarah Fischer's testimony, saying she was trying to figure out why she had been called as a witness. "To tell you the truth, I have no idea why they brought her here. I thought she was a lovely young woman, and I think it just proves exactly what we're saying."

X

From: Peter Porco
To: cp002m@mail.rochester.edu
Sent: Thu, Oct 7, 2004 9:50 AM
Subject: Citibank Loan Letter with W-2 attachments

Chris,

Hope all is well with you.
Attached is a Citibank letter dated September 24, 2004 asking for you to supply certain information. I have attached copies of your 2003 and 2002 W-2 forms, which is all I can provide. Let me know if you want me to forward the original letter and/or hard copies to you by mail.

P.S. Yesterday was Mom's birthday. I sent you a text message reminder. Maybe you can call her tonight around 9:30 p.m. Love, Dad.

*

Goshen, New York
July 6, 2006

Michael McDermott stopped for the cameras lining the barricades outside the Orange County Courthouse. Reporters asked what testimony he expected to get in if all went well. "Today I anticipate Dr. Paul Spurgas the neurosurgeon will testify. Dr. Hubbard may testify this afternoon, and we have some witnesses from the New York Thruway Authority," McDermott said.

"What will the neurosurgeon say?" asked a reporter.

"How catastrophic Joan's injuries were. I mean, it's a miracle she survived. It's a testament to his skill as a surgeon. The type of injury she sustained to her frontal lobe would not necessarily mean that she had no memory of the attack, and that she would be capable of communicating," he added.

Another reporter asked how Joan could have remembered the attack, but soon after forgot key details. "Sometimes after surgery, memories are lost," he said, then thanked the reporters and walked inside with Rossi.

Kindlon declined to make a morning comment, as he would from time to time. He usually tried to talk with the journalists, but his priority was to be inside a few minutes early, even though court usually began late anyway. Most of the time Christopher walked in with Kindlon and Shanks, but occasionally he walked in by himself, carrying a few notepads or folders for his attorneys.

Reporters followed an unwritten rule not to ask Christopher anything even though he passed by them every morning. Kindlon had made it clear if his client was asked questions, he wouldn't grant too many more interviews. After this case concluded, all the reporters knew they would need to speak with Kindlon at some point. After all, he almost always had a high profile or interesting case in the pipeline.

Even now, Kindlon's office had been preparing for an upcoming federal trial involving two men accused of laundering money in an FBI sting operation. Investigators said the suspects were willing to support the fake United Nations missile plot, but Kindlon would argue there were major problems with the evidence. Additionally, there was the state-level gay marriage case Kindlon had taken on, where he argued for equal rights. And those were just the cases he was involved with *now*.

Investigator McDonald took the stand for a second time as soon as everybody was seated. McDermott continued where he had left off, and the witness described the basement through pictures. He discussed an open safe with a few dollars and an old cell phone inside. There were clothes in the Porco's dryer. McDonald said the important part about the downstairs was an identifiable fingerprint they had found. A picture of the basement door, spotted with the amino black powder, revealed the only print found in the house that investigators could trace back to Christopher.

Then, jurors were taken on a mental tour of the garage. McDonald said they had found a few drops of Peter's blood there, and a broken bottle he had apparently handled as he stumbled around. A red-stained tissue had been tossed in the blue recycling bin. McDonald said the garage window had been opened, but only a few inches. It took a few photographs and some explaining to make it clear that Peter had at some point bolted the top part of the window to the bottom part, so the two pieces became one. The configuration only allowed for a small opening. Outside, the screen had been cut in a "C" shape, with the top part folding over the bottom. As pictures of investigators looking at the window filled the wall in back of him, McDonald pointed out that the window was up about six feet, making it difficult for anyone to get in even if the window hadn't been bolted.

"There are also spider webs on the corners of the window," he said. They had been undisturbed. "This was not a point of entry."

A video of investigators trying to open the window began to play. Kindlon objected, but jurors saw the window, in fact, could only move an inch or so up or down.

Then the lights came on. The prosecutors turned off the projector. For the record, McDermott identified a long object wrapped in brown paper. He gave it to McDonald, who held it and identified it as the ax used in the murder. "It's approximately three feet in length. There was blood on the handle," said the investigator. He told the court it weighed less than three pounds.

McDermott looked briefly at Kindlon and then asked McDonald if the ax was a fireman's ax. "No," the witness replied. "A fireman's ax is different. It's a little bigger. And the other end has a side to pry with. It's a totally different ax."

McDonald made mention of Peter's shotgun, which had not been loaded. He said there was no sign of how the assailant may have left the scene. Prosecutors thanked McDonald, who would return later for cross-examination. For now, he would be replaced by neurosurgeon, Dr. Paul Spurgas, a gruff man who made it obvious he preferred to be in Albany saving lives.

He answered questions matter of factly, saying things like, "there are witnesses of her following commands" and "the jaw injury would impair speech."

"Was any portion of her brain damaged so she couldn't understand the words spoken to her?" McDermott asked.

"None," Dr. Spurgas said.

Shanks took her turn, talking about how no one had given Joan a mental status exam at any point. The most she got out of the neurosurgeon was that he said Joan could have lost part of her memory after surgery.

Investigator McDonald took the stand once again, and Kindlon stood at attention in his Marine-style. He asked McDonald if the garage door had been closed or not. He was trying to prove the garage could have been another point of entry, but McDonald doubted the theory.

Kindlon also tried to deduce that Peter was the one who put the key in the front door. "Would the door lock behind you?" he asked.

"I'm not sure."

"And you are not able to say if the person or *persons* were men, women, or both?"

"My opinion is it's one person."

Kindlon cited grand jury testimony where McDonald had said "the person or persons," but the investigator repeated his current conclusion.

"Peter was struck between 10 and 30 times with an ax," Kindlon said. "We don't know if another ax was involved. There's no way to tell if the attacker was left or right handed?"

McDonald said there wasn't, but his voice sounded skeptical of what Kindlon was getting at. The witness was excused, and two neighbors took the stand, one after the other. Both said they had their own codes to get inside the Porco home if they were asked to take care of Barrister.

Then, Rochester Police Officer Michael Cotsworth took the stand. He said he ran into another officer who had been looking for a yellow Jeep. The murder scene had just been discovered three hours away in Albany County. "I knew of a similar Jeep on the other side on Genesee Street on the south side," he said.

He went to the street, blocked it off, and unrolled crime scene tape to keep people from the vehicle. He said he didn't touch the car, nor did he remove anything from it. He did look inside though. "The only thing that caught my attention," he said, was "what looked like a pellet gun or a rifle in the back." Cotsworth said he later canvassed the neighborhood, mostly made up of University of Rochester students living off-campus.

Kindlon made an objection to the November 15th police report, and members of the jury were ushered out of the courtroom. He told Judge Berry police ignored someone they had talked with. Celestina Brown lived in the neighborhood and had apparently told them the car was parked in the same spot for days. "Police already selected their suspect and information came their way that went against their case and it was ignored," he argued.

But the judge disagreed. He said this attempt by Kindlon to show police didn't do a thorough job was not going to fly. "The truth is, it's hearsay." Berry argued Kindlon couldn't have it both ways. He couldn't introduce the Brown statement to demonstrate the police may have ignored information, and then not have her testify that what she said was true. Kindlon believed whether it was true or not, the statement was important because he said investigators hadn't followed up on it.

Rossi later explained to reporters what the controversy over Brown's statement apparently meant. "It's a bit of a figure of speech: 'the vehicle has been there a couple of days.' And she didn't have any other information specifically of when it was there at 12, 1, 2, 3, 4, or 5 in the morning."

Jurors came back to take their seats. A Bethlehem Policeman briefly took the stand. He explained the yellow Jeep was put on a flatbed truck and transported out of Rochester. He rode with the truck driver to the State Police headquarters just outside of Albany.

And with that, another short week came to a close. Berry had local cases to deal with on Friday, so he told everyone to arrive at around nine Monday morning.

Outside, reporters gathered around the microphone stand for the usual afternoon debriefing. McDermott took questions first, as Rossi stood to the side. The key testimony from the neurosurgeon, he said, was that "there was nothing about the brain injury that would have prevented her from having a memory of the attack."

The Chief ADA said that wasn't the only damning evidence. He said the discussion of the window and cut screen was also important. "Our allegation is the cut screen is something Christopher Porco has had success with in the past. The Bethlehem Police weren't able to solve those burglaries, (but) the jury will see the commonalities. It also is very telling that the window where the screen was cut was the only window where there was no alarm to."

A reporter asked McDermott what he thought about the Frankie "the Fireman" theory. "It's not important at all because the whole Frankie "the Fireman" Porco thing is ridiculous. I just wanted the jury to know if they didn't know, that this isn't a fireman's ax."

The prosecutor also seemed surprised by the pellet gun testimony. "We weren't going to bring it up because, I mean, obviously Mr. Porco wasn't assaulted with a pellet gun."

Kindlon would later say he hadn't heard about the rifle-style pellet gun until it came out in court.

Members of the prosecution walked to their cars in the mostly empty parking lot as Kindlon stepped up to the microphones. Christopher stood to the side, listening to the miniature press conference. His attorney began in typical Kindlon-fashion: "The prosecution succeeded in proving beyond a reasonable doubt that Peter Porco is dead. And that is really the thrust of that evidence. What this was all about was the murder of Peter Porco. But there's no evidence at all that's been presented through investigator McDonald that has anything to do with Christopher."

He took a question about the window, but dismissed the prosecution's theory. "I think the window is a red herring. The fact is, there's the front door, two back doors, there's a garage door, and based on all the forensic evidence it's impossible to know which was the point of entry."

Kindlon also didn't think his Mob snitch theory had been destroyed either. "The fact is an ax is an ax. And I think a fireman's ax, Paul Bunyon's ax – an ax is an ax." He continued to explain what he thought happened. Frankie "is a famous figure in the world of Mafia bosses and there are plenty of people who want to take revenge on him. They couldn't because he was serving all of 24 months on murder with convictions."

Earlier, Laurie Shanks had criticized the neurosurgeon's testimony, arguing it made no sense that Joan could have been coherent while her husband walked right by two cell phones as he unloaded the dishwasher. "They not only have attacked Christopher Porco, they've attacked the entire family," she said.

The defense team left for home, where Kindlon and his wife would plan out their argument that mistakes had been made throughout the two weeks of trial. They would ask that it be shut down.

XI

From: "Porco" pporco@nycap.rr.com
To: cp002m@mail.rochester.edu
Sent: Wednesday, Oct 20, 2004 6:22 PM
Attach: amexpress – chris.PDF; chris – cap auto finance.PDF; irs payment 2003 chris_4.PDF; irs chris.PDF
Subject: Fw: IRS Levy notice; Capital Auto Finance Late Notice; American Express Bill

------Original Message ------
From: Peter Porco
To: cp002m@mail.rochester.edu
Cc: peter_porco@yahoo.com
Sent: Tuesday, October 19, 2004 10:20 AM
Subject: Fw: IRS Levy notice; Capital Auto Finance Late Notice; American Express Bill

Hi Chris,
Yesterday was an interesting mail day for you. Attached are .pdf files of what we received. I trust you will bring your car loan up to date. It distresses me that you have accumulated so much debt on your AmX card. I don't see how you can possibly make those payments, your car payments and take on another $525 monthly payment in March for a loan to Citibank. I think we should discuss that loan further so, please call tonight, if possible. I want to know exactly when the Bursar needs the money. If I don't already have it, email me a copy of the Bursar's bill for the Spring Semester. Finally, and most upsetting is the IRS levy notice. It appears you simply don't have the proof to convince them that you returned the previous check. If you think Paypal can wreck havoc with your checking, you've no idea how miserable a tax levy can be. Therefore, I'm going to pay the $340.98 today, so that's put to an end. Talk to you soon. Love, Dad

p.s. Your chrisporco@sprintpcs.com is returning e-mail. The message reads "over quota."

*

Goshen, New York
July 10, 2006

Prosecutors told reporters the first day of the third week of trial would be all about tollbooth tickets and trying to put Porco's Jeep on the thruway the night of the attack. But first, Kindlon had some points to make. It meant the jury would wait in the back room for a good portion of the morning.

Kindlon was still angry about the hearsay ruling made at the end of the day last Thursday regarding Celestina Brown. He asked Judge Berry to reconsider his decision not to allow the fact that Brown said she saw the Jeep parked for days, even though Rossi said she couldn't account for it at specific times. "The information wasn't for the truth it contained," but to show how the police responded. "That argument is always material," the attorney said. "I am asking the court to reconsider."

The prosecution made a brief statement arguing the Brown issue was, in fact, hearsay, so it couldn't be let in.

"Mr. Kindlon, my ruling stands," said Judge Berry.

Kindlon continued with the second motion of the day. He said he was concerned about statements attributed to his client that might sound bad, but may not mean he was guilty. "It's a persistent problem in this case," he said. The problem had to do with a statement supposedly "made by Chris at the hospital, which is too ambiguous to infer guilt from." Someone had apparently asked Chris, "What are you going to do with your mother's house?" Kindlon told the court. Chris, he continued, said, "Maybe sell it."

Kindlon then moved to another issue. His voice got louder. "And this…this is the big one. Christopher was subjected to six-and-a-half hours of interrogation by police in violation of his rights. The court suppressed the statement." However, Kindlon said so much of the investigation had been based on what had happened during the taped ordeal. "Items of clothing, biological evidence, the drawing of the map of his jogging route were taken…The reality is, when we threw out the statement, the prosecution's case was still based on that tape," he said. "To permit the prosecution to continue to reference the information in the interview shouldn't be allowed." He cited the example of the jogging route Christopher told police he took the morning of the 15th, which Kindlon believed prosecutors might not have even known about had it not been for the long chat. "They went forward on a massive scale with information from that interview. You can't use the fruit of the poisonous tree." His voice was getting louder, his gestures more extreme. "We need to shut down this trial and have a hearing. Otherwise we'll be forced to object to anything that came from the interview as its source."

Berry asked Kindlon to continue with his final motion for the morning. The attorney said proof about the gasoline level in the yellow Jeep should also be barred. There was no proof of a fill-up in Albany, something the prosecution accepted as part of their reasoning behind why the amount of gas remaining in the Jeep meant anything. "You would have to assume to have this mean anything," he argued.

The prosecution said that the statement made by Chris about selling the house "shows Chris knew about his inheritance which is important." They reiterated that the gasoline was yet another piece of the puzzle.

Once again, the judge said the trial would continue.

The New York Thruway Authority's Senior Accountant, Craig Slezak took the witness stand. It took some time for him to go through the basics of how the toll tickets are handled, distributed, and collected. After being used, they end up in a security room for a certain period of time. He said he was asked to recover tickets handed out for travel from Rochester exits 45 and 46, to Albany exits 23 and 24. He was given a specific time period: between 12AM and 3AM for the Albany exits, and up to 10AM for the Rochester ones. He said he wore rubber gloves as he looked through the tickets, and added he was confident only three people could have touched them. Then, they were turned over to police and the DA's office. Seven vehicles fit the exits and the timeline, and the documents were photocopied, he said. After that, DNA analysis was done…

"Objection! Motion to strike…any testimony should be struck…" yelled Kindlon. He didn't want to hear anything about DNA.

Judge Berry ordered the prosecution to continue, nonetheless. He said the question and the answer were both fair and based on facts pertaining to the discussion at hand.

The cross-examination continued. Slezak said four tickets, which meant four different vehicles, arrived at exit 24 early the 15th: they read 12:10AM, 1:51AM, 1:56AM, and 2:02AM. Later that morning, four tickets corresponded to vehicles that had traveled from Albany to exit 46 after 8AM: 8:14AM, 8:18AM, 8:36AM, and 9:16AM.

The judge stopped the witness and asked that everyone return in an hour after lunch. Everybody stood, and the jurors left the courtroom. Then the reporters emptied the seats to jog down to their cameras for their live shots outside. After updating the public on what had happened so far, they also headed out to grab some lunch. Today, as usual, the owner of Steve's Deli had a bit of gossip to share. This time it was that Porco had been eating there, which he felt awkward about. He seemed happy to let the daily group of four or five jurors sit at their usual outside table. He let them keep to themselves.

As everyone returned to court, the hallway filled up because the doors were locked shut. Kindlon came over to one of the reporters. Often the conversation was light. Everyone enjoyed joking with the man. After all, he almost always had something interesting to say. But not this time. "Your report was inaccurate," he snarled at the journalist, who asked him what he meant. "I've been watching. You need to watch your facts," he said. It was a warning that seemed to come out of nowhere. Some of the other reporters wondered what that outburst had been all about. After all, he hadn't cited a specific report, and all the reporters had all been writing stories based on similar information throughout the trial.

Kindlon seemed on edge, but then again, so did Shanks. She had confronted a print journalist about one of his recent reports. She told him he should highlight the accurate parts of his story in blue, and the rest of it in yellow. "It's called yellow journalism," she said.

A few minutes later, court officers unlocked the doors, and everyone took their seats. Slezak answered a few more questions from the prosecution, and then Kindlon began his cross-examination, focusing on the tollbooth ticket. "Do you know where the paper is manufactured?" he asked.

"It's shipped from North Carolina," said Slezak.

"But you don't know where it's manufactured?" Kindlon asked again. Slezak said no.

Kindlon picked up a box of toll tickets to use as a prop and placed them in front of him. "Now if the tickets fell out," he said dramatically, as he spilled the tickets all over the court floor, "someone could touch the tickets."

He asked Slezak how many people can fit in a typical car. "The ticket can be passed around in a car. More than three people could touch it...And you can put money on the ticket and hand it over simultaneously," he pointed out. Slezak admitted that was possible.

The next witness, State Police Investigator Kelly Strack, spent only a few minutes on the stand. She said she used a different set of gloves with each ticket she touched and added that the chain of custody was solid because State Police kept the tickets for months.

James Buono testified that he worked with Slezak to secure the tickets. He said he wore gloves too, though he didn't change them each time he touched a new ticket. Another worker testified similarly.

That brought the prosecution to John Fallon, who had since given up his tollbooth job to work for the post office. Taking a seat, he reached for the nearly empty cup of water the previous witness had sipped from. "Can I have some water?" he asked, as he looked around, not sure who would help with his request. His voice sounded low and raspy from a lifetime of smoking. He filled his cup once the pitcher was replenished, then he took a long drink. He looked up as if to ask them what they wanted to talk to him about. He didn't seem too pleased to have been forced to make the long trip from Rochester.

He told the people in court he had been a toll collector at exits 45 through 48, and 48A. In a typical day he saw about 1,000 cars. But he said, "I only pay attention to the car I'm interested in." It just so happened, that meant Jeeps. "My whole family has Jeeps."

In mid-November, 2004, Fallon said he remembered working at the Henrietta exit, #46, from three in the afternoon until eleven. "I saw a yellow Jeep right before quitting time," he said. "I was sneaking a smoke," he explained, and was worried he might get caught by his boss, so he had been on the lookout. "I saw it had wide tires. It was yellow. I thought it might be nice for my son."

McDermott asked if Fallon had seen who had been driving the Jeep. The witness described the driver as a white male in his early 20's, wearing a baseball cap. McDermott pointed to a toll ticket that had Fallon's code number on it. It had been handed out at 10:45PM, November 14, 2004.

McDermott took his seat.

Kindlon asked if anyone had shown Fallon a picture of a white male driving a Jeep.

No.

The attorney then asked if he had been shown a picture of a yellow Jeep. Kindlon was insinuating that someone could have put the idea in the witness's head. "Yes they did. They showed me a Jeep picture," said Fallon.

He told Kindlon he couldn't remember how many Jeeps he saw on any given day. But this one, he said, stuck out in his mind. This one was different. "Because the color and the tires and time right before my shift," he said. Kindlon shrugged and smiled as if this witness was ridiculous, then he sat next to Porco. Fallon walked out just as quickly as he had come in.

Karen Russell, the next witness, was an Albany toll collector. She said she remembered a yellow Jeep come through just before 2AM. Asked how she could have remembered one car out of all the vehicles that came through, she explained it was "because of the speed it was going." That, and she was about to go on break like Fallon.

Russell stepped down, and the Judge allowed a brief afternoon recess. Journalists milled about in the hallway. Prosecutors talked privately in a nearby room.

Then Laurie Shanks walked by, and one reporter asked if she was OK. It looked like she had been crying. She stopped, turned, and just shook her head with tears streaming from her face. She walked into the courtroom.

Moments later, Judge Berry announced the trial had ended for the week. He said Laurie had a family emergency. The Judge asked that everyone keep Laurie and her mother in their thoughts. Court would continue on Monday, giving Laurie enough time to fly to Arizona and grieve over her loss.

No one knew how to react, so everyone followed the daily routine. Reporters went to their tents outside to give quick live updates and then waited by the microphone stand to see who would talk.

"We've got to get going," Kindlon said as he walked quickly past everyone. Laurie walked by his side, obviously shaken. They left the parking lot immediately. Christopher Porco walked out a few minutes later holding a few folders and drove off in his Jeep.

McDermott and Rossi emerged from the courthouse slowly, having spent a few minutes discussing what the delay meant for their case. "Obviously we want to extend our condolences," he told the reporters. His concern for the length of the trial had begun to grow, however. "We're testing the patience of the jurors, but under the circumstances, there was nothing else that could be done," he said.

McDermott also took time to explain the tollbooth testimony, which he thought was very good for their case. "It fits in with our timeline. It fits in with everything that Bethlehem Police began to build back on November 15th."

McDermott laughed when one reporter asked if Fallon might be *too* good a witness. "Who would have known Mr. Fallon has a thing for Jeeps? His son has a Jeep and his wife has a Jeep, and the fact he's being vigilant because he's sneaking a cigarette." He didn't doubt that Russell had good reason to remember the Jeep either. "I'm sure the pet peeve of every toll taker is someone who goes too fast," he said. He added that the tickets only enhanced their timeline, and the upcoming DNA testimony would bolster what they had been saying. McDermott reiterated for reporters that the tickets put the Jeep arriving in Albany at 1:51AM and returning to the Rochester exit at 8:18 that same morning. He said the DNA evidence came from the ticket collected in Albany.

A reporter asked if it was even reasonable to think Porco's DNA could be found on a toll ticket. Rossi stepped up to the microphones. "When you hear the numbers on the DNA," he said, "it's not going to be very reasonable to think it just happened to match Chris Porco's DNA also."

Most everyone involved with the trial returned to the Albany area, except Laurie, who left for Phoenix. In the meantime, her husband nearly died too.

"The first picture of the artery," explained Dr. Augustin DeLago, "the artery looked practically closed." According to the doctor, Kindlon could have died from a blocked coronary artery, but a cardiac catheterization had saved him. DeLago explained that he had numbed an area in Kindlon's leg, passed a "very small tube up into the heart, and actually made a roadmap of the blood vessels that surround the heart." He described it as a relatively simple procedure.

"Monday, in court, we had the terrible news that my wife's mother, Lilly, had passed away out in Phoenix," said Kindlon from his Albany office just a few days later. "Judge Berry was kind enough to shut the trial down."

He seemed rested, in good spirits, and full of energy. The exact opposite of how he had been just days ago. "We had intended to keep this a secret," he laughed. Before the trial, he said he ran every morning. Then, with the heavy workload, he said he had been forced to stop. Plus, he just didn't have the energy. "It's like a fuel injected engine and one of the injectors is plugged, and consequently the engine just doesn't work as well as it's supposed to. By Monday, energy levels were really quite low, and this chest pain had developed and it was pretty much constant." He said it came to a head on a walk with Laurie, and he couldn't walk any further. "Tuesday morning at 9 o'clock the cardiologist came in. At 9:30 - catheterization. Done."

Now, he felt good. "All this energy that was missing is back. All that pain that had been present is gone. So I want to say to all the 59-year-olds out there," he said, looking directly into the Capital News 9 camera lens, "go have your heart checked because you may be suffering from something like this and you may not know it."

He continued: "I wish I could have a do-over for a couple of my cross-examinations on Monday, quite frankly, because at the time I was doing it, I was having some pretty significant chest pains."

Then, his mind shifted to the other case he had been involved with. He shared the Court of Appeals ruling on gay marriage that had been handed down just a few days ago. They had ruled against it - against his arguments. He had the ruling framed. "This is Plessy v. Ferguson for me," he said.

XII

From: "Chris Porco" cp002m@mail.rochester.edu
To: "Porco" pporco@nycap.rr.com
Sent: Thursday, October 21, 2004 9:50 AM
Subject: Re: Second time sent- all your boxes are full!!!!!!!!!!!!!!!!!!!!!!!!!!!!IMPORTANT!!!!!!

Hey guys,
I am in between classes, both american express and the car loan are supposed to be auto paid.. I will talk to HSBC and get it fixed and paid up. I will also go to the bursar and see what the problem is. Thanks for the heads up, I will give you a call tonight.
love
chris

From: "Porco" pporco@nycap.rr.com
To: "Chris Porco" chrisporco@sprintpcs.com
Sent: Thursday, October 21, 2004 6:35 PM
Subject: Please call after 9:30PM

Hey Chris-
Another problem today- your license is going to be suspended because you did not answer a ticket???in Saratoga- violation date- 7-3-04

Please call after 9:30!!!!!!! The pile is getting deep- your credit is in shamblesMOM

*

Goshen, New York
July 17, 2006

It had been a tough trial, mostly because it had already lasted longer than some had predicted. And everyone knew there were plenty more witnesses to go. While Kindlon and his wife reminded journalists and jurors alike that it was tough for Christopher because he lost his parents and was on trial for the crime, the young man's attorneys had dealt with enough too. But even beyond the death of Laurie's mother, and beyond Kindlon's heart troubles, there was additional emotional strain on the couple.

Kindlon talked about it a few times, airing his frustration, but it hurt his wife more. A blog created by the NBC affiliate urged anyone to type what he or she wanted about the evidence, Christopher Porco, or the case overall. Reporters from the station said the comments were screened, but Shanks said that didn't seem to make much of a difference. The blog, deleted soon after the trial would end, consisted of valuable insight for everyone unable to make the trip down to Goshen, but also went further. More than one person commented about Shanks' hair or teeth. She called the attacks cheap, hurtful, and wondered aloud how such comments could be allowed.

More blogs would be created throughout the trial. Some that already had a following in the Capital Region covered the latest gossip in the case. A newer one, hosted by "LadyRuby," had the title of "Porco Fact Checker." Each new post discussed the emotional drain the case had caused everyone in the Porco family. The writer also aired her frustration about how the defense had proceeded with the case, even complaining that "K + S" had taken $200,000 for Christopher's defense, but didn't sit down and speak with the family to reassure everyone. K + S wouldn't say whether the number was accurate or not.

While discussion outside the court involved everything from gossip to fact, once inside, the reality of the situation came into sharp focus. Peter Porco's sister, Patty, attended the proceedings when she could. She was thin, with neatly combed black hair reaching past her shoulders. She didn't want to be bothered by all the reporters, gossip, or the public's take on things. This was deeply personal. Asked if the end of the trial would help her find any closure after the death of her brother, her eyes became misty, and she said she didn't think there could ever be a feeling of closure. She sat on the prosecution's side of the courtroom.

Week four began with another protest by Kindlon. An automotive technician in Albany took the stand, but had to step down only to return after a brief discussion. Kindlon believed anticipated testimony from a witness was once again "from the fruit of the poisonous tree." He said Joseph Catalano, a youth minister who Christopher had confided in, became a witness based on information gleaned from the police interrogation that was tossed out. Prosecutors said a detective at the hospital had seen Catalano talking with Chris, and therefore Judge Berry said he would allow the testimony.

Then the technician took his seat. He said once the yellow Jeep had been brought to his garage by way of a flatbed truck, he emptied the tank and measured the gas that had been left inside. He said about a half-pint typically remained in the lines.

The next witness, Joseph Killian, from the Albany County Division of Weights and Measures, testified that 87 octane weighs 6.1 pounds per gallon. After some basic math, it meant that 4.8 gallons of gasoline had been removed from the Jeep.

To put the gas issue into perspective, prosecutors then called in Daniel Lawler, a Rochester gas station owner. He testified that on November 13th, a credit card with Joan Porco as the account holder's name had been used to purchase $35.64 worth of gas.

Kindlon asked if the receipt would show what type of gas had been purchased. Lawler said it didn't.

Prosecutors later explained they were trying to show the amount of gas in the Jeep was about what you'd expect if you drove from Rochester to Albany on a full tank. It assumed a cash purchase of gas in Albany, but with no receipt, or proof of any purchase in the Albany area, the defense argued there were simply too many variables to prove the measurements meant anything.

Catalano, the youth minister, testified that he had known Christopher since Porco's junior year in high school. McDermott asked about a conversation Chris had with Catalano about a month before the attack. Catalano said Chris "needed an unsecured loan." He was led to believe the loan would pay for the next year of school.

Catalano said when he heard of the brutal attack, his first thought was to head to the hospital, "to offer support for Chris and his family." He said he spoke with Chris for about three hours once he arrived. Chris told him he had seen his parents Saturday after saying goodbye to his girlfriend. Porco also said that he had slept in the lounge the following night because a fraternity houseguest had come to stay in his room. Catalano discussed Chris' frustration over how police were treating him and said the young man mentioned the house alarm system either had not been working, or had been disabled.

The defense soon asked for another sidebar once Kindlon and Shanks realized that the comments Porco made about the house alarm system being broken could have come from that police interrogation. Shanks argued Christopher had been told the alarm wasn't working during the interview. McDermott said police had never said anything about the alarm system. "The only thing Christopher was told," he said, was that "the phone wire was cut." He "independently believes this could affect the alarm system." The judge asked that in this instance questions be specifically tailored to avoid the interrogation controversy.

Then the University of Rochester students came to the stand, starting with Marshall Crumiller. The young witness said he had graduated in 2006 and grew close to Christopher not only because they were fraternity brothers, but because they lived only two doors apart at school.

The young man began to discuss what he remembered from that November weekend with the aid of some pictures of the places he was mentioning. The frat brother said he saw Chris in the afternoon on Sunday and then had dinner with him around 9:30 at "the pit." The attorneys all chuckled at the dinnertime. Crumiller said he remembered it being cold that night, which is why after dinner he offered to drive Chris to his car parked off-campus. Chris apparently joked about moving his Jeep to the lawn in back of Munro and leaving it there. The two thought of it as a mini-protest against the parking situation. Chris accepted the invitation for the free ride and parked his Jeep in back of the building for the night, according to the witness. "He said he needed to help his Aunt and Uncle mulch in the morning." Crumiller added he didn't know about anything that happened in the lounge because he had gone back to his room and stayed there. The drive to pick up the Jeep had happened around 10:30 at night, he remembered.

Crumiller said the following morning he went to class at nine and hadn't seen Christopher. When he came back at around 12:45, he said he saw Chris wearing shorts and watching TV in the lounge with a few others. Around three in the afternoon, Chris told his frat brother someone on his street had been killed. Then, Chris' phone rang. "He answered questions about the names of his siblings," Crumiller said. "He came out of his room and said his parents were dead."

David Rossi asked him one final question before the cross-examination. Did you know Christopher Porco as someone who would jog in the morning?

"I didn't know him to jog in the morning, except for ROTC. I never saw him jog that semester," Crumiller said.

Shanks stood up and asked if Chris had been wearing shorts like someone who had just taken a jog. Crumiller said, "Yes." He added that Chris would often sleep somewhere other than his bed because he and others would allow friends or girlfriends to stay in the building. Shanks reiterated that on the weekends Chris could have parked closer to campus because many people left and parking problems eased, but he parked in back of the building as a joke. Crumiller agreed again.

Rossi stood to make the point that Chris could have parked closer on weekends, but didn't. Instead, he parked really close. Conveniently close, his voice seemed to say.

More students would step up to the stand, but first, prosecutors called Barbara Balzano, who had been waiting quietly in the hallway with her husband. Without saying much to him, she entered the courtroom. She said the last time she had seen Chris before the murder was September 16th, 2004, for her husband's birthday celebration. She said they hadn't asked him to help with any yard work just a few weekends later.

As McDermott sat, Shanks stood. Her goal was to paint a different picture of the family, so she asked her to describe her sister-in-law. "Joan puts herself last," Balzano said. She described Mrs. Porco as a "perfectionist," and "very religious.

"Peter was very outgoing and friendly – a wonderful host during family gatherings. He liked gadgets and computers. He was very supportive of his children," she said. Then, she described getting the news and waiting at the hospital. Balzano explained she and her husband stayed at Albany Med from nine in the morning until nine at night. She even moved into Sunnyview to be with Joan and help her recover. She recounted the medications she had to help Joan take – pills for everything from her eyesight, to pills that would help ward off infection.

McDermott stood and asked how the Balzano's relationship with Christopher had changed. "Chris had more freedom at college," she said. They were concerned about his studies and about how much he might have been drinking. "There wasn't much communication."

Tisha Abrams, the next former University of Rochester student to answer questions, said she had asked Chris if he would be at movie night on the 14th. They were good friends who would hang out and party on the weekends. Movies were an almost weekly tradition. They were set to watch "Shrek" in the lounge, but he didn't show, she said. "I saw Chris less frequently in October." On November 14th, "He wasn't there. I didn't see Chris." She said she had hung out in the lounge for four hours that night. Around 2:30 in the morning, she returned to her room. But she came back to the lounge around 3:15 to give someone a CD, and said she still didn't see him there.

"Did he ever jog?" Rossi asked.

"No."

Kindlon asked Abrams if she had seen another student in the lounge that night. She said she hadn't. Too bad, Kindlon insinuated. He told her the student had been there.

Jason Novak replaced Abrams. The young man with dark hair and a confident walk had grown up in the small town of Durham, Connecticut, and still had his senior year at Rochester ahead of him. He said Christopher told him he was "paying for tuition himself." Novak had been doing homework in his room until about 2AM, he told the courtroom. At that point he went to the lounge where he saw a few people still socializing after "Shrek" had finished. "I stayed in the lounge until around 3:30," he said. He went to bed close to four, and slept through several classes until he woke at around 11 Monday morning. That afternoon he saw Chris and followed him into the suite. Novak testified Chris said he was worried about his parents, that he had been trying to call them but couldn't get a hold of them. He said Chris' phone rang and it sounded like he was being questioned for about five minutes. Then, Christopher walked out and said, "My parents are fucking dead."

More students corroborated different aspects of the same stories. All agreed that Christopher had not been in the lounge. No one remembered him to have ever jogged. They said Christopher told them he had trouble reaching his parents.

Gregory Whiteside said Porco "seemed tired and stressed about not being able to reach his parents."

Shanks got Whiteside to admit that Christopher may not have jogged, but he had worked out regularly. And one of Porco's favorite places to go off campus was to Wendy's. It was not uncommon for him to leave and grab a snack.

McDermott asked the witness, "Did Chris ever explain where he was during those hours?"

"No," said Whiteside - - and Kindlon erupted.

"Objection!" he shouted.

Judge Berry knew where this was going, and dismissed the jury, telling them to return for 9AM tomorrow.

Kindlon held the steam inside as jurors filed out of the courtroom. "The prosecution desperately wants to make this an alibi case," he said. "But they've thrown a nuclear bomb in the middle of the courtroom."

Kindlon argued the question that had been asked shifted the balance to the defense to prove where Christopher was when it was the prosecution's job to prove their case beyond a reasonable doubt. "The only remedy," he said, "is a motion for a mistrial."

McDermott countered that the door had already been opened for his question. He said he hadn't offered anything that Shanks hadn't when she asked whether it was unusual for Chris to be somewhere off-campus, or to be unaccounted for.

Judge Berry warned McDermott not to ask the question again, but denied the mistrial request. "The jury will follow my instructions," he said. "I will give them a charge tomorrow morning." That charge would include explaining that a question never constitutes evidence, and that under U.S. law the defendant doesn't have to prove anything.

Outside the courthouse, Kindlon was eager to speak with reporters. He sounded upbeat and optimistic about how the day had gone.

A reporter asked about the students all saying Christopher had not been in the lounge. "I think we've demonstrated college students stay up late, sleep late, and don't know who's with them all the time," Kindlon replied. Earlier in the day he said the idea of a timeline was bogus anyway. "There is no timeline. There is no timeline, OK? There stopped being a timeline when the confession or the statement was thrown out. If they want to bring all of that stuff in, they're just rigging their case with explosives."

But McDermott stuck by his claim there was a clear timeline based on the evidence. The Chief ADA walked up to the microphones: "I didn't think I was going overboard on that," he said. "Mrs. Shanks got a lot of leeway without objections from me that Chris could have done this and could have done that so I thought it was fair game to ask and see whether he did any of those things."

McDermott downplayed the differences in the student testimonies. "He gave up his room that Sunday night because there was a visitor to the fraternity. A regional director. And he told people he was going to sleep on the couch in the lounge. The following morning when people started to get up on the Monday morning, he said he had spent the night on the couch in the lounge...Maybe slight lapses in their memories, but they were all uniform in that Christopher wasn't there. That came across loud and clear." With that, he thanked the reporters, and the prosecutors walked to their cars. Christopher had jumped in his Jeep and jetted out of the parking lot as soon as court ended.

XIII

From: "Chris Porco" cp002m@mail.rochester.edu
To: Peter Porco PPORCO@courts.state.ny.us
Sent: 10/22/2004 11:59:14 AM
Subject: Re: Driver's license suspension notice

Hey dad,
I think the ticket is for a uninspected car. But I was under the impression that I never received the ticket when I was pulled over.. I was going to a concert that day at SPAC, and when I pulled into the parking lot a state trooper waved me aside and noticed I didn't have an inspection.. I showed him my DMV extension slip, because I had just registered the car, and you have a certain amount of time to get the car inspected…as far as I know I do not have any copy of a ticket. I am 90 percent positive that he did not hand me anything. I will look in my car to make sure, but if I had gotten a ticket I would have sent it in along with proof of inspection, and they would have dismissed it right? I will look in my car and let you know if I find anything, or I will call the court I guess and ask them whats up, or what I owe.
Also, all of my financial stuff is taken care of, the problem was that shitty auto bil pay wasn't paying my bills. I have stopped that service, and will be manually paying the bills from now on… the bursar is taken care of too, they really couldnt give me a straight answer as to why you received a bill notice. They agreed that I am paid up through and have no problems. I will email you after I look in my car, thank you for sending me the notice, sorry you've had to waste time with this.
love
chris

*

Goshen, New York
July 18, 2006

Just like each day before it, reporters and their cameramen lined up behind the barricades to catch both sides for a few sound bites to fill the top of the noon hour. Today, Kindlon put his briefcase on the ground and ripped into the gas evidence. "That is the most idiotic evidence or non-evidence I've ever heard of in my life. He's got four gallons of gas in his tank. How many gallons of gas do you have in your tank, and what does that prove you guilty of? Seriously…it's calling on the jury to wildly speculate, and it's as meaningless as a lot of the other crap we've encountered so far."

But as boisterous as Kindlon was, McDermott told reporters to wait for the gas evidence "loose ends" to be tied up by a final witness. "On Saturday when Mr. Porco returns to Rochester, he fills up the tank. On Monday, there's only 4.8 gallons left in the tank. He never accounted for a long trip after he got back Saturday."

McDermott said the main focus of the day would be on the Jeep's travels. "The video puts him on his way to the thruway, and more importantly shows him coming back in the same direction those morning hours."

Inside the courtroom Kindlon started the day off with his now almost expected objections and motions. He argued that the interviews of students by investigators, as well as the video of a yellow Jeep leaving and coming back to campus, should all be thrown out because their original source was that initial police interrogation.

But Judge Berry seemed ready for the argument, telling Kindlon, to the prosecution's satisfaction, that the location of Christopher was established through others, and not the interview necessarily. "The People have an independent source…it defies logic that the People wouldn't have investigated."

Kindlon asked that his objection be made part of the record. He objected to each student's testimony as being "fruit of the poisonous tree."

With that out of the way, and the trial once again beginning late in the morning, Dana Perrin, the Security Department Manager at the University of Rochester, took the stand. He began by providing background on just how complicated the surveillance system at the University was in November of 2004. With over 100 cameras overlooking parking lots and roadways, it made for plenty of hours of footage. Perrin said images are stored for between 17 and 19 days before they're deleted. Each camera would move back and forth about once a minute. Software at the surveillance hub would sync the time and date with the video images, and it automatically accounted for daylight-saving time. Because of privacy concerns, there were no cameras in the dorms.

Perrin said investigators wanted him to save footage from a 22-hour time frame, to see if they could catch Porco in his Jeep leaving and returning at just the right times. Perrin said that request, using 40 cameras, meant 300 gigabytes worth of video. That was because 22 hours times 40 cameras meant 880 hours worth of video to sift through. Perrin was told to look for a yellow Jeep, which he located, moving through the parking lot just after 10:30 the night of November 14th.

Shanks objected to the time and date on the images. She told the judge since there was no record that anyone had checked the time to make sure it was accurate that day, the time and date had to be thrown out. Judge Berry agreed. He told Perrin that if he could get more information about the time being accurate, it could be allowed in later. They would go back and forth on the issue throughout the day, but Berry told jurors to ignore the time and date on the pictures. One of the jurors made a face at that, but managed to keep what looked like a sarcastic laugh inside.

Perrin went over the various cameras that showed a yellow Jeep, with mud on the lower side of the vehicle, traveling around campus and leaving on a road that prosecutors argued led right to the thruway.

But Shanks disagreed. She asked Perrin if he or anyone else to his direct knowledge had checked the tapes for the times between 11 that night and eight the next morning. He said he had no idea if the Jeep had been seen between those hours.

She also asked if he was aware of several fast food restaurants situated next to each other near the path Perrin seemed to put Porco on. "Did prosecutors ask to check for surveillance from the fast food shops there?"

He said he didn't know.

She asked if he had known about Wendy's receipts littering the floor of Porco's Jeep. He said he was never told about that. "It's perfectly normal if cars leave – you wouldn't see where he went. He could have gone to Wendy's," she cleverly stated.

He agreed and reiterated that he hadn't looked at all of the surveillance shots. If the Jeep returned at 2AM, Perrin acknowledged he wouldn't have known about that.

Shanks then asked about the plastic EZPass boxes that most people put in their car's windshield. Porco's had been found jammed in his vehicle's console. Perrin said there had been a safety campaign on campus, urging students to secure their valuables. He admitted that could mean hiding an EZPass.

Perrin remained on the stand while Rossi tried in vain to link the time code on the video images to a picture of the student who would testify she saw Christopher jogging on campus at a certain time Monday morning. Judge Berry still didn't allow the time to be considered by jurors.

The second witness of the day was a Daimler-Chrysler employee who billed himself as an expert on the mileage of the company's vehicles. His testimony was brief, but to the point. He calculated the Jeep Wrangler owned by Christopher could travel 210 to 345 miles depending on all the variables, he said. This meant if he had made the trip, Porco couldn't have gone from Rochester to Albany and back on one tank of gas.

The final witness for the day, Grant Fredericks, took the stand. He told jurors his job title was "forensic video analyst" – someone who compares video images with known objects. Televisions were setup on either side of the jury box, which took several minutes. Small screens faced out towards the public area, but they were too small to show much. The lights in the courtroom were dimmed, and the forensic video analyst pointed out that mud on the Jeep in the University of Rochester surveillance video matched the mud found on Christopher Porco's Jeep when it was brought to Albany for analysis. He also pointed to a spot on the back of the Jeep – a small oval object that usually didn't appear on other jeeps. Looking at the pictures of Christopher's Jeep, he pointed out the similarly shaped "W '04'" sticker.

Outside, the defense team seemed excited about another strong day; Shanks thought she had destroyed the importance of the surveillance video. "The only thing they have all the bells and whistles for is to prove Christopher left campus – which he had to do because he wasn't allowed to park on campus," she said. "They're going to prove conclusively that it was Christopher's Jeep that left campus -- which we already know because it was later found on Genesee Street."

Asked about the timestamps on the cameras, she said it was up to the prosecution to prove the times are accurate, but added, "I don't think the pictures are worth anything whether they enter the timestamps or not…They don't want the truth. They want to convict Christopher."

One of the reporters asked about what some began to call the "Wendy's Theory," wondering if any of the fast food receipts had a date that matched the night of the attack. She admitted there wasn't one, at least in the car.

As Christopher moved from his listening spot in back of the reporters to follow his attorneys to their car, Mike McDermott took his turn. He seemed to be as upbeat as the defense team, even though the time/date stamp had been thrown out. "It's just a minor inconvenience. The logs that substantiate the tuning of the equipment and calibration will be on the way here. As soon as the logs are located, we'll recall Mr. Perrin, and he'll show that they were properly maintained." He also denied that whole chunks of the video surveillance weren't viewed, possibly leaving a hole of time when a yellow Jeep could be seen going back and forth on campus. He told reporters that State Police and Bethlehem Police had also looked at the video. Perrin was only able to talk about the certain parts he had seen.

McDermott called the "Wendy's Theory" a red herring. "There was all kinds of junk and old receipts in the vehicle. I'm sure he habituated those places, but not on the morning in question."

Goshen, New York
July 19, 2006

Wednesday began quite cloudy and humid. It seemed fitting. The length of the trial had begun to wear people out. Prosecutors looked tired though they said they weren't. Some of the reporters complained that they didn't know if they could continue to live over two hours away from their families and work out of a live truck and hotel room. One journalist talked about getting out of the business altogether. She said she was burned out. Another reporter couldn't wait for his wedding – scheduled to take place in just a week-and-a-half. Everyone joked that if the trial didn't pick up speed, he might have to postpone his honeymoon and wait for a verdict instead.

The grueling schedule each station demanded of their reporters was partly to blame for their growing frustrations. Some woke each morning around five to get ready, do a radio interview, complete a morning story, interview both sides in the case, put together a story for noon, go back to court, interview the players again for the evening story, put that story together, race to dinner before the restaurants in Goshen closed, then begin writing the next morning's story before bed, and finally grab a few hours of sleep before waking to start all over again the next day...week after week. Not everyone complained because it was the big story. But it had its price. Thinking about murder all day for weeks on end would wear almost anyone out.

McDermott made a solo appearance in front of the microphones by the barricades. Kindlon and Shanks said they were running short on time so they walked by. McDermott said he was still focused on getting the timestamp on the video of the yellow Jeep, but it wouldn't be easy. "It's going to be interesting because the gentleman who maintains those business records of the DVR has no independent recollection so he's not going to shed any light. But there's more ways to skin a cat until the cat gets skinned." He admitted that since jurors technically couldn't take the date/time into consideration, "the impact of that video is diminished. And especially when the timing from the nighttime video matches up with the ticket he got at the thruway to come back within minutes, and the same thing in the morning - the time stamp coincides with the ticket he got coming back."

Inside, court began with a discussion, this time led by Shanks. She argued any e-mails between Christopher and his parents were hearsay and shouldn't be let in. After all, with Porco not testifying, and with Peter dead, there was no one to vouch for the contents of the electronic communications. If the e-mails were allowed in, she wanted to make sure "it wasn't just the bad ones."

Judge Berry agreed and asked that they all be put in, especially if Joan could remember any. McDermott wanted them all in whether Joan vouched for the ones she sent and received or not. He added that she refused to meet with prosecutors. "She's still angry over a leak to the newspaper."

The jury entered. University of Rochester investigator Roger Keirsbilck brought additional timestamp records and told prosecutors he reviewed the archived video. In it, he had found an outside clock in the background. Its time matched within a minute or two of the time superimposed on the images.

Shanks didn't let it go. She asked if the witness knew whether the newly found clock in the picture was accurate or not. She asked if it had been calibrated. He said no. A couple of jurors rolled their eyes. Judge Berry allowed the clock shot in as evidence, but told the jury they had to decide how much weight to give it.

More students were called in to say if they had seen Christopher the night of the attack. All said they hadn't. Matt Ambrosio shared an instant message conversation he had with his friend and frat brother, Christopher, a few weeks after the attack. Porco's IM name was Jeffsalosa; Ambrosio's was PygmyHippo1:

> PygmyHippo1: I pray for her every night.
> Jeffsalosa: She's doing better. She will nod and shake her head and give a thumbs up sign and stuff.

*

> PygmyHippo1: They were playing good cop bad cop with me.
> Jeffsalosa: Hey dude, they pulled that shit with me on Monday night for 8 hours.

*

> Jeffsalosa: For a week or so the cops have been leaking lies to the press to keep it in the news.

*

> Jeffsalosa: They told the vet I worked for that even they couldn't make the trip to my house and back in the time allotted.

*

But the part of the conversation that seemed to grab jurors' attention the most was where Ambrosio had typed, "I didn't c u till next morning." He asked Porco to tell him he wasn't in Albany that night. Porco told him to relax.

Later, McDermott said the conversation sent a clear message. "His friend is worried about him. He's asking, 'please tell me you were somewhere Sunday night to Monday morning,' and he says, 'don't worry I was in the hall.'"

Shanks, not surprisingly, said exactly the opposite. "Frankly, I think it helped us. It showed he had friends and all were supporting him. That the police really pressed them to say anything bad about Christopher and they didn't."

Ambrosio continued to testify about the police coming to Christopher's dorm room. They took a pile of his clothes, and one seemed "pushy," he said. Ambrosio said he told Chris he was concerned his friend might have to go to court. In the instant message Christopher reassured him. "Once they talk to my Mom it will all be over."

Ambrosio's testimony ended with him explaining that Chris was a big fan of Wendy's, and that he slept in other rooms frequently. Chris smiled at his college friend as the witness left.

Tyler Graham described that Sunday on campus. He said he saw Chris at the "Anchor Splash" charity event. They had also both been at their fraternity meeting earlier. But he said when it came to movie time in the lounge, he "didn't see Chris at all."

Twenty-four-year-old Jason Wortham answered questions next. He was the Sigma Phi Epsilon Regional Director. He spoke about living out of his car as he traveled from campus to campus, talking with the different fraternity chapters. He told McDermott he arrived around 8:00 Sunday night for the scheduled Sunday through Tuesday visit. He met with several members and then, because he acknowledged he was a little older and on a different schedule, went to his room around 9:00 or 9:30, where he saw Chris and his roommate. He wanted to make sure he wasn't putting Chris out of a bed for the night. Chris, he said, assured him the arrangement was fine. Wortham said he went to sleep around 10.

Sunday, there was conversation about Chris not being able to contact his parents. The house phone didn't seem to be working, and Chris said he couldn't reach them on their cells either. "The brothers suggested calling for help," Wortham said.

He woke up the following morning around nine. He saw Chris an hour later sleeping in the lounge in front of the television – in gym shorts and a t-shirt. Later that afternoon, Wortham said he saw him pick up the phone after it had been ringing repeatedly. It sounded serious. Christopher sounded like he had a cold as he spoke. Porco hung up and told Wortham that his parents were dead.

Wortham stepped down and another student, the Vice President of the fraternity, came in to tell a story that closely matched the other students. Lewis Ortiz said Christopher had told him he stayed in the lounge and couldn't contact his parents. Ortiz said he had chastised his friend for giving up his bed at the last minute after another frat brother had backed out of his promise to give up his room to the regional director.

Christopher sat quietly and calmly throughout the testimony. And while the question often came up, the defendant would never testify. Even so, prosecutors were about to bring in e-mails they believed showed a young man spinning more and more out of control as November 14, 2004 approached.

PART IV
VERDICT

XIV

Goshen, New York
July 19, 2006

Testimony was interrupted by questions about whether Peter Porco's last will and testament should be allowed in as evidence. Shanks argued it should not be – because she said there was no clear sign that Christopher had ever seen it or had wanted to see it. "They manufactured a story of him thinking he inherited money, but that doesn't mean the will should come in," Shanks said. She added the Porcos actually had relatively little money, and Christopher had more to gain with his parents alive. She put their net worth at around $100,000 and said that the money would have gone to Joan first.

Rossi tried to make it simple. "Peter is dead. The jury has a right to know who gains from that." The judge agreed. He also placed limits on what could be discussed, and jurors reentered the courtroom. "When you account for their indebtedness and the death benefits, it would have come to about $1.1 million. But again, proving that Christopher knew that is something I don't think we can establish," McDermott had said earlier in the day.

Julia Cannizzaro had worked alongside Peter for about 25 years. She described the awful day when she had found out something was wrong and told the court all she could think was, "I always knew they were a loving family." Rossi asked her to tell the jury if the way Peter had spoken about Chris had changed at all leading up to the murder. She said it had. The courtroom became utterly silent.

Shanks got up to try and put that fire out. "Do you think Peter ever stopped loving either of his children?" she asked in a soft voice.

"That's hard to answer with a yes or no." Cannizzaro breathed in and let it out. Rossi later described it as "a dramatic moment in the courtroom."

She was dismissed, which brought in two witnesses, one after the other, who testified they printed out all the e-mails between Peter and members of his family. One testified he looked for any violent threats in the writings but didn't find any. Three months of e-mails had been archived – e-mails that McDermott said were important to get in because "you can see it progressing and escalating over time." He believed they showed more than financial worries. "Deception. Money had a big part in it, but it was more than that. Christopher was deceiving his parents on a variety of issues, his parents at first accepting everything at face value."

With jurors about to hear the e-mails, it seemed an awkward time to end the trial for the day, but it was already getting late.

Prosecutors were optimistic that even though the defense objected to almost every witness as being "fruit of the poisonous tree," McDermott smiled as he told reporters, "It's OK, because a lot of the fruit's getting in, you know?"

Laurie Shanks, who had been cross examining the witnesses all day, believed as she'd been saying all along that the e-mails would show the average American family struggling to pay college bills. Asked about Bethlehem's police chief showing up to watch parts of the trial throughout the day, Shanks said "I think if they had done a better job, perhaps we wouldn't be here, and perhaps the person who killed Peter Porco would be on trial." The chief said he wouldn't make a comment until after the verdict.

A reporter asked Shanks what she thought one of Peter's coworkers would say tomorrow when she took the stand. Shanks told reporters, "I think she'll testify Peter was a wonderful father."

The witness would say much more than that.

Goshen, New York
July 20, 2006

The final day of week four began with an air of anticipation, as reporters wondered how much of the e-mails would be seen by the jurors. Kindlon said he wasn't worried about their contents, though he reiterated the defense team didn't think they should be allowed as evidence. He dismissed Peter's loan concerns. "Peter Porco did the same thing he always did. He got really angry, and then he forgave Christopher."

The attorney just didn't buy the idea that the e-mails meant his client was a murderer. "The fact is there are some cranky e-mails from Peter to his son at a time when he was upset with how his son was acting, and as a father who has had a son in college, I can assure you that this is not unique to Peter Porco."

Inside, Daniel Kidera, who described himself as a "good friend" of Christopher's, said he had an internship with Northwest Mutual. He told McDermott the two had a number of conversations where Chris said he would be gifted $2.8 million on his 21st birthday.

Jurors were ordered to leave the courtroom as Judge Berry anticipated the legal wrangling over the money issue. McDermott defended his question that had elicited the high dollar figure by saying the testimony showed Porco had knowledge of the actual wills as well as their location and what they said. The $2.8 million figure wasn't brought in for the truth of the matter.

Judge Berry agreed that $2.8 million was not accurate. Kindlon added that it was in the context of what he called "imaginary money" that Kidera knew of any wills. The attorney said if they continued down the money path, it would shift the burden to Christopher to prove he was "better off with his parents alive," which he said meant "we'll be here until it's snowing outside." The Judge didn't laugh at that. A few of the folks sitting in the public area whispered about the judge becoming snippy to keep the trial moving. It seemed he was getting tired of the legal debates that slowed the trial each day.

McDermott countered that just because the dollar figure may be inaccurate, it didn't mean the rest of the testimony would be. Judge Berry decided prosecutors could get in the testimony that Porco knew the content of his parents' wills without the specifics.

Kindlon asked that his frustration over the ruling be made a part of the record. Jurors came in, and McDermott asked his carefully crafted question. Kidera said Chris told him he had seen his parents' wills, and knew where they were kept.

He stepped down as Lieutenant Rachel Boylan, dressed in her United States Marine Corps uniform, walked to the stand. She said she knew Christopher because they had gone to college together and knew of him through ROTC. She said on November 15th, she had an aerobics class at 9AM. She left early from her dorm to grab breakfast, and then walked over a bridge on campus as she made her way to class.

Rossi asked what she saw when she was on the bridge.

Below her and to the left, she said, she recognized Christopher Porco. She said he was wearing a dark sweatshirt, khaki shorts, a ball cap, and glasses as he continued on what looked to her like a light jog towards Munro. She said she saw him around 8:45.

Rossi showed a picture from the surveillance cameras of what looked like a young woman on the bridge. Boylan identified herself as the person in the picture. She said the time encoded on the picture looked accurate to her.

Setting up the e-mails that were to come, Julio Lopez of Capital One Auto Finance came into the courtroom next. He explained that Porco had applied for a car loan on May 17, 2004. He was approved, Lopez said, and the check for $17,000 "was over-nighted to the customer." McDermott asked about the signatures on the request. Lopez said there were two – Christopher's, and the reported signature of Peter Porco. He went on to explain that by November the payments had become two months late. On November 4th, he received an inquiry from Peter Porco asking for a copy of the contract. Two payments were made shortly thereafter.

Shanks asked Lopez if the account was brought up to date once those two payments were made. "Yes," he said. He admitted after a further question that "many people are late with their payments."

Other financial workers testified similarly. One discussed the $31,000 student loan. A man named John Coffin said Peter Porco, who had apparently signed for it, canceled it around the beginning of November 2004.

Prosecutors brought Julia Cannizzaro back to the stand to look at the loan documents. She said she was very familiar with Peter's signature and told the court, "No, this is not Peter's." She was shown a few other financial documents and said Peter's signature had been forged on all of them.

While jurors pondered the testimony, prosecutors switched gears. Once again, because of the move to Goshen, the linear story prosecutors tried to tell was broken up. Verizon Corporate Security investigator Jon Nicholas told the courtroom he had received a subpoena for a "special computer run," that would show the incoming and outgoing calls from the Brockley Drive home at a certain time.

"Cell phone calls from a certain time or date would show up?" Rossi asked.

"Yes," Nicholas answered. Even with the phone line in the backyard having been cut, he said, "you can see what calls were made to the house."

Rossi asked if any cell phone calls had been placed to 36 Brockley Drive between November 12, and November 15, 2004.

"Two," Nicholas replied. He said they originated from a Nextel at 11:11AM and 11:12AM on the 15th – from the court officer who had come to the house. The duration was recorded as zero, meaning no one had picked up.

Kindlon acted confused, or, perhaps intended to confuse, a few reporters thought. Would one "flat rate service" calling another "flat rate residence," show up on the report?

Nicholas admitted that there wouldn't be a record if two flat rate phones were involved and one called the other. But more than a few jurors shook their heads, looking like they were trying to understand the different hypothetical phone situations as Kindlon continued. "If a cell phone with a 518 area code called a flat rate 518 phone," will it show up on the flat rate landline even if it just rings?

Nicholas said it would. Kindlon continued. What about if a downtown office called to the Bethlehem home? Would that show up?

That depended on the service of the office, Nicholas replied.

Kindlon asked about what would happen if a calling card were used. The investigator told him it was possible it would show up, but locating the actual place the caller had dialed from would be difficult.

Next, Kindlon took aim at the cut phone line in the backyard. He asked if there had been service calls to the Porco residence. Nicholas said there had been. On August 12, a service call was made after a utility box on the telephone poll had been damaged.

"How did it get damaged?" asked Kindlon.

"A tree branch hit it," Nicholas said, adding the box had to be replaced. He said fingerprints had been taken from the technician who had come out that day. They were compared to the fingerprint found near the telephone pole as police searched the property immediately after the attack. The print they found on the box simply didn't have enough points of identification to match with anyone specifically. The witness was then dismissed.

Michelle McKay took the stand next. She appeared a bit nervous as she took a sip of water. McKay had worked in the office with Peter and said they often spoke about day-to-day happenings and Peter's family.

Then the courtroom went awkwardly quiet. Jurors perked up as McKay told David Rossi that a week before the murder, Peter told her he "thought his son was a sociopath." She said it was a very uncharacteristic comment for Peter to make.

How serious was he? Rossi asked her.

"He was dead serious." She added that Peter had told her he decided to bail his son out once again. He continued to talk about his concern, she said, and came to the conclusion he would have to talk to Christopher.

In the afternoon the trial continued with dozens of e-mails. Each one was projected onto the courtroom wall. Prosecutors believed them to be possibly the best glimpse into the relationship between Christopher and his parents.

From: "Chris Porco" cp002m@mail.rochester.edu
To: "Porco" pporco@nycap.rr.com
Sent: Monday, October 25, 2004 9:23 PM
Subject: good evening

Hey guys,
Your phone has been busy the couple times I have tried tonight, I will try again a little later on..sorry I havent been around the past couple days I had a massive midterm today in my fluids class.. I think I did pretty good on it. About the american express shit.. I paid their asses, they called because it probably hadnt shown up yet, I paid online. Everything financially is taken care of, hsbc was giving me problems with auto bill pay, I have since discontinued the service, and am paying bills manually every month. The loan that you sent me stuff for will go through, the letter is an automatic letter sent after 20 days of inactivity on the account. I spoke with a lady with citibank today, and the loan will be approved and all set to go for next semester. Other than that im doing fine, a little sick again, no big surprise there I guess... have been taking the vitamins you sent me awhile ago. Will try to call again in an hour or so, hope all is well.
love
chris

From: "Chris Porco" cp002m@mail.rochester.edu
To: pporco@courts.state.ny.us
Cc: "Chris Porco" chrisporco@sprintpcs.com, "Chris Porco" cp002m@mail.rochester.edu, "Peter Porco pporco@courts.state.ny.us, peter_porco@yahoo.com, "Porco" pporco@nycap.rr.com
Sent: Thursday, November 4, 2004 12:17 PM
Subject: Citibank Loan

Hey dad,
The school and citibank talk to each other to figure out how much the school will be getting. The final loan amount will be 2000. The amount was given a ceiling of 31,000, but not all of that will be used. I haven't signed anything yet either, I assume that we both sign when the loan amount is all figured out.
chris

From: Peter Porco
To: Chris Porco
Sent: 11/4/2004 11:28 AM
Subject: Citibank Loan

I'm calling the bursar. I need to know what the truth is about all of this. What you're saying about the $2,000 is ridiculous. Citibank has already electronically sent $15,000 to the school. That's either to pay for next semester or its to pay for the current semester, in which case you haven't been truthful with us about free tuition for this semester.

From: "Porco" pporco@nycap.rr.com
To: "Chris Porco" chrisporco@sprintpcs.com, "Chris Porco" cp002m@mail.rochester.edu
Sent: Thursday, November 4, 2004 8:47 PM
Subject: Citibank Loan

Chris,
A letter arrived yesterday from Citibank indicating that <u>my $31,000 loan</u> had been approved and the first disbursement was going to be today. I did not authorized my credit on a $31,000 loan! I authorized only a $2,000 loan commitment. I don't care if your position is that you're only going to take $2,000. The loan amount affects my credit rating. You're making it impossible for me to finance another car. If I was going to be on the hook for another $31,000, I would have borrowed it through the Federal Government. Moreover, I have never

been permitted to review or approve any loan documents. I'm an attorney. I don't approve things without review. I have not even signed a loan instrument. Did you forge my signature as a co-signer? What the hell are you doing? You should have called me to discuss it. As a consequence, I cannot permit this current loan to go through with me being liable on it. I'm calling Citibank this morning to find out what you have done and am going to tell them I'm not to be on it as a co-signer. As far as the letter to the Court, I haven't received it. When did you send it? Send another original if it was several days ago. If you don take timely action, you can drive down to Saratoga and handle it yourself or risk a criminal conviction for driving on a suspended license. Dad

From: "Peter Porco" PPORCO@courts.state.ny.us
To: cp002m@mail.rochester.edu, chrisporco@sprintpcs.com
Sent: Friday, November 5, 2004 10:24 AM
Subject: Come Home

Chris,

I found out yesterday that you also obligated me on the car loan by signing my name to the check used to purchase the jeep. I got the paperwork from Citibank and confirmed it with a check of my credit history. That being the case, I immediately paid the October and November, 2004 payments to bring the loan current so that no default is reported on my credit history. I want you to know that if you abuse my credit again, I will be forced to file forgery affidavits in order to disclaim liability and that applies to the Citibank college loan if you attempt to reactivate it or use my credit to obtain any other loan, without my express knowledge and permission. Also, American Express keeps calling but won't discuss anything with me so I presume you're in trouble there too. Things are obviously spinning out of control with you. I think you should come home so we can talk. We may be disappointed in you, but your mother and I still love you and care about your future. We can't help you problem solve without information and input from you. Dad

From: Chris Porco cp002m@mail.rochester.edu
To: "Peter Porco" PPORCO@courts.state.ny.us
Sent: 11/5/2004 1:54:11 PM
Subject: Re: $31,000 loan and Car loan

Dad,
The loan was not supposed to be for that much money at all. I have enough money to pay for this year of school, except for the 2000

dollars. I will find a way to get the extra money in time for registration. They are pretty leinant with payment options and time periods here. Ill talk to you tonight.

chris

From:	"Peter Porco" PPORCO@courts.state.ny.us
To:	cp002m@mail.rochester.edu; chrisporco@sprintpcs.com
Sent:	Monday, November 08, 2004 10:46 AM
Subject:	Why won't you call

Chris,

We waited for your call all weekend. We stayed in all three evenings hoping you would call. We are extremely worried about you. You appear to be in serious financial trouble with the school and perhaps other creditors, yet you don't seem to be facing it. If you have the money to pay for the current semester, why haven't you paid it? If you had the money to pay for your car loan why didn't you pay that timely? I still haven't received the letter to the Saratoga Springs City Court and the clock is ticking away on that. After November 20th, you won't be able to drive legally. These problems are not going to go away by ignoring them. They will only get worse. There may still be time for me to assist with tuition for this semester through an additional Parent Plus loan, but I can't take action without knowing all the facts. I can't act unilaterally. I just don't understand your refusal to talk to us. Will you please call us! Dad

From:	Chris Porco cp002m@mail.rochester.edu
To:	"Porco" pporco@nycap.rr.com
Sent:	Tuesday, November 09, 2004 1:17AM
Subject:	Re: 11/8-Monday- Call tonight or I'll be there tomorrow

Hey Guys,
I am very sorry for not communicating with you recently. I intended to call you tonight to talk but I went with my friend to the hospital around 5 tonight because he had abdominal pain, turned out to be appendicitis. He is getting operated on tomorrow morning. I have enough money to pay for this semester, and I think I am ok for the second one as well, the whole point of the loan was so that you guys were not paying for any more of my schooling. I did not intend on financing my entire year through a loan with a high interest rate.
I feel like for the first time in my life I really have a handle on schoolwork. The capability is there for me, and always has been, but

the will has not been present. I have always just coasted along. This year for some reason I have really figured out how to study, and get more than a C. I really think my time home helped me realize the stakes of everything. I have been a little too absorbed in work lately I think, which has led to me neglecting other things, namely finances and you guys. I cannot appologize enough for the shit you have been through in the past couple weeks, my intentions were exactly the opposite.
I will call you tomorrow, just tell me when to do it. I have 2 tests tomorrow during the day so I will not be around till around 5 or so. Im going to go to the library shortly to make sure I know the material. I am speaking with a student financial assistance rep tomorrow also, to figure out my situation. I am confident that I can secure payment without your assistance, you have already done enough for me, and I cannot thank you enough for it.
I lost my cell phone late last week, and havent had time to get another one, I will be doing that this weekend, I also plan on stopping home this weekend also if you guys are going to be home.
Thank you so much for everything, and again I am so very sorry for all you have been through. I love you guys.
love
chris

From: Peter Porco
To: Chris Porco; Christopher at U of R
Sent: 11/12/2004 9:18 AM
Subject: Are you coming home?

Chris,
In your last email you indicated that you might be coming home this weekend. It would be great if you can manage it. Do you know if you are coming and, if so, when? If you can't come, would you at least call. Mom will be home from her conference by 5:00 p.m. on Saturday.
Also, I've received repeated calls from American Express. A woman named Ms. D'mello would like you to call her. A representative from Sprint also called but hung up before I could get a call back number.
Dad

From: Chris Porco cp002m@mail.rochester.edu
To: Peter Porco PORCO@courts.state.ny.us
Sent: 11/15/2004 2:09:24 PM
Subject: yo dad

Hey dad,

I talked to the financial aid office today and everything is set for next semester... so I guess just the plus loan for the past one. I don't have a lot of time right now, ill give you guys a call tonight. Give my love to mom
love
chris

*

Prosecutors maintained the e-mails showed a crescendo of frustration, culminating in the brutal crime. While Porco's attorneys disagreed with that assessment, the judge told jurors the e-mails were entered not for the truth of what they contained, but to show Peter's and Christopher's state of mind.

Outside the courthouse, as everyone's eyes adjusted to daylight from reading e-mail after e-mail with the courtroom lights off, McDermott took a swipe at Kindlon's contention that Porco thought his parents were worth more alive than dead. "If his parents were still alive he could be in jail for forgery, so I don't know if that's necessarily true. Plus, I think they were about to cut him off."

Beyond the issues discussed during the day, word had spread that Christopher's brother, Johnathan, might testify soon. McDermott said he wasn't sure.

Reporters also wanted to know if Mrs. Porco would take the stand. The issue was more complicated than anyone had thought. A meeting had apparently been scheduled between prosecutors and Mrs. Porco to figure out if they should have her testify. But earlier, during a break from court, McDermott said, "I don't know if we have a meeting with her today. We have requested a meeting and we're waiting to hear whether that meeting is going to occur." Then, after the e-mails had brought the day to a close, the Chief ADA said he still didn't know whether they would meet with her. "We plan to meet with her. I don't know if it's going to be with her today. It's going to have to be at her convenience. We're asking for a meeting but it hasn't been granted yet. We can't force her to meet with us. We had talked with Mr. Kindlon and Ms. Shanks, and they said they would facilitate it. But they have yet to tell us it's a done deal."

It would have to happen soon because prosecutors might try to get in some of the e-mails between Mrs. Porco and her son. Of course, that was if she could remember sending or receiving any of them. It was just one possibility prosecutors were looking at.

Kindlon took his spot in front of the reporters and downplayed the importance of the e-mails. "The last e-mail, the final one, is of the – everything is forgiven, everything is under control. We're going to take care of your tuition."

Someone asked if Kindlon would let Joan meet with the prosecutors. "We have offered to have her meet with the prosecution. It's going to be up to them," he said. Another reporter told him McDermott had just said prosecutors were waiting on *him*. "I feel like a chicken talking to a duck. We said right to Michael McDermott at a speaking distance of 18 inches - which is standard in America - sure we'll set it up. You can report to him we're ready willing and able."

XV

Goshen, New York
July 24, 2007

Court began with a discussion of the usual motions. This time, Judge Berry decided not to allow Porco's forged Hudson Valley Community College transcript. McDermott later shared his frustration with reporters because it had seemed to him like it was going to be allowed in. "I'm a little concerned if he changes his ruling at this point because the jury's going to be left to speculate, 'well the prosecutors said they would prove this, and they never did.' So that puts us in an awkward position."

But the issue seemed to fade away as a young man with short, reddish hair and a focused, stern look, walked quickly into the courtroom. Heads turned as he marched through the aisle and took his seat. He stared straight ahead, purposefully avoiding eye contact with his brother. Johnathan Porco poured himself a cup of water as a chill came over the courtroom. A few jurors sat up, aware of an intangible tension that enhanced the utter silence in the courtroom.

David Rossi began questioning the Lieutenant, who said his family had moved to their Delmar home when he was in the 5th grade. From there, Johnathan helped provide details about a typical day and night at the house. If you stood at the foot of his parents' bed, Joan slept on the left side, Peter on the right. His father usually wore a device for sleep apnea over his face. You could hear it's quiet operating noise if the door wasn't shut all the way.

Rossi asked the witness to describe the backyard. There are woods and a telephone pole, Johnathan said.

Would Chris have known about that? Rossi asked.

Yes, he said. When the two boys were younger, they shot paintballs at the phone box, just for target practice.

He recalled the 2002 burglary that had shaken his family. "Someone broke in," he told the court. The window was opened, police investigated, footprints were found outside, and a camera was dropped. That incident, he said, led to the family installing an alarm system. "You had to type in the code. 4416 was the master code."

"Who had the master code?" asked Rossi.

"Dad, Mom, Uncle John, Margaret Fennell, and my brother had it." He said the alarm was usually set at night. If you opened any doors, you'd get a beeping sound and enough time to enter the code to deactivate it.

Johnathan talked about Barrister. The dog was 14-years-old now. As a puppy, he had been kept in a crate, but as an adult dog, he had the choice of several beds, one on each level of the house.

He also said his parents owned an ax. "A regular ax you can buy at the hardware store." They kept it in the garage.

After Johnathan ascertained that he and Chris both knew they were beneficiaries, he said his relationship with his brother "had been strained recently."

Johnathan said he was in South Carolina attending Navy School in November of 2004. Christopher told him he slept in the dorm lounge that night after he gave up his bed to the fraternity director.

Shanks stood. Instead of asking questions from in front of the attorneys' desks, she didn't move from Christopher's side. It was as if she was trying to force Johnathan to look at her – and make eye contact with his brother. But he didn't.

Johnathan said his mother had told him she saw a stranger in the driveway – a shadow – just a few weeks before the attack. Someone had walked up the driveway, tripping the motion sensor lights. The person then walked away.

Shanks asked Johnathan about his parents. Once again, she wanted to put a human face on the case to show her client had feelings and a loving family. "Dad was a hardworking, great guy," he said. "He loved the law. He did that his whole life. I think he was an excellent father." He told Shanks he talked with his mom from time to time and said, "She's a great mother. A great person...She's a speech pathologist who's very dedicated to all her children."

Rossi asked a few questions and pointed out Joan had only told her son about the stranger in the driveway after the attack. Judge Berry thanked the witness for coming to testify and for his military service. Without looking at his brother, Johnathan walked out of the courtroom.

A few more witnesses gave brief testimony to tie up loose ends. If Christopher told everyone the University of Rochester had given him a free semester because they lost an exam, one University official said it wasn't true.

Another witness from U of R discussed the phone records for room 222 in Munro. As far as they could tell, no calls were placed to Christopher's parents' house except on November 15th in the afternoon.

After the judge told everyone to take a recess, most headed over to the few restaurants in town. Some of the jurors took their seat at a table outside Steve's Deli to enjoy the perfectly warm, sunny day. Reporters ate inside, careful to avoid any signs of impropriety. It was annoying with such beautiful weather, but necessary. Once in a while Christopher Porco would also eat inside in the tight dining area. The overall scene made for a slightly awkward lunch for everybody. Jurors came inside to grab extra bags of potato chips. Reporters looked for scarce seats while the young man sat with his friends. Within an hour everyone returned to the sterile, air-conditioned courtroom.

New York State Police Investigator Kelly Strack, a forensic investigator with five years experience who had testified previously, said she had dressed in a white Tyvek suit and booties as she scoured the murder scene back in 2004. She spoke about the cut wires in the backyard. A fingerprint had been lifted from the phone box. She had also thoroughly looked through Christopher's yellow Jeep. Though it had been brought up onto a flatbed for transportation, she didn't believe any of the contents – like the EZPass - had shifted. After all, there was a Dunkin Donuts cup in the cup holder that still contained a brown liquid.

Thirty-four tollbooth tickets were taken from the Thruway Authority for analysis. Investigator Strack verified that they were brought back to the State Police Troop G Headquarters in Loudonville where they stayed. "No latent fingerprints were found," she said. The tickets were eventually transferred to the Bethlehem Police Department on January 26, 2005.

Strack told Laurie Shanks on the cross-examination that she had taken every precaution possible so she wouldn't contaminate any evidence. Specifically, she said she had changed gloves after handling each toll ticket.

The investigator said she then focused on finding blood in the Jeep. Often, a murder can mean a struggle, so it wouldn't have been uncommon to find some – if the suspect was responsible. With that in mind, Strack said even the floor pedals had been taken off to see if the driver's feet could have transferred blood onto them. None was found.

Instead, Strack found an old t-shirt, a towel, running socks, and a Maglite flashlight. She said blood that matched Christopher Porco was found on a floor mat. But she insinuated it didn't mean much. After all, it was his Jeep.

After another witness discussed Porco's abysmal college grades and corroborated other witness testimony that no one had lost any of Christopher's exams, the prosecution said the end of the trial was in sight. "We fully intend to rest on Monday," McDermott said.

The Judge seemed upbeat about that. He also said there would be no court Tuesday because Laurie Shanks was receiving a prestigious law award. Attorneys not connected to the case admitted that putting the trial on hold for such a thing seemed a bit odd, but prosecutors didn't seem to mind. It gave them more time to plan.

Outside, there seemed to be a slight feeling of optimism from reporters after hearing the end might be near. The case continued to strain some of their personal relationships. Most were tired. The hotel room scene had gotten old for everyone involved with the case. Even the jurors seemed ready for it to be done; a couple alternates had nodded off for brief moments. "I know," said McDermott, "and the problem is we still have to present a legally sufficient case, not just a persuasive case. So in the event someone looks at this case down the line they see all the *i*'s were dotted and the *t*'s were crossed."

A reporter asked McDermott about the Porco brothers' "strained" relationship. "I think the jury found it was strained as well. There didn't seem to be too much goodwill going back and forth between the two." Another reporter asked why neither he nor Rossi had asked for details. "If we had asked the question about why it's strained and he had given an honest answer, I'm sure Mr. Kindlon would have jumped up and called for a mistrial."

Kindlon declined to comment at the usual afternoon microphone stand, but said earlier in the day, "Johnathan is very reluctant to have any contact with the media." When asked if Johnathan supported his brother, Kindlon replied, "I believe that he is supporting him against these charges. Yes. Absolutely."

Joan Porco would testify very soon.

Goshen, New York
July 26, 2006

"Horse Head Harassment: Councilwoman Target of Sick Prank." It was a headline no one could miss. Each day as reporters hung out by the barricades and waited for interviews, some would crack jokes about the local newspaper. The headlines always seemed a bit over-the-top. But this one was just bizarre. The article described a creeped-out local councilwoman who had found a horse's head in her pool. The paper theorized she might have been targeted because she was the only Democrat in a town of Republicans, though no one knew for sure. Later in the day, it would also be an issue in the Porco case.

But the first concern at the trial was getting a seat. For those who were watching first-hand, the seats had been mostly empty throughout the proceedings. But now the public seemed to get the feeling it would soon come to an end, and they wanted to see it. Reporters and local attorneys, who had no problem finding a seat before, had to get in as early as possible. One young girl, barely a teenager, had traveled down with her dad to see what the trial was really like. She said from watching the news it seemed Porco was guilty. Being there in person, she wasn't so sure anymore. The seats would fill even faster in the coming days.

In the meantime, Detective Bowdish took the stand. Both sides knew his testimony would be important, mostly because the defense kept pointing to a failed investigation, and Bowdish was their punching bag. Prosecutors said they were confident, but behind the scenes some wondered how well he would really do. A simple slip or two about how the evidence was handled or how a certain procedure was or wasn't followed might be enough to convince even one juror that there was enough doubt.

Bowdish told jurors he had worked in law enforcement for 20 years. During that time, they had investigated three murders. For the past 12 years, he was a detective. He said Bethlehem's population is about 25,000. Forty-four officers work in the department. He described the burglary call he had responded to back in November of 2002. It matched his previous testimony.

On November 15, 2004, he heard a call for a man down at 11:20 in the morning and arrived at 36 Brockley Drive to see an officer running into the house. He noticed a court officer outside. There was a key in the door, and when he went in, he noticed blood "everywhere."

"I saw signs of a struggle," Bowdish said. "I considered it unsafe." He walked through the kitchen and living room. He remembered hearing officers say the house had been cleared.

Upstairs, he saw Mrs. Porco lying on the bed. He told paramedics to follow him. "She had her hand up and motioned to come in." Bowdish told the jurors the familiar story, where he called down to Lt. Heffernan to get the names of her sons.

Then Bowdish said he asked her the set of questions. He listed them in order for the courtroom. "I asked her if she could hear me. She nodded her head several times." He said he then asked, "If a family member had done this." *Yes*. "If Johnathan had done this." *No*. He added that she had indicated with her hand back and forth as well. He asked again "If Christopher had done this?" *Yes*. He asked yet another time for each boy and got the same response. Then, he said he apologized to her. "I felt bad. She had very bad injuries."

He said he went back downstairs and decided to put out a BOLO for Christopher. "I called the State Police Forensic Unit out of Loudonville, and they responded within an hour." He said as he dusted for a fingerprint found by the telephone pole in the backyard, he realized the sheer magnitude of the scene.

The thruway tickets that might have been used by Porco the night of the murder were sent to the Bethlehem Police Department after the State Police looked at them. Bowdish said the tickets went right to the evidence room and weren't touched until they were sent to another lab. By the middle of March, all the tickets had been sent to the District Attorney's office as part of their growing collection of evidence.

Bowdish began to talk about the yellow Jeep. He had investigators check businesses for surveillance video and found the hard drive of saved images from the University of Rochester's cameras. The detective also had them look through dumpsters to see if any evidence had been discarded.

And with that, Shanks shot up for her cross-examination. She was ready to pounce. "Did you or anyone else look at the 800 hours of video? Are there logs of people watching 800 hours of video?"

Bowdish said he knew of one person who did watch it "consecutively."

After some back and forth on the issue, the questions turned to the room where the attack had occurred. Was the ax left on the bed as a sign? she asked. She emphasized that he took plenty of pictures of the crime scene, but hadn't taken any of the upstairs windows. Shanks asked if there had been a ladder in the garage to point out another possible way the suspect (or suspects) could have entered the house. But Bowdish wouldn't bite.

"Did you consider an ax left at the foot of the bed significant?" Shanks walked over to her wooden desk and picked up a newspaper. She asked if Bowdish knew what a sign might be. "A horse's head would be a sign," she said, holding up the front cover of the local newspaper for everyone to see. While some thought trying to bring in the article as "evidence" of symbols in a crime was ridiculous theater, others inside thought it just might strike a chord with a juror or two. The judge denied the request.

After Shanks got Bowdish to admit he did not wear a Tyvek suit while inside, she asked if he had ever heard of a mental status exam which could have been used during the questioning of Joan. "Did you ask 'were you awake,' 'was it one person in the room,' 'more than one person in the room?'"

"No."

"Her jaw is fractured. She has one eye on her face. She's covered in blood. 'Do you know where you are,' 'where your sons are?' No. You didn't ask those questions," she said, sounding utterly surprised at the thought. "Did you ask if medicine was given before you asked the questions?"

He said he knew no medicine had been given at that point.

After he went downstairs to put out the Be On the Lookout notice, Bowdish said he spoke with someone from the Times Union. He guessed that was when they had called Christopher for comment about the attack on his parents. Bowdish added that the State Police offered helicopters to pick up Christopher if he could be located.

Shanks directed the conversation to the fingerprint found on the phone box in the Porco's backyard. Bowdish said they compared Christopher's prints to it, but they didn't match. After talking to Verizon, he found out the box had recently been replaced, though the print didn't match the worker who had come out to fix it. The alarm technician, who had been sent once to the house to see if there had been trouble with the phone line, also did not have a fingerprint that matched. Bowdish said he had no idea whose fingerprint was left on the box and added that prints quickly degrade in the weather.

Laurie Shanks returned her questions to issues that had come up from the investigation in the Porco's upstairs bedroom. Bowdish said he had found two men's watches in bed. One was broken. The other was on the nightstand. Bowdish said there was an unidentifiable fingerprint on the watch found in bed, and the DNA on it didn't match Peter's or Joan's. She hinted that the watch might have been left as some type of "sign."

Shanks then turned to the questionnaires that were created to find leads from University of Rochester students. "There were questions about whether Chris ever said anything bad about his parents, but there were no questions about whether he said anything good about his parents," she said.

She continued by asking if they had ever tried to find who had been working around 10:30 at night on November 14th at the Rochester Dunkin Donuts near campus. There were receipts from Wendy's in Christopher's car, she noted. "He liked to hang out there." Bowdish admitted he had not checked those sites.

Then, Shanks took issue with the investigation of Chris' vehicle. "Did you ever do a lineup with the Jeep?"

"No."

She came to the conclusion through her carefully worded questions that Arduini showed pictures of the Jeep to toll collectors. If he didn't use a lineup, it could mean witness's answers were biased.

"You never went to Dunkin Donuts to see who was working then, even though there was liquid still in the Dunkin Donuts cup in the Jeep…you never spoke with ROTC students and others who knew Chris."

She sounded angry as she asked about the GPS tracker that had been placed on Chris' Jeep. She explained how her client had brought the small object to his attorneys, who in turn told investigators to desist. She wondered why a tracker had also been placed on Joan's car since she wasn't driving.

Shanks continued with the Mob theory. "Peter is the oldest living relative," she said, trying to explain why he and his family might be targeted if someone wanted to get back at their distant cousin. Shanks added that roofers had access to the house only two months before the attack.

Next, she asked Bowdish if he inquired about the stranger in the driveway who had "frightened Joan." She also wondered if he asked about a man who had made threats against Peter and his family before.

"There was an incident 15 years ago," Bowdish said.

Seemingly satisfied, she sat; Rossi stood.

Bowdish seemed frustrated. Shanks had been good at getting him to answer the questions with a simple "yes" or "no" response each time. The way the questions were asked made the simple answers feel inadequate to him, and anyone who read his face could tell.

Rossi fired off several questions to try and clear up any confusion. Bowdish said he had wanted to talk with Joan in September of 2005 in Rochester. They spoke, and though he said Joan was cordial, the conversation was brief.

Bowdish said he hadn't worn a Tyvek suit at the murder scene because every second counted and he was responding to an emergency. The list of investigative explanations continued: the BOLO resulted from the head nod, the victim of the crime gave him the information he needed to put the word out, and the watch from the bed had been submitted to the lab. He clarified for the prosecution the timepiece had *both* Peter and Joan's DNA on it. He added that there was a warrant from a judge that allowed the GPS to be placed on Christopher's vehicle.

Rossi referenced the questionnaires and asked if Christopher used drugs or alcohol. Most students said Christopher was drunk all the time, Bowdish answered. He added that they had checked the receipts in the car. Christopher had apparently gone to Wendy's on September 21st.

Shanks followed up on the "Wendy's Theory," and pointed out no students had seen him on the thruway that night. She returned to the watch question. Bowdish admitted he didn't quite know the results of the DNA test.

Then the jury was ushered out.

The defense team moved for another mistrial. While Shanks had been asking the questions, Kindlon had been stewing over the question Rossi had asked about whether Christopher had done drugs or not.

They interviewed three or four hundred students, said Kindlon. Some said Christopher was always drunk in college – but the defense felt that drinking was different than insinuating drug use. "This is a clear attempt to prejudice the jury... It's prosecutorial misconduct, it's unethical, and has no basis."

Judge Berry allowed Rossi to respond. "There are dozens of cases where students said he was drunk and skipped class."

Judge Berry seemed angry. His tone revealed he was taking this one seriously. He had given immediate instructions to the jury not to read into the question, which, he reiterated, was never considered evidence. Then, he admonished Rossi. "That was a bad faith question. There was no basis for it, Mr. Rossi. When you stoop to that level it's not professional or fair." Judge Berry underscored the seriousness of the matter by telling the prosecutor he would report him to the Grievance Committee if there were any similar conduct.

It seemed both sides left the courthouse feeling a little worn. McDermott said no harm had been done by Rossi's drug question. Rossi himself stepped up to the microphone, wanting to clear up what he obviously felt was a misunderstanding. Alcohol is a drug, he said. Students had told them Porco drank plenty.

McDermott also explained that the two watches found in bed were easily explained. He believed Peter wore one watch during the day. That one had been found on the nightstand. The other one was the cheap watch he liked to wear at night because it was easier to read in the dark.

Goshen, New York
July 28, 2006

State Police Investigator Gary Kelly was the man police had sent to track down some of the more bizarre leads and explain what prosecutors called the defense's red herrings. First, he looked at whether the man who had made threats against Peter, Judge Cardona, and another attorney 15 years ago could have possibly returned to kill. Next, he corroborated testimony from other witnesses that Christopher Porco had stolen his mother's work computer. He also spoke about Kindlon's Mob theory.

"Did you do any investigation into someone named Frank Porco?" Rossi asked.

"As part of my investigation I spoke to federal agents and federal prosecutors involved in an investigation of Frank Porco," the investigator said. "He had been indicted and pled guilty to racketeering charges – federal – related to sports betting and loan sharking acts alleged to have occurred in the early 90's. As a result of that, he received a two-year sentence. He was incarcerated at the time of the homicide in a federal penitentiary in Petersburg, Virginia.

"As part of the investigation, I also spoke with family members. Frank Porco has a daughter...and a son with the exact same name...who lives in New Jersey. He practiced medicine there as a medical doctor for 20 years, retiring two years ago. Both...are living and have never received any threats. In addition to that, I spoke to other family members. I also flew to Virginia and spoke to Frank Porco at the federal penitentiary about this time last year."

Rossi asked if Peter was Frank's oldest living male relative, something Shanks recently discussed in court. "Frank Porco has a nephew...who lives in New York City, born in 1944. He's nine years older than Peter," Kelly said.

"Were you able over the course of your entire investigation to find any connection between Frank Porco and his illegal activities and the death of Peter Porco?"

"Nowhere in the 421 leads in a year-and-a-half investigation has Frank Porco's name ever resurfaced."

Before Rossi took his seat and let Kindlon have a shot at the witness, Kelly said he had "painstakingly" gone through all the e-mails and contents of Peter's computers. He wanted to see if there were any blatant or veiled threats against him, but he didn't find any.

"Good afternoon," Kindlon said. He asked if the investigator had ever talked to Mrs. Porco to get her opinion on the crime. Investigator Kelly said he had not. "Now on the subject of Frank Porco, did you ever see the indictment that Frank's name was on?"

Kelly said, "Yes."

"And that the United States attorney indicates that the Bonanno crime family is operated through groups of individuals headed by captains...and that the little groups that they run are called crews, regimes, capodecinas. And the little groups consist of made members of the Bonanno crime family which are also referred to as soldiers?" Kindlon asked. Kelly said he had only read the indictment. "Now, when you look at this indictment," Kindlon continued, "did you happen to notice that Frankie 'the Fireman,' also known as "Big Frank" Porco, was charged with racketeering?

"Correct," Kelly said.

"And that he was charged with conspiracy?"

"No, I don't know that."

Kindlon began to explain further, and Rossi objected. The jury was dismissed as Investigator Kelly stepped down. The debate centered on some vague wording in the indictment. "Big Frank," as Kindlon referred to him, had been brought up on a racketeering charge. The question came when the document went on to discuss a murder conspiracy charge, which named another man as being involved. The defense believed it meant "Big Frank" might have been under the umbrella of that charge. Prosecutors argued that wasn't at all what the indictment indicated.

Kindlon called the docket sheet attached to the back of the indictment "significant." He said since the case was adjourned "numerous times," it was likely the man in question was a snitch.

"(Frank) Porco was never charged with murder," argued Rossi. He seemed more than a little frustrated. "Even though Mr. Kindlon can talk about it in his opening and all of his questions," that's what the investigators say. "Mr. Kindlon now wants the jury to speculate because he said it's obvious to him that Frank Porco must be a snitch because his sentencing was adjourned several times...As we know, it occurs all the time in our system."

Kindlon fired back, saying he had to bring up all the accusations because he felt prosecutors had painted "the Fireman" as "a choir boy."

Rossi looked like he had had enough of Kindlon's arguments. "Mr. Kindlon raised in his opening - misled the jury – to believe that Peter Porco was the oldest living male relative, that this is some sort of retribution. I am responding to his opening to things he's misleading the jury with...Mr. Kindlon's questions and rags with horse heads and pools, and

I think at some point it's fair to set the record straight regarding Frank Porco with this jury. That's all I want to do."

The judge clarified that the indictment "does charge a conspiracy and it does charge the conspiracy to murder," but said the only named defendant as far as the murder conspiracy was not Frank Porco.

Kindlon argued that because conspiracy was the major charge, it meant everyone listed in the document had some part to play in murder. Prosecutors rolled their eyes.

Once the legal battle ended, the jury returned and Kelly took his seat. He was asked about the counts in the indictment. "The only conspiracy I am aware of is conspiracy to commit sports betting and loan sharking," said Kelly.

The attorney tried to get the investigator to say Frank Porco was somehow involved with the murder count alleged in the indictment, but he wouldn't budge. "Loan sharking and sports betting," he repeated.

"You went to see Frank Porco at the federal correctional facility in…Virginia, correct?" Kindlon asked.

"That's correct."

"And when you went to see Frankie 'the Fireman' in the federal penitentiary where he was doing time, he told you he was there because he was framed, right?"

"That's what he told me." Investigator Kelly added that he knew the man had pled guilty. Kindlon asked how involved "Big Frank" was in the crime family.

Kelly said Federal prosecutors and federal agents told him "his role with the Bonanno crime family has been detached for many years." He added that when police told Porco he had been mentioned as someone who might have had an impact on the upstate trial, he had laughed at them.

Next, Kelly answered questions to dispel the other big theory the defense had floated. He basically said the man who had threatened Peter's family over a decade ago couldn't have been involved. The person in question had swiped in at 7:02 on the morning of November 15th at the high security military building he worked at, located in Arlington, Virginia. Kelly testified that the man threatened Peter almost two decades ago. The defense argued the man had been unaccounted for before then, but Kelly said they were sure he was home before he went to work.

A few other witnesses throughout the day offered their focused testimony to tie up loose ends for prosecutors.

Jurors seemed to lose their interest from time to time, but McDermott and Rossi knew they had to create as airtight a case as possible. With Kindlon asking for so many mistrials, they were already bracing for an appeal -- *if* they could get a conviction first.

Mrs. Porco hoped to avoid just that and would testify next. Prosecutors still wanted to get in as evidence e-mails between her and Christopher, even though they predicted the woman who had almost died would do everything she could to keep her accused son out of prison.

XVI

Goshen, New York
July 31, 2006

There would only be one witness on the first day of the sixth week of trial. Once again, the courtroom filled quickly with local attorneys who had heard about the case, folks from the Capital Region who just wanted to be there, and reporters from the various local and national news outlets. Peter's sister, Patty, took her seat on the prosecution's side of the courtroom. John Polster walked Mrs. Porco into court, taking a seat on the opposite side. Then Joan was called up.

She took her seat carefully. Her scars were visible. Christopher kept eye contact with his mother throughout; she was his first ally to testify. McDermott acknowledged earlier he would have to be careful questioning the "hostile witness."

And so McDermott changed his tone dramatically. He apologized for asking certain questions and referred to her as Mrs. Porco, instead of by her first name. Her voice was at times hard to hear in court because she was so soft-spoken. Jurors didn't seem to blink as she told her story.

A few days before the attack she said she remembered going to the YMCA to get a membership. She recalled working on the lawn and going to church. She said she also remembered the last few days of her stay at Albany Medical Center when she couldn't see well. And she didn't remember anything else in between. She said she hadn't discussed the case with either of her sons.

Surprising some who expected the testimony to last all day, McDermott thanked her and sat down. Little did they know she would remain on the stand, but not because of prosecutors.

Laurie Shanks began by asking about Joan's quiet voice. The witness said her throat had been damaged in the attack.

Shanks took Joan to the beginning. The witness explained her family had grown up in Gloversville, about an hour west of Albany, in Fulton County. They had worked in the glove business for which the city was named. She had earned her master's degree in Speech Language Pathology from SUNY at Albany. While attending college, her parents had died. Mrs. Porco acknowledged that was probably one reason why her family was so important to her.

Few noticed, because everyone's eyes were on Joan. But in the public seating area, Patty couldn't bring herself to look at her sister-in-law. Mrs. Porco continued, saying she met Peter in 1972 while at SUNY and married a little less than two year later in June of 1974. She said she now lived with her brother, John, in Rochester.

She told the court that Peter had worked very hard as an attorney. He left that job and took another as a law clerk to spend more time with his family. She approved of the move and said they had been as close as ever, right up to the point when she lost her memory. She knew they had celebrated their 30th anniversary, and remembered they were devoted to each other.

Chris smiled as his mother spoke. It was the most anyone had seen him react in some time. He continued smiling as Mrs. Porco said her youngest son shared her husband's personality.

Then Shanks asked her about a typical day at the Porco home, starting with Barr. Mrs. Porco said the dog occasionally had to be taken outside in the middle of the night. It was one reason they sometimes did not set the alarm. Other times, they forgot to turn it on altogether. She continued by saying the dog would be put in the basement if company came over. They would often shut the door.

Mrs. Porco told jurors about a letter she had written to her son in 2001. In it, she described him as "a gift," and said she was proud of his loyalty, kindness, humor, and independence. She said she knew he had kept that letter until it crumbled in his wallet.

Shanks asked about Mrs. Porco's bedroom to try and shed light on whether Joan could really have seen her attacker. Specifically, Shanks wanted to know how dark it would be on a typical night. With the shades drawn and the light off, Joan said it was difficult to see anything.

Christopher's mother said he had a B average in high school. She said she always thought he was capable of doing better, but his grades fell after a nasty bout with mononucleosis when he was in college. That's when he dropped a few classes, she said, adding that she visited him to help in any way she could. She told the courtroom her son had stopped swimming, something he had always excelled at. He failed out of school his sophomore year. He didn't tell her or Peter about the situation right away because he had wanted to please his parents, she said.

She admitted it was in the fall that they had found out he lied about paying for college. However, she pointed out he had never been violent. She said Chris was headstrong, but respectful. Sitting next to Kindlon, Christopher smiled and laughed as she spoke. "He's as gentle as his dad." Then, they began to discuss e-mails between her and her son. The first came after Chris told his parents everything was fine while he vacationed in London.

From: "Porco" pporco@nycap.rr.com
To: chrisporco@sprintpcs.com
Sent: Sunday, March 21, 2004 9:47 AM
Subject: Amen Alleluia!

3/21/04

Hi Christopher- Thank you for the e-mail…
Glad that you're safe! Glad that you are feeling confident at school. You can't imagine the feelings that we've had. We love you so much – we couldn't imagine what the problem was- We start to look at ourselves… to you….

Anyway- it is your brother's birthday and we're going to Syracuse this afternoon to meet Johnathan and Aunt Barbara and Uncle John. We'll send your best- you might send him an e-mail…. So, we're off to church soon – and then on to Syracuse… Tomorrow night Dad will be working late and Tuesday night he has Judge Keegan's retirement dinner. You might call between 4:30 and 5:30 on Dad's cell phone today while we're at dinner with everyone and that way you could wish him a Happy 23rd, if it's convenient, or you could call us at home tomorrow morning between 6AM and 6:30 AM. We found a bed that we really like- the furniture part…

Love you BIG- MOM & DAD XOXOOXOXOOXOXOXOOX

From: "Porco" pporco@nycap.rr.com
To: chrisporco@sprintpcs.com
Sent: Tuesday, July 27, 2004 9:40 AM
Subject: TRUTH NOW

Tues 9:35

Where are you? Vet called- come in at 3PM. What are you hiding? We can take the truth- try us. Dishonesty is crumbling our relationship with you. MOM

From: "Porco" pporco@nycap.rr.com
To: "Chris Porco" Jeffsalosa@hotmail.com
Sent: Monday, August 30, 2004 11:06 AM
Subject: third send just to be sure…let me know if you receive this…

8/30

Hi Christopher,

Do you have a place to walk, sleep and work yet? Hope all that is coming together for you. I know that you don't neeeeed my advice but I am compelled to give it only because I am lucky enough to be your mom and I want to do it the best I can…. I am wondering if you plan to go to the bank today and get yourself straightened out? Remember that if you have any direct payments from your account that if they change the number that you will have to notify each of them. How did you lose your card? Also, are you planning to visit your advisor again to possibly change any courses, like taking the intro now so that your cumulative average can begin to recover? Michele Wickert had some big problems trying to get courses because they are only offered at certain times of the year. Please remember that you have time and try not to overextend. Most especially, take what you have a passion for and you will find that your energy level will soar. Get a schedule together for yourself with classes, ROTC, and study hours. Then you'll know that you can get your things done and have some time to socialize…etc…. The crunch at the end can bring you poor grades just because time runs out. Ya know? Johnathan's schedule begins at 6am with classes until 4pm. Then each week for now he has to spend 25 hours a week studying. This level of studying will probably assure a high level of success, won't it?

Hurricane Francis paid a visit on Charleston yesterday and left high levels of water and some limbs down. JD lost power for a time. Marty is taking an LSAT course in Charleston and he and JD went to lunch yesterday. Today is the beginning of JD's program. There are mostly academy guys in his class although he has met Lamar's classmates also. He bought a computer desk and he's looking for a bed.

It took us 5 hours both ways yesterday. The rain was horrific and there was a serious accident on the thruway. Did Malary's team play? Those storms really packed a punch.

I'm off to Milford, CT for the wake and funeral for Sherry's grandmother. Thought that you might like Joe's cell: xx, and Sherry's xx. Sherry also is a great resource if you should have questions about school...

Your brother, Barr is visiting your room and lying outside it also. He's sniffed everything each time. I know he's lost without you.... He wants you to be the best that you can be, he told me, and he can't wait until you come home next time.

I'm off. Set yourself up for success!!! What did your Lieutenant have to say? JD was pleased to hear that you were going to see him yesterday. Talk with you soon. I'll be back Tuesday night. Love you BIGGGG,
MOM
XOXOXOXOXOXOXOXOXOXOXOXOXOXOXOXOXOXOOO

Last chance, do you have my card? If not I'm going to change it on Wednesday... Honesty and integrity are the most precious to have in life. If lost, they can almost never be completely recovered and many opportunities will be taken away from you. Suck it up and tell the truth always...

*

As Ms. Shanks and Mrs. Porco made their way through the e-mails, it wasn't lost on anybody that the situation seemed to get worse as time went on. But Joan said in the end things were "getting under control." She believed her son was sorry for what he had done and was acting responsibly by getting a loan and talking with his parents about it.

Questions next turned to life after the attack. Joan said everything had become so much more difficult. She told the court she found herself asking both her sons where their father was.

Shanks asked Mrs. Porco if she could remember when the police first tried to speak with her. She said she could not. As she had been doing without any objection (because no one wanted to upset her further), Joan added on her own that she soon realized the police weren't trying to find the truth. "They were out to get my son, Christopher." In fact, she called it "absurd" when John Polster informed her that police were interested in Chris. She said police never really asked for her input.

She spoke about the letter she wrote to the Times Union out of frustration. The defense tried to enter it as evidence, but the judge denied the request.

After a recess, the testimony continued with Shanks asking the witness if there had been any strange events she might have noticed before the attack. Mrs. Porco said she remembered the phone line in the back of the yard had been cut some time before November 14th. She also said she was concerned when she noticed a stranger approach the driveway one night. The motion light had gone on and the shadowy figure vanished. She told the court she had a "good sense" of what that person looked like. Shanks asked if the police had ever followed up on the possible clue, but Joan said no one had ever asked her to sketch what she had seen.

By now, Joan seemed tired after sitting all day on the stand, having to constantly think about what she was left with in the wake of the attack. Jurors were dismissed and Christopher went over to his mother, talking with her as they left the building together.

Outside at the daily reporter gathering, Shanks blasted investigators for not following up on Joan's concerns, from the stranger in the driveway, to the "fact" that it was dark in the Porco's bedroom. The attorney concluded that her client's mother couldn't have seen the attacker. Later, Kindlon would tell reporters he was baffled by how the police - in his words - had looked at clues "dressed in suits" with the words "I'm a clue" written on them in bold letters and had still ignored them.

McDermott said the lengthy testimony from Mrs. Porco meant the trial would likely last an extra couple days. He said they'd be ready to follow up on her testimony.

XVII

Goshen, New York
August 1, 2006

Before any of the jurors, attorneys, or witnesses arrived, journalists were buzzing about Joan's testimony, wondering if what she said would create just enough doubt to acquit her son. But a few felt she came off as a mother willing to do anything to keep Christopher out of prison.

McDermott walked up to the barricades and the bank of cameras and placed his briefcase on the ground. He said prosecutors were ready to show Joan was confused or unclear about a few issues. "Her claim is that the phone lines were cut sometime before November 16th," he said, though he meant the 14th. "So actually we're going to bring in someone from the phone company to talk about that."

A reporter asked about the stranger in the driveway. Could that have been a precursor to what happened?

When she first met with police, McDermott said, "She wracked her brain and the story about someone coming up the driveway never was mentioned. I'm not saying she fabricated this, I'm claiming at the time she thought her son was a suspect she was trying to help the police and the significance of that was really nothing."

Shanks told reporters the idea that Joan would lie to protect her son – especially when she's the victim – was ludicrous. "She's been painted sort of as this wimp who would cover for her son, who is gullible. She's one of the strongest women I have met in my entire life."

Inside the courtroom the seats were already filled. Because everyone knew Joan would be on the stand for a second day of testimony, several families had traveled hours to see the courtroom drama. Security guards at the courthouse saved a couple rows of seats for reporters who had attended the trial from the beginning. Even so, the tight seating wasn't comfortable. On top of that, the trial began closer to noon because Judge Berry had local cases to handle, which he dealt with in front of his packed courtroom.

Before jurors came in, McDermott wanted the judge to rule on whether or not to admit a family photo album as a defense exhibit. Shanks argued it should be allowed in because "one of the prosecution's arguments is that this family is so broken. They would have you believe he would kill over his grades and credit card debt." Judge Berry sustained McDermott's objection to the book coming in because it had been specially prepared for the case. After further protest, Berry allowed a few photographs, but not the full album.

Laurie Shanks and Mrs. Porco began where they had left off. Shanks asked about a relative of Peter's. Joan said she met Frank Porco, a great uncle from New York City, in Brooklyn 30 years ago. She said he attended their wedding and remembered he wore lots of gold jewelry. "He was very tall. Well built," she said. She explained he caused a stir at their wedding. He sat down and crossed his legs when she noticed he had a revolver holstered to his leg. She said he told her he owned a restaurant and dealt with a lot of cash, so it was for protection.

"Was he a member of the Mob?" Shanks asked.

Just as Joan was about to answer, McDermott stood and said, "Pardon me, Mrs. Porco. I apologize. Your honor, I object."

Judge Berry told Shanks to ask a different question.

Shanks asked about the threat directed at Mrs. Porco's husband.

"Peter was involved with family court cases," she said. He "was a law guardian who represented children in cases in family court." She said Peter had represented a child, and the father threatened him. "We were very concerned about our children's safety. We went to the schools to make sure they weren't taken by anyone," she said.

Joan continued to explain just how seriously they took the threat. Two shotguns had been given to Peter from his father, and they had kept one by the bed at night. Joan said she thought the man was apprehended soon after that and believed he had served some time.

Shanks asked about the Judge Peter had worked for. Mrs. Porco said he "called Peter, 'Gentle Peter,' much like Christopher is." She said Peter wanted to buy a handgun at one point, but had talked with Judge Cardona and the purchase never happened. It helped that there had been a high-profile case around that time which led to an increase in security at the Albany courts. She said the Judge himself has a bodyguard.

Shanks thanked the witness, and McDermott took over. He asked how long ago the threat against her family had been made.

"Fifteen years ago," Joan said. She also told the courtroom they had long since wrapped up the shotgun and put it away in a closet.

McDermott asked about her son's first semester at the University of Rochester -- when she believed he had mono. She said she wanted him to come home, but her son "insisted he could do it." At one point Joan said Peter went to check up on their son and found him sleeping in a locker room. During his second year of college, Chris was involuntarily separated from school. He received two different transcripts at home, even as he traveled to Acapulco and Europe. She said she and Peter might have helped pay. Chris had trouble with PayPal so she had loaned him some money.

Joan added that she saw letters sent to Chris' business, "Computers Direct 2000." She wasn't sure how long the business had been operating, or when the letters had been sent. As she spoke she seemed to lose track of her thoughts. She had to ask several times what she had just said and then picked up from there with her quiet words.

McDermott asked about a talk she had with the Balzanos as the problems seemed to build. "Did you tell them you were so frustrated with Chris that you had just given him up to God?"

The defense objected as Joan said she didn't remember.

But she did remember being asked questions by officials as she recovered at the hospital. She said she believed it was just casual conversation, had no idea Christopher was a suspect, and was shocked to find out what she said later became her grand jury testimony. "I am angry about the way I was treated." Christopher continued to smile at his mother, trying to reassure her from 20 feet away.

McDermott asked about suspicious people on her property. Joan explained she didn't immediately tell police about the "stranger in the driveway" because she only thought about the backyard when they wanted to know if she had seen anything suspicious.

She said a Verizon worker had informed her lines were cut by the telephone pole out back just before she had dinner with some friends in late September or early October.

"I was concerned." She said people up and down the street had phone problems and around August, a technician came out to the house.

She told McDermott neither she nor her husband had any enemies. The prosecutor reminded her that during her grand jury testimony, she said the only person who had any animosity towards her family "was the person who took the laptops."

The prosecutor discussed the Thanksgiving burglary from a few years earlier. Mrs. Porco said her son was living at the house at the time, so he didn't break in. "He didn't tell us about his needs," she said.

Laurie Shanks followed up on McDermott's questions, asking about the grand jury interview. Joan said she had known Paul Clyne, the DA who talked with her from her hospital bed, and thought he was friendly. But when she found out what she told him became her testimony, she felt "he was conning me." She said, "I only answered seven or eight questions the second time when he came two days later. So I don't understand about this. I thought that-"

Judge Berry interrupted. "Mrs. Porco" – He wanted to keep her focused on the question at hand.

"I'm sorry. It's very frustrating because I feel they have done things they haven't informed me about." Mrs. Porco wanted to share her side of the story as Judge Berry did his best to calm her down. She apologized and said, "I just have anger about the way I was treated."

"Have you ever gone back in your mind?" asked Shanks, wondering if Joan might somehow remember who had nearly killed her.

"I believe the person, or persons, are still out there. Were they after both Peter and I?" The question hung in the air for a brief moment. "It's scary for me."

Joan's testimony concluded with her saying she was "incredulous police would think Christopher would do this…They were not investigating anything." Both sides thanked her, and she stepped off the stand. She took a seat between a group of young, good-looking girls who had been attending court on and off for a couple weeks in support of Christopher. More than one of them said they couldn't believe such a fun, genuinely nice, and intelligent man, known for his low-key dry sense of humor, could be accused of such a disgusting crime.

Next, prosecutors called a Verizon worker. He verified he had been called to the Porco residence to fix a cut phone wire sometime that August when it was damaged by a tree branch.

After that short testimony, Dr. Terry Melton, the President of Mitotyping Technologies took the stand – one of the People's last witnesses. Melton, from the University of Pennsylvania, said she had extensive "experience in the field of mitochondrial DNA analysis."

Kindlon jumped out of his seat and jurors had to be ushered out of the courtroom. Once again, the attorney was concerned about that interrogation being dragged into the trial after it had already been tossed out. The first DNA sample had been taken from Porco's clothes the night he talked with Bethlehem police. They all agreed not to discuss a "first sample of DNA" so they could avoid the quandary as best as possible.

Melton continued with her curriculum vitae and was recognized by the court as an expert. She said she completed doctoral research that dealt with using mitochondrial DNA as a forensic tool and then began educating everyone in court. She explained nuclear DNA is what you get from your parents. It determines your hair color and other specific features. Mitochondrial DNA, however, is passed down from the mother's side only. It is not a unique identifier, she explained. Nuclear DNA is, except in the case of twins.

More than one juror yawned as Melton went over what amounted to complicated high school biology. She explained the letters A, C, G, and T stand for parts of DNA called nucleotides. Two nucleotides connect to become base pairs. "It's the order of the bases that tell you what you need to know," Melton said, just prior to the Judge ordering a lunch recess.

After lunch, court resumed. Melton continued by saying the sample that was tested was relatively small. She said the point of looking at any DNA would be to find out if the sample was large enough to draw conclusions from. She said it was. It therefore brought her to the main point of DNA as evidence in a criminal trial. With mitochondrial DNA, she reiterated, you want to figure out how many people would not be excluded from possibly contributing the sample. "We can use the FBI database to find out."

The FBI database contains over 5,000 samples with which to compare profiles. She said private industry has access to 4,839 of those sequences, which was large enough. Melton gave an example of what you could do with a DNA sample when compared to the database. Using complex equations, she said one could predict with 95 percent certainty no more than X amount of people have the type of mitochondrial DNA in question.

McDermott asked Melton to describe what she had received from the New York State Police. "I received three items," she said, including bits of a tollbooth ticket in tubes and a sample of Porco's known DNA. The first item showed "a negative control," which meant that toll ticket sample was not clean. Any results would be meaningless.

She said she moved to the other tube which held bits of a ticket and found a small amount of DNA, consisting of only 85 bases. "It was a partial bit of DNA," she explained, but emphasized she found the same pattern twice.

She took the known sample of Christopher's DNA and was able to "identify and make a full profile" of his genetic code to compare to the tollbooth ticket DNA.

Kindlon objected at that point, protesting that the "Sorcerer's Apprentice" was assuming facts that are not in evidence. "DNA has mystical qualities in the public's mind," he cautioned. Kindlon said out of the 85 bases that had been found on the ticket sample, only one matched with his client's DNA – "which is next to nothing." Usually, the more the better, Kindlon argued. Not 85 bases with one match.

But Melton countered that you only had to have enough DNA to show differences or similarities in key spots between the evidence and known DNA sample. "It depends on the piece of profile you have," she said. In other words, it wasn't the quantity, but the quality because some parts of the DNA sequence were more informative than others. One piece might show a rare combination of "base letters" which would eliminate the possibility that the DNA had come from most people. But another slice might match with most humans, thereby having little value for figuring out whom it belonged to. "This very small piece had the ability to exclude a very large number of people," said Melton.

More specifically, the prosecution's expert said it meant 12 people out of 4,839 had the same stretch of 85 bases. She said about half a percent, at the most .39 percent, might have mitochondrial DNA that matched up. It meant 99.61 percent of North Americans wouldn't match with the mitochondrial DNA.

During "voir dire," when one side tries to flush out how competent a particular witness is, Kindlon made his skepticism known. "You used 85 base pairs to compare – which is about 12% of the overall database," he said, adding that Melton's sample was minimal and degraded. "You can exclude people as possibilities, or you can fail to be able to do that," Kindlon continued, almost asking it like a question. He then pointed to the wall where the DNA sample was represented by letters projected in back of the witness. Kindlon asked what "nd" meant. The two letters filled a number of spots where the A, C, G, or T letters should have been.

"'nd' is not determined," replied Dr. Melton.

At one position, noted Porco's attorney, there was a "mixed site." Kindlon asked if that meant more than one person's DNA was involved. He then objected to the testimony, but was denied.

As to how credible the sample might be, Melton said she had already accounted for the DNA of the State Police who had handled the evidence, as well as the toll takers.

Kindlon asked if mistakes happen during testing. "Oh sure, always," replied Melton.

"Was this lacking in quantity and quality?" he asked.

"The result was good," the witness said. She admitted she had never had such a minimal sample before. Either way, all 85 base pairs matched with the Porco sample, according to Melton, and at one site in particular, there was a "more rare match. Most people have a G, some an A, a few a C. Based on one site we can reach a conclusion. G to C confers a great deal of rarity."

Kindlon asked several questions to clarify points and got Dr. Melton to say mitochondrial DNA is not a unique marker. It meant you only know you can't *exclude* Christopher from having a match to the toll ticket. Kindlon finished up by asking how much her DNA work had cost the county. "$21,000 to $22,000," she said.

Another day came to a close. Once outside, Christopher Porco stood by reporters as they asked about the DNA testimony. Prosecutors seemed optimistic that yet another brick in their case had been laid. Kindlon said there were too many variables for the evidence to mean much to the jury. "We don't know what other forms of corruption or contamination were inflicted on that ticket prior to the time people started to handle it with rubber gloves," he said.

Reporters told their Albany-area audience the defense might start calling witnesses as soon as tomorrow.

Goshen, New York
August 2, 2006

"It's going to be a short day for the prosecution," said McDermott from in front of the cameras outside the courthouse. "We will put on the 'records person' from Verizon and then Mr. Gokey. I can't imagine they'll have too much in the way of cross-examination. Then we will rest."

Mr. Gokey was the neighbor prosecutors called another important part of their case. He claimed he saw Porco's Jeep in the driveway the morning of the attack. "He's telling it like he sees it and he's an unbiased witness who should come across like that to the jury."

Asked to reflect on how well things were going, McDermott said, "I'm very pleased at how the prosecution's case has gone in. I'm very disappointed we didn't get to put in all our proof in front of the jury."

Shanks stopped for the cameras too, albeit briefly, so she could make her way from the steamy outdoor air into the chilly air-conditioned courthouse. She said she was eager to get to the defense witnesses. She called most of them "character witnesses" who would try to add some positive perspective on her client's behalf. "I think people will be able to see who the Porco family really was, as opposed to what Christopher Bowdish needed them to be to support his made-up theory." As far as the neighbor who would say he saw the Jeep, she dismissed the whole thing. "I think he was someone who probably really wanted to help, and he just really is mistaken."

The mercury would top out at 97 degrees later in the day, one reason most were happy to be inside for once. Up north in Albany, the temperature would reach a record 104 degrees for the city. Nearby in Troy, a state record would be broken with a reading of 108.

While the air heated up outside, prosecutors wrapped up their case inside. Deborah La Croix introduced herself as a

Verizon field foreman. Looking over documents and logs related to job orders originating out of the Porco home, La Croix said on August 12, 2004, a technician went to Brockley Drive. McDermott asked when someone had been called to the same address before that. "December 31, 2003," she responded. After August 12, there were no records of any other visits. Except for November 15, 2004.

Shanks took her turn by asking for more details on the August call. La Croix said the technician did not go out for cut phone wires at that time because none were cut. And there were no other service calls. Shanks then asked if a person might call about a problem and not be aware of what was causing it. Therefore, cut wires might not show up on the paperwork. La Croix acknowledged that might be possible, but she said it likely didn't happen in this case.

La Croix left almost as soon as she had come and was replaced by Marshall Gokey. He said he was a construction worker who had lived on Brockley Drive for 8 years. He said he often spent time around the house on weekends and was "very familiar with vehicles in the neighborhood."

Gokey went on to say he specifically knew of Porco's Jeep because the defendant liked to speed up and down the street. The witness said the vehicle was yellow with a canvass top and wide tires.

McDermott asked what Gokey was doing during the pre-dawn hours of November 15, 2004. He said he had a construction project that required him to leave his house early. He went to his car around 3:45 or 4:00 in the morning when he saw what looked like Christopher Porco's Jeep sitting in the Porco's driveway. He said he didn't think much of it at the time.

Shanks asked Gokey if it was even possible to have seen the Jeep from where he was. She asked him if there were streetlights because if there weren't any, she wanted to know how he could have seen more than ten feet in front of his face. Gokey said with the leaves off the trees, it wasn't a straight shot, but he could still see the spot in question even though the sun had yet to come up.

Shanks asked if police had shown him a lineup of different vehicles when they questioned him, or if they had shown only one picture. He believed it was one picture. And he remembered a brush guard. Shanks asked if Porco's Jeep had a brush guard because there wasn't one. Gokey explained he assumed the winch – which the Jeep did have - was a brush guard.

She asked him if there was more than one Jeep in the neighborhood that could have caused some confusion. "More recently, there's another one in the neighborhood," he said. He knew of one person who lived in Delmar who drove a similar yellow Jeep. McDermott then asked for clarification on which side of the driveway Gokey had seen the vehicle, and Gokey stepped down to leave Goshen.

McDermott and Rossi entered a few additional items into the record as evidence, things that had not officially been brought in. There were no objections. At 2:30 in the afternoon, McDermott said to Judge Berry, "Your honor, the prosecution rests."

As was standard, Kindlon made a motion for the Judge to dismiss the case based on a lack of evidence. But Berry said they had provided enough evidence of possible guilt. "The case is not dismissed."

XVIII

Goshen, New York
August 2, 2006

Margaret Fennell, the first defense witness called to testify, winked at Christopher as she walked up. After swearing to tell the truth, she told the court she was a retired teacher. Several people sitting in the public area said she looked and acted the part. She seemed to choose her words carefully as she spoke – not so much because she might say something wrong, but because she had been an English teacher who valued the proper word. She said she met Joan years ago while working with her at a school in Voorheesville. They quickly became friends. Fennell said she befriended Peter as well and met Christopher the day he was born. She even helped take care of him and his older brother from time to time. When asked about Peter, she tried to stay strong as she described him as a wonderful man. "I miss him a lot."

She said Joan was one of her best friends and was always meticulous about her home. Mrs. Porco had constantly updated her knowledge about computers so she could be successful as a speech therapist, Fennell told the courtroom. "Christopher is a very intelligent young man," she added, and said he would mow the lawn and keep the family computers running.

Shanks asked Fennell if she remembered a conversation with Joan about a stranger in the driveway. She said she did. Joan looked out the window in September of 2004 and saw a figure walk up the pavement. Motion lights had clicked on and the person was scared away, she said.

Fennell explained it was the evening of the 15th when she found out there was a murder at the Porco home. She said she went right to the hospital and eventually told Polster about the stranger. In December of 2004, Fennell said she told McDermott about the stranger. By then, she had also heard about someone breaking into the phone box out back at some point before the attack. She spoke with police, but said she didn't believe they followed up on either the stranger in the driveway or the phone box leads.

Finally, in May of 2005, Fennell said McDermott did meet with her to discuss "the stranger." The prosecutor apparently told her not to talk with Joan about the attack so that her memory wouldn't be altered in any way. The whole thing was difficult, she said, because there was media attention "24 hours a day."

Christopher sat still, occasionally smiling at his parents' friend. McDermott asked how many times Mrs. Porco mentioned the stranger in the driveway, trying to prove it wasn't a serious concern. She said Joan had only mentioned it once, but that it scared her. She also said at several different times her friend complained about the phones not working. The Chief ADA asked if she thought Peter or Joan were close to a breakdown before the attack. The defense objected, and McDermott had to back off.

Fennell said the couple had been concerned enough about the Thanksgiving 2002 burglary to get an alarm system. She said Peter never looked like he was close to a nervous breakdown, and she admitted because of the stress on everyone, it took awhile for her to remember Joan had discussed the stranger with her. She said she had last seen Joan in early October for her birthday and saw Peter briefly in November when they had talked for a few moments.

Linda Polster replaced Fennell on the stand and had a similar story to tell. The tall, elegant woman said she met Joan and Peter in 1974 after her husband, John, started law school. She said their families would get together, the kids would play, and they'd even have the occasional sleepover. Polster said the Porco boys and her son, who suffers from a neurological impairment, had gone their separate ways as they grew older, but they still got together for the holidays. Polster said Peter was a loving father who would put young Christopher in "timeout" if needed.

Polster said she learned about the attack around 3PM on November 15th. John had called her on the cell and told her to "get here as soon as possible." She told the courtroom she asked if their son was all right. "Yes," said John, "but Peter's been murdered." She said she heard through the news that police were looking for Christopher. She remembered hearing Christopher should be considered armed and dangerous.

She arrived at the hospital around six at night to spend time with Joan. Polster said Christopher "was subdued," and that he was always concerned about his mother. Chris visited her whenever possible in the hospital and "was very concerned about her condition," she added. He was "a little boy who was hurting." She said police never asked her any questions.

McDermott stood, and asked one question to point out how irrelevant he thought Mrs. Polster's testimony was to the investigation: "You do not know about the murder, do you?"

"No, I do not."

With that, court was adjourned for the day. Jurors were told to return for 9:30 the following morning. There would be no trial on Friday, but Judge Berry warned everyone once deliberations began, he might allow jurors to work from 8:45 in the morning until 8:00 at night. He said they would not be sequestered.

Outside, McDermott seemed upbeat, though everyone appeared to lose steam as they walked outside and hit the wall of heat that had descended on New York. "I'm glad we're at this point in the trial. The end is in sight," McDermott said. He thought Gokey had done well, even if every detail wasn't perfect. "It's a big yellow Jeep with wide tires and a canvass on top. I don't think anyone's going to expect him to know the exact model number. If he had come off and spouted off the chapter and verse of the make of the tires, it would have come across as rehearsed. Here's a neighbor who really doesn't care about the Jeep, other than it's a yellow Jeep and it goes up and down the neighborhood and he described it to the best of his ability." McDermott admitted prosecutors had tried to deny the defense's character witnesses from taking the stand, but the judge refused.

Shanks said their witnesses were important. "Now we're going to fill in the pieces with the people who knew him and the people who worked with him: his godmother and the other people who have known him his entire life and are standing with him today."

A reporter asked her opinion of the case that had been presented so far. "I think the prosecution's case is a desperate attempt to sort of take different pieces of circumstantial evidence and build them into something they're not…I think the jury really wants to know who the killer really is. Not the Detective Bowdish version of who he is." She dismissed Gokey once again. "I think he was someone who wanted to help, and that's all I can really say." She and her husband walked to their car to escape the heat.

Goshen, New York
August 3, 2006

"You know if we proved that Christopher was one of the 12 apostles, it would not prove to these people that it was a defense to the murder of his father. Their minds were made up in the first 30 seconds," Kindlon told reporters. One asked about the DNA witness who said the odds were low it was someone other than Christopher who had touched the toll ticket. "The DNA expert, Dr. Shields, from Syracuse University, will demonstrate today through *intelligible* testimony and a *clear* explanation of mitochondrial DNA - rather than through the gobbledygook from the prosecution's witness - that indeed Christopher could not be excluded from being a contributor of DNA in this case, just like 71 percent of the population couldn't be excluded." Kindlon explained Dr. Shields would have very different numbers that would eliminate far fewer people from ever having touched the ticket, rendering the prosecution's results meaningless. "So that narrows it down to 70% of the population, which I don't think is very compelling proof of guilt," he said. He told reporters Dr. Shields had been involved with some big cases, including the O.J. Simpson, Unabomber, and Scott Peterson trials.

He also took another chance to attack Gokey's testimony. "You'll remember Mr. Gokey saw a Jeep Cherokee or a Jeep Wrangler or a Liberty or a G.I. Joe Jeep – I don't know. Given the realities of the circumstances on Brockley Drive at 4AM on a November morning it is extremely unlikely that Gokey would have had an adequate opportunity to have looked at that driveway if he had been able to look at the driveway at all." Kindlon went inside the courthouse. As he had been doing lately, Chris Porco came in by himself a few minutes later, carrying a few folders.

McDermott stopped for the cameras to preview the day and to stick up for the prosecution's DNA expert. "Just like the toll takers seeing him on the thruway, and Mr. Gokey seeing him in the driveway, his mitochondrial DNA being consistent with the DNA on the toll ticket is just another piece of the puzzle."

He also criticized the defense's "DNA expert" as a man who evaluated the "building blocks" of caviar instead of the human type. "Mr. Shields is a well-known gadfly in the

DNA community. He doesn't do any testing himself. Never has. Doesn't work in an accredited lab, but he testifies all over the country." McDermott also made it clear he was ready for the case to conclude with a verdict. "I think there's sufficient proof on the record for them to deliberate on the case."

Dr. Shields introduced himself to the judge and handed over his resume to the court reporter to be entered as evidence. He said he had been a biology professor since 1979 and explained that his background wasn't so much about forensics, but overall genetics.

McDermott stood to question whether Dr. Shields should be allowed in. The witness agreed with everything McDermott said: You're not a forensic scientist. You have no degree in forensics. You don't do medical genetics. You're not a member of any professional society concerned primarily with human genetics. You've never worked in a crime lab. You've never done mitochondrial or DNA tests.

Dr. Shields didn't agree with the last statement, though. He said he had done tests on caviar for a case where authorities wanted his help.

McDermott continued. "You've never amplified mitochondrial DNA, quantified, or sequenced it."

Dr. Shields agreed again and then frustrated the prosecutors as he explained that he could look at results of certain tests and come to a conclusion with "a reasonable degree of scientific certainty."

McDermott said that sounded too unclear. What did "degree" mean?

"Certainty is a very rare event in the real world," explained Shields. He told the court he earned his degree in genetics and previously looked at DNA test results for wolves and other animals. He insisted, "DNA is DNA." Two students of his were currently working on ducks and plants. He had worked on 20 mitochondrial DNA cases, he said.

Over the People's objection, Judge Berry allowed Dr. Shields in as an expert DNA witness.

And so began a long day of dense statistical DNA discussion. Over time those in court who could follow the testimony realized Dr. Shields was speaking more like a statistician than a geneticist. He had more of a problem with how the results of the DNA tests were interpreted than with the actual tests themselves.

Dr. Shields said he examined the Mitotyping report and noted that Dr. Melton said 99.61 percent of the population could be excluded from having contributed the DNA found on the toll ticket. But he didn't believe that was true.

Dr. Shields said the DNA was not a perfect match. At one spot on the DNA sample from the toll ticket another "letter" replaced the predicted base. He said it was likely a *mutation*, though it still didn't eliminate Christopher. That's because he said mitochondrial DNA tests are never 100 percent accurate since each person is capable of producing a DNA sequence that's slightly different than the next. Dr. Shields said that meant you shouldn't exclude anyone who had one difference with the known sample.

He continued to explain what that meant by going back to Dr. Melton's report. Dr. Shields pointed out that 12 out of 4,839 of the DNA database samples were an exact match. But 3,0002 of those in the database still matched with one difference, and that would exclude far fewer people.

It took quite some time to get the witness to explain what he was saying in a way that was easy to understand as evidenced by several jurors who battled sleep. One yawned every 10 seconds or so. A visitor from Albany later said the trial seemed much more exciting on the evening news than in person.

Dr. Shields told the struggling jurors the toll ticket could also be contaminated. That possibility – or the potential of a mutation - might explain the difference in base letters. Either way, he said he had never heard of a DNA sample that was so small and part of a criminal case.

One of the alternate juror's eyelids must have felt like concrete. He was doing everything he could to stay awake. Though he never actually fell asleep, it looked like he was losing the battle. Christopher simply sat calmly, occasionally writing a few notes.

Dr. Shields also explained the FBI's database was not appropriate to compare results to. That database included wide-ranging DNA samples from around the world. But in North America, in the United States, and in New York, the witness argued a different sample should be used, one with more Caucasian, Hispanic, African American, and Asiatic samples. He said if you considered all of his arguments, instead of the over 99 percent who could be eliminated from having possibly contributed the DNA found on the toll ticket, only 27 percent of people would be eliminated.

The witness for the defense continued by saying if you looked at the results his way, five of the eight investigators and toll ticket handlers who had likely touched the sample could not be excluded.

McDermott stood for the cross-examination. Dr. Shields reiterated the same ideas and wouldn't budge from his interpretation of the results. The prosecutor did get the witness to discuss his research on barn swallows, bats, and squirrels, though. Shields said he was also involved with a seminar for defense attorneys titled, "How to win with DNA." He rarely testified for prosecutors.

The testimony took all day. The one juror never did quite fall asleep, but it was close. Judge Berry ordered everyone to return for 9:30AM on Monday. The sixth week of trial had come to a close.

Outside, McDermott seemed to think Dr. Shields' take on the DNA evidence was irrelevant. "He doesn't have the background. He's a zoologist. He does a lot of work with animals. We don't have any caviar in this case." But he said it didn't contradict the prosecution's witness because "he agrees the DNA on the toll ticket is consistent with Christopher Porco. He can't be eliminated." The prosecutor said the different numbers arrived at by the defense witness were simply due to faulty reasoning. "They cannot make an assumption about the ethnicity of the person who contributed it so they have to look at the entire database."

McDermott left the courthouse with Rossi and the team from the District Attorney's office, and then Kindlon came out swinging. "The overall point is Terry Melton cooked her results. Let's keep it as simple as we can. If she had been honest, the first thing she would have done is not file a report because the evidentiary sample is of such a poor, degraded quality, it didn't give her enough of a sample to do her report. If she had been honest about the results concerning Christopher, she would have shared with the court the reality that 70 percent of the Caucasian population cannot be excluded. Is that not exactly consistent with what happened when they did testing on the eight people who had handled the ticket? The people from the thruway and police lab - out of those eight people, five of them could not be excluded."

Kindlon said it meant his client would be found not guilty. "I think this is game over, this testimony, quite frankly. It just shows you how they've been going around trying to cook up evidence and they fell flat on their faces here...all the double-talk and gobbledygook in the world can't change the fact that seven out of ten people can be contributing the DNA, and that's meaningless."

Within a week jurors would begin deliberating – and reach a verdict.

Goshen, New York
August 7, 2006

"Today we're going to hear from Steve Meyers who is a neighbor, who made a report to police about something extraordinary on something that occurred in the neighborhood around two in the morning on the 15th and they didn't care," said Kindlon during the usual morning interview right outside the courthouse doors. "We've been pointing out repeatedly that what the police did in this case was they decided in the first two or three minutes Christopher had committed this crime." He said the defense expected to start with Meyers on the stand, and continue with a neurologist who he said would contradict Dr. Spurgas. Then, one of the vets who had employed Christopher would offer her testimony.

Inside, Stephen Meyers told the court he was a funeral director in Delmar who supplemented his income with a part-time job at the Albany County Airport. He said he would "throw bags" from seven at night until around two in the morning and had done so on Sunday, Monday, and Tuesday nights for the last six years. Meyers said he lived at his funeral home located a block or so from Brockley Drive.

"What, if anything, unusual occurred on November 15th, 2004, in the early morning hours?" Kindlon asked him.

Meyers said he was on his way home. In the five or six years he had been working the extra job, he said he had only seen two cars on the roads around his home at that hour. One was a police car. But that night, around two or a quarter after, he said he saw two coming at him at the intersection of Charles Boulevard and Orchard Street – one street down from Brockley Drive. He said he slowed down because he thought it might be a police car and pulled to the right to avoid getting hit. The pair seemed to be going 40 miles per hour and accelerating. "One was right on the bumper of the other. I had to veer all the way to the right."

Meyers said it was tough to see the vehicles, but the first one had a New York license plate. It was a sedan with a chrome grill. The second car was "right on the bumper," so he couldn't really see it, he repeated. He said he arrived at his funeral home moments later and went to bed, not thinking much of it.

After waking up, Meyers turned on his scanner just before noon and heard chatter about Brockley Drive. The funeral director said he walked over to see what was going on. Neighbors told him there had been a homicide, and he immediately remembered the two cars he had seen. Meyers told the courtroom he went to the Bethlehem Police Department to tell investigators. He gave them a description of what he had seen.

Did anyone call you back? Kindlon asked.

"No one ever contacted me."

David Rossi asked several questions of Meyers, who said the police dispatcher who took his name down said she would forward his information to the proper person. Meyers stepped down and drove back to Albany County.

Dr. John Kearney, the next witness to take the stand, wore a seersucker suit and an almost permanent smile. But jurors were ushered out of the courtroom by court officers once Kindlon made it clear he wanted to bring up the controversial decisions Detective Arduini had supposedly made during the investigation.

Kindlon told the court where he hoped to go with the testimony. The Bethlehem Veterinary Hospital had employed Chris since he was 16-years-old. The Arduini family had several dogs that were treated there. Kindlon said Arduini had two daughters, which was significant because Mrs. Arduini had apparently approached Dr. Kearney to fire Christopher. Kindlon said Det. Arduini was upset with Chris since he had dated their older daughter. According to the defense attorney, the younger daughter had taken an interest in Chris, but the feelings weren't reciprocated.

Kindlon said on November 15th, almost immediately after the murder, Arduini, who was off-duty at the time, showed up at the Vet Hospital and told Kearney, "Things look bad for Christopher." Dr. Kearney gave the detective Chris' contact information. Kindlon told the judge that Arduini then went to the High School to see if his daughter had run off to Mexico with Christopher. Arduini, Kindlon added, had shown the veterinarian a bag marked "evidence," and told him, "Christopher isn't the person you think he is." Kindlon paused, then explained that Arduini had died in April and was not available to testify. Yet, he said the detective's actions were significant.

The judge asked McDermott to respond. "It's all hearsay," the Chief ADA said. If Arduini was to testify, it might be OK – but he couldn't. He added that jurors had heard no proof about Arduini's involvement and doubted he would have been called to testify in the trial had he been alive. McDermott said as far as he knew, Arduini had actually taken a step back from the case because of his daughter's friendship. As for that evidence bag, it wasn't part of the evidence at the trial.

Kindlon fired back by telling the judge that Arduini had his daughter go online to see if Christopher would make a confession to her. Arduini had also "moved the toll ticket," he said. "I mean no disrespect to Mr. Arduini, but he had an obvious bias."

Rossi jumped into the fray. He said Mrs. Arduini had explained to him that her husband had been showering when he got a call. He called back around the time the BOLO went out, and the dispatcher told him to go to Brockley Drive. Arduini asked if there had been another burglary. After some discussion, Arduini went to the vets first to see what he could find. McDermott added that Arduini had only handled *copies* of the toll ticket, not the actual toll ticket itself later on in the investigation.

Judge Berry told the attorneys if he allowed any of the supposed Arduini story the defense wanted to get in, it would "open up a lot of speculation…it would be hearsay." He said he would allow a basic discussion of the so-called bag of evidence shown to Dr. Kearney.

Jurors returned, and Kindlon discussed what he could with the vet. Dr. Kearney said one of Peter Porco's judge friends had urged him to consider hiring the young Porco. He didn't usually hire young kids, but found the judge persuasive and was happy with Porco's work.

McDermott took a different path. He asked what Christopher's duties at the animal hospital included. Dr. Kearney seemed eager to answer each question to the best of his ability and explained how Christopher would keep the clinic clean, assisting in the examination room by restraining cats and dogs and noting each pet's history.

McDermott asked if they performed animal surgeries at the clinic. Dr. Kearney said they did. They had to follow certain protocols just like a hospital. They would wear caps, masks, gowns, and gloves. He said if liquid touched a cloth gown, it would likely soak through to the skin. Work at the vets could be "very bloody and messy," Dr. Kearney said. Surgical disinfectants would be used for cleaning up. Christopher would wipe down the table and launder the caps and gowns. Even though the Dr. admitted he knew Christopher might not have been completely honest with him when it came to stolen property, he was pleased to have the young man working for him. "He was a valuable, great employee."

Kindlon asked Kearney if he had known his employee to be violent. "He's not capable of violence," he –

"Objection."

"Sustained," said the judge, tossing the statement out. It wasn't up to the witness to make that conclusion one way or the other.

Dr. Kearney stepped down and was replaced by a thin woman with short, spiky blonde hair and intense eyes. Dr. Mary Dombovy identified herself as Joan's neurologist after the attack. She explained that a neurologist treats injuries to the nervous system, whereas a neurosurgeon is trained in such matters, but primarily performs surgeries. Shanks wasted no time in getting to the point, asking about when a mental status exam should be given.

It would be used if a patient might have an injury and can respond, Dr. Dombovy said. They went through what kind of questions would be asked: what month is it, where are you, spell a word backwards, give the patient something to remember for later. There were many ways to find out if "yes" really meant "yes," and that a person's short-term memory really worked.

After a traumatic brain injury, there can be erratic movement of arms and legs, said the Dr. A "yes" or "no" question might therefore get a response, and it might even seem to make sense. But, she said, you would expect to get a correct yes/no answer half the time simply by chance.

Shanks asked if it meant something if someone seemed to be covering themselves with their clothes when someone walked in the room. Dr. Dombovy said it might mean a person had some awareness, but it didn't give any insight into memory or orientation. "It's not possible to tell what she understood," she said.

She added it was extremely unlikely, if not impossible, for Mrs. Porco to remember the attack because of her injuries. Months afterwards, doctors noticed she had what they call "attentional impairment," which means Joan processed information more slowly. She noted that her patient had improved since then. Now "I think she's doing very well."

Shanks asked about Peter's injuries. Because he had stumbled around the house and didn't use his cell phone to call for help, she wanted to know if that was because his brain injury made it impossible to put two and two together. Dombovy agreed it was possible.

McDermott asked about what it meant if someone with a traumatic brain injury responded not just with head nods and shakes, but with hand movements as well. He repeated for the courtroom that according to testimony, Mrs. Porco had pulled her nightgown down when emergency responders walked into the bedroom. Dombovy said it could show she knew she wasn't alone, but "memory is different from responsiveness."

McDermott pushed further, explaining that Joan was a speech language pathologist and would have known to use nonverbal means of communication. Dombovy agreed that might be true, but said bottom line, it was guesswork. The finger movements would add no more insight than the supposed head nods.

After Judge Berry thanked Dr. Dombovy for her time, and after a break, the defense brought into evidence several audio recordings from November 15, 2004. The grainy recordings were made by the Town of Bethlehem Police Department and sounded like those muffled 911 calls occasionally played on the evening news.

The first clip involved police discussing what they had to go on almost immediately after they found out about the attack. Christopher's name was mentioned. They said they were putting out a BOLO. "Use extreme caution...could be armed with any weapon."

"OK Lieutenant, putting the BOLO out. Homicide…method unknown. Use extreme caution."

One said Christopher is a suspect. "We don't know the victims yet. Is it a Jeep, yellow Jeep still?" Another asked if Chris was still working at the vets, or if he was back in school.

"You want to swing by the vet clinic on your way? See if there's a yellow Jeep there?"

The dispatcher was told Chris had last worked at the vets in August. He was still driving the yellow Jeep. They discussed Chris' cell phone number and who was attacked. "I think it may be his dad and mom."

Police were laughing about the crime in another audio recording -- until one officer heard it was Peter Porco. "Holy Crap," he said. They would need to call the forensic unit in Loudonville, the voice added.

The courtroom heard another recording where an investigator discussed the yellow Jeep with the dispatcher. They were laughing. "What happened to my town?" chuckled the investigator.

"I'm telling you," she said.

They decided to call Rochester police to let them know they should look for Porco. "He's a suspect in a murder here," they said.

Then the dispatcher told an investigator, Chris Porco's on the phone right now. "He's in his dorm room." She was told to tell him the police would call him back.

Another portion of the audio revealed that a 2nd grade teacher had called once she heard about what happened. She told police someone had threatened the Porco family years ago. The teacher mentioned Peter: "It had something to do with his profession. He's a lawyer."

Already the day had come to an end. Judge Berry reminded the jurors what they just heard was not for the truth of the matter, but was played so they could understand the state of everybody's minds. Judge Berry told the jurors as he did every night not to watch or read any accounts of the case. He wanted them to avoid the news and asked them to return at 9:30 the following morning.

Outside, McDermott set his briefcase down by the microphone stand and basically said he had heard a whole lot of nothing throughout the day, beginning with Meyers' testimony. "I don't think there's any significance" to the speeding cars, he said. "They weren't on Brockley Drive, they were on Charles Boulevard. Mr. Meyers didn't attach any significance to it that night. It was just someone speeding in the neighborhood." A reporter asked how the incident fit in with the prosecution's timeline for the attack. "It doesn't," was the reply. "He said at 2:10. The alarm's not even deactivated yet. I think it's a desperate attempt to throw something unusual in the area on that day."

McDermott thought the veterinarian testimony had helped him and Rossi prove their case. "Yeah, he works in a job where he cleans up bloody messes. He's trained in how to do it and trained in how to protect himself, and that's the kind of protection he's trained to wear. It's an interesting component for why police weren't able to find blood in the Jeep."

McDermott criticized the defense's decision to have so many character witnesses testify. Then, he thanked the reporters and left the courthouse.

Kindlon was just as optimistic about how the day had gone. He said Meyers' testimony was significant. "Again, what you're seeing is a big juicy clue laid at the feet of the Bethlehem Police Department. And they thought it didn't match their theory so they kicked it aside."

A reporter asked about how it fit into the timeline – the timeline he maintained didn't exist because it was built on faulty assumptions. "I think it fits like a glove. If the timeline fits you must acquit – can I say that? Look, this extremely unusual event occurred at a very peculiar time, and (the witness) said, 'here's a piece of information,' and they said, 'OK, thanks a lot,' and slammed a door in his face...It could be whoever was driving that car was responsible for Peter's death. It could be it was someone on the way home from playing checkers. We don't know."

Kindlon called the audiotapes "distressing" and thought Dr. Dombovy's testimony created incredible doubt when it came to the meaning of Mrs. Porco's movements. He said the prosecution's insinuation that his client would have known how to clean up a crime scene was far-fetched. "Was there any indication anyone had cleaned anything up in the house? And the answer to that is no."

Christopher walked to his yellow Jeep and drove off.

Goshen, New York
August 8, 2007

Kindlon arrived at the courthouse early and gave more time than he usually did to reporters before he went inside. He said the defense team expected to wrap up with testimony from John Polster. Then he criticized the police for their investigation. "This cockeyed house of cards theory that the district attorneys and the Bethlehem Police have concocted in this lame effort to come up with some sort of a motive involves this theory where Christopher was spinning out of control. The reality is, there is no evidence of Christopher spinning out of control except in the malignant imaginations of the police. We're showing that his conduct right up until the time in question was perfectly normal, and right from the day in question was perfectly normal. I guess if you want to believe their theory, you have to believe he got psychotic for a couple of hours in the middle of the night."

He took the opportunity to remind reporters about the audiotapes that had been played the previous day. "They were disgusting. They were appalling. Yucking it up. 'Ha ha. Now we're in the big leagues.' You know? I wish we could play for you the tapes the judge wouldn't let the jury hear, because what they show is clearly a small-time, two-bit police department that is so far over its head it's just amazing that they didn't suffocate."

He said the other Bethlehem veterinarian, Elaine LaForte, would testify later. "Stay tuned. I want you to look forward to it. You're really going to enjoy it."

Kindlon couldn't help but criticize the prosecution's case once more before he headed in. "The DA has taken a football and has pasted feathers to it, and wants you to believe it's a duck. And it's not. It's a football with feathers on it. Our summation is going to point that out." He smiled at the thought, and left reporters to ponder what he had just said.

McDermott soon arrived for the morning interview. He was told Kindlon called the prosecution's case a football with feathers on it that they were calling a duck. "Terry said what?" asked a confused McDermott. "I'll think about that one and get back to you after lunch."

McDermott said they were considering one or two rebuttal witnesses after the defense rested, but nothing that would hold the trial up for more than 30 minutes or so. He said summations would last longer than normal because "we have seven weeks of material and we want to make sure we do it justice. We're trying to trim out what we can let out by the wayside and keep the important stuff. But even that is going to take awhile."

He reiterated he was confident in the strength of the case. "I think it's brick upon brick upon brick of circumstantial evidence that cannot be explained away. Christopher Porco was initially identified by his mother as the attacker; the police found it wasn't his brother, Johnathan, just like the Corporal said it wasn't Johnathan. Mrs. Porco said it wasn't Johnathan. Then they look at Christopher and every place they turn -" he said, letting everyone else finish the sentence for him. He felt good about the jury. "I think they got it. I think they got it. If they didn't get it all, they'll get it during summations."

The first witness's testimony was brief. Alexandra Hallock said she had met Joan years ago when they both had kids growing up. In August of 2004, she said she tried to call Joan to invite her to a get-together. She tried reaching her on the 18th, 19th, and 20th, but couldn't get a hold of her. She said the phone would ring and ring. When she finally did reach her friend, Mrs. Porco told Hallock that "the telephone box was tampered with." The witness said she remembered the conversation because "it's not normal."

Hallock said she talked with McDermott on December 14th, 2004 about the incident. He never returned her call, she said, but admitted that in January Detective Rinaldi spoke with her about the tampered box. On cross-examination she clarified that it was the box, and not wires, that had been the concern.

Richard Hanft replaced Hallock on the stand. He said he was an attorney. He knew Peter Porco through work, he said, and then got to the heart of the matter. Hanft told jurors there had been a case involving a dispute over the custody of children. In 1987 Judge Cardona had decided the couple involved in that battle would share custody. However, the husband made it clear he wanted the children taken away from his wife, apparently saying she should never see them again.

Hanft said Peter was the children's law guardian and was "a good lawyer and a very nice guy." He told the courtroom that the court proceedings dragged on, lasting into 1989 as the husband went through about a dozen lawyers. The case got into issues of house ownership, mortgage payments, and all the other tough stuff one might imagine was part of a two-year divorce proceeding. In the end Hanft said the man was not happy about Judge Cardona's ruling. He remembered getting a phone call from Peter in March of 1989. Peter told him the man had threatened his, the judge's, and Hanft's lives. Hanft dismissed it as "a lot of hot air."

Unfortunately, Hanft said, it didn't end there. Another attorney shared a recording of the man threatening to kill the three. The attorney told them "it should be taken very seriously." According to Hanft, the recording caught the man saying he was going to go to Kmart to get a gun and was going to "get that 'Guinea' Porco, and he was going to get that 'Guinea' Cardona too."

Hanft said he and Peter discussed pressing charges with the judge. Peter gave instructions to his wife to get out of the house and get the children and even asked for a sheriff's car to pass by the neighborhood. Both attorneys filed a criminal complaint, and the man eventually pleaded guilty at some point, according to the witness.

Hanft then jumped to November 15, 2004, when he received a phone call from Tina Brigham, a former secretary, who asked if he was OK. "Did you hear Peter Porco was murdered?" he said she asked, wondering if the man who had made the threat years ago had done it. Hanft said he called the Bethlehem Police to tell them the story, and said he would cooperate in any way. They took his name, number, and Social Security number. The witness said they never called him back.

Hanft said it didn't end there. Just before Election Day in 2004, there was "an incident with a character" who sounded a lot like the man who had made the threat. The attorney said he wasn't in the office at the time, but the whole ordeal stayed in his memory. Then, a few months later in 2005, Hanft said he had just finished a swim at the Troy YMCA when he saw the man. He looked angry, and walked right towards him. And then disappeared.

Judge Berry clarified for jurors that the testimony was not to show the threatening man may have committed the crime, but to show the police may not have followed up on what could have been a lead. Hanft stepped down.

The crowded courtroom watched John Polster give his name for the record, and then he took a seat. He explained who he was, where he worked, and how he knew Peter. "Peter was a great guy. He was a spectacular attorney. A very strong family man. He enjoyed his kids." Polster said his best friend had been a soccer coach and went to all the sports games to catch his children in action.

Polster said Peter didn't have a temper but he admitted during the last week of October that his friend expressed concern about his son. Peter was "rather upset with Christopher. He was mad. Very mad." Polster said he expressed his sympathy, but told the jurors he didn't think Peter was close to a breakdown.

Polster last spoke with Peter the Thursday afternoon before the attack. The Porcos and the Polsters had gone to New York City together in 2004, he said. He wanted to do it again, so they discussed some dates in November and December when they all might be able to make the trip. Polster characterized the conversation as "jovial," and said they decided they wanted to see the Statue of Liberty.

At around 2:45 Monday afternoon, Polster found out that Peter had been murdered. He said he left work, called his wife, and went home to meet up with her. On the way he said he listened to WGY, a local radio station, which he said was reporting police were looking for Christopher's yellow Jeep. Once at home he turned on the television. "Capital News 9 is the 24-hour local news station. It was their lead story."

Polster said he stayed at the hospital all day Tuesday and most of Wednesday. He told jurors he made it clear he was Joan's attorney because he wanted to make sure if she woke up, it was her memory of the events that would be explained and not what someone had told her. Polster said there had been a leak about the so-called DNA evidence about a week before the trial started. It upset Joan, and she declined to be interviewed by prosecutors. Polster stepped down.

The defense called Elaine LaForte as their final witness. The Bethlehem veterinarian had a small frame and a soft voice. She told Shanks, "Christopher has always been kind and caring." She said Porco lived with her and Dr. Kearney from the end of 2004 to the present day and added that she never noticed any violent behavior. She said she had also become close friends with Joan.

Shanks asked if any investigators had visited her after the attack.

She said Detective Arduini had come. "He told me" –

"Objection," said the prosecution.

The jury was dismissed for a few moments as the attorneys discussed with Judge Berry how far the Arduini discussion could go.

A few minutes later, the testimony continued. LaForte said Arduini had told her what had happened, and that he wanted Christopher's contact information. She said she gave him Christopher's Instant Message name. The detective asked if she knew anything about his yellow Jeep, or if he had been depressed or on drugs or alcohol. She said he still had the Jeep and told him Porco had no problems as far as she knew. The detective left, and she called Dr. Kearney to tell him what was happening.

Then she said she began to worry about Barrister. She drove to the police station later that night and asked Detective Rudolph if they could tell him when Porco returned. She said she was concerned because Christopher didn't have any parents at the time. She also picked up the Porco's pet. She said Barr was an older dog who didn't bark much – even at strangers. Barr likes to sit outside, she said, watching people and things go by.

After a few questions about surgeries at the animal hospital, LaForte told the courtroom that police never came back to talk with her.

At 3:20 in the afternoon, Kindlon and Shanks spoke with each other for a moment, and then told Judge Berry, "Your honor, the defense rests."

McDermott announced the prosecution had one witness for a rebuttal. Tina Brigham had worked at the law offices of Richard Hanft. She said around Election Day in 2004 a strange character had come inside. Police came to investigate, and she said the person was not the man who had made the threats against the three men those years back. Brigham then stepped down, both sides took their seats, and Judge Berry announced summations would begin tomorrow. Jurors would be charged in the afternoon, and he would allow them to deliberate until six at night.

Kindlon made one final motion to preclude Mrs. Porco's possible head nod from being allowed in as evidence because she couldn't be cross-examined on the matter as a result of her memory loss. The main question, he said, was whether she could be considered competent at the time she may have nodded. If she wasn't, it had to be thrown out.

Judge Berry denied the request. A dying testimonial is allowed in – even if the victim survives, he said.

Both sides didn't want to spend too much time talking with reporters because they knew they had a long night ahead of them to prepare for summations. McDermott said he had wanted Hanft's testimony about the threats to be barred. "It's the defense's hope to only show police didn't follow up the leads," he said, but "we already showed police did follow up on it. Ultimately they verified the whereabouts" of the man. "The fact that they don't get to investigate a threat from 15 years ago for three weeks I don't think is unreasonable…it's been established that (he was) alibi'd for the time that Mr. Porco was attacked. It defies common sense he would be back after 15 years."

But Kindlon said, "It's entirely possible he may have had something to do with this – at least as a matter to be investigated by police. We're not trying to prove the man is guilty, or that Frankie 'the Fireman' Porco is guilty, or that the two guys driving the cars at a high speed away from the residence at 2AM the day that Mr. Porco was killed are guilty. We can't do that because we don't have police forces…In the case of Mr. Hanft, they said, 'alright, thanks, see ya, goodbye.'"

Kindlon said there was "a failure of proof in this case," and left reporters to consider another of his Kindlonisms. "Under our way of doing things in the American Justice system, the ball is in their court, and it's just sitting there on the ground in their court and the air is all leaked out of it at this point."

Goshen, New York
August 9, 2006

"If police have a theory and they test it, and evidence comes back and they ignore it and they don't look for evidence, an innocent person's life can be lost." Laurie Shanks had just begun summing up the defense's contentions as jurors listened intently. Albany visitors packed the courtroom. Several dozen waited in line out in the hallway, hoping at some point to see the trial first-hand.

A freelance cameraman hired by 48 Hours ran a single camera set up in the public seating area. Wires ran from inside the courtroom to a small room just outside in the hallway. Reporters logged their sound bites from their edit machines in the cramped room.

Inside the courtroom the visitors sat in complete silence. "Did they look for all the evidence?" Shanks asked jurors. She described the murder scene and told jurors that Christopher's prior acts had nothing to do with the crime they were all here for. "This wasn't a burglary. This wasn't a theft," she said.

Shanks urged jurors to doubt the head nod. "There was no agreement on who found Mrs. Porco. There was no agreement on who did what. There was no agreement even on who asked her questions, how many were asked, and no agreement over hand gestures." The attorney said no one had asked Joan if she knew where she was or who she was. She paused for effect. "What there is agreement on is Joan was near death."

Shanks turned to her client, who seemed to be trying to smile. "Christopher gave his fingerprints just like other innocent people...we know with 100 percent certainty Christopher did not put his hand on the box where the cut (phone) wires were...They tested everyone they could think of who could have given that print, and it didn't match any of them." She reminded them that police had pursued her client, nonetheless.

Shanks next discussed the watches found in the bedroom with some mixture of DNA on one of them. "We know at least two male donors touched this watch, and it's not Christopher."

She then took on the role of an investigator as she spoke: "We'll just ignore it. It doesn't fit our conclusion, doesn't fit our theory," she said. She asked if the "stranger in the driveway" lead had been followed up on. She said the defense couldn't prove the man who made threats against Peter committed the crime or that Frankie "the Fireman" was involved, but it wasn't up to them to do so. "How can we not have a reasonable doubt," she asked, as Joan leaned forward in her courtroom seat.

Shanks said no one had ever tested the alarm system after the phone wires in the backyard were repaired. And she shared a much different timeline than what prosecutors had worked hard to build. She said investigators had only looked at the alarm system times to build their case. The attack could have happened at another time that didn't fit with the prosecution's theory, she said. She referenced a brief statement most hadn't caught earlier in the trial. She said a forensic pathologist who gave gruesome details of Peter's injuries put the victim's time of death at sometime between 1:30 and 6:30 on the morning of November 15, based on the condition of his body. Shanks said the Dr. believed Peter had survived several hours because of the amount of cell damage he found. Shanks said that meant it was possible if he had lived for four hours, for example, that the attack could have happened between 9:30PM and 1:30AM. The attorney reminded jurors that Christopher's friend said both he and Christopher were finishing up dinner at least three hours away in Rochester around that time.

Shanks put up another chart to show the fast food restaurants around the University of Rochester. She pointed out that a Dunkin Donuts cup - with liquid still inside – was found in the Jeep's cup holder. Shanks said investigators asked scores of students if Chris did drugs. "The only way a child could do this to a parent is if he was in a drug-induced rage, and every student said no."

She continued. "The nature of the crime suggests this was one of rage – a professional killer who could do this and walk away." Shanks said the e-mails proved nothing because any parent stressed about finances would likely have had a similar discussion with their kid. And the last e-mails all stated the issues would be resolved. They'd meet over Thanksgiving break.

She brought up the yellow Jeep that was sitting out in the parking lot as she spoke. When Marshall Gokey was shown a picture of it with crime scene tape on it, "he said, 'Oh yeah, I've seen that before.'" She looked at the jurors and asked, "Can any of you remember what you saw in your neighborhood this morning?"

Shanks next attacked the prosecution's motive. "It's just silly he'd want to kill or maim his parents for money…Chris was a lot better off financially with his parents alive than dead."

She next pointed out "there's no physical evidence tying Christopher to this scene." Then, she asked a question and waited a moment so it could sink in. "What if - at the end of the trial - we just don't know who did it?"

She told jurors they didn't need to share the same reasonable doubt – they just had to have reasonable doubt to let her client go free. She reminded them of the watch she said was left behind in bed, the alarm system, the e-mails, and how police hadn't followed up on leads. "Chris' life will now be in your hands."

In all, Shanks had taken about two hours for the defense's summation. McDermott would take about the same amount of time for the prosecution. In the meantime, a few people left their courtroom seats to stretch their legs, and people who had been waiting outside the courtroom quickly filled them.

McDermott began by outlining the questions the jury had to answer – namely, did Christopher Porco cause the death of his father and intend to cause the death of his mother early one morning back in 2004.

"The house had been secured with an alarm, deadbolts, and broomsticks in the sliding door." As he said those words, a picture of Peter Porco's bloody, slumped over body flashed up on the wall. The crowd in the courtroom let out an audible gasp. McDermott spoke about Mrs. Porco, explaining that her head nod proved she was aware of what had happened. "She was using her fingers to tell who committed this crime." He paraphrased the questions she was asked – questions with answers that investigators believe pointed right to Christopher. The prosecutor raised his voice slightly and pointed towards the defense table where Christopher Porco was sitting calmly, showing little emotion as he jotted the occasional note. "All answers indicate that man, right there, was responsible – Christopher Porco."

Before summations began Kindlon said he had talked with his client about the tough days ahead. He said Christopher had been doing as well as could be expected for a young man accused of murdering his parents. He felt Christopher was as ready as he could be to be pointed at and called a killer.

"This was the most horrific crime not only in Delmar, but in Albany County," McDermott continued. "'Where's Christopher Porco?' turned out to be a complicated question." He said Marshall Crumiller was the last to see Porco that night, and clarified that it took a yearlong investigation involving hundreds of leads and hundreds of interviews to reach the conclusion that Christopher had done it. "There was no rush to judgment."

The prosecutor said Porco told four of his frat brothers he was sleeping in the lounge that night. One of them, Matt Ambrosio, pleaded with Christopher when everyone had heard what happened to his parents, McDermott said. Then, the prosecutor pretended to be the student: "Dude, please, just tell me where you were Sunday into the morning. Anywhere. 'Cause I didn't see you in the hall until next morning." He reminded the jury that Tisha Abrams said she didn't see him there either. No one saw him there.

He discussed the issue of where the blood had gone if Christopher had committed the murder and jumped in his Jeep as the prosecution believed. "All of the blood is away from the assailant," he explained. "If you're swinging the ax back and forth, you'll get droplets but there's none of that...And the assailant had the benefit of a room full of clothes. He lives there." The prosecutor said the timeline put Christopher in the house for two hours and 40 minutes – and this was someone used to bloody messes.

Christopher also had the master code. "The only people with the code are Peter, and he's dead; his mother, who was attacked; Johnathan, who is in the Navy; and Chris." McDermott took a moment to make eye contact with a few jurors, then he raised his voice. "Using the master code is like leaving your wallet at the crime scene."

He said the killer knew where the spare key was, and that the only window with a cut screen just happened to be the one that wasn't hooked up to the alarm system. It wasn't the first time there was a cut screen, either.

Of all the places where police dusted for fingerprints they found one on the downstairs door. McDermott said Christopher put it there as he shut his dog in the basement so he could commit the grisly act.

He briefly explained away the mixture of DNA found on the "extra" watch in bed as normal for something that had casual contact with other things and people. "The killer spared the family pet, the killer staged a break-in...Nothing was taken. Despite all the computers and crystal, the valuable property was still there."

McDermott then spoke to the jurors about the gas left in the Jeep. The only thing that would explain how much fuel remained in Christopher's fuel tank, he said, was if "Chris Porco did a substantial amount of driving after he got back to the University of Rochester."

He criticized the defense's DNA witness, Dr. Shields, and mentioned the witness had been involved with the O.J Simpson and Scott Peterson cases, and had disagreed with prosecutors in both cases.

Kindlon shot up from his seat. "Objection!" he yelled.

Berry quickly announced it was a good time for everyone to take a break. Jurors left through the back.

"I motion for a mistrial," said Kindlon. It seemed he was ready and willing for a fight. Bringing up other well-known cases and connecting their verdicts with testimony to a current case made for a complicated legal situation.

Judge Berry said he would reserve judgment, meaning a mistrial might be granted at a later time. It was a message to prosecutors to be more careful, said Paul Der Ohannesian, an Albany attorney who had commented on and followed the proceedings closely.

McDermott explained he felt the comment he made wasn't out of bounds because it was in the record that Dr. Shields had testified in those cases and that he mostly worked with defense teams.

Jurors returned moments later. Judge Berry told them Mr. McDermott was "admonished for making that remark." Shanks later said she was startled when she heard it and said she hoped it was just because he was tired.

Either way, McDermott continued with a discussion of the toll tickets, which gave Porco just over three hours to travel one-way. He dismissed the idea that investigators had only looked for the yellow Jeep at certain times of day. "Every hour on every tape was reviewed until past 8:30AM," he said.

He reminded jurors about the e-mails. "The house of cards is starting to unravel," he said. "Peter Porco is finding out about the deceit." McDermott almost poked fun at the last e-mail Porco sent to his parents, saying it was only a ruse. "Give my love to mom, love Chris…I can't get a hold of you guys."

The Chief ADA said the Porco's neighbor, Marshall Gokey, not only put Christopher's Jeep in the driveway, but he also put it there at the time of the attack.

McDermott spoke for about two hours. Towards the end he explained Mrs. Porco's head nod could be used as direct evidence if a juror believed it to be credible. If one did, he or she could convict based on that possibility alone. But he said there was also plenty of circumstantial evidence that could lead them to the same conclusion.

"Mr. Porco is either guilty, or he is the unluckiest man on the planet," McDermott said emphatically. Joan vehemently shook her head while sitting between family and friends who supported both her and Christopher.

"Use your common sense and judgment, and if you do, you will return a verdict of guilty on both counts." McDermott sat down.

Judge Berry thanked both defense attorneys and prosecutors. He told jurors they were to arrive the following morning at 8:45 when they would be read detailed legal instructions on how to proceed. After that, they would decide Porco's fate.

Goshen, New York
August 10, 2006

Attorneys arrived early. Reporters arrived earlier. Christopher Porco arrived dressed in a sharp looking dark suit. He walked inside as Laurie spoke with reporters. No one knew it would be the last day for the morning interview ritual. Both sides tried to calm down the rhetoric as the case left their hands.

"Probably the most awesome responsibility you can have as a lawyer is to represent an innocent person," said Shanks. "And you always say to yourself, 'have we done enough? Is there anything we could have or should have done?' Hopefully we'll have done enough. We'll know when the jury wants us to know."

McDermott stopped for a brief chat as well. "Today is the day the jury gets the case. It's the most important day of all." After jurors heard his summation, he said he wanted them to come away with "a clear understanding of how each piece of circumstantial evidence fits together."

Inside the waiting game began. Judge Berry charged the jury for several hours. White sheets of paper taped to the outside of the courtroom doors warned people not to enter. Anyone who had been inside once the instructions began was not allowed to leave. The television screens inside the media room just outside the courtroom showed nothing, at least for now. The camera inside had been turned off until the jury reached a verdict.

Around lunchtime the doors opened, and reporters who sat through the charge were happy to be let out. Attorneys left the courtroom as well. Shanks reiterated her near disbelief that it all came down to this. "We've been involved with this case for two years," she told cameras from every local news station. "I think the jurors were extremely attentive. I've felt that way since day one. I've been very impressed with them. They take notes. They pay attention. They get here on time."

Kindlon also answered a question on how Christopher was doing. "Christopher is just going to have to be stoic as he's been from the start here. And we'll have to wait and see what happens. There's probably nothing less pleasant for a criminal defendant or his lawyers than waiting out a jury. It's a little bit like being the recipient of a mortar attack, or a root canal without anesthetic. It's not fun. It's a tough time for everyone." A reporter asked him for a prediction, but he balked: "The sun will come up tomorrow."

He said Joan was in the worst position of all. "Mrs. Porco is not only the strongest woman I've ever met, she's also the unluckiest. She lost her husband, her life is blown apart, her son is a murder defendant whose fate is about to be decided by a jury. It doesn't get more difficult than that."

McDermott agreed and said just like everyone else, he had no idea when the case would be decided, especially after it had lasted for seven weeks. "I'm not going to begin to guess. I'm not going to speculate. They have a lot to go through. I wouldn't be surprised if it takes them awhile." Neither the prosecutors nor the defense attorneys would even take a guess at what the verdict might be if it came quickly - or took days. But McDermott admitted he was ready for whatever jurors decided. "It's been a long, drawn out affair. It really has. I'm glad it's over. There were a lot of logistical problems that consumed our time rather than being able to spend a lot of time on legal work." He said he wished the trial had stayed in Albany and that some of the barred evidence had been allowed in.

Although he had declined to say anything before, Bethlehem Police Chief Lou Corsi traveled to Orange County and wanted to set the record straight. He was waiting like everyone else for the verdict and felt it was time to respond to the intense criticism his department had taken from the defense team. "This was more than a personal attack," he said.

"We had a job to do and we were focused on that job. Not on the banter back and forth."

The attorneys on both sides left the courthouse, not wanting to wait around for a verdict that might not come for some time. Once jurors made a decision, both sides would get a phone call anyway.

Which is exactly what happened at 1:45 in the afternoon. It took a few minutes for everyone to assemble in court. Once they did, the jury entered. They requested pictures of the area around the Porco home and the house itself, including the windows, the basement, the alarm system, and the telephone poll in the backyard. Judge Berry told them they would have access to the evidence right away.

No one tried to read the jurors' minds. The issues related to each of the pictures were too numerous. But at 2:20, the jury returned.

"We, the jury, request testimony from Kurt Meyer from Time Warner Security," the forewoman said. "Plus People's exhibit 180 and 184, plus the alarm system event buffer."

Jurors sat as the court reporter read a transcript of David Rossi's direct examination of Meyer. It was a discussion of how the alarm system worked, as well as what codes did what. Meyer had said the event buffer kept track of when the alarm was turned on or off, or had its clock changed. He said that timeline was intact, even though the phone line in the back had been cut and the alarm system's keypad had been smashed. The testimony stated that at 6:17PM on the 14th, the alarm was disarmed. At 9:54PM it was armed until 2:14AM on the 15th when someone had entered the master code into the system. Only a few moments before five in the morning, the alarm registered a problem with the telephone line as the voltage dropped.

Jurors returned to their back room. McDermott was cautious not to read too much into the first read-back. "I think the alarm system is critical. I'm not sure what they were looking for. I'm assuming they wanted to make sure punching the alarm code and breaking the faceplate wouldn't affect the alarm system."

Shanks seemed slightly more optimistic, but she wasn't making any predictions either. "I think that when I mentioned in closing arguments they had never tested the alarm system, you know, they planned their whole case around it being accurate, literally to the minute. And they never even tested it to see - one - if it was accurate and - two - if it was working."

After more waiting around, word came that the jury wanted to rehear more testimony, or scrutinize another piece of evidence. Some had to know that this time it was different, but the rumors and confusion couldn't be stopped. Because it was approaching dinnertime, a couple reporters joked that perhaps the jury wanted to place a food order. Dozens filed into the courtroom. Christopher took a seat next to his attorneys. Court officers lined the room. The 48 Hours freelance cameraman walked in and fired up his camera. Journalists tried to call their news organizations, but the court officers asked them to shut their cell phones off. The jurors walked in and found their seats. They didn't make eye contact with a single person.

Judge Berry announced the jury had reached a verdict. "Will the defendant stand with his attorneys please?"

They stood. Christopher Porco was stoic, just as Kindlon had said. Judge Berry told the courtroom he didn't want any outbursts, no matter what the decision was.

A woman began reading a statement. "The People of the State of New York against Christopher Porco. Count one. Murder in the second degree. What's your verdict?"

"Guilty," the jury forewoman said.

"Count two. Attempted murder in the second degree. What's your verdict?"

"Guilty."

Porco showed little reaction, staying calm, just as Judge Berry had asked. His ears turned bright red.

"Was that verdict unanimous?" asked Judge Berry.

"Yes, it was."

The judge went through a brief discussion of legal matters as a court officer placed handcuffs around Porco's wrists. Shanks rubbed his back. The judge told the defense team he would not be granting their motion for a mistrial and said he wouldn't rush them on the expected and usual motion to set aside the verdict.

As the judge spoke, there was pandemonium outside the courtroom. Reporters ran through the courtroom doors – some not even sure where they were going. Several spoke quickly on their cell phones so websites could be updated. Others dashed down the long hallway and out the doors to go live. A group of girls – Christopher's friends – cried loudly as they held hands and ran from the courtroom.

Jurors had deliberated fewer than six hours.

EPILOGUE

Joan Porco missed the verdict. Defense attorneys said they hadn't expected it to come so quickly. Some thought perhaps they were simply protecting her, but Kindlon said they had told her that she could rest at the hotel down the street where she had been staying because jurors couldn't possibly have reached a decision so soon.

Almost immediately after the verdict, Kindlon's assistant and one of Christopher's friends raced to the hotel to offer their support. The two ladies spoke with Mrs. Porco in a hallway off the main lobby. They held hands and shared their concerns. A reporter who left the courthouse found the three and apologized to Mrs. Porco for all she had been through. He asked how she was taking the news. In her soft voice, she said, "I'm very upset. That's all I can say right now."

Cameras back at the courthouse caught Porco being placed in an Albany County Sheriff's vehicle. Several reporters yelled questions at him, but he didn't respond. Others tried to chase down the jurors who had been let out. A few would talk as long as cameras weren't in their face; some wanted nothing to do with the crazy scene and asked for time to think about what they had just gone through.

Just outside the courtroom Kindlon stopped for the crush of cameras assembled around him. "We are deeply disappointed. This is obviously a crushing blow for our client and a terrible disappointment to his attorneys. Needless to say, we intend to file an appeal in this case. We're told we have the transcripts so we can begin working on that immediately. This was a terrible, terrible disappointment."

After taking a few more questions, he offered a brief olive branch to investigators and prosecutors. "Obviously the DA's office and the State Police and Bethlehem Police Department spent a huge amount of time and money on this and brought an incredible wealth of talent to this case, and obviously it worked with this jury…It was a very quick verdict, and we are very surprised. It actually intensifies our disappointment." He called the change in venue and the suppression of the interrogation significant. Then, he walked with his wife to their car.

Outside by the media tents, McDermott spoke with a Capital News 9 reporter on live television. "It's not a time to crow," he said. "It's a very sad affair. I mean, I feel terrible for Mrs. Porco. Peter's dead. Mrs. Porco – I'm not sure where she's going to go from here. I don't take any joy in increasing her misery. I do feel, however, that justice was served. Christopher Porco obviously did this, and he should be off the street."

McDermott said he didn't think any appeal would survive scrutiny. "Judge Berry gave more breaks in my opinion to the defense and excluded a lot of evidence. I think if the Appellate Court looks at the record - and I'm sure they will - they'll find that Judge Berry was very fair. The defense got most of the benefits." McDermott said he was heading back to Albany, but would also help pack up the office of the District Attorney's makeshift planning room.

Detective Bowdish also spoke for the first time with the same reporter on live TV, happy with the verdict. He said he finally felt vindicated. "We followed all leads to the very end. We had 444 leads, and whenever there was another person's name that was given to us, we followed it right to the point where we eliminated or alibi'd that person. We got to the point where there was no other suspect. I know what we did was correct."

Within just a couple hours the attorneys had left, and Christopher was on his way to the Albany County Correctional Facility. The news crews packed up their tents, rolled up their wires, and filed their last reports from outside the courthouse.

Cars left one by one, emptying the large parking lot, leaving Porco's yellow Jeep in the middle of the pavement with nothing but empty spaces surrounding it.

*

About a month later, 48 Hours turned Brockley Drive into a production studio. The street was blocked off at night as film crews recreated parts of the murder scene inside and out. Just before Halloween they aired the special they called, "Memory of Murder." In it, Christopher gave his only on-the-record on-camera interview since, reiterating that he would never kill or try to kill his parents. A handful of willing jurors spoke at the end of the program. They discussed how Mrs. Porco's supposed head nod had nothing to do with their decision to convict her son. Instead, they said the timeline fit like a glove.

On December 12, 2006, Christopher Porco, his attorneys, and prosecutors came to the Albany County Courthouse for sentencing. Before Judge Berry decided how many years Christopher should remain in prison, Peter's sister, Patty, was allowed to read her impact statement to the court. She told everyone how her family would never be able to escape their memories of that November day. "We had once been a happy group of 12 gathered for holidays and summer vacations for the last two decades, but we are now a small band of survivors of murder and our time together is overshadowed by our unspeakable grief. Our loss is massive, and the circumstances of that loss are impossible to fathom…Although it crossed my mind that I might outlive my brother, it never entered my thinking that he would be ripped away from me at midlife and in such a horrific manner. I am so angry that my future with my brother has been taken away, and especially that after giving years of his life for others, he did not get to live out his own dreams and potential.

"It is hard for me to accept that Peter is gone forever. His absence from my life is staggering. I will never again hear his cheerful voice on the phone, or exchange silly e-mails with him. We will never go on a trip together again, or meet for dinner, or celebrate a holiday or milestone together. I will never again be able to confide in him or seek his counsel or count on his support in times of need. We have been robbed of the chance to grow older together."

Peter's mother, Jane, who wasn't able to attend, had asked that McDermott read a letter she wrote: "I depended on Peter for his always good advice, loving understanding, and wonderful hugs. I am very proud of his achievements but am most proud of the man he had grown to be."

"I do not fully understand what happened to my grandson, and I hope and I pray that he can be cured, but unless that happens he must not be allowed to kill again."

Joan Porco also read a statement, asking for leniency for her son in her soft voice. "I cannot accept that Christopher could have – or would have – chosen to butcher us in any conceivable way, for any conceivable reason. Christopher is the product of a loving and supportive family."

"I know that Christopher has made some unfortunate decisions in his life, but Jesus Christ said that the man without sin should throw the first stone. Christopher has spoken, and shown his remorse for his indiscretions…I know my son, and he could not have committed these very violent acts. And I wish the court to continue to find the person or people who did this to us."

Mrs. Porco asked for concurrent sentences for her son, which would allow him to get out of prison earlier than a consecutive sentence. "Please allow Christopher the opportunity to attain freedom in my lifetime. I believe him to be innocent with all my heart. Please give him a chance to use his talents to make a significant contribution to society. Please give him the chance to be home with me in his lifetime, and in my lifetime."

Kindlon stood and asked for leniency as well. There was no prior criminal history, he said, and added that he believed his client to be innocent.

Then Christopher stood and spoke to the courtroom, reading a prepared statement. "I will be the first to admit that I made some mistakes in my life, and I have certainly done things that I am not proud of. I was not always honest with my friends and family. And my desire for people to view me in a positive light at times overcame who I actually was. A minor dispute between my father and me was taken completely out of context and then multiplied by the police and the prosecution because they needed to invent a reason why a person who has never been violent his entire life would randomly decide one day to partake in unspeakable destruction of life.

"If my desire to absolve my parents of the financial burden of college was my only intention, I only wish that I had been more up front with my mom and dad about it. My family has done nothing but cooperate in an attempt to help police and the DA's office for the past two years. I have freely given DNA, fingerprints, clothing, and hours of my time in an attempt to aid the authorities. All that we have received in return is contempt and a complete lack of interest to any information that did not fit the theory that the police created minutes after this case began.

"Unbridled media leaks by the police and the DA's office have been a direct attempt to paint me as an evil person and my family as dysfunctional. These lies perpetuate to this day and what saddens me is the public still does not know much about this case that I feel resembles the truth. Ultimately, I have faith in the system that my father held so dear. I am confident that with time, wrongs will be righted. But I hold no illusions that there will ever be true justice for my mom and my dad - or my family as a whole. Any possible chance the police had of catching the true perpetrators evaporated long ago.

"Crimes are not solved by plucking a motive out of a cloud of conjecture and half-truths and attempting to shape pieces of the puzzle so they all fit together. By caving in to public pressure to hold the most convenient suspect responsible, the police deprived all of us of the justice we are entitled to.

"My father was taken from all of our lives, but the man he was and the legacy he left will always be with those who were touched by his life. I miss my dad so much and my heart aches for my mom, who is the strongest person that I will ever know. Despite her horrible treatment by the authorities, despite all of her physical and emotional anguish that she has suffered over the past two years, she has kept an aura of love and contentment that has helped me carry on day to day. My mother has been cast as naïve and irrelevant by the police, but she knows her family above all else. Only because she told the truth did the police ignore and discount her words. I worry about her constantly, but I am confident that she will be OK living without her sons and husband nearby day by day. My only wish is to join her soon.

"I was never able to say goodbye to my dad before he was taken from us. The idea that he was disappointed in me before he died will always haunt me. We can never know when our time is going to come, but I know that my dad is with all of us now. Even though I can't hug him and tell him face to face, he knows that I love him. The pain and anger that I feel over what has happened to my parents is only surpassed by the love that I have for both of them. I cannot fathom hurting any person, let alone my parents, in this way. And for me it is enough that every person important in my life knows that. Thanks."

Judge Berry thanked Christopher, and told him he was a very intelligent person. He said he would not set aside the verdict, and felt Christopher had received a fair trial. "It is without a doubt (your mother) has no memory of the events which occurred in the early morning hours of November 2004. It's very understandable that she is upset with the system. It is very understandable to me that she feels the police didn't do enough. That's because it would be the most difficult thing in the world for a parent to believe that their child - who she gave birth to and raised and took care of – would be capable of being the perpetrator of these violent, heinous acts…

"When I sentence you today, I just want you to understand that all sentences that I impose, I never permit myself to get angry or upset or things like that, because quite obviously, if I did that, then I would be abdicating my job to be a fair and impartial jurist. However, in sentencing you today, I've got to explain to you and make you understand that the sentence that's being imposed upon you is a sentence because I fear very much that what happened in the early morning hours of November of 2004 is something that could happen again."

Judge Berry sentenced Christopher Porco to the maximum 50 years to life in prison.

*

The total cost of the trial to Albany County, according to the comptroller's office, came to $206,010.43. If there is an appeal, officials say the overall cost would likely rise significantly because Christopher Porco is now considered indigent and would need public funds to help pay for his continued defense. His various possessions have already been sold.

Kindlon still promises an appeal that, as of publication, has not been made. He says he is looking at a number of issues, but won't elaborate.

Michael McDermott is now practicing law with the prestigious Albany law firm, O'Connell and Aronowitz. He is part of a team pursuing lead poisoning cases, and in 2007 settled one of the largest such cases in upstate New York history.

David Rossi continues his work with the District Attorney's Office, prosecuting some of the more high-profile local cases in Albany County.

Laurie Shanks no longer practices criminal law, but continues to teach at Albany Law School.

Terence Kindlon continues to be involved with some of the biggest cases in the Capital Region.

Before the 48 Hours crew shot their special on Brockley Drive, Mrs. Porco sold the house she and Peter had lived in. She moved to the Rochester area to be with family, but has since returned to the Capital Region.

Christopher Porco is serving his sentence at the Clinton Correctional Facility in upstate New York. He says he is innocent.

About the Author

Steve Ference is an award winning television news reporter who lives in New York's Capital Region, covering the top stories for the local 24-hour news channel. He covered the Christopher Porco case extensively, filing live and recorded reports for radio and television several times a day - each day - during the trial.

Steve graduated from Ithaca College with a degree in both Politics and Broadcast Journalism. He got his start in Hartford, Connecticut, at the CBS affiliate where he helped to cover the Michael Skakel (Kennedy Cousin) murder trial. He also worked in Washington, DC, and reported for the NBC station in Savannah, Georgia, covering military deployments and various local news stories. In Albany he has reported on everything from state politics, to the so-called Albany "Terrorism Trial" in Federal Court.

Steve thanks his father for all his editing help, as well as attorney Paul Der Ohannesian for his constant insight, suggestions, and perspective.

Most of all, he would like to thank his wife for her patience, help, and support.

He would also like to thank Jim Cuozzo from the local Spotlight Newspapers. His help throughout the trial was invaluable. He also thanks the District Attorney's office, including Michael McDermott, the Bethlehem Police Department, New York State Police, as well as Terence Kindlon and Laurie Shanks, and all the others who – even through the most difficult of moments - opened up in the hope of getting at the truth.

BIBLIOGRAPHY

CHAPTER I

Cannazzaro, Julia. Court Testimony. Orange County Courthouse, Goshen, NY. 19 July 2006.
Hart, Michael. Court Testimony. Orange County Courthouse, Goshen, NY. 29 June 2006.
Bowdish, Christopher. Court Testimony. Albany County Courthouse, Albany, NY. 18 May 2006.
Bowdish, Christopher. Court Testimony. Orange County Courthouse, Goshen, NY. 26 July 2006.
Bowdish, Christopher. Live interview. 8 August 2006.
The People of the State of New York v. Christopher Porco. Ind. No. DA848/05. Sworn Affidavit. Exhibit D. Christopher Bowdish. 13 November 2006.
Bowdish, Christopher. "Dear Tony Pemezopto." 12 May 2005. Letter.
Wood, Dennis. Court Testimony. Albany County Courthouse, Albany, NY. 18 May 2006.
Wood, Dennis. Court Testimony. Orange County Courthouse, Goshen, NY. 29 June 2006.
The People of the State of New York v. Christopher Porco. Ind. No. DA848/05. Sworn Affidavit. Exhibit B. Dennis Wood. 11 November 2006.
Robert, Kevin. Court Testimony. Albany County Courthouse, Albany, NY. 18 May 2006.
Robert, Kevin. Court Testimony. Orange County Courthouse, Goshen, NY. 29 June 2006.
The People of the State of New York v. Christopher Porco. Ind. No. DA848/05. Sworn Affidavit. Exhibit A. Kevin Robert. 13 November 2006.
McDonald, Drew. Court Testimony. Orange County Courthouse, Goshen, NY. 5 July 2006.
Balzano, John. Court Testimony. Albany County Courthouse, Albany, NY. 16 May 2006.
Balzano, Barbara. Court Testimony. Orange County Courthouse, Goshen, NY. 17 July 2006.
Bethlehem Police Department. BOLO. 15 November 2004.
Noone, Father David. Court Testimony. Albany County Courthouse, Albany, NY. 16 May 2006.
The People of the State of New York v. Christopher Porco. Ind. No. DA848/05. Sworn Affidavit. Exhibit F. David Noone. 13 April 2006.
The People of the State of New York v. Christopher Porco. Ind. No. DA845/05. Sworn Affidavit. Chief Assistant District Attorney Michael P. McDermott. 1 May2006.
The People of the State of New York v. Christopher Porco. Ind. No. DA848/05. Sworn Affidavit. Exhibit G. Kenneth Gregory. 14 April 2006.
The People of the State of New York v. Christopher Porco. Ind. No. DA848/05. Medical Records. Exhibit C. 15 November 2004.
The People of the State of New York v. Christopher Porco. Ind. No. DA848/05. Sworn Affidavit. Defense Exhibit. Christopher Porco. 17 April 2006.
Polster, John. Court Testimony. Albany County Courthouse, Albany, NY. 17 May 2006.
The People of the State of New York v. Christopher Porco. Ind. No. DA848/05. Sworn Affidavit. Defense Exhibit. John R. Polster. 17 April 2006.
The People of the State of New York v. Christopher Porco. Ind. No. DA 848/05. Defense Exhibit. Bethlehem Police Interview with Christopher Porco. Audio Transcription. M.L.S. Transcription Associates, Inc. 15 November 2004. 2, 3, 23.
Carter, Lt. Steven. Court Testimony. Orange County Courthouse, Goshen, NY. 7 July 2006.
Porco, Johnathan. Court Testimony. Orange County Courthouse, Goshen, NY. 24 July 2006.
Polster, John. Court Testimony. Albany County Courthouse, Albany, NY. 17 May 2006.
The People of the State of New York v. Christopher Porco. Ind. No. DA 848/05. Defense Exhibit. Bethlehem Police Interview with Christopher Porco. Audio Transcription. M.L.S. Transcription Associates, Inc. 15 November 2004. 207, 211-212, 217-218.

CHAPTER II

Porco, Peter. Personal E-mail. 10 January 2004. Times Union. TimesUnion.com.
Porco, Joan. Personal E-mail. 14 January 2004. Times Union. TimesUnion.com.
Porco, Christopher. Personal E-mail. 16 January 2004. Times Union. TimesUnion.com.
Various Capital News 9 Reports.
Crumiller, Marshall. Court Testimony. Orange County Courthouse, Goshen, NY. 17 July 2006.
Abrams, Tisha. Court Testimony. Orange County Courthouse, Goshen, NY. 17 July 2006.
Novak, Jason. Court Testimony. Orange County Courthouse, Goshen, NY. 17 July 2006.
Culverwell, Eric. Court Testimony. Orange County Courthouse, Goshen, NY. 17 July 2006.
Whiteside, Gregory. Court Testimony. Orange County Courthouse, Goshen, NY. 17 July 2006.
Bowdish, Christopher. Court Testimony. Albany County Courthouse, Albany, NY. 18 May 2006.
Bowdish, Christopher. Court Testimony. Orange County Courthouse, Goshen, NY. 26 July 2006.
McDonald, Drew. Court Testimony. Orange County Courthouse, Goshen, NY. 5 July 2006.
McDermott, Michael. Court Testimony. Orange County Courthouse, Goshen, NY. 28 June 2006.
Meyer, Kurt. Court Testimony. Orange County Courthouse, Goshen, NY. 5 July 2006.
Cotsworth, Michael. Court Testimony. Orange County Courthouse, Goshen, NY. 6 July 2006.
Radliff, Charles. Court Testimony. Orange County Courthouse, Goshen, NY. 29 June 2006.

CHAPTER III

Porco, Peter. Personal E-mail. 19 March 2004. Times Union. TimesUnion.com.
Porco, Christopher. Personal E-mail. 20 March 2004. Times Union. TimesUnion.com.

Briana Tice. Court Testimony. Orange County Courthouse, Goshen, NY. 29 June 2006.
Audio Recordings. Town of Bethlehem Police Department. Played in Orange County Courthouse, Goshen, NY. August 7 2006.
Polster, John. Court Testimony. Orange County Courthouse, Goshen, NY. 8 August, 2006.
Polster, Linda. Court Testimony. Orange County Courthouse, Goshen, NY. 2 August 2006.
Sig Epsilon New York. Website. http://www.sigepnyxi.com/chapterinfo.shtml
Crumiller, Marshall. Court Testimony. Orange County Courthouse, Goshen, NY. 17 July 2006.
Capital News 9. Various reports 21 December 2004 – 5 May 2006.
Porco, Joan M. Times Union. Letter to the Editor. 23 August 2005. The Times Union. www.TimesUnion.com. Porco E-mails. 18 November 2005.
Kindlon, Terence. Opening Statement. Orange County Courthouse, Goshen, NY. 28 June 2006.
Porco, Joan M. Letter to Judge Jeffrey Berry. 13 November 2005.
Porco, Johnathan D. Letter to Judge Jeffrey Berry. 13 November 2005.

CHAPTER IV

Capital News 9. Various reports. 7 March 2006 – May 2006.
Corsi, Lou. Bethlehem Police Chief. Public Statement. 30 March 2006.
The People of the State of New York v. Christopher Porco. Ind. No. DA845/05. Sworn Affidavit. John Dalfino, M.D. 27 April 2006.
The People of the State of New York v. Christopher Porco. Ind. No. DA848/05. "Memorandum of Law Regarding the Admissibility of Communications Had Between Joan Porco and Members of the Bethlehem Police Department and Albany County Paramedics at 36 Brockley Drive on November 15, 2004." 17 April 2006.
The People of the State of New York v. Christopher Porco. Ind. No. DA848/05. "Molineaux/Ventimiglia Application." 17 April 2006.
Lyons, Brendan. "Porco defense to key on tape." Times Union. 19 April 2006.
The People of the State of New York v. Christopher Porco. Ind. No. DA848/05. "Memorandum of Law in Support of Defendant's Motion to Suppress Statements." 17 April 2006.
The People of the State of New York v. Christopher Porco. Ind. No. DA848/05. Sworn Affidavit. Exhibit F. David Noone. 13 April 2006.
The People of the State of New York v. Christopher Porco. Ind. No. DA848/05. Sworn Affidavit. 17 April 2006.
Corsi, Lou. Bethlehem Police Chief. Public Statement. 11 May 2006.
Kindlon, Terence. Interview. 19 April 2006.
McDermott, Michael. Interview. 19 April 2006.
Egan, Terri. Interview. 12 May 2006.

CHAPTER V

Porco, Joan. Personal E-mail. 1 September 2004. Times Union. TimesUnion.com.
Porco, Christopher. Personal E-mail. 2 September 2004. Times Union. TimesUnion.com.
Balzano, John. Court Testimony. Albany County Judicial Center, Albany, New York. 16 May 2006.
Noon, David. Court Testimony. Albany County Judicial Center, Albany, New York. 16 May 2006.
Ruby, Mary Louise. Court Testimony. Albany County Judicial Center, Albany, New York. 16 May 2006.
Berben, Robert. Court Testimony. Albany County Judicial Center, Albany, New York. 16 May 2006.
Kindlon, Terence. Interview. 16 May 2006.
McDermott, Michael. Interview. 16 May 2006.
Rudolph, Charles. Court Testimony. Albany County Judicial Center, Albany, New York. 17 May 2006.
Bowdish, Christopher. Court Testimony. Albany County Judicial Center, Albany, New York. 17 May 2006.
Polster, John. Court Testimony. Albany County Judicial Center, Albany, New York. 17 May 2006.
Interrogation Transcript. Bethlehem Police Department. 15 November 2006. Page 23.
Interrogation Transcript. Bethlehem Police Department. 15 November 2006. Page 208.
Kindlon, Terence. Interview. 17 May 2006.
McDermott, Michael. Interview. 17 May 2006.
Polster, John. Court Testimony. Albany County Judicial Center, Albany, New York. 18 May 2006.
McDermott, Michael. Court Testimony. Albany County Judicial Center, Albany, New York. 18 May 2006.
Rossi, David. Court Testimony. Albany County Judicial Center, Albany, New York. 18 May 2006.
Baynes, Christopher. Court Testimony. Albany County Judicial Center, Albany, New York. 18 May 2006.
Robert, Kevin. Court Testimony. Albany County Judicial Center, Albany, New York. 18 May 2006.
Court Testimony. Albany County Judicial Center, Albany, New York. 18 May 2006.
Wood, Dennis. Court Testimony. Albany County Judicial Center, Albany, New York. 18 May 2006.
Helligrass, Robert. Court Testimony. Albany County Judicial Center, Albany, New York. 18 May 2006.
Bowdish, Christopher. Court Testimony. Albany County Judicial Center, Albany, New York. 18 May 2006.
Kindlon, Terence. Interview. 18 May 2006.
McDermott, Michael. Interview. 18 May 2006.

CHAPTER VI

Porco, Christopher. Personal E-mail. 15 September 2004. Times Union. TimesUnion.com.

Porco, Peter. Personal E-mail. 20 September 2004. Times Union. TimesUnion.com.
Porco, Christopher. Personal E-mail. 20 September 2004. Times Union. TimesUnion.com.
Lyons, Brendan. "Toll ticket called Porco clue." Times Union. 2 June 2006.
Porco, Joan. Letter to the Editor. Times Union. 2 June 2006.
Kindlon, Terence. Interview. 6 June 2006.
Various Interviews. Albany, New York. 14 June 2006.
Anson, Scott. Interview. 20 June 2006.
Kindlon, Terence. Interview. 20 June 2006.
People v Christopher Porco (2006 NY Slip Op 04864). Supreme Court of the State of New York Appellate Division: Second Judicial Department. Change of Venue Ruling. 13 June 2006.
Rossi, David. Interview. 15 June 2006.
Kindlon, Terence. Interview. 15 June 2006.
McDermott, Michael. Interview. 15 June 2006.
Court Arguments. Albany County Judicial Center. Albany, New York. 15 June 2006.
Lyons, Brendan. "Porco video likely barred." Times Union. 16 June 2006.
Der Ohannesian, Paul. Interview. 16 June 2006.
McEneny, Rachel. Interview. 19 June 2006.
McEneny, Rachel. Interview. 23 June 2006.
Conners, Michael. Interview. 23 June 2006.

CHAPTER VII

Personal Notes. Orange County Courthouse. 26 June 2006.
Court Notes. Orange County Courthouse. 26 June 2006.
Court Notes. Pool reporter notes for parts of jury selection. 26 June 2006.
Kindlon, Terence. Interview. 26 June 2006.
McDermott, Michael. Interview. 26 June 2006.
Court Notes. Orange County Courthouse. 27 June 2006.
Court Notes. Pool reporter notes for parts of jury selection. 27 June 2006.
Kindlon, Terence. Interview. 27 June 2006.
McDermott, Michael. Interview. 27 June 2006.
Court Notes. Orange County Courthouse. 28 June 2006.
Kindlon, Terence. Interview. 28 June 2006.
McDermott, Michael. Interview. 28 June 2006.

CHAPTER VIII

Porco, Peter. Personal E-mail. 1 October 2004. Times Union. TimesUnion.com.
Porco, Joan. Personal E-mail. 2 October 2004. Times Union. TimesUnion.com.
Court Notes. Orange County Courthouse. 29 June 2006.
Hart, Michael. Court Testimony. Orange County Courthouse. 29 June 2006.
Shanks, Laurie. Orange County Courthouse. 29 June 2006.
Radliff, Charles. Court Testimony. Orange County Courthouse. 29 June 2006.
Robert, Kevin. Court Testimony. Orange County Courthouse. 29 June 2006.
Wood, Dennis. Court Testimony. Orange County Courthouse. 29 June 2006.
Tice, Briana. Court Testimony. Orange County Courthouse. 29 June 2006.
Kindlon, Terence. Interview. 29 June 2006.
McDermott, Michael. Interview. 29 June 2006.

CHAPTER IX

Personal Notes. Orange County Courthouse. 5 July 2006.
Kindlon, Terence. Interview. 5 July 2006.
McDermott, Michael. Interview. 5 July 2006.
Fischer, Sarah. Court Testimony. Orange County Courthouse. 5 July 2006.
Carter, Steven. Court Testimony. Orange County Courthouse. 5 July 2006.
Meyer, Kurt. Court Testimony. Orange County Courthouse. 5 July 2006.
McDonald, Drew. Court Testimony. Orange County Courthouse. 5 July 2006.

CHAPTER X

Porco, Peter. Personal E-mail. 7 October 2004. Times Union. TimesUnion.com.
Personal Notes. Orange County Courthouse. 6 July 2006.
McDonald, Drew. Court Testimony. Orange County Courthouse. 6 July 2006.
Spurgas, Dr. Paul. Court Testimony. Orange County Courthouse. 6 July 2006.
Cotsworth, Michael. Court Testimony. Orange County Courthouse. 6 July 2006.
Kindlon, Terence. Interview. 6 July 2006.
McDermott, Michael. Interview. 6 July 2006.
Shanks, Laurie. Interview. 6 July 2006.

CHAPTER XI

Porco, Peter. Personal E-mail. 19 October 2004. Times Union. TimesUnion.com.
Personal Notes. Orange County Courthouse. 10 July 2006.
Kindlon, Terence. Court Testimony. Orange County Courthouse. 10 July 2006.
Slezak, Craig. Court Testimony. Orange County Courthouse. 10 July 2006.
Strack, Kelly. Court Testimony. Orange County Courthouse. 10 July 2006.

Fallon, John. Court Testimony. Orange County Courthouse. 10 July 2006.
Kindlon, Terence. Interview. 10 July 2006.
McDermott, Michael. Interview. 10 July 2006.
Shanks, Laurie. Interview. 10 July 2006.
Kindlon, Terence. Interview. 13 July 2006.
DeLago, Dr. Augustin. Interview. 13 July 2006.

CHAPTER XII

Porco, Joan. Personal E-mail. 21 October 2004. Times Union. TimesUnion.com.
Porco, Christopher. Personal E-mail. 21 October 2004. Times Union. TimesUnion.com.
Personal Notes. Orange County Courthouse. 17 July 2006.
McDermott, Michael. Interview. 17 July 2006.
Rossi, David. Court Notes. Orange County Courthouse. 17 July 2006.
Shanks, Laurie. Interview. 17 July 2006.
Kindlon, Terence. Interview. 17 July 2006.
Montanie, Douglas. Court Testimony. Orange County Courthouse. 17 July 2006.
Killian, Joseph. Court Testimony. Orange County Courthouse. 17 July 2006.
Lawler, Daniel. Court Testimony. Orange County Courthouse. 17 July 2006.
Catalano, Joseph. Court Testimony. Orange County Courthouse. 17 July 2006.
Crumiller, Marshall. Court Testimony. Orange County Courthouse. 17 July 2006.
Balzano, Barbara. Court Testimony. Orange County Courthouse. 17 July 2006.
Abrams, Tisha. Court Testimony. Orange County Courthouse. 17 July 2006.
Novak, Jason. Court Testimony. Orange County Courthouse. 17 July 2006.
Culverwell, Eric. Court Testimony. Orange County Courthouse. 17 July 2006.
Whiteside, Gregory. Court Testimony. Orange County Courthouse. 17 July 2006.

CHAPTER XIII

Porco, Christopher. Personal E-mail. 22 October 2004. Times Union. TimesUnion.com.
Personal Notes. Orange County Courthouse. 18 July 2006.
McDermott, Michael. Interview. 18 July 2006.
Rossi, David. Court Notes. Orange County Courthouse. 18 July 2006.
Shanks, Laurie. Interview. 18 July 2006.
Kindlon, Terence. Interview. 18 July 2006.
Perrin, Dana. Court Testimony. Orange County Courthouse. 18 July 2006.
Kennedy, Jim. Court Testimony. Orange County Courthouse. 18 July 2006.
Siko, Steve. Court Testimony. Orange County Courthouse. 18 July 2006.
Fredericks, Grant. Court Testimony. Orange County Courthouse. 18 July 2006.
Personal Notes. Orange County Courthouse. 19 July 2006.
McDermott, Michael. Interview. 19 July 2006.
Shanks, Laurie. Interview. 19 July 2006.
Kindlon, Terence. Interview. 19 July 2006.
Keirsbilck, Roger. Court Testimony. Orange County Courthouse. 19 July 2006.
Ambrosio, Matt. Court Testimony. Orange County Courthouse. 19 July 2006.
Graham, Tyler. Court Testimony. Orange County Courthouse. 19 July 2006.
Wortham, Jason. Court Testimony. Orange County Courthouse. 19 July 2006.
Ortiz, Lewis. Court Testimony. Orange County Courthouse. 19 July 2006.

CHAPTER XIV

Personal Notes. Orange County Courthouse. 19 July 2006.
Rossi, David. Court Notes. Orange County Courthouse. 19 July 2006.
Cannizzaro, Julia. Court Testimony. Orange County Courthouse. 19 July 2006.
Nixon, William. Court Testimony. Orange County Courthouse. 19 July 2006.
Rossi, David. Court Notes. Orange County Courthouse. 20 July 2006.
McDermott, Michael. Interview. Orange County Courthouse. 20 July 2006.
Kindlon, Terence. Interview. Orange County Courthouse. 20 July 2006.
Shanks, Laurie. Interview. Orange County Courthouse. 20 July 2006.
Kidera, Daniel. Court Testimony. Orange County Courthouse. 20 July 2006.
Boylan, Rachel. Court Testimony. Orange County Courthouse. 20 July 2006.
Lopez, Julio. Court Testimony. Orange County Courthouse. 20 July 2006.
Coffin, John. Court Testimony. Orange County Courthouse. 20 July 2006.
Cannizzaro, Julia. Court Testimony. Orange County Courthouse. 20 July 2006.
Nicholas, John. Court Testimony. Orange County Courthouse. 20 July 2006.
McKay, Michelle. Court Testimony. Orange County Courthouse. 20 July 2006.
Porco, Christopher. Personal E-mail. 25 October 2004.
Porco, Christopher. Personal E-mail. 22 October 2004.
Porco, Peter. Personal E-mail. 4 November 2004.
Porco, Christopher. Personal E-mail. 4 November 2004.
Porco, Peter. Personal E-mail. 4 November 2004.
Porco, Peter. Personal E-mail. 5 November 2004.
Porco, Christopher. Personal E-mail. 5 November 2004.
Porco, Peter. Personal E-mail. 8 November 2004.
Porco, Christopher. Personal E-mail. 8 November 2004.

Porco, Peter. Personal E-mail. 12 November 2004.
Porco, Christopher. Personal E-mail. 15 November 2004.

CHAPTER XV

Personal Notes. Orange County Courthouse. 24 July 2006.
Rossi, David. Court Notes. Orange County Courthouse. 24 July 2006.
McDermott, Michael. Interview. Orange County Courthouse. 24 July 2006.
Kindlon, Terence. Interview. Orange County Courthouse. 24 July 2006.
Porco, Johnathan. Court Testimony. Orange County Courthouse. 24 July 2006.
Crowley, Kate. Court Testimony. Orange County Courthouse. 24 July 2006.
Strack, Kelly. Court Testimony. Orange County Courthouse. 24 July 2006.
Krause, Marcy. Court Testimony. Orange County Courthouse. 24 July 2006.
Personal Notes. Orange County Courthouse. 26 July 2006.
"Horse Head Harassment: Councilwoman Target of Sick Prank." Times Herald-Record. 26 July 2006.
Bowdish, Christopher. Court Testimony. Orange County Courthouse. 26 July 2006.
McDermott, Michael. Interview. Orange County Courthouse. 26 July 2006.
Rossi, David. Court Notes. Orange County Courthouse. 26 July 2006.
Shanks, Laurie. Court Notes. Orange County Courthouse. 26 July 2006.
Kindlon, Terence. Interview. Orange County Courthouse. 26 July 2006.
Kelly, Gary. Court Transcript by Cummings, Robert. Orange County Courthouse. 26 July 2006.

CHAPTER XVI

Notes. Orange County Courthouse. 31 July 2006.
McDermott, Michael. Court Notes. Orange County Courthouse. 31 July 2006.
Shanks, Laurie. Court Notes. Orange County Courthouse. 31 July 2006.
Porco, Joan. Court Notes. Orange County Courthouse. 31 July 2006.
Porco, Joan. Personal E-mail. 21 March 2004.
Porco, Joan. Personal E-mail. 27 July 2004.
Porco, Joan. Personal E-mail. 30 August 2004.
Shanks, Laurie. Interview. Orange County Courthouse. 1 August 2006.
Kindlon, Terence. Interview. Orange County Courthouse. 1 August 2006.

CHAPTER XVII

Court Notes. Orange County Courthouse. 1 August 2006.
McDermott, Michael. Court Notes. Orange County Courthouse. 1 August 2006.
Shanks, Laurie. Court Notes. Orange County Courthouse. 1 August 2006.
Porco, Joan. Court Notes. Orange County Courthouse. 1 August 2006.
Kindlon, Terence. Court Notes. Orange County Courthouse. 1 August 2006.
Melton, Dr. Terry. Court Notes. Orange County Courthouse. 1 August 2006.
Kindlon, Terence. Interview. Orange County Courthouse. 1 August 2006.
Kindlon, Terence. Interview. Orange County Courthouse. 2 August 2006.
McDermott, Michael. Interview. Orange County Courthouse. 2 August 2006.
Court Notes. Orange County Courthouse. 2 August 2006.
McDermott, Michael. Court Notes. Orange County Courthouse. 2 August 2006.
Shanks, Laurie. Court Notes. Orange County Courthouse. 2 August 2006.
Kindlon, Terence. Court Notes. Orange County Courthouse. 2 August 2006.
La Croix, Deborah. Court Notes. Orange County Courthouse. 2 August 2006.
Gokey, Marshall. Court Notes. Orange County Courthouse. 2 August 2006.

CHAPTER XVIII

Court Notes. Orange County Courthouse. 2 August 2006.
McDermott, Michael. Court Notes. Orange County Courthouse. 2 August 2006.
Shanks, Laurie. Court Notes. Orange County Courthouse. 2 August 2006.
Kindlon, Terence. Court Notes. Orange County Courthouse. 2 August 2006.
Fennell, Margaret. Court Notes. Orange County Courthouse. 2 August 2006.
Polster, Linda. Court Notes. Orange County Courthouse. 2 August 2006.
McDermott, Michael. Interview. Orange County Courthouse. 2 August 2006.
Shanks, Laurie. Interview. Orange County Courthouse. 2 August 2006.
Court Notes. Orange County Courthouse. 3 August 2006.
McDermott, Michael. Interview. Orange County Courthouse. 3 August 2006.
Kindlon, Terence. Interview. Orange County Courthouse. 3 August 2006.
Shields, Dr. William. Court Notes. Orange County Courthouse. 3 August 2006.
McDermott, Michael. Court Notes. Orange County Courthouse. 3 August 2006.
Kindlon, Terence. Court Notes. Orange County Courthouse. 3 August 2006.
McDermott, Michael. Interview. Orange County Courthouse. 7 August 2006.
Kindlon, Terence. Interview. Orange County Courthouse. 7 August 2006.
Court Notes. Orange County Courthouse. 7 August 2006.
Meyers, Stephen. Court Notes. Orange County Courthouse. 7 August 2006.
Kearney, Dr. John. Court Notes. Orange County Courthouse. 7 August 2006.
Dombovy, Dr. Mary. Court Notes. Orange County Courthouse. 7 August 2006.
Various Audio Recordings. 15 November 2004. Bethlehem Police Department. Orange County Courthouse. 7 August 2006.

McDermott, Michael. Interview. Orange County Courthouse. 8 August 2006.
Kindlon, Terence. Interview. Orange County Courthouse. 8 August 2006.
Court Notes. Orange County Courthouse. 8 August 2006.
Hallock, Alexandra. Court Notes. Orange County Courthouse. 8 August 2006.
Hanft, Richard. Court Notes. Orange County Courthouse. 8 August 2006.
Polster, John. Court Notes. Orange County Courthouse. 8 August 2006.
La Forte, Elaine. Court Notes. Orange County Courthouse. 8 August 2006.
Brigham, Tina. Court Notes. Orange County Courthouse. 8 August 2006.
Court Notes. Orange County Courthouse. 9 August 2006.
McDermott, Michael. Interview. Orange County Courthouse. 9 August 2006.
Shanks, Laurie. Interview. Orange County Courthouse. 9 August 2006.
Court Notes. Orange County Courthouse. 10 August 2006.
McDermott, Michael. Interview. Orange County Courthouse. 10 August 2006.
Kindlon, Terence. Interview. Orange County Courthouse. 10 August 2006.
Shanks, Laurie. Interview. Orange County Courthouse. 10 August 2006.
Corsi, Lou. Interview. Orange County Courthouse. 10 August 2006.

EPILOGUE

Court Notes. Orange County Courthouse. 10 August 2006.
Kindlon, Terence. Interview. Orange County Courthouse. 10 August 2006.
McDermott, Michael. Interview. Orange County Courthouse. 10 August 2006.
Bowdish, Christopher. Interview. Orange County Courthouse. 10 August 2006.
Porco, Joan. Interview. Goshen, New York. 10 August 2006.
"Memory of Murder." 48 Hours Mystery. 4 November 2006.
Court Notes. Albany County Courthouse. 12 December 2006.
Mayo, David. Court Transcript. Albany County Courthouse. 12 December 2006. 8,9, 14-17, 19-23.
Szostak, Patty. Court Statement. Albany County Courthouse. 12 December 2006.
Whalen, Jane. Letter. Court Statement. Albany County Courthouse. 12 December 2006.
Porco, Joan. Court Statement. Albany County Courthouse. 12 December 2006.
Kindlon, Terence. Court Testimony. Albany County Courthouse. 12 December 2006.
Porco, Christopher. Court Statement. Albany County Courthouse. 12 December 2006.
Berry, Judge Jeffrey. Court Statement. Albany County Courthouse. 12 December 2006.
Dott, Chip. Interview. 4 October 2007.